THE DHARKAN

TIMELESSNESS
BOOK 2

Susana Imaginário

ISBN: 978-1-9161402-5-7 (hardback)
ISBN: 978-1-9161402-4-0 (paperback)
ISBN: 978-1-9161402-3-3 (ebook)

For my pups

INTERLUDE 0

Ramblings of a Restless Soul

Time is relative, a wise man once said. I reckon he was a Wyrd, cursed to live amongst mortals. That's the punishment given to gods who know too much, for mortals don't give a fuck about their wisdom.

He was right, of course. Chronos, the God of gods – the only God, some would say (but don't let Kali or Gaea hear it) – is kin to the gods, but he's not one of them.

And that is his curse.

∞

Psyche is my name, but everyone calls me Butterfly. I don't mind. Not anymore. It's funny how easily we get used to the things that annoy us…

I was born a mortal, and now I'm a goddess. The goddess of the soul, of all things. The Universe must have been running out of talents to give its gods.

I've lived free for millennia, hiding amongst the stars, far away from the worlds and their petty inhabitants, until one day, driven by a senseless whim, I answered a dryad's prayer. That mistake dragged me helpless into the very pit of what I tried so hard to escape.

I'm no longer a Wyrd, having broken the curse that bonded my soul to Ileana, and yet I'm more a prisoner now than I was before. Before, I was hidden inside her; my thoughts mingled with hers. Now I'm exposed, forced to deal with my true self and the horrors of my own mind. In her I was powerless; now I'm bound to my power. The power I didn't know I'd asked for until I got it.

I've accomplished what I came here to do, yes, but victory is a double-edged blade with no hilt; it will cut you either way just to teach you not to fight.

∞

A tremor spreads through the walls to the sound of metal grinding on wood. I'm unable to Reach its source, as if the world doesn't exist beyond the boundaries of this vault. Zeus' empty eyes stare down accusingly at me. I suppose I should be flattered, but being locked in a tomb with the King of Olympus was not what I had in mind when I imagined myself amongst the gods, nor was his death my idea of revenge for the way he treated me. Imagination is a treacherous thing…

Another tremor. Stronger this time. It's hard to tell what caused it. Niflheim is a world tormented by the dead, the living and the divine alike. I suspect these are caused by neither, though. This is caused by something else. Something the gods are unable to understand, the same way mortals fail to understand the gods. And so they turned to me, for who would know more about either than the creature who used to be both? First, they attacked me with questions, then with accusations. Now they locked me in here to 'reconsider my answers.' Fucking gods… I'll give them answers. I'll give them all the answers they want to hear, for those are the only ones I have! My memories, from the time I answered Ileana's prayer to the moment I woke up in this forsaken world, were taken by Mnemosyne, the Titan goddess of memory herself, and I'm not sure I want them back at this point… I refuse to suffer punishment for other gods' schemes.

And I'll do anything to be free again.

CHAPTER ONE

Iva

The blue sun went silent.

Its burning light still shone above, and yet something had changed. Iva wished she understood what, exactly.

The Dharkan shifted at her side, silver eyes darting at the sky and at each other, confused. No one spoke, nor dared to step out of the shade either. Instead, one by one, they settled their gazes on her. Iva swallowed. There were disadvantages to leadership – some more fatal than others. Hel had promised that no Dharkan would have to fear the Olympians' light again after this day, but gods lie as often as they breathe, and Hel hadn't been Iva's goddess since she abandoned the Dharkan to their enemies. For all she knew, this could be a trick, something devised to end her and her followers once and for all as a punishment for their lack of faith.

"Very well," she said, licking her lips. "Only one way to find out," she added to gain a few more moments to gather her courage, then stuck her bare hand out under the sun, palm facing down. A few moments of exposure to the harmful light wouldn't kill her, but to not be able to feed properly until the hand healed would be an inconvenience she wasn't willing to risk.

As soon as Iva stretched out her hand, the blue sun vanished, leaving the world duller, dimmer and a great deal safer for the Dharkan under the illumination of its white counterpart.

Iva, caught between relief and annoyance, forsook all caution and stepped into the light. It hurt, as it always did, burn it. The white sun wasn't enough to kill, but even when hosting a deity, walking in daylight would never be a pleasant experience for the Dharkan. *One battle at a time*, she said to herself, ignoring her discomfort. She had endured much worse to get where she was; and to prove her strength, she tilted her head up and faced the punishing star, then grinned to the others in triumph.

"Come out, brothers. What doesn't kill you will only make you tougher." It was something her goddess often said. Iva figured if she remained in the sun, she'd be hard as diamonds by the end of the day.

Tentatively, one by one, the Dharkan moved out of the shade, doing their best to show no fear, or pain, or trip over themselves half blind on the rocky ground.

Something boomed in the distance, and at once her followers retreated under the shade. *Cowards*, Iva thought with disgust. Another blast. It sounded like thunder – if thunder could shake mountains.

She ran up the hill to get a better view, leaving the rest of the group behind to find their courage at leisure.

Lightning crashed above the Stump in a magnificent display of power and destruction. *Beautiful*, she said to herself. She could only hear the storm and see the bursts of energy crossing the outline of the felled World Tree, but that was enough. Death was always beautiful.

The ground shook under her feet, and the Boiling Lake roared behind her, hotter than ever.

"It's happening!" she shouted back to the others still clinging to the shade of the cave. The Dharkan cheered, and some even ventured up the slope to stand at her side and admire the event. Emil was one of them. She hadn't thought the boy had it in him, always so timid and cynical. She supposed that, like her, he had to see this for himself.

"He did it," Iva said through clenched teeth. Jealousy threatened to overcome her joy. She closed her fists and allowed herself one breath, for she would not let such a thing as emotion rule over her. She was better than that. *Better than him*, she thought again and had to take another deep breath.

Emil grunted. "So much for discretion, though. Every creature on this side of the Mountains will know something happened," he said reproachfully.

She glanced at the young boy. He seemed to have aged a decade in the last few days. And he was right, which was annoying. She would have handled the attack on the Suzerain much better, of course. *Breathe.* She should have been the one chosen to bring the Suzerain to his knees. She had done more for the Dharkan since the Merge than Aedan had in his whole existence. The dozens of followers by her side were proof of that. But alas, no one chooses who they love. Not even the gods. And if it was true that the Olympian gods were involved, those idiots did nothing without a spectacle.

"The living will know something has happened, but hopefully they will not know what. As long as they think the Suzerain is still in power, it won't affect our plans," she told him. It was an easy conclusion to make, for the man, like his gods, often loved to impress and suppress his subjects by setting the sky ablaze.

Emil snorted and walked away whistling to himself. Iva watched him go, intrigued. When had the boy become so… manly? She blamed the blinding light of Aegea for making her fail to notice such things. He looked so much like his brother, back when he still had his looks, that is. Before the Suzerain burned his wits along with his skin. She sighed and focused back on the dead Tree.

The storm above it kept expanding, burning trees and shelters randomly across the land. The Dharkan retreated to the cave, having seen enough. Apparently they'd rather celebrate in the shade with their prey than in the sunlight with her. That stung.

Iva remained atop the hill, defiant and alone. Back at the cave, the celebration would continue until the Dharkan took every life stolen from the temple in Lagus. She was famished and longed to join her brothers, but she paced along the ridge instead, watching Aegea burn while she waited for a better, more fulfilling prey to arrive.

∞

It was almost dark when Ulcan finally showed up. She didn't hear the hunter approach until his spit landed in front of her boot. Burn the man.

The hunter chewed on a piece of straw – gathering saliva for his next spit, no doubt – and grimaced at her with disgust. "You look like raw steak. Have you been in the sun all day?"

Iva fought the urge to throw him off the cliff. How dare the boorish creature comment on her looks? Spitting was the least of the hunter's appalling features. He was all brown, and hairy in the wrong places. The hair that should have been on his bald head sprouted from his cheeks and chin instead, all the way down his equally hairy shoulders and chest. Even his hands and fingers had hair! She could not fathom for what purpose. The rest of the man's body remained hidden from view (Narrum, unlike dryads, were extremely self-conscious of their bodies – thank the goddess!) but she suspected it would only get worse below the waist. Had the gods created Narrum so ugly to make them unappetising to Dharkan? Well, if so, it worked. She'd rather starve than touch him. Still, there was no avoiding dealing with the man. He was resourceful and hated the Olympian gods as much as the Dharkan did. When survival is at stake, one can't be too picky about their allies. Not while they are still useful, of course.

"Do you have the Ambrosia?" she asked dryly, doing her best not to ice him then and there for his insolence.

He sucked his teeth and spat. "More or less."

Iva's eyelid flinched. She knew she had to be patient with the Narrum. Their minds worked too slow for a proper conversation, but patience was hard to summon after so long under the sun. She struggled to keep her tone reasonable. "Either you have it or you don't, and you would not dare come here if you didn't. Where is it?"

Ulcan brought forth a Narrum cub she had not noticed was there. *Burn this light!* Hel should have got rid of both suns. To be fair, the whelp was barely tall enough to reach her thigh and so was easy to miss. It stared up at her with wide eyes and a finger in its mouth. *Courage or ignorance?* Iva wondered. They often looked the same.

"I'm fairly certain *that* did not come from a tree." Iva scowled, her patience thinner than the early morning mists.

"She ate it," Ulcan said matter-of-factly.

Iva blinked. "I thought you people only ate meat."

The hairy man shrugged. "The hunt has been scarce. There are more Narrum born each day than deer or… anything else, really." He glanced toward the pens down below. There was no way he could see the other cubs from there. "Too many and not enough for them to eat," he said.

Indeed. If there was one thing the Narrum did well, it was eat. Iva would like to meet the god who created these predators and give him a piece of her mind. Life, like energy, should be transferred, not butchered. The amount of waste they produced plus the extra energy required to cook their sustenance made them an unsustainable race. Someone had to eliminate them.

It gave her no pleasure. Like most Dharkan, Iva preferred to take the Prana of dryads, but sacrifices had to be made for the greater good.

Iva crouched down to the cub's eye level. Fair-skinned and grey-eyed, it could almost pass as a Dharkan child if not for the yellow hair. It showed no fear as it stared back at her, only curiosity. Narrum took longer to develop a self-preservation instinct and were instead driven by their curiosity and greed right from the womb.

"Does it hurt?" it asked, pointing at Iva's sunburned nose. She didn't answer. Iva would never indulge a question with such an obvious answer.

"Is it true? Did you eat the resin?" Iva asked instead.

The whelp looked sheepish and tried to hide behind Ulcan. Such typical Narrum behaviour. It was not afraid of Iva, only of the punishment she might inflict. Narrum would do anything if they thought they'd get away with it.

"It's all right. I'm not mad," Iva lied. "Did you really eat your father's treasure?" she asked with fake admiration in her tone.

The cub nodded proudly.

"What did it taste like?"

The cub licked its lips, and something rapacious crossed its face. "Like gods' blood."

"That good, huh?"

The young predator nodded enthusiastically.

"Did you save some for your family?"

The cub pushed its bottom lip out and glanced at the forest, then shook its head, morose.

That was disappointing. Iva had expected a supply of Ambrosia large enough to sustain a dozen Dharkan, at least. A whelp this small probably would not endure multiple feedings, even if infused with the resin.

"Her father wishes me to convey to you his greatest apologies for not realising the importance of the resin sooner. In truth, he only kept it because it was shiny and he thought it might be worth something. He hopes this makes up for the oversight and that it pleases you enough that you won't seek further retribution. He has other children, you see – other children he wishes to keep," Ulcan said.

"Sure." If only this one ate the resin, then it would not make a difference, anyway. Let the logger keep the rest of his cubs.

"Are the gods angry because of what I did?" the whelp asked, glancing at the Stump. The lightning had long stopped, but many of the fires it started still raged across Aegea.

"Oh, no. Not at all. The gods would never be angry with *you*." Iva poked its belly with a finger. "You are their favourite creatures."

The cub giggled. "Maybe they are angry with the tree huggers. Mother says they make everyone angry, but we can't eat them or the Suzerain will punish us. He's one of them," it added in a conspiratorial whisper.

Iva frowned up at Ulcan.

"She's one of the forest folk," he explained.

Ahh, a stray from the settlements, then. Not that it made much difference to Iva. To her, all Narrum were uncivilised. This explained why the whelp was not afraid of her. It'd never seen a Dharkan and didn't know what they looked like, apparently. It never ceased to amaze Iva how well the Narrum thrived given how little they taught their offspring.

"You are absolutely right, he was," Iva said to the cub. "But you won't have to worry about him or the tree huggers no more."

The girl grinned.

Iva grabbed her neck and lifted her off the ground. She kicked frenetically. "Hold it still!" Iva ordered Ulcan.

The hunter hesitated long enough for Iva to send an icy glance in his direction, then complied.

Iva hated to take Prana from a Narrum. They had so little of it, and it was often tainted with the many other lives they'd consumed. To a Dharkan it was like ingesting regurgitated Prana. Fortunately, this one hadn't lived long enough to consume much and had its life force filled with the flavour of the Ambrosia. It was wonderful. *Gods' blood.* Exactly as the whelp had described. Immediately Iva's skin healed and her vision improved, almost as if all light had vanished from the Universe. She told herself she had to leave the whelp alive for the others, but its Prana was so sweet, so powerful, so… gone.

Iva dropped the small lifeless body on the ground, cold as ice. Blazing sun, she got carried away. Still, she felt too good to feel bad about what she'd done. Iva felt as if she had a god's soul in her. No, it was better than that; she felt *alive*.

"I am ready," she said, breathing heavily, relishing her fast-beating heart.

"The deal still stands." Ulcan extended his forearm to her. It wasn't a question.

The nerve of the man to invite her to touch him after what she'd just done. Hairy, yes; coward, no. Too bad he was so ugly and so… Narrum. She could use a man like him in her pack. The right thing to do was to ice him, but that would spoil her meal. Besides, he might still be useful.

Overcoming her aversion to the man, Iva wrapped her forearm in his and clutched it firmly.

He grinned a rotten-toothed grin she'd never noticed before and spat on her hand. Then he simply… vanished.

That had not been the hunter, Iva realised too late. She blamed her goddess for not being with her during their meeting. She could have warned her, protected her. Why do gods always find ways to be busy when you most need them? *It doesn't matter*, she told herself. Iva's heart beat faster than ever – too fast, and not in a pleasant way. She wiped the spit on the girl's dirty dress, wishing for the blue sun to come back to cauterise the skin off her hand. *Burn the gods!* Iva cursed and kicked the girl's body into the ravine so the others wouldn't find it.

Yes, she'd made a mistake, but so did he, whoever *he* was. For she had Ambrosia now, and she could take on any god who dared to challenge her.

CHAPTER TWO

Iosh

Iosh stood on the teleportation ring, twitching with impatience. "Work, you worthless piece of slush," he spat at the bracelet after he frantically rubbed and twisted every gem on the key to no effect.

Iosh was late to the Tribute – very late, in fact. Not that it made much difference: the Suzerain severely punished even the slightest amount of tardiness. The cursed event was not supposed to take place for another few days, anyway. Why change it? If that half-witted Isko made him come all the way there for nothing, Iosh would permanently revoke his privileges at the temple. Oh yes, he would.

Why Iosh had to be present in the first place was beyond him. It wasn't as if he were personally making the offers to the Nephilim. The Suzerain just liked to humiliate him, to show who was in charge – as if anyone in Aegea could ever forget. It only took one glimpse at the mutilated World Tree looming above them to know the old gods no longer held power in Niflheim. Alek probably thought it hurt Iosh to see his children swallowed by that dark pit he called a portal.

If only the Suzerain knew how little children meant to him, especially his own. But while Alek believed this, he wouldn't endeavour to find other ways to hurt him.

Eos' light vanished from the grey sky. *Already? Frost.* That meant Iosh was even later than he'd thought. What a freezing nightmare. It was that Dharkan's fault. No, it was Odin's fault. What had possessed the Wyrd to invite such an abomination to his temple, anyway? Everyone knew those creatures were death and left nothing but death in their wake. Now, as a result, Iosh had lost his best friend and – personal loss aside – finding a reliable replacement for Fabrian at the temple was proving to be quite the challenging addition to his duties which kept him busy until the last moment. Then his mount lost a shoe at the Grove and since there are no blacksmiths amongst the wayfarer Anann, he had to walk the rest of the way. And now here he was, exhausted, alone and late for the most unpleasant event in the forsaken land.

Lightning cracked in the clear sky above the massive tree trunk; a cold wind bit into his skin, sending shivers down his spine. Something dramatic was happening up there, and he was missing it. "Why don't you work?" Iosh hit the bracelet again and prayed fervently. Nothing. "For frost's sake! Argh!" By the gods, how he hated this 'technology', as the Suzerain called it. It was as if every device had been created arbitrarily by children: they looked like toys, had to be used as such and rarely worked the way they were supposed to, when they were supposed to.

Something moved past Iosh's shoulder from above.

The sound of its impact on the metal at his feet startled him, but what made him jump was the ice-cold debris thrown up his bare legs. He kept his hand motionless on the bracelet and just stood there for a long moment with his mouth hanging open, unable to come to terms with the realisation that the birch-tree-patterned chunks of skin at his feet with green-and-black hair attached to them were part of the shattered head of the Suzerain.

Caught between shock and utter confusion, he looked up, half dreading, half expecting more body parts to fall.

"I need to get inside, now!" Iosh said to his forearm. The bracelet clicked, and before he could move or think anything else, the metal circle glowed and light engulfed him.

When Iosh could see again, he was staring at what looked like the Suzerain's frozen nose snugly wedged between his toes. He shook his foot vigorously. The nose dropped on the smooth, blood-spattered floor of the Stump's common room. Iosh blinked several times while his eyes adjusted to the dim light, trying to make sense of the shadowy shapes across the floor. "Gods…" he muttered to himself.

Countless body parts lay strewn beyond the teleportation ring. Cold had not shattered those. Those men had been crushed and clawed apart limb from limb by powerful jaws. The sight didn't bother Iosh as it would a pure-blood dryad, but he hadn't eaten since the previous morning, and thanks to his Narrum ancestry, he couldn't help but feel both nauseous and hungry while contemplating that much meat. He swallowed and had to hold on to his shock to quench the unwelcome appetite.

This turn of events meant Iosh no longer feared the Suzerain's wrath for being late; he now hoped he was late enough to miss whatever had caused such butchery.

A growl reverberated through the walls of the great hall. No such luck, it seemed. Blood rushed to his legs, prompting him to run. Run where, from what? He spared one look at the bracelet, then felt a presence looming behind him. With a pounding heart and a quick prayer to any god that might listen, Iosh half turned, half peeked over his shoulder, expecting to find the largest canine in creation. Instead, he had to look down to see a young Narrum boy, grinning up at him with crooked teeth.

"Hello," the boy said cheerfully.

"Er... hi."

"Iosh! Get me out of here!"

"Occa?" Iosh dismissed the boy and traced the voice to a dark corner. "Occa, is that you?" The girl was barely recognisable. She was on her knees with both hands tied to her ankles behind her back. He walked over to her, taking care not to step on anything that used to be part of someone. Her face was a bloody mess with one eye completely purple and swollen shut, a split lip and a broken nose from which a sluggish stream of blood ran down her chin to soak into her once lovely sky grey dress.

Next to Occa, a familiar face looked even worse. Despite having no visible injuries or restraints on him, the Wyrd was the personification of hopelessness:

slack-jawed, blank rheumy eyes, rocking back and forth and murmuring something that, if Iosh didn't know any better, he would swear was a prayer.

"Odin? Er… Agnar? What happened here? Who did this?"

He didn't answer. Occa's eyes widened when the Narrum boy, still grinning excessively, came to sit behind the Wyrd. Iosh reckoned he was probably one of the Suzerain's cup bearers and felt sorry for the boy. Whatever happened in that room clearly had broken his mind. He smiled back, unable to think of anything better to do or say to the poor child.

And then his heart sank when a thought struck him: If that was the state of the queen's sister and her *uncle*, what had happened to the queen herself?

Please gods, no. "Where's Arianh?"

Occa, eyes darting between him and the opposite corner, didn't answer. The Wyrd didn't seem to have heard the question at all.

The ground beneath Iosh's feet shook hard enough to make his teeth rattle. He gripped Occa by the shoulders, partly to steady himself – for he didn't want to fall on the bloody floor – and partly to make her answer him. "Where is she!"

"Hey! Hands off. Don't you dare remove her restraints." The command came from a petite dryad with wild blue hair. She stood across the room, on the other teleportation ring, and seemed frustrated with a bracelet of her own. Her huge blue eyes shined like those of an owl in the dim light when she fixed them on his forearm.

"Hey, handsome, how do I get to the top?" Her bracelet looked familiar. He glanced at the many broken body parts scattered across the room. "Is that Oric's?"

"Yes."

Iosh had no love for Oric, alive or dead. Still, the answer, and the careless way she gave it, chilled him to the bone. He swallowed. "It won't work without him." That much he knew about the accursed things. He had to give the Suzerain some of his blood to be infused into the metal of his bracelet for it to work. *Technology… right.* More like sorcery.

"I have him right here." She lifted a small leather pouch stained red like most of her shabby yellow dress and gagged, obviously nauseated, but the involuntary response seemed to only annoy her, as a hiccough would. "Will you help me, or do I need to be more persuasive?" Her voice was soft and her tone cheerful, but Iosh heard the threat in it loud and clear nonetheless.

The Suzerain had once explained to him how the devices worked, of course. Yet he had failed to understand the full extent of the instructions the first time around and had been too intimidated to ask again. Alek was not a man who liked to repeat himself, after all.

"Er… I think you need to press… Wait, I need to see it." He joined her inside the ring and compared the bracelets. The larger gems were similar on both keys, the other smaller one wasn't. "Try that one."

She smiled at him. Like most dryads, she had perfect teeth, made for smiling, not chewing.

"Makes sense," she said. "Mika, will you keep an eye on those two until I return?"

"Sure." The boy scratched his ear vigorously. "Can I have a treat as well?"

The girl glanced around the room. "All the treats you want – not the main course, though. Remember what your father said."

"The boy growled low and nodded."

The Stump shook again. Harder this time.

"What's happening up there?" Iosh asked.

"The end of your Lord," she replied while she twisted the gem the wrong way around, nearly plucking it out of its socket. She was even less adept with the keys than he was.

"Good grief, woman. Let me do it," he said, taking the key and the blood-stained pouch from her hand.

She immediately snatched them back. "You're lucky you're cute or I'd scratch your eyes out," she said with the most innocent and alluring of smiles. Iosh was still holding his breath when light engulfed them.

They found themselves at the edge of a long corridor. He could hear children crying behind the walls along with the desperate shushes of their mothers. He felt a pang of aversion mixed with guilt. Many of these children were probably his, and yet he did not care for their misery. If anything, he was annoyed by the sound of it, for it muffled any other sounds that might be important.

"Where are we?" she asked him.

"Where you shouldn't be." A stout Narrum woman stepped from behind a wall. She held a club studded with blades in her hand. He had met her before: Rita, her name was. She assisted with the women in labour and cared for them and their babies before they were sent to the Nephilim.

"Woman, I'm Judoc of Relicum. I'm here for the Tribute. Let me through."

The matron was silent a moment, then grunted. "And you?"

"I'm Ideth. I'm here to take my son and will shave your moustache with those blades if you don't let me through."

Iosh gaped at her. *What sort of nymph talks like this?* The crazy little creature would get them both killed! Rita was a Narrum, and they didn't shy away from threats, especially when armed.

Rita laughed. "Judoc of Relicum: go, your Lord needs you. Ideth, is it? We're going to have a conversation."

The Stump shook again, and Iosh didn't wait to see whatever the two women were about to do to each other. "Much obliged," he said, running up the spiralling tunnel before the matron changed her mind.

He could already see light from the surface when he heard a familiar voice call out for help.

"Arianh?" The relief he felt reflected the tension he hadn't realised he held. "Arianh, where are you?" He followed the sound to one of the cells used to house the more headstrong women.

"Judoc, is that you? Thank the goddess! What is happening out there?"

"I don't know." Another shake and the wood groaned around him. "I don't think I want to know…"

he said to himself, and then to Arianh, "The Suzerain is dead."

There was a long pause to the sound of angry women fighting.

"Are you sure?"

"Fairly sure," Iosh said, grimacing at his legs.

"How?"

"Frozen to pieces." He ran his hands over the wall, trying to find a crack, an opening, something. Eventually he found a small shallow hole, large enough to insert the tip of his finger. He pressed it, but nothing happened.

"And… Occa?" Arianh asked tentatively.

"She's fine." That was an overstatement, but he didn't want to alarm the queen. "Alive," he corrected himself.

"Good," Arianh said. "Open the door so I can teach the thorny little weed a lesson."

A howl of pain echoed from the depths of the corridor, followed by an inhuman screech. "What was that?" Arianh asked.

"Nothing," he said. Iosh pressed the shallow hole again, harder, to no effect. "Freezing technology," he muttered.

"Judoc, just open the door!"

"What do you think I'm trying to do?" he snapped. His hands searched frantically along the panel. There was nothing else he could find to work with. "How does this thing open?"

"Occa had a ring. She touched it to the wall and…"

More cries came from the shadows. Iosh ceased his search and eyed the long dark corridor warily. Not far below, a female yelped. From above came the sound of sleet on metal and lightning splitting wood. Apparently neither fight was over yet. "Er… Arianh, are you in any immediate danger or discomfort?"

"What? No. Apart from being locked in here, you mean?"

"Then hold on. I'll come back for you soon. I promise!"

"Back? Where're you going? Don't you dare leave me in here! Judoc!" Arianh's voice faded quickly as he walked away.

Iosh knew that once the queen got out of her cell, he would not hear the end of it. Well, she said it herself; she was used to being upset with him. At least there she was safe. *Maybe she won't be too upset this time,* he lied to himself.

He could sense the cold even before he'd made it up the ice-covered ramp, and the first thing he saw when he reached the surface was a voluptuous woman in the ripe stages of womanhood lecturing Oreth, the Suzerain's boy, crouched atop the Suzerain's pet, Xylo, who was completely wrapped in vines, thick as ropes.

"What a…?" Iosh said. He lost his footing on the slippery ice, nearly crashing into a large winged horse. Its master – Iosh assumed that was what the satyr standing next to it was – scowled at him. Not a pretty sight. Iosh had seen such creatures in the forest. One of them had tried to do things to him he would not go into detail about. This one had his arm around a Dharkan – a female Dharkan and an attractive one, no less. Those were rare. Not that Iosh had ever considered praying with a Wraith, but he never failed to notice an attractive woman.

There were no signs of the Nephilim. The Suzerain was there, though. Or what was left of him, held together by the fabric of his dress. Another Wraith, a particularly large and ugly specimen, knelt close to his remains.

"Argh! Gods! Who are you people? How did you —"

He strongly considered going back inside and taking his chances with the crazy nymph, Rita, and her sharp baton. But then, beyond the hulking Wraith, he glimpsed an unmistakable shade of holy green hair. "Illy!"

Iosh half ran, half slid to Ileana's body lying on the icy floor. Her eyes were glazed, and she had what looked like rotten veins streaking from a wound in her chest.

"Illy, no… please gods, no." *Not again*, he almost said. He knew the woman lying in front of him was a Wyrd, that he'd never really got Ileana back, but she still felt like her to him. Worse, he'd grown fond of the Wyrd herself and wasn't sure which loss grieved him more.

"What did you do to her, daemon!" he demanded, all sense of self-preservation momentarily forgotten.

The Dharkan growled something vile, and Iosh saw he was crying. Or something like it. Iosh wasn't sure *tears* was the right word to define the sleet falling from the Wraith's eyes. Regardless, the Wraith sure looked more miserable than he was. Iosh knelt next to him, too stunned to let proper tears well up in his eyes.

"My lady, Niflheim is ours," said the satyr. "What happens now?"

∞

The Stump shook again. Someone was trying to activate the portal from the other side. The satyr cursed and immediately got into a heated argument with the female Dharkan over how to use the Suzerain bracelet to stop it.

There was one thing Iosh knew about the devices: the gems worked as keys to open and close doors between spaces. Remove the key when the door is locked, and it should remain locked. For a time, at least.

Iosh stood up slowly, his anxiety gone, his thoughts seemingly as frozen as the woman he once loved and the ice under his feet. He walked to the quarrelling couple, snatched the bloody bracelet from the satyr's forearm and twisted the largest gem. At once the circle stopped glowing. He then pulled the gem from its socket and dropped it onto the icy surface. Both satyr and Wraith stared at him with blank faces.

"Thanks, man. What shall we call you?" the satyr asked.

"Judoc," Iosh said curtly and turned away.

"I'm Hades."

Iosh stopped in his tracks and peered back at the copper satyr with an outstretched hand and a fiendish smile. "You're Hades? *The* Hades of the Underworld?"

"In the flesh. Disappointed?"

Iosh wasn't sure disappointment was the right word for the clash between the mighty dark god forged in his childhood imagination and the bestial creature in front of him. He turned to the female Wraith next to Hades and frowned suspiciously.

"Yes, mortal, I am the goddess Hel."

"Good grief!" Iosh had to sit down, so shocked and distraught he barely felt the cold. Not immediately, anyway. The thing about dramatic gestures was that they often lost gravitas when faced with adversity. And what adversity. Being late was the least of his problems, it seemed. He should not have come at all.

"I'm Chiron. A pleasure to meet you, friend."

"What the frost…?" Iosh looked up, mouth agape. The words definitely came from the winged horse. Either that or Iosh had lost his mind for good.

"I'm not a horse, I'm a Titan," the horse – Chiron – said without moving his mouth.

"Ah…right." *What the frost is a Titan?* Iosh wondered vaguely. He did not really care. Sure, if horses can fly, why not talk?

"I am Gaea, Mother of Life," the mature woman announced proudly.

"Of course you are…"

"Hey, Chiron!" called a girly voice from the ramp.

I guess we know who won that fight, Iosh thought, somehow impressed. Rita was not a woman he would ever want to confront.

The girl hugged the horse and then danced around and under his wings. "Wow! Look at you! You got to take me for a ride. Promise you'll take me, please."

There was a jarring chuckle mixed with an equine snort. "I was getting worried, unbridled one."

She stopped paying attention to the horse and fixed her sight on Xylo. More precisely, on Oreth, still sulking on his shoulders, and began walking gingerly to them.

Iosh overheard a torrent of protests and curses from the boy, followed by her shouting, "I am your mother!"

"Huh?" It was getting worse. How could she be his mother? She looked even younger than him! No, Iosh didn't want to know what drama afflicted those two as well. He shook his head and prayed to wake up. The day had gone from bad to worse to something indescribable. Had he been enthralled by some devious creature back at the Grove and was imagining all this? Could Chronos finally be taking his claim on his life? He never figured the old God to be fond of mind tricks, and yet this was by far the strangest series of events he'd witnessed in his life. It was all too much. He was too cold to think properly. His mind was numb. Maybe he was dreaming it all? No, why would he dream such things? His stomach rumbled. He'd better eat something soon or he would faint.

A young woman appeared out of thin air. Now, she was more like something found in a dream, or in a hallucination. She had an ethereal sort of beauty, like a proper goddess from the stories of his childhood.

"Aaah, let me guess," he said to the newcomer, "you must be Aphrodite, then."

The look she gave him was one of pure contempt. Before she could add words to it, the big Dharkan was on her with vicious intent. He grabbed her by the throat and lifted her one-handed off the surface, snarling. Lightning flashed again, wind roared, and an unnatural chill came upon them from everywhere.

Iosh stood up and then stood there, for what could he do against a Dharkan?

The Dharkan grunted, released the goddess and fell to his knees, holding his head with both hands.

"You don't get to do that to me ever again!" she shouted at him. Everyone stood still. Even Xylo, who never showed interest in what went on around him, seemed confused by the exchange.

The goddess walked gingerly towards Ileana, sparing a glare in his direction. There was something inadvertently sensual in the way she lifted her eyebrow when she did it. Under different circumstances, Iosh would like to know her better, but for once, surrounded by gods, he wasn't inclined to pray to any of them.

Gaea intercepted her path.

"Think again," the new goddess said with a hand raised to Gaea's face.

"I only wish to know what happened, dear. How you felt, how much you took, where you've been all this time!" Gaea pleaded.

"The name is Psyche, not *dear*, and the answer is still no."

Psyche... Iosh mused. He could swear he'd heard the name before.

Roots sprouted from the ice, wide as trunks and flexible as vines, they wrapped Psyche from feet to mouth. "*You* think again, dear," Gaea said in a crone's voice.

In that moment, something cracked in Iosh's mind. It was as if a trapdoor he didn't know was there burst wide open and everything that used to be him fell right through it. Apprehension and confusion gave way to anger and bitter resentment. *Were these gods?* The gods of his world? Had this group of petty, monstrous creatures really defeated the Suzerain? He was disgusted.

"Girls, behave," Hades said in a mocking tone. "This isn't over yet. We still need to find Zeus."

Iosh disagreed. The way he saw it, their little uprising would be over once the Nephilim arrived. How he regretted disabling the key. It didn't matter. They would come, he was sure, and when they did… well, it might be too late for Ileana but not for him. He would take Arianh and go away, far away to a time and place where there were no gods, nor Tributes or portals.

"Zeus is dead," Psyche said in a muffled voice, and it all went downhill from there.

INTERLUDE 1

The Spoils of Victory

"Wait!" Ileana shouts as I crush the Suzerain's neck.

A wave of immense energy hits me from within, its power almost palpable in the lightning striking around us.

I did it. I finally destroyed the creature who took over Niflheim and ostracised my people. *Wasn't even that hard,* I admit to myself with pride. Hades had been right: all we needed was to cast out the Olympians' sun to succeed. The usurper was no match for a Dharkan on even terms. *He was no match for me.*

The Suzerain's life force is unlike any other. I fear it might burn me from the inside, but it exhilarates me instead. *Is this how it feels to be a god?* I wonder. *It explains their egos.*

I laugh and roar my victory to the world.

"We did it," I say to Ileana. She does not share my elation. Her eyes are unfocused, her expression blank. "Ileana?"

Gaea's roots shatter the Suzerain's frozen body, and Ileana's left holding her father's head by the hair, his face frozen in a malevolent grin. She sways. Thinking she's about to hug me and rejoice in our victory, I hold her just in time to break her fall.

"Ileana! Talk to me!" She doesn't speak; she doesn't move. I lift her head to face me and fear she does not see me either. This makes no sense. I took no Prana from her.

Dread overtakes my triumph when I see something stuck in her chest, deep red tendrils spreading from it under her skin. I pull out the strange object. There's no blood; the tip's thinner than a nail, surely that can't – *It was piercing her heart*, I realise.

The Suzerain's tremendous power still rushes through my body, but I'm powerless holding the woman I love. *She will heal*, I tell myself. Her Wyrd won't dare let her die. Except… I look at the empty sky.

"Bring back the sun!" I shout to the gods. I do not care if it burns me to ashes. "Now! Bring it back NOW."

"It's gone," Hel says, her tone mildly surprised. She stands a few paces away, staring at the sky with a wide grin. "Eos' light is gone. Loki – *father* – was true to his promise."

I curse. Ever since I can remember I've prayed for the absence of that murderous aberration over our land, now I would give anything to have it back for a little while longer. Without the blue sun, the Wyrd can't feed, they can't heal their host's bodies, and if they can't heal…

"Please don't die," I beg Ileana under my breath. There's so little warmth left in her.

"You!" I point at the buxom creature entangled with what looks like a tree with limbs. "Come here."

Gaea glares at me in reply, not used to being addressed in such a way. "Ileana is dying," I explain to her.

The tree man stops struggling with the roots pinning him in place. The Goddess of Life takes a deep breath, then composes her dress. Gods have no sense of urgency whatsoever. "Hurry!"

Gaea finally comes over and touches Ileana's chest. *Why is she shaking her head?* Ileana is not dead. She cannot be. She is NOT dead.

"Is she dead?" Hel asks.

"She should be," Gaea says. "She's not alive."

What is that supposed to mean? "She is either one or the other, burn you!"

Gaea shrugs. "I don't know how else to put it: she's not alive."

I shake Gaea by the shoulders. "You are the Goddess of Life! Make her alive."

Lightning webs around us and blinds me in its glare. I can't control it. I hear a scream. The plump Goddess wraps me in her vines. "I cannot!" she shouts.

"You lie!" I growl back.

I freeze her vines off and shatter them so I can grab Gaea by the neck. *She'll obey me now.* The Goddess radiates outrage for a moment, then fear, and the next thing I know, I'm flat on the ice with Hel's boot on my chest.

"Don't," she commands in an icy tone.

"How dare you!" Gaea hisses. "I cannot make her alive, same as I cannot make a stone alive. Understand?" Her voice echoes beyond the clamour right through my senses. I nod.

Hel releases me, and I roll from under her boot to Ileana's side.

"What happened here?" asks the satyr looming behind Hel. Hades is the Olympian god of the Underworld and a friend of Ileana's Wyrd. If the Goddess of Life cannot help, maybe he can.

"Bring her back!" I plead. My fortitude is fading along with the life force of my woman.

Hades leans down and touches Ileana's forehead, then grimaces like a man bracing himself for a fall. "I can't."

"Why not?"

"I've liberated Ileana's spirit – at her request!" Hades adds before I ice him. "I can't bring her back, for her spirit is no longer linked to the Underworld. I don't even know where to look for her now."

"You did *what*?" Hel asks, strong disapproval in her tone.

"It was part of our bargain. She wanted to have a say in her fate, so..." – Hades smiles sheepishly – "I let her have her way."

"How could you? To leave that decision to a mortal is beyond irresponsible."

"It was not my brightest moment, I admit. And I was working slightly under pressure, if you remember." Hades exhales. "Why don't you help me find her instead of chastising me. Above or below, she has to still be in your world."

"Oh, it's my world now, is it?"

"Find her!" I thunder. Those two would argue for eternity given the chance. "Please," I add to the goddess of Niflheim. Hel is not the kind of deity you bark orders at. "Bring her back."

Her eyes flutter for a moment. "She's not with the dead in my realm either. Actually, I can't find any trace of her anywhere in Niflheim. If not for the fact that I can see her *right there*, I would not know she even exists." She speaks as if she doesn't believe her own words.

"That is not good enough!" Lightning hits the weird tree man again, the sound similar to when lightning hits an actual tree, except for the surprised cry and the smell of burned flesh.

Gaea gasps and goes to him. "Control your minion, or I will," she says with a finger pointed at Hel.

I cradle Ileana closer. She's growing cold, and I try to give her as much warmth as my body can muster. It is not much; Dharkan are creatures of cold and shadow, after all. How can I be surrounded by some of the most powerful gods in the Universe, myself now capable of bringing down the sky it seems, and none of us is able to accomplish something as simple as reviving flesh?

"Ileana, come back to me. It is over. He is gone. We won. Please, look at me!" Her green eyes remain staring into nothing. She's not breathing, her heart is not beating, and yet she's not dead either. I know how death feels, and this is not it. Dead creatures still have a presence, some vestige of energy. Not Ileana. It's like Gaea said: she's lifeless as a rock.

I pluck the Suzerain's head from her grip and feel the same emptiness in it. "What have you done to her?"

I ask the frozen face grinning back at me. "I destroyed you. I won!" And yet, without her, what is the point?

I throw the head over the edge of the Stump.

A tear crystal falls on Ileana's beautiful face, melts and runs down her cheek as if it's her own. The next ones remain frozen and roll off her silver birch skin to make a clicking sound when they hit the icy surface.

There's no more warmth in her body.

She's gone. *This cannot be. Please goddess, do not let it be so*, I pray.

Hel places a hand on my shoulder. "I'm sorry, Aedan. She's beyond my Reach. Know that I'm eternally grateful for her sacrifice. And yours."

I throw my head back and howl at the sky. A lightning storm burns destruction over the world. I wake up covered in ice, the Suzerain's tyrannical laugh still echoing inside my mind.

∞

The dream is always the same. Not a dream – a memory. Every time I close my eyes, I relive that moment, and every moment awake I am reminded of what I have lost. *Ileana.*

It was all for nothing.

I'm in the Suzerain's chamber, lying in his bed. I wear his jewellery and command what's left of his power. Burn the gods! I wanted to ice the usurper, not replace him.

"Aedan? Aedan, wake up."

Hel's voice comes from the large gemstone on the wall. The gods can't Reach inside this room; it's the reason I chose it. Unfortunately, their aversion to the Nephilim's magic is not strong enough to stop them from using it. I roll over, covering my ears with a pillow. Gods have little need for sleep but I, despite having taken the power of a god, still require rest, even if only to relive my worst memories.

"Aedan, get up here!" Hel's voice again, distorted by whatever power the Suzerain gods use to make words travel through gems.

I groan in annoyance. "All right. I'm coming." I take the Suzerain's ring from the bedside table, still set on his frozen thumb, and move to stand on the dark circle at the corner of the room. From here I can teleport anywhere in the Stump, as long as I hold the ring and there's a matching circle in that destination. In principle, anyway.

"You better work this time," I grumble. Often it does not. One of the Suzerain's faithful who survived the initial attack by hiding with the women described the failed attempts as 'user errors'. I iced him. In retrospect, that might have been rash. We could definitely use more insight on how these things work. Then again, the idea had been to destroy them, not use them.

Light engulfs me, and I find myself in a small anteroom staring at a panel with a glaring red snake biting its tail. *Blazing sun.* I swear the flaming thing brings me here every time as if to aggravate me on purpose.

Maybe I should take the opportunity to go in. And this time, I'll show no mercy. I clench my jaw and step outside the circle, determined to be ruthless.

"Aedan! I need your help!" Hel's voice comes from somewhere in the ceiling this time and is tainted with

alarm. Must be serious, then. No god asks for help lightly.

I step back inside the circle. "Later," I promise the snake and work the black ring again.

Light blinds me once more, and I find myself back in the Suzerain's bedchamber. *Burn this.* I walk to the door. It slides to reveal Ideth standing behind it with a raised fist. Her eyes widen when she sees me, then travel from mine all the way down to my hip. I'm pretty sure I forgot to put on a shirt.

"Hel called for you, *Lord*." Despite her mild flirtation, Ideth sounds as tired as she looks. Her long hair is matted and dishevelled, her bright owl-like blue eyes sunken and dull in their sockets. I bet she has had little sleep since her old master's demise either. That and the failed reunion with her son have taken a toll on the pretty nymph.

"I heard." I point at the wall, then throw the finger and its ring on the bed in frustration. "And don't call me lord. I'm not Hades."

"Yes, milord."

It's pointless to argue with the nymph. If there's one thing I learnt about Ideth, it's that nothing short of ripping her tongue out would stop her from using it to exasperate others. She might be beholden to me, but her obligation only stretches so far. I storm past her and wind my way to the surface on foot.

The Stump, once a great World Tree, symbol of life and eternity, is now an artificial labyrinth of rectangular caverns, many of them unexplored since we killed everyone who knew how to access them. Walking through the narrow tunnels connecting the spaces might take longer than using the teleportation rings, but it's a surer and less aggravating way to get to where I need to be.

I'm in the last tunnel, already squinting at daylight, when the Stump shakes violently enough to throw me back and forth against the walls. I curse. The mighty tree trunk has been shaking since the Suzerain's shattering end – *How long ago?* I can't tell. It's hard to count the nights inside this metal cage – but this was no ordinary tremor. The whole structure creaked and groaned – not a good sign. Probably means the great teleportation ring on its surface has been activated – again. A worse sign. I run towards the light.

The white sun's energy prickles my bare skin, but daylight cannot burn me anymore thanks to Ambrosia and Loki, who tricked Eos into closing her eye. At least that is what Hel believes her father did. Sometimes I think I can still feel the blue sun, burning just beyond the icy Mountains, dormant, waiting to be summoned to Aegea again.

I wait for my eyes to adjust. Dharkan see perfectly in the dark but poorly otherwise. Regardless, I don't need sight or a god's Reach to know the whole surface is covered in thick ice again.

Hel stands alone at the edge of the hungry snake outlining the metal ring; it's dark centre shimmers like the Boiling Lake under the night's sky.

"What is it doing now?" I ask, wary. The large circle sometimes glows and spins grudgingly like a grinding stone, causing the old tree to groan and shudder with it. This, however, feels different and looks far more menacing.

"The Nephilim are coming to claim their Tribute," answers Oreth's petulant voice. I scowl at the dryad boy chained to Xylo and wonder whose brilliant idea this was.

Xylo, the bizarre hybrid creature created by the Suzerain's gods, now somehow miraculously restored from my lightning attack, appears – as usual – unflappable like a tree, staring up at the sky, seemingly unaware of the commotion, the chain around his tree trunk of an ankle or his reluctant companion. The boy, very much aware of his restrains, stands on his shoulders, as far away from the ice as possible, and grins maliciously at us.

"You're all going to pay for what you did," he says in that infuriating tone of his.

Oreth used to be the Suzerain's cup-bearer – whatever *that* is – and remains fiercely loyal to the tyrant and his gods. I should have iced him already, but I'd rather remain on good terms with Ideth. She owes me her life, and the debt increases every moment I spare her obnoxious offspring.

"What are you waiting for?" Hel asks, eyes blazing bluer than the banished Olympian sun.

Before I can react, something hits the frozen layer and cracks Hel's shield; the force of the impact throws me off balance.

"Where is Hades?" I ask. Or everyone else, for that matter. The gods keep finding excuses to be away from the dead Tree.

"Calling in a favour," Hel replies between clenched teeth. "He took the keys. Now, come here and help me, burn you!"

Took the keys?! Where? What favour? Why wasn't I in-formed? There is no time for questions. The snake spins faster and faster, the circle glows a deep red as if made of lava, and judging by how fast the ice melts above it, I reckon it's similarly as hot.

"Are you sure, goddess?"

"Yes! We can't let them through," Hel shouts as another thick layer of ice spreads over the one already in place. I move to her side, delighted by the opportunity to ice something.

∞

After the storm's power source became clear – that it came from Zeus and not the Suzerain – Hel advised me not to use any of my talents for fear of how they might interfere with the god's powers. Xylo hadn't been the only victim of the lightning storm brought down by my grief. All of Aegea suffered for it. But how am I supposed to learn how to control Zeus' power if I don't use it?

Another violent thump and the tree trunk quakes. The ring glows redder.

"Come on, Aedan! Show me what you've got," Hel demands and adds another layer of ice over the ring.

I grin and do not hold back. This is my moment. Now we'll find out just how useful the Olympian King's magic can be. And if I hit Xylo again, or maybe even Oreth... Well, tough luck. Gods never spare much thought for those caught in their power. Why should I?

I will show them.

Lightning flashes above, and a now familiar exhilaration rushes through my body along with a bleak sense of ignorance. I feel capable of shattering the world with a thought, if only I knew how to think the right one. I know I can plunge a bolt all the way down to the deepest pit in the Underworld, but I don't know where it is. So all I can do is gather energy from the sky and hope for the best.

I focus on the ice and channel all my strength and all my anger, plus Zeus' power, into that burning circle.

It is not enough.

Not smiling any longer, I double my efforts with a mighty roar. The ice layer gets thicker, stronger, colder. Lightning crashes all around us in a storm of wrath. The surge of energy running through me becomes painful and chaotic. I can't control it. I don't want to control it. I want to unleash it. Another quake. This one nearly knocks me off my feet. Whoever or whatever is trying to get through is close to succeeding.

Hel utters a curse so coarse even the dead would shy away from but holds her ground. She is a sight to behold. I can freeze better than most of my kind, but the goddess of Niflheim would put any Dharkan to shame. As soon as the ice weakens, she pours more cold into it. She makes it look easy, but even gods have their limits. We won't be able to hold it for much longer.

Not like this.

"Aedan!"

"This is all I've got," I'm forced to admit. As it turns out, Zeus' power is of little help in this situation. He was a god of thunder, not of ice, and the Suzerain, despite being as invulnerable and arrogant as a god, seems to have had no talents of his own. At least that I've yet to discover.

Hel's strength falters; my own is close to exhausted. Part of me wants to just let them come and be done with this. After all, I am better at sucking life than heat, but with no way to know what we are facing on the other side, how many or how strong these beings are, it is not wise to do so. *Know your prey*, my father used to say. It applies to enemies too, and of this enemy we know nothing save that it is formidable and relentless.

"We can't stop it like this!" the goddess cries out. I sense her exhaustion, fear and frustration inside my mind as if it's my own – she is Reaching for me to host her. Clever. Together we can hold a lot more power, enough to fight off whatever is on the other side of this sorcery. And if we fail, as a host I can still protect her identity from the enemy.

I let her in, for there is no denying Hel. Any Dharkan would kill for the honour to host his goddess. The truth is, I yearn to experience her mighty power first-hand. The goddess hesitates. Why? She knows how much I need to fight and destroy those on the other side. I need revenge for Ileana. I need –

The glow ceases. The snake stops chasing its tail, and the ring becomes dark and cool again.

∞

"There," Hades says, fiddling with the gems on the Suzerain's armlet, the only device that doesn't require his flesh to work. I growl in frustration. The

Underworld Lord always shows up in the nick of time and takes credit for solving a situation he created in the first place. Together, Hel and I could have defeated whatever is on the other side without his timely intervention.

"Oh, thank goodness," says the Titan, Chiron. He's another one I wouldn't mind freezing. The creature makes no sense, even for a god. I still don't understand how he speaks at all. He used to be part horse, part human, and now he's part horse, part bird, and somehow he still sounds like a human. Gods are bizarre creatures, especially Titans.

"Not bad for a goat," Chiron says to Hades. He must be extremely relieved to give such a compliment to the god.

"The perks of having opposable thumbs." Hades sneers back at him.

Chiron snorts and turns away, 'accidentally' hitting Hades on the head with one of his outstretched wings.

"Ow! Stupid horse! You were saying?" Hades asks the disappointed boy glaring at him from atop Xylo's shoulders. Oreth's teeth rattle; he has frost in his hair and the beginnings of an icicle under his nose. Even Xylo shows hints of discomfort – or maybe just annoyance – standing half buried in ice. He spares us a sour look while he brushes away the frost from himself with the care one applies to brushing away a bee.

The Stump shakes again, and the circle glows anew. Oreth grins. "They'll just keep trying until they get through. You are all going to regret this."

"Aren't you the merry oracle?" Hades twists the gems again, and the glowing ceases.

Hel, barely able to stand, collapses on the icy surface. Hades is at her side in a blink of an eye. Real gods don't need portals to move from place to place in an instant, it seems.

"I'm fine," Hel says, pushing him away half-heartedly. "Was it worth it?"

Chiron tucks his wings close to his equine body and shakes his head. "I fear Hephaestus is reluctant to assist us."

Hades snorts. "Understatement of the millennium!"

"I thought you said he hated Zeus," Hel says.

"He does – er… he did." Chiron ruffles his feathers and flares his nostrils in my direction. His horse face looks reproachful, like Cornus' whenever I took an action he did not approve of. I dislike Chiron for reminding me of him and wish he would revert to his previous form.

The death of the King of Olympus still has not settled well with the gods. Not because they cared for Zeus, for they did not, but because he did die – by my hand. I'm well aware of how they look at me sometimes, even Hel, for she knows I would ice any deity if it would bring Ileana back.

"Who are you talking about?" I ask. The name Hephaestus means nothing to me.

"The blacksmith in the forest," Hel answers as if I should know who that is, and after a moment's denial, I realise I do.

"You mean the Crafter? He's a *god*?" *What sort of god would choose to look so grotesque*, I wonder. Then I glance at Hades and dismiss the question. "You went to *him* for help?" Any Dharkan knows not to trust the Crafter's weapons, but apparently he is an Olympian and gods are not Dharkan. What they are, clearly, is desperate.

"Have any better ideas?" Hades asks rhetorically. Sparks crack between my fingers in an involuntary response, triggered by a lingering effect of Zeus' life force and his hatred for Hades, I guess. Not that the Underworld lord requires his brother's influence in me to inspire hostility.

"And?" Hel prompts impatiently. The gods are only using words for my benefit, and so I let them speak.

"As it turns out, there is another god he hates more than Zeus," Chiron says with a hint of annoyance, kicking at the ice.

"Who?" Hel asks.

"Loki," Hades replies in an 'I told you so' tone.

It seems this Trickster god has made enemies in every pantheon. Having been his host and knowing how he thinks, I'm glad he's not *my* enemy.

Hel looks dead serious, which means she's confused. "What has my father done to the cripple?"

"Nothing. But he offended his beloved wife."

"Ah… the altercation with Aphrodite, right," she whispers to herself. "But that was ages ago!"

"You better than anyone should know how long gods can hold a grudge," Hades says pointedly.

"Did you explain to the cripple that whatever is

beyond that portal doesn't care about our grievances and if it takes my world, it will go after the gods in it first? All the gods, regardless of their pantheon."

"He's not too worried about that, apparently. And, my lady, if you hope for his favour, I suggest you stop calling him cripple."

"I've heard you call him worse often enough," Hel protests. "Isn't he worried I can permanently freeze his furnace if he refuses to cooperate?"

Hades shrugs. "No, not particularly either. He even had the nerve to challenge me to take him to Tartarus. Tempting, oh so very tempting."

"Why didn't you?" I ask. I often find the gods' motives puzzling. So much power and so much reluctance to use it.

Hades gives me an exasperated glance. "Why didn't I give the god of blacksmithing access to the best forge in the Universe, you mean?"

It's still your forge, I think, but remain silent. Hades has no more control over his furnace than Hel has over Aegea, judging by the number of Dharkan in Hades' Underworld, working to keep it contained.

Hel shakes her head. "I cannot believe it. Aphrodite is probably off in Olympus with that brute who calls himself a god of war, and he refuses our request for her sake?"

"What can I say, my lady. Love is stupid." There is something forced in Hades' cheeky tone. Almost as if he believes his words for a change.

Hel snorts. "Men are stupid, especially gods."

"Is that your answer to every man who disagrees with your wishes, my lady?"

Hel's eyes flash blue for a moment. Hades never misses an opportunity to rattle the goddess. I struggle to understand their courtship, for I would never speak to Ileana this way.

Chiron whines and creeps away. I consider following his example before the headache that usually follows their arguments manifests. This particular argument happens far too often, and it bored me the first time I heard it.

"Did you offer him anything in exchange, or just made demands?" I ask instead. In my experience, gods often skip the giving part of negotiations.

Hades fakes offence. "We offered him plenty: power, respect, freedom to go beyond Aegea, and all the nymphs in the forest besides!"

"He said he might take Hel if she begged him," Chiron says to the wind, avoiding Hel's gaze.

"He said what?!" Hel stands, and the ice underneath her feet splinters into shards.

Hades holds on to his horns, sighs and shoots a 'you shouldn't' glance at the Titan, who has already taken flight with a whinny that sounds suspiciously like disguised laughter.

"He said he would take you as payment for both his help and as payback for your father's insult to Aphrodite." Hades keeps looking the livid goddess in the eye as he speaks. "I figured you wouldn't be interested in that deal."

Hel practically shatters with rage. Her eyes burn like blue coals. If not for her exhaustion, I suspect the whole Stump would have frozen by now.

Oreth, catching up with the conversation, bursts

out laughing. Xylo sprouts a branch and forces the dryad from his shoulder. He hasn't spoken, has barely moved since we took the Stump in fact. Never perturbed, disturbed or seemingly aware, and yet there is something there, behind those blank eyes of his, that makes me think his mind is not as empty as the gods say it is. Xylo might look like a tree, but as any Dharkan knows: trees can't be trusted. I wonder about his Prana, and ice forms on my palms. My recent efforts have left me peckish.

"My lady, spare yourself. He's not worth your rage." Hades must have said something else to her in their hidden language, for her eyes return to silver and she eases herself back down, subdued. After her own ordeal with the portal, this display of anger probably cost her more energy than she could spare.

The portal might open again at any moment.

"And where is Loki?" I ask. The Trickster has been absent since we took the Stump. If what Hades said is true, maybe he should be the one making amends.

Hel's eyes flicker for a moment. "On the other side, tending to a personal matter – and taking his time about it," she grumbles, sounding more suspicious than upset.

"You know how easy it is to lose time on the other side, my lady," Hades says sheepishly.

He had kept her captive for a generation. How the gods can lose track of so much time is beyond me.

"So now what?" I ask.

No answer. I suspect no one has one. I don't see Loki apologising or submitting to any sort of deal. Hel's even less likely to do so. She'll follow through with her threats first, no matter the cost. I have a mind to speak with the Crafter myself. Perhaps he won't dismiss a request from the man who killed Zeus. Anything to get me away from this place. Except… I grind my teeth in frustration. I can't leave yet.

∞

"Is it safe?" Arianh asks, poking her head up from the ramp.

"Define safe," I reply to the queen.

My once betrothed narrows her violet eyes at me and emerges fully, elbows locked with the Wyrd.

"It's over, uncle, come."

Odin, the fated Aesir King, drags his feet behind her. His ravens, Huginn and Muninn come to perch on his shoulders. He pays them no attention. Once unable to keep silent, he has not said a word since we took control of the Stump. Not even when we discovered that Zeus, his arch-rival, had perished. I thought the news would please him, but it sent him deeper into a stupor instead. He whimpers frequently as if in pain and stares off at horrors only he can see. His host's hair, once a bright shade of green similar to Ileana's, has turned black overnight. Occasionally a tear forms in one of his murky green eyes and dries there unshed. I do not know or care what afflicts the man, but he'd better get over it soon. For once, I'd like to hear Odin's thoughts on the recent events. Ideally, a plan. The Wyrd always had a plan.

I used to think the eccentric creature was brainsick, a consequence of being fated. Now that I've spent some time amongst other gods, Olympians in particular,

I've changed my definition of sanity altogether. I almost miss the constant meddling and scheming of the Wyrd. At least his plans made sense; they worked, after a fashion. One thing has to be said for the Wyrd: he always knew what to do. He had initiative, took action, and worried about the consequences afterwards, much like a Dharkan.

The Olympian gods go about things the other way around: always too concerned with consequences to take any action. Even Hel, once so decisive, now hesitates before acting. I blame Hades. She changed after her time in his Underworld. And Chronos, of course. The unspoken name on everyone's mind. I would fear him too if I had as much to lose as they do: their worlds, maybe even their very existence. Then again, I did lose my world. *Maybe if I had been more cautious, I'd still have Ileana.* No, I push the thought aside. It's restraint that leads to regret, not the other way around.

A young Narrum boy follows the Wyrd. Like a faithful hound, he has not let Odin out of his sight since we took the Stump. He flashes a ghastly grin at me. The boy has big teeth and is always showing them – quite unnecessarily. He makes my skin crawl, for that creature is neither boy nor Narrum. He and Hel are both children of Loki, and I doubt I could ever confront that one in his true form.

"Hey, pup," Hel says tiredly. The boy howls at her, a playful howl that puts a smile on the goddess's face and a frown on Hades', who obviously dislikes children and puppies alike.

The Aossi queen removes her exquisite dress, indifferent to the boy's lustful gaze, then helps the Wyrd out of his cloak and looks to the sky with regret. The fated god has already shed some flesh from his bones. All Wyrd must be starving without the blue sun. Instead of just a few minutes basking at dawn, they now need to spend every moment of daylight under the white sun to sustain themselves.

"Any word from Judoc?" Arianh asks.

No one answers. Judoc, the Suzerain's living shrine in Relicum, has taken the horde of women and children held inside the Stump back to his temple, and no one but Arianh has missed him since.

"Shouldn't your sister bask too, or is she still afraid to show her face?" I ask.

"I'm the one who can't look at her face," the queen grumbles. "Fasting will do her good. She needs to think about what she's done."

Arianh's anger seeps through every syllable. I smile at her petty rage and wonder, had Ileana not prayed to Chronos, if we would ever have worked as a couple, the way Odin planned. Underneath her warmth lies a cold resolution I admire.

"Don't starve her too much. I like my meals well fed," I say to her. Oreth scowls defiantly at me, while Arianh throws me a look half horrified, half hurt. It's not a tease. The Suzerain's mistress failed to provide us with useful information. I only left Occa alive as a supply of Prana – and Arianh knows it. The girl has yet to leave her chamber, though. Like Oreth, she's waiting to be rescued by her gods, or maybe she's just avoiding Ideth. After the beating the nymph gave her, I wouldn't be surprised if she feared her more than me. As for the queen and I... No, it would never work.

I watch the way she tends to the Wyrd: a fated god, not even from her own pantheon; a creature willing to sell her and her people to benefit himself. I sigh. She's too soft for me.

Chiron lands beside Xylo. "What if *Psyche* talks to the Blacksmith instead?" he suggests in a small voice.

The gods had to have been talking amongst themselves, and this is his way of including me in the conversation. My fists freeze at the mention of the goddess who took Ileana as host. *The one responsible for her death.*

"She should be ready to cooperate by now," Hel says, glancing at me.

I scowl. I've been doing all I can to persuade Psyche to talk, and the only things I get from the goddess are insults and nonsense. It has occurred to me her mind might be broken. Who knows what the Suzerain's weapon did to her? Maybe icing the goddess of the soul would be a mercy to us all, but the gods don't let me use any *hands-on* measures. They want me to believe she's worth more alive, that her power is too dangerous to meddle with. The truth is, they all fear her. Their fear and my need for answers keep the goddess alive and useless, locked deep inside the Stump. I itch to squeeze every bit of Prana out of the creature, and grow more impatient each passing night. Unlike them, I don't have eternity to waste.

"She claims she's quite comfortable down there," I say.

"Comfortable?! Like a fish in the desert, I imagine," Hades says.

"She probably feels safer there," Chiron snorts,

introspection in his large equine eyes. He was against her imprisonment. He wanted to use his self-proclaimed wisdom and charisma to reason with Psyche instead. Except he can't fit on any of the teleportation rings, and without Gaea around, the gods would rather not risk letting her out of the vault for questioning.

Hel grimaces. "You haven't been down there. That place is a god's worst nightmare. *Powerless* doesn't begin to describe what it does to you. It's like a weight, a deep sense of loss." Hel shakes herself. "She won't be able to take that pressure much longer."

Hades grunts. "It's probably no worse than being a Wyrd."

The corners of the Odin's mouth twitch into what might be a smirk.

"In any case, Aphrodite hates her as much as Loki, if not more," Hades continues with a shrug.

"Why is that?" I ask, curious.

"Oh, it's a long family feud involving worshipping rights."

"Care to elaborate?"

"Oy." Hades scratches his bushy ears and glances at Hel sideways. "Apparently some humans believed she was more worthy of worship than the goddess of beauty herself."

"She's not *that* beautiful," Hel grumbles. I agree. Humans are small, ugly creatures. They have little appeal to the senses, or sustenance.

Hades laughs and immediately raises his hands in a placating gesture. "Humans, my lady, they have strange aesthetic ideals. But it's worth a try. Let her speak with Hephaestus. After all, Psyche is sort of his daughter-in-law. Who knows, perhaps he'll take her apology in exchange."

The implication makes me cringe. Olympians are all a bunch of inbred perverts. No wonder their creations are skewed. Except for Ileana, of course.

"I thought you two were friends," says Chiron, one ear flat against his equine head, the other stretched out, suspicious.

"All I'm saying is that she might be willing to swallow some of her pride in exchange for freedom. We've already established men are stupid." Hades glances at Hel. She's not amused. "The only thing we know for certain is how much Psyche wants to be free of us, of this place. And how persuasive she can be. It's just a thought." He waves a dismissive hand and lies back on the ice.

"Feel free to go ask her, then," I sneer, daring him to do it. Hades attempts to burn me with his gaze. "No? Then I guess she's mine until she gives me what I want. You can use her afterwards."

Suddenly Hades is no longer lying at Hel's side but standing right in front of me. A distant fire burns behind his black eyes. I blink. Never noticed that before. "You play a dangerous game, Aedan, son of Eghan. You think dangerous thoughts and speak rash words. Don't make the mistake of overestimating your… *abilities*. You don't want to bring down the wrath of real gods upon your oh so flammable flesh."

This is the first honest thing he's ever said to me, far from the speech of the character he plays. Now his relationship with Hel starts to make sense. The goddess would never compromise to a weaker god. It makes no difference. Psyche is the only link to Ileana I have left, and I'm the only one willing to enter the room she's in. Maybe Hades can burn me right here and now, but I'm confident he won't ever enter that chamber. I hold his gaze and smile.

"This discussion is pointless," Chiron says. His hoofs scratch at the ice nervously. "We still don't know if the cripp – he snorts – if Hephaestus can help us or not."

"Oh, I know he can – if he wants to," Hades says without taking his eyes off me. Still sounding sincere.

There's a silent pause while the gods exchange meaningful glances again. I hate when they do that. I can see by Arianh's confused frown that she's not pleased to be left out of the conversation either. Mika, on the other hand, looks fairly entertained.

"You guys are hilarious," he says, giggling to himself.

"I'll talk to Psyche," the Wyrd says, breaking the silence. *Burn him.* Days without a word and he chooses *now* to comment. This can't be good.

"Look who's alive! Welcome back, old friend," Hades says sarcastically. The fire in his eyes vanishes behind the mask that slides back into place. "Yes, Odin should convince her. Thank you. Bring her up. Let's get it over with," he orders, almost daring me to disobey. Sparks crack between my fingers.

"I want to talk to Psyche alone," Odin says. Then he whispers something to his ravens and they fly off. His eyes are focused and cunning. He's his old self again.

"As if I'll ever leave you two alone," I say.

"Agree," Hel says.

Odin rakes a hand through his raven hair. "She's in that room, right? Gods are powerless there, as I understand." Hades and Hel shift uncomfortably. The gods avoid that room like a Dharkan avoids the sun. It can't just be because it makes them powerless, can it?

Odin laughs. "But I bet it doesn't affect me. I'm already powerless. Besides, if she's powerless, what can she do to me in there? Nothing. I know she can help us, and I know how to persuade her to do it."

"Then by all means, do share," I say, unhappy with the direction the conversation is going.

Odin gives me that look of his that says 'you're an idiot'. "I need to have her trust. She won't be ordered about or judged. The woman is more stubborn than a mule! She'll defy you even if she agrees with you, just to prove that she can."

"That's absurd," I say.

"No. That is true," Hades says, amused. "The butterfly, like most humans, can be quite stubborn. Wouldn't you be if you thought you had nothing to gain?" He directs the question at Hel.

"I don't like it, Odin. Why would she even talk to you? There is something you're not telling me." She narrows her eyes, trying to Reach into the old Wyrd's mind.

He shrugs nonchalantly. "I'm a Wyrd. She used to be a Wyrd. We are both in a powerless position. I can use that to build some rapport, at least."

"It's not enough." Hel steps closer to him; her frown deepens.

Odin clutches the air below his chin a few times, then exhales deeply. "I know how to talk to her, Hel." He lowers his voice in a conspiratorial tone. "Listen, you need to trust me on this."

"No, *you* listen," she says loud and clear. "I will not let you burn this up." Cold spreads from her, forcing Arianh, who's been standing between the two with her mouth agape, to take a few steps back, shivering.

"Oh," Odin says, also moving away from the frigorific goddess. Hel and Hades exchange glances again. Arianh looks to me for clarification and catches Mika staring at her breasts, unaffected by the exchange or the cold.

"Believe it or not, I'm on your side. I can bring her into the fold," Odin repeats gravely. His good eye rests on the grinning, almost drooling boy standing next to him. "You have my word as the King of Asgard."

"Very well," Hel says after a moment's consideration. "Odin will convince her."

What just happened? I wonder. Suddenly all eyes are on me.

I clench my fists. "With all due respect, goddess. Psyche is my prisoner. I have a personal interest in her and –"

"And have you had any success questioning her?"

"Well no, but –" I bristle. "I have tried everything short of freezing the creature."

"My point exactly. Perhaps a little empathy is in order. Let me talk to her. Wyrd to Wyrd," Odin says in his old calculating tone.

"No," I insist.

"You catch more flies with honey than sour wine,"

Arianh says. All eyes shift from me to her. She blushes. "It is a Narrum saying. I think I finally understand it now." Arianh smiles at her uncle, who smiles back at her fondly. Hades and Hel are suspiciously silent. Chiron flaps his wings, while Xylo crosses his arms. If they hadn't moved, I'd completely forget they were there. How can creatures so large go unnoticed in such a way? Oreth, standing on one leg between them, couldn't look more perplexed.

"I'll go with him," Mika says casually.

Hel narrows her eyes at her brother, then turns to me. "Very well. Aedan, I order you to take them to the goddess of the soul. Make sure she cooperates this time, then bring her to the great hall so I can take her oath." Her tone's final and leaves no room for argument. I clench my jaw and reluctantly obey.

CHAPTER THREE

Ideth

Ideth's stomach churned as she held the Suzerain's finger to the snake. Freezing goddess, handling the digit was not getting easier with practice. She wondered if this flesh-based magic of the Nephilim had been devised purposely to deter dryads from using it. It made no sense; the Suzerain had been a dryad, after all. Then again, he was far from a good example of one.

A violent quake swept the floor from under Ideth's feet. She flailed about with nothing to hold on to until she landed painfully on her knee, dropping the gem key in the process. *Frost.* The clinking of metal on metal told her the ring had rolled some distance away. She cursed again in the near darkness, regretting not bringing one of the flameless torches with her, then began searching the smooth floor with her fingertips, praying for whatever was happening on the surface to last long enough for her to return the finger and its ring back to Aedan's room before he missed them. The last thing Ideth needed was to further aggravate the Wraith. Ice, but the creature was a boulder about to roll down a mountain, felling every tree in his path. She had no intention of being one of them.

Aedan was not like the other Wraiths; that he'd spared her that fated dawn was proof of that. He could have taken her life then and a dozen other times since, but he'd rather have her as a friend, someone loyal to him, the way he was to the goddess Hel. Loyalty was more important to Aedan than killing. He had the Aesir notions of honour and a soft spot for dryads. Ideth had used both to her advantage, but she doubted those traits would spare her this time. If the Wraith found out she was there, against his wishes, he would suck the life from her just for the fun of it.

A muffled buzz, akin to a bee caught in a pot, interrupted her thoughts. It came from behind her, from a panel no one had managed to open yet. The whole thing now glowed alarmingly bright, and the sound made the hairs on her nape stand. It reminded her of the day the World Tree fell.

There were plenty of bizarre objects inside the Stump, and most of them glowed and made strange noises, but nothing like this. She half expected a swarm of wasps to pour out of the snake at any moment. Never prone to eerie feelings or shivers, in that moment Ideth had plenty of both.

The glare allowed her to spot the gem key only inches away. She hastily picked it up, her nausea replaced by something close to panic, and promptly pressed it in place. The wall clicked and drifted slowly aside. Too slowly. Behind her, the buzz was taking on a life of its own. The whole room vibrated with it.

She considered going back to the teleportation ring, but then she might not get another chance to talk to Psyche alone. *Move!* Ideth urged to the wall. She had no time to stand around and watch walls drag themselves to the sound of angry wasps. She slid through the opening as soon as she could fit in, and once on the other side, she breathed out, realising she had forgotten to do so for some time.

What the frost was that?

The Suzerain once told her he had coated the walls of the Stump with a god's blood, and she figured that was what the gods sensed and feared, but blood did not explain what she'd just witnessed.

Behind her, the anteroom was dark and silent once again, as if nothing happened. Would it happen again when she left? *One problem at a time*, she told herself, taking another deep breath, remembering where she was and what she came there to do.

The vault, as the gods called it, was a stark and gloomy room, not much different from the one she'd just left. Every room in the Stump was like that, as if purposely designed to be uncomfortable and unnatural. At least this one didn't buzz. Ideth took it as an improvement.

At its centre, an old man in a white toga floated in mid-air, wrapped in light. She curled her lip at him. Had Ideth any respect left for the Olympian gods, she'd discarded it then. Why would their king take human form? Olympians had no issues changing appearance, but even Chiron, at his best, presented himself as a centaur: half horse and half *human*, not dryad.

Floating next to Zeus was Ileana: the Suzerain's daughter; the dryad Ideth plucked out of time through the Chronodéndron. Death suited her, for she'd never looked so serene, but Ideth knew *serene* was probably the last word anyone would use to describe the woman. When they'd met, all Ileana had wanted was to die, so Ideth spared no pity for her now. At least someone got what they wanted out of this mess.

Ideth put herself at the mercy of Chronos to bring Ileana through time. *A son for a daughter*. That had been the deal with the Suzerain. Unfortunately, things had not turned out exactly as planned. They never do. Somewhere along the way, Ileana had been replaced by a Wyrd, and instead of her baby boy, Ideth came back to find a young man. A young man raised by a tyrant who'd filled his head with notions of godhood. A young man who all but despised his mother, almost as much as Ileana had despised her father. Ideth told herself she'd got the best end of the bargain, since she still had her life and her son, even if the reunion had not gone as she'd hoped, while the Suzerain… she considered the frozen finger in her hand and sighed. There was no winning with the Suzerain. He'd lost, sure, but so had everyone else. The gods were fools to believe otherwise.

Ideth's shoulders slumped. She felt so drained. *No. I haven't lost yet*, she reminded herself. That was why she risked Aedan's anger by coming here. Oreth had a problem, and problems could be solved.

The solution stood between the two bodies. The Wyrd who'd taken Ileana to get to the Suzerain. A goddess that all the other gods feared. She was small, barely as tall as Ideth herself, and not quite Narrum, for she had a slender bone structure and was almost as lovely as a nymph. The differences between her and the Narrum were subtle, as subtle as Anann and Aossi, but there was no mistaking her race. She *was* human. Beautiful or not, all humans were sick creatures.

"You're early. The sun's still up. Have you fallen out of, oh –"

Psyche went silent when she turned around and found Ideth, obviously not who she'd been expecting. Aedan was the only one who dared to come down here to interrogate her.

"Well, well, unbridled one. What a surprise. Last I saw you, you were clawing at Occa's face. I figured you'd win."

Ideth blinked. How could she have seen their fight? *She's not a Wyrd anymore*, Ideth reminded herself. Not a friend; nor an ally either.

"And before that," Psyche continued, "you were stuck between a furious Dharkan and a vengeful goddess. How did you get yourself out of that one, little snake?"

Snake?! Does she know how much I hate snakes as well? To call *her* a snake: the most revolting of creatures with their unblinking eyes and appetite for vermin. The freezing human had the nerve to compare her to *that*? She'd teach her a few things about snakes.

Ideth took a step forward, and the Stump shook again. That made her pause. There was no time for insults, so she lifted her chin, took a deep breath and gave the infuriating goddess her best smile instead.

"Aedan saw the value of keeping me alive," Ideth said. She almost sounded calm.

"Did he?" Psyche crossed her arms and raised an eyebrow in an appraising look. "So you're his pet now. Good for you. He does like his meals seasoned with Ambrosia. Has he tasted you yet?"

Ideth's lip curled. "I don't have time to fill you in on the details of my life choices."

Psyche smiled, amused. "No, he has not, and he doesn't know you're here either. Alone with his prisoner. Holding the key to the cage. Tsk tsk, you naughty girl."

You naughty girl. That had been what Ideth said to her when she'd seen Ileana basking under Eos' eye. She'd thought it part of Ileana's self-destructive tendencies, for the blue sun, although exhilarating, was also noxious to most beings.

The goddess ambled towards her. "Have you come to take me on a journey to a better world?"

"No." Ideth cursed her lack of planning. Psyche was supposedly powerless inside the room, but could she take the gem key from her by force? Ideth took in the goddess's confident, knowing smile and didn't like her own chances. They were of a similar size, but Psyche looked nimble and had more muscle on her than Ideth, and she was a goddess to boot, not some stiff, old hag like Rita. To Ideth's surprise, the goddess just circled around her.

"So, why are you here?" Psyche asked coldly.

Ideth swallowed. "I need to ask you something."

"Aahh. I have a few questions for you myself. Shall we trade?"

Ideth cursed. Nothing was ever free with the gods.

"Go on," the goddess insisted. "I can't read your thoughts in here. What do you want to know?"

Ideth had prepared a summary of her troubles for Psyche. When the Stump shook again, she decided it was probably still too lengthy. In truth, Ideth wasn't sure how to ask what she wanted to know, or what the goddess could do to help her, but she was the goddess of the soul. It stood to reason she must know all there is to know about the things.

"Can a soul be sick?" Ideth finally asked.

Psyche tilted her head, confused. "Define sick."

Ideth clicked her tongue. For once, she wished Psyche could just read her mind and give her the answers to the questions she wasn't sure how to ask. "Forgetful. Can a soul forget?"

"Ah, you're talking about your son."

"Yes."

"He was a baby when you left. Of course he forgot you."

"Yes, but, his father…"

"Was a god."

"Yes, well, he was a Wyrd, actually. When his host died, he transferred his soul to me – to Oreth, I mean – so he could live again. Shouldn't he remember?"

Psyche's eyes went wide, then she burst out laughing. "Seriously?"

"What's so funny?" Ideth wasn't amused, and the goddess quickly sobered.

"Listen, I won't even go into how fucked up that idea is. First, souls are not commodities, Ideth. They can't be passed around like that. As far as I know, only

I have that power, and I would not make you give birth to your dead lover. Second, memories are linked to the mind, not the soul. And third, I've met Oreth. There's no proper soul in him. He's just like all other dryads. You, however, are not."

"Because his father's soul is still in me?"

"No. That's not it. Even you don't possess what gods call a soul."

Ideth's lip quivered at Psyche's harsh words. "Oreth's father had a soul. What happened to it, then?"

"I don't know. If his host died, chances are he's in the Underworld. Have you asked Hades or Hel?"

"No. I know he's not in the Underworld."

"How?"

"I just do."

"You're not giving me much to work with, unbridled one." Psyche sighed. "Perhaps he's free and far away."

"He would never leave us." Of that, Ideth was certain.

"Maybe he didn't have a choice. Maybe he intended to return and now he can't. Maybe he never left this world and is still cursed in another mortal. I honestly don't know. Ask me again when I'm not in here. This room clouds my insight." Psyche scowled at it, then pointed at Ideth's hand. "You hold the key to all your answers."

Ideth looked at the large black gem set on the ring around the Suzerain's finger. "I can't let you out. You'll have to kill me for it, for if you leave this room because of me, they will."

"Then I can't help you."

Ideth hesitated. She did not trust Psyche, and she probably would not believe her, anyway. Then again, at this point, what did she have to lose? "I feel him with me," she admitted in a whisper.

Psyche frowned. "What, exactly, do you feel?"

"I feel protected. Loved. Warm. It's like he's always standing behind me. Watching over me. Whenever I turn around, I expect to see him there. He's always with me from the moment I wake up until I go to sleep."

"How... disturbingly intimate," Psyche said cautiously. "Do you feel him now?"

"No... not in here..." Ideth admitted. There was only a deep sense of loss and emptiness inside the room.

"And you didn't feel him in Ileana's time," Psyche mused.

Ideth bristled. "How the frost do you know that?"

"You told me about your... *feelings* back in the forest, remember?" Psyche sneered.

"Oh... right." Ideth cursed with irritation. She al-ways had a tendency to say too much and thought it best to get back on the subject.

"So what are souls, anyway? Why are they so special?" *Why are you?* she almost asked, but bit her lip instead.

"Souls are what powers a god's will. It gives them the ability to bend the rules of the Universe in order to get what they want."

Ideth wasn't impressed. "That's it? I'm wilful. Caused me nothing but trouble."

Psyche laughed. A sharp sort of laugh with more triumph than mirth in it. "Yes, that you are. Who knows, maybe you do have something akin to a soul in you. After all, you can taste souls," she said conspiratorially.

The memory of that tasting still haunted Ideth. "I don't know why," she said truthfully. "It's something I've always been able to do, and so far it's been a hindrance, not an advantage."

"Most gifts are…" Psyche said morosely.

The Stump shook again. There was no more time to beat around the bush.

"I need to find Oreth's father. Can you help me or not?"

"Very well," Psyche said, understanding the urgency. "I promise to help you find him once I'm free of this place. Good enough?" Ideth nodded. A god's promise was as binding as a curse. "Now, you have your answers. I still have my questions."

"Then ask them."

"My mind's been violated. I have too many of Ileana's memories, and too few of my own. I want you to kiss me and tell me what you see."

"What? Kiss you again? Here? *Now*?" The request was abrupt and unexpected, especially considering how the Wyrd, er… the goddess had reacted to it the first time.

"Fancy taking me for a stroll in the forest first? Yes, now, before this whole structure collapses. What is going on up there?"

"Something to do with the portal."

"It can't be good, then. So, come on. Kiss me. Before I change my mind."

Ideth did as she asked.

At least she's an attractive human. It was a strange thought to have. Her second thought was that Psyche was not a bad kisser, kissing back with a passion reserved for clandestine lovers. Afterwards there were no more thoughts, only darkness.

That dark taste – for lack of a better word – filled her senses and twisted her mind. A flavour rich with anger, ambition, desire, lust. Ideth felt herself falling into it. It called to her, pulling her in, tearing her apart with need. Ideth opened her mouth to breathe, and Psyche plunged her tongue deeper, breathing her in instead. The darkness overwhelmed her.

A light flickered: a candle, maybe? The glow was too dim or the darkness too vast to be sure. It burned cold and distant. She couldn't see past it. Something called to her. Ideth pulled Psyche closer, curious. More darkness.

Next Ideth was falling off a cliff, falling off the world. Then she was flying above the clouds in an alien, bright blue sky. The wind took her to a palace made of light and gold. Greater than any temple. There she felt empty, sad; so sad and lonely. She wanted to leave; she had to get away, but there was nowhere to go. Hidden eyes watched her every movement. They watched her as she watched the sun set, and her misery turned to dread. He was coming. He was coming to take her in the darkness. She wanted to scream, to cry, to hide. She wanted to die. Ideth tried to pull away from the kiss.

Psyche held her closer, kissing deeper. There was that candle again… It burned. It burned away the darkness and blinded her with starlight: warm and beckoning, almost too bright to look at. Ideth focused on the light. It called to her, sang to her, danced with her, and then it was burning her from within, hot and bright and as dangerous as the blue sun. And then…

Ideth opened her eyes. Psyche had hers open too. She tried to pull away, but it was Ideth's turn to pull the goddess close, for she saw Orion there, in that brightness, his smile spread across the stars.

The goddess was stronger, and their lips parted.

"What did you see?" Psyche asked breathlessly.

Ideth couldn't answer.

"Tell me. What did you see!" Psyche pleaded, desperation in her voice.

"What did you do to him?" Ideth murmured.

"Who?"

"Orion."

Psyche opened her mouth and frowned, confused. "Who?"

"I saw him in the stars – with you!"

"Ideth, I don't remember anyone by that name. I swear."

Psyche took a step towards her.

"Just stay the frost away from me!" Ideth warned, walking back to the wall. She was shaking, her lips burned, and she felt sick. She took a long look at Psyche with disgust. "You are wrong. Everything about you is *wrong*."

Psyche looked hurt. Ideth didn't care. She couldn't

breathe. She had to get away from the creature, from the room, from all its ghosts. She opened the panel and walked through it, all memory of eerie buzzing forgotten beneath the surmounting horror that filled her mind.

INTERLUDE 2

A God's Grave

I take my leave ahead of the group and walk the long way down to the Suzerain's private chambers to clear my head. I often imagined the Suzerain living in opulence, like a king or one of the Olympians, but apart from the bed – which is comfortable, I have to admit – an absurdly large mirror and a few dresses hanging from the wall, there's not much in here. Either he wasn't as pampered as I thought, or he didn't spend much time in the room.

It doesn't take long for Ideth to materialise through the ring. She holds the Suzerain's frozen digit with its large onyx ring by the tips of her fingers, as if to not taint herself with it.

"Was it worth it?" I ask.

She freezes, just about to turn on the light, then clenches her jaw and lifts her head high to stare at a point a couple of inches to my left. Her face is wrecked with concern, guilt and disappointment, but even sleep deprived and grieving, she has the ability to look enticingly vulnerable. Not that I've ever considered taking any dryad except Ileana, of course.

I touch the button on the wall, and light floods the room, leaving me half blind and her able to see the anger on my scarred face. She blinks, then rubs her eyes from the sudden glare and adjusts her tear-streaked gaze to meet mine.

"Not really," Ideth says with such weariness I'm inclined to believe her. "But I had to try."

She drops the stolen gem key in my hand. "Do what you have to do."

I have to give it to the nymph. For someone who just got caught under the blazing sun with no shade in sight, she has nerves of steel. And no shame.

"Did the Titan put you up to this?"

"No. It was my idea."

I believe her. Unlike the others, Chiron has showed little to no interest in the goddess of the soul, and he's very protective of his unbridled one. Besides, I know the nymph well enough to know she has her own mind, and it's not like Ideth subscribes to the idea that it's better to ask forgiveness than permission, for she does neither and she's more efficient because of it.

"So, what did you talk about?"

"We didn't talk much." Ideth brushes her lips with the tips of her fingers and grimaces. "Words are not her forte."

I disagree with that. Psyche can be more laconic than a Dharkan, true. She is frugal with words, but she knows exactly which ones to use for maximum effect.

"Did you ask her about Ileana?" I ask patiently.

"No, I had more pressing concerns," she replies in a similar tone.

Ice spreads over my skin. "Ideth, when I spared

your life and saved you from the mad huntress, you promised me allegiance." I keep my voice low and even, trying to keep the room temperature bearable for her.

She nods once. "Our deal still stands. I'm beholden to you."

My patience for vague answers runs out. I push her against the wall. The room grows colder. "Then *what* did you two talk about?"

"Oreth!"

I would believe her, for I know few things occupy Ideth's thoughts besides her precious son, if not for the fact I could smell Psyche's scent on her. And… fear. Ideth is not a woman to frighten easily, the goddess knows I try. Even pinned against the wall, she stares back at me defiantly, letting me know I am not the thing she fears.

"What else?" I growl.

Her pretty face hardens. "You're not the only one who lost a loved one, Aedan."

I shake her once, hard.

"Our conversation was personal!" she protests, large owl-like eyes open wide with apprehension.

I start draining Prana from her. The Ambrosia flowing through her body is delicious, and yet the dryad's life force brings no joy, no warmth or sustenance. Ideth has an all-consuming hunger of her own.

"Tell me!" I command angrily.

She snorts a bitter laugh. "I didn't go there for you! We didn't talk about you or your precious Ileana. I only questioned her about Oreth's father and his soul. That's all, I swear!"

"Why?"

"Because my son is lost. I thought... I thought maybe, maybe she could help him..." Her teeth rattle as she speaks and she speaks the truth. This motherly obsession is as out of character as it is vexing. Ideth, one of the most pragmatic creatures I've ever come across, loses all sensibility when it comes to that rotten twig of hers. Mother's guilt for abandoning him to the Suzerain can only justify so much.

"Help him how?"

She purses her lips and looks away. I have to punish her.

"I believe Oreth's soul is sick," she cries out. "I hoped she could help him remember –"

"Oreth has no soul, woman! He's not lost; he just does not love you."

Tears well up in her eyes. "No. No, he does not." And she breaks down sobbing.

I don't have patience for this. I push her aside and activate the teleportation ring, disgusted with her weakness. Her full punishment will have to wait. I need to get some answers of my own first.

"Aedan," Ideth calls as the light blinds me. "Be careful with her!"

∞

The ring works on the first try. Of course it does, the flaming thing never fails to bring me here.

Why would Ideth urge me to be careful with Psyche? I'm not the one in danger. She should be more concerned with herself and what I can do to her.

Flaming nymph… I'm not angry because she talked to Psyche behind my back. After all, I left the key behind on purpose hoping she'd do just that. I'm angry because she did it for her own selfish reasons and failed to learn the information I need.

After I spared her life, Ideth promised to serve me, but I know I'm not her only master. Chronos took hold of the little dryad long before I did, and he owns Psyche as well. They've both been through the Chronodéndron along with Ileana, and I'd bet my right hand there is something about that journey that neither of them is telling me.

Speaking of masters, the Wyrd is already here, escorted by Arianh and Mika.

"Finally," Mika says. He sounds angry but looks relieved.

"Is this where you found him?" the Wyrd asks, aghast. He stares at the room's angular ceiling as if it might collapse on him at any moment. I have no idea what holds it in place, so he might have reason to think so.

"Over there, behind that wall," I say, pointing at one of the light-encrusted snakes ingrained in the metal.

Arianh hugs herself. "It's cold…"

"That's my fault," I admit. The altercation with Ideth left me on edge. Dryads are sensitive to temperature the way Dharkan are to light, Arianh more than most.

"I don't like this," Mika says. His yellow eyes narrow to slits, and he's not grinning for a change. "We should not be here."

I bet he can see better than me in the dim light gleaming through the walls, but judging by how he frowns at them, his objection comes not from what he can see, but what he can't.

"If you don't like it, leave, for you'll like what's behind that wall even less."

The pup bares his teeth at me. I ignore him. "Wait here," I command the group.

This space we find ourselves in, located deep within the Stump, is the grim antechamber to something much worse: a room sculpted from a different material – darker, thicker and, as far as I can tell, indestructible by force, elements or a god's will. No sound or thought escapes it; no natural light can penetrate its darkness. Even Seshat failed to make one of her tiny suns burn within. Whatever it is, it seems to only affect gods. To me, it's just another lifeless room, like all the others inside this prison.

I use the gem on the Suzerain's large ring to open it. A loud crack echoes through the mutilated structure of the Stump, and the wall slides into itself, revealing the stark interior of the vault, then closes as soon as I cross the threshold. How it knows when I'm through is beyond me, and I don't like to consider the implications of that knowledge. Ice spreads further across my skin, betraying my discomfort. *Goddess give me strength*, I pray out of habit, for I know Hel can't Reach me in here even if she was inclined to answer prayers.

Several luminous rings mark the floor. Above one of them, like a statue suspended in mid-air over an invisible plinth, rests the lifeless Zeus wrapped in some sort of liquid light pouring from a large gem fixed above. I find it hard to believe that this is the embodiment of a god. The only awe he inspires comes from disappointment, not grandeur. He looks Narrum, and I reckon he fashioned himself after the traits of a similar tribe as Psyche. His youthful body is at odds with the wrinkled face. He has dark skin, and hair as long and white as mine. The beard, also white and hanging down to his chest, is the most deific feature he possesses since no Narrum would ever keep their facial hair that lustrous.

Hovering next to the Olympian King is Ileana, frozen by Hel's magic hoping somehow she can be revived. Ileana loved light and warmth. To have her frozen like that seems wrong, but if her spirit's going to be recovered, it'll need a body to recover to, and none is more perfect than hers. She looks so peaceful, as if she's only asleep. *She is not dead*, I reassure myself.

I'm assaulted by the usual torrent of regret: *I should have acted sooner, faster, done better.* Burn me for being weak and greedy. I was so consumed with lust for the Suzerain's life, I did not notice hers dwindling away. "Forgive me," I whisper, doing my best to ignore the tightness inside my chest.

Between the two figures stands Psyche. Not as short and stocky as a regular Narrum, she's still quite short, with alabaster skin, and hair the colour of chestnuts held loosely in a braid over her shoulder. *Cornus used to love those nuts.* The thought comes unbidden every time I see the cursed creature's mane. She wears a simple white tunic, cinched with a rope at her waist, and a crown of lilies on her head for whatever reason.

I knew who she was the moment she materialised

out of nowhere, right after Ileana ceased to breathe. Hades and Chiron rushed to her side, and no mortal would ever react so calmly to a satyr, never mind the winged horse. I should have iced her there and then. I tried… *Maybe if I'd tried harder, I would have saved Ileana?* I push the thought away.

The fallen – or fated, or whatever she is – goddess has her back turned to me, her attention split between the two frozen figures. It's like she hasn't moved since last I left her there. And she's not concerned with my return either. I hoped whatever terrifies the gods about this room would make her more cooperative. So far it hasn't. If anything, she looks comfortable, and that, like everything about her, perturbs me. Small and innocent-looking, the goddess of the soul looks too young, too vulnerable and too… human to be a deity. But if there's one thing I've learnt, it is that you can't judge gods by their looks.

"To be entombed next to a god; Ileana would love that," Psyche says when I'm close enough to hear it. She always speaks casually, as if merely voicing her thoughts.

"Would she? Would she love to be dead?" My words bounce off the walls, loud and harsh.

Psyche shifts her weight and turns to face me with a bitter smile. "Yes."

The simple candour of her answer burns deeper than the blue sun. She's telling the truth, and my father always said you cannot argue with the truth. You can, however, argue with the truth sayer. "And then she met you, and you granted her wish."

Psyche sighs. "After a fashion, yes. She convinced me it was the right course of action. Your lover was a good liar."

"Better than you?"

She raises her eyebrows as if surprised. "Oh yes, much better."

"She never lied to me," I say and immediately regret it upon seeing the pity on Psyche's face. They had shared one mind, after all. "She might have kept things from me, but her emotions didn't lie," I insist.

"What about your emotions? Are they true?"

I'm not pleased with her tone. "Where are you going with this?"

Psyche tilts her head, pretending to consider an answer. "You spent one day together, and suddenly she's the love of your life? Either you had a very short, boring life, or you have Eros' arrow up your arse."

I blink, unsure of what to do with that. The words made no sense to me. "Huh?"

She pins me with her dark eyes. "Why do you love Ileana?"

"What?"

"It's a simple question."

A simple question? Burn her. I'm not comfortable with this conversation, but this is the most she's talked since I locked her in here. It'd better lead to something.

"Love doesn't require reason; it has none. It just… happens."

Psyche twists her mouth, radiating annoyance. Clearly she expected a different answer. I remember what Hades said about the animosity between her and

Aphrodite and use the information to elaborate an answer in terms she might relate to. "She's the most beautiful woman I've ever seen."

"Tsk. That's not love; it's lust. What drew you to her?"

Now I'm the one annoyed. "She made my heart beat. She is the one."

"Ah! Zeus also made your heart beat. Why isn't he the one?"

The room turns colder than Helheim with my indignation. "That's different!"

"How so?"

"Ever since the moment I saw her, she was all I could think of. Everything I did after that was for her – because of her. I could not defeat the Suzerain before. Not for my father, not for myself, nor for my people or my goddess. But I did it for her. And all I want now is to have her back. Nothing else has meaning without her."

The words spill out of me. Burn the creature. No wonder the gods fear her if she's able to make them babble like this.

"You did it for *her*…" Psyche echoes, nodding to herself. "Dharkan, you're an intelligent, educated man. Can't you hear yourself? Don't you find that passion a bit disproportionate? Think: What do you really know about Ileana?"

I like her praising my intelligence even less than her dismissal of my feelings. "I know we were fated to be together."

"Fated! Yes, exactly. Fate is not random, Dharkan. It's not a choice, and it's often fatal."

"What do you mean?" Is the creature implying

I'm responsible for Ileana's state? Many times I have wondered if I am. But if I were, I'd feel her inside me, as I do Zeus and that meat eater in Relicum. I did not take Ileana's Prana. Not that time, anyway. Then again, I should be able to feel her from when I fed on her back at the cave, and yet there's nothing of her in me. There's nothing of the Suzerain either. Just an all-consuming sorrow mixed with resentment. And that, I realised, came from Psyche, not Ileana.

The goddess twists her mouth again before she speaks. "What if I told you that there's a god whose talent is to make you fall in love? That love is just another curse, similar to the one used to bind a Wyrd, actually."

"Are you comparing our love to a curse?!"

She chuckles. "Yes, I guess I am."

"That it was not natural or mutual?" The room freezes. *How dare she!*

"Oh, it was mutual, all right. Ileana would do anything for you. She sacrificed all her carefully laid out plans. She betrayed both her father and herself. I lost control over her the moment she met you. No, I'm not questioning the emotion, just its cause."

I keep forgetting Psyche was there, hidden inside Ileana during the time we were together. How much does she remember? Dharkan can hide their thoughts from the gods when they host them. Can dryads do the same?

I look up at Ileana longingly. "You're saying it wasn't real?"

"No. When you truly believe something to be real, your mind makes it real. I'm just... suspicious."

"Of course you are. Who would love a creature like me, right?"

"That's not what I said."

I know the goddess is playing games with my mind. That's what she does. No, I won't let her ruin my memories of Ileana.

"You cannot love, so you'd rather believe in a god's curse than admit Ileana could truly love me." Upon hearing myself speak these words, it does sound improbable. I grind my teeth in frustration. "And what if it was a curse? Does it make our love less significant? Or my grief less painful?"

"No. Eros' magic is strong," she admits with a heavy sigh. "I'm sorry."

"So why are we having this conversation?"

"Because I need to know if I can trust you."

This surprises me. I gathered the argument was part of a test, but not one aiming at trustworthiness. "You should have started with that question, little goddess. Here's the simple answer: you can't. You don't deserve my trust. If you want it, you need to earn it."

She twists her mouth unfalteringly. "How?"

"You still have Ileana's memories." It's not a question.

Psyche nods agreement. "Even the ones she worked so hard to hide," she teases.

Oh goddess, how I want to grab her slender neck and break it. If only I could extract memories as easily as life, we would not be here exchanging words. Nothing fazes the burning creature, not force, threats or imprisonment. She's not even afraid of me, standing this close to her, and why would she be? So far, all I've done is threaten her. Well, enough of that. I step closer, commanding enough cold to freeze embers. "Tell me what I need to know. Now."

Her eyes widen. "Is this how you honour your beloved, Dharkan? By demanding to learn her deepest secrets?"

"Only the ones that might concern me and her father. Since I cannot ask her myself."

"No, it seems you cannot." She crosses her arms.

There is a long silence. Psyche has no intention of revealing Ileana's secrets. Part of me respects that, while the other… Ice spikes jut through my fingers.

Psyche's eyes lower to my hand, then up to my bare chest where the butterfly pendant rests. The necklace is the only thing she seems to care about.

"Why did it turn amber?" I ask. The thing was nearly black when Ileana wore it. Now it glows like Mika's eyes when he's upset.

"Because it's not on me?" The tone implies as much a question as an answer.

I take it off and press it roughly against her face, enough to hurt, or so I hope. She keeps her eyes on mine and doesn't even flinch. "Still amber," I say.

"Are you accusing me of lying again?" Her words come out mumbled with the pendant pressing hard against her cheek.

"Lying is the natural language of the soul."

She laughs. "Who told you that?"

"My father." I take the pendant away and place it back around my neck in case it does possess some magic in it that she might exploit.

"An expert on souls, is he?"

"Yes. He hosted many. And he liked none of them."

"Why not?"

"He called them 'the dark passenger', a disease of the mind. I agree. Souls make the gods want things, things they don't need. For most creatures, motivation comes from what they need. Gods tend to go after the things they don't. And they'd do anything to get them. Lying is the easiest. Same goes for humans. It's like they have a void inside them that can never be fulfilled. They consume and they hoard anything they can get their hands on because of their souls."

The goddess acts as if the thought had not occurred to her. "Gods and humans…" she murmurs. "Your father sounds like a wise man. Where is he?"

"He was the first Dharkan burned in Relicum."

Something ugly crosses her face. "I'm sorry," she says.

"Burn your sorries. Tell me what I need to know!"

She steps closer, unafraid of my temper. "I will not tell you about Ileana, for you'd never believe me if I did. You must experience her thoughts first-hand. And that means, the only way you'll ever know her mind is if you offer yourself as host to me."

"You… You can't be serious."

"Oh, but I am. This is what I want, Dharkan: I want my freedom. Failing that, I want to know which gods you hosted and what their thoughts were. I want to know their souls." Psyche's big dark eyes burn as they stare into mine, greedy for an affirmative answer. Sparks crack between my fingers. "You now have a god's power, but you don't know how to use it, do you? You need a soul to wield it properly. I can teach you. What do you say?"

"Souls are overrated. Like their goddess," I reply with scorn.

"Isn't that the truth!" Psyche laughs again, a genuine laugh, feminine and free of pretence. Then she turns her back to me to stare at Zeus. "Your choice," she says.

This Olympian is not like the others in her pantheon, that much I know. Chiron believes she was sent here to kill Zeus. *A Trojan horse*, he called her – whatever breed that horse is, it must be a good one, for Zeus is dead. Now she dares me to host her in exchange for Ileana's memories? Something's not right. She's after what's left of Zeus' power. Can she take it from me? Does she think she can control me? *Goddess, maybe she can.* My hands itch to wrap around Psyche's neck. *You miserable piece of ash, I should ice you right here, take your Prana and…* I clench my fists just inches away from her skin.

"Go ahead," she says, guessing my thoughts, and pulls her braid up, tilting her exposed neck – the insolence.

And therefore we get nowhere. I can feed on her and never learn what she knows, or I can let her take me and hope to access Ileana's memories while… no, that is *not* a good idea. The last thing I want is to have Psyche's twisted soul inside my mind. If I set her free, would she honour the agreement? I would make her promise. Gods always need to follow through with their promises.

"Or you can let me go, and once I'm safe, I'll tell you anything you want to know, but all you'll have now is my word, no promises," she says in a meek tone. She can't read my mind, I'm sure.

"I need not read your mind, Dharkan," she continues. "I know how you think. I know what you need as well as you know what I want." She glances over her shoulder, teasing.

The room temperature drops to freezing, and her breath puffs between us. She shows no sign of being cold, though. She seems amused by it, blowing it out like smoke.

"Why do you breathe?" she asks causally.

The question throws me off my intent. I frown and have to think about it, for never has such a question occurred to me before. "I don't know. I just do. Why do *you* breathe?"

She shrugs. "Habit. Breath is life."

How has this conversation derailed into this nonsense? Next we will discuss why hair grows. Anger surges again.

"Come on. I won't stop you this time. *I promise.*" She winks.

The first thing I did when I realised who she was, still intoxicated with Zeus' power, was to take her Prana. She forced me to my knees with her will and left me feeling like a discarded glove. That feeling has not quite worn off yet. But here, here she's powerless. Here I can harm her. Gods can feel pain, and Loki only said I couldn't kill her, not that I couldn't hurt her. She'll live. Gods are resilient creatures, after all.

She turns back around. "Not angry enough? What

about this?" She slaps me across the face. "Go on! Take my life force, Dharkan. What are you waiting for?" She slaps me again. "Take it!" She's about to hit me again, and I grab her wrist.

Ice spreads over her hand and I break the bones in it, one by one.

She makes a strangled sound with each fracture, eyes glistening. "There he is: the real Aedan." Her teeth rattle as she smiles, still defiant. Goddess, how I want to ice her. Everything about this creature frustrates me. All Wyrd are crazy, true, but this one is even crazier than Odin. The ice spreads up her arm towards her face as I feed on her. She has enough Prana to sustain a hundred Dharkan. I want to take it all; I want to destroy her, annihilate her. A wave of nausea hits me along with the elation her power brings. Then a darkness, cold and familiar, follows.

She only laughs. Behind her I see Ileana's face, lifeless, disapproving. She will never laugh again if I… No! I push Psyche away. She gasps and cradles her arm, still laughing mirthlessly. She truly wants me to kill her, and if I stay here any longer, that's exactly what I'll do. I refuse to play her game. Let's hope the Wyrd has better luck than Ideth or I.

"You have a visitor," I growl.

"Another one? Must be my lucky day." Psyche scowls, then curses when she tries to open her hand. Her fingers are crumpled and deformed like gnarled twigs. Tears wet her cheeks; from pain or anger, I don't care. I'm just glad they are there. It's a small victory.

CHAPTER FOUR

Odin

Odin waited for Aedan to return. This was what the Aesir King had been reduced to: waiting in the dark like a lesser mortal. Not that there was much to see apart from the two hungry snakes glowing through the walls like they were guardians of the entrances to the Underworld. He had to give it to the Suzerain's gods; their magic was deeply unsettling.

As a Wyrd, Odin wasn't affected by whatever ward surrounded the Stump, for he perceived reality with only the basic senses of a mortal. What perturbed him wasn't so much that he couldn't Reach inside certain areas but that he couldn't even access them by more mundane means.

Arrogance had been his downfall, he knew that. He'd underestimated his enemy. Not for the first time in his long life as a warrior god, but definitely for the last. A god's glory is something to behold; it ripples through the Universe like gravitational waves – and so do his failures. Gods do nothing halfway.

This battle with the Nephilim turned out to be one

Odin could no longer win for himself. He took a petty comfort in the fact that he had not been the first nor the only one to lose. Zeus had lost first, and he'd lost worse. The King of Olympus was gone, as gone as a god can be. The thought still didn't sit well in Odin's mind. After the initial vindication came a deep sense of loss and frustration. He'd spent ages fighting the Olympian King and never even considered the possibility of him being vanquished. Not by anyone else, that is. Had Odin been free, he might even be sad at the loss of a worthy rival. Things being as they were… he was beyond sadness.

Behind Odin stood Fenrir. He didn't need to see the wolf to know he was there in the form of a Narrum boy – a shepherd, no less. The creature's idea of a joke, surely. Fenrir had flourished in Niflheim after the Merge. The once lifeless world was now a feasting hall for the little monster.

And to think he'd sent him there to starve… Odin would pull the hairs from his beard in frustration if he had any. Another miscalculation in a long list of miscalculations involving Loki and his offspring. And now there he was, always by Odin's side, guarding, following, waiting, ready to claim his prize. The only thing stopping the creature from ripping him to shreds was his father. Odin cringed at that insult added to the irony. Loki, the Trickster, that daemon, that traitor, that aberration of the Cosmos. *He* was the enemy Odin would happily be without. He should have been the one vanquished instead of Zeus. For what purpose the Trickster wanted Odin alive, he could not fathom.

It could only be for a fate worse than the one Fenrir would deliver himself. It didn't matter, though, for he would not oblige either of them.

Arianh, standing next to him, moaned, hugging herself for warmth. The room was indeed painfully cold. Odin still remembered when he used to like the cold. And meat, and have a beard and... Suddenly he realised he felt jealous of Zeus, for memories no longer tormented him.

The queen shuffled closer and gripped her elbow around his arm. She was tense, of course she was. The last few days' events, hard as they were on the gods, must have shaken the sheltered girl to the core. But at least for mortals, no matter how bad things got, their suffering never lasted long. They were lucky that way. He sighed and leaned on her, breathing in Arianh's floral scent enhanced by the lack of stimuli to his other senses.

Arianh was a kind mortal. Kinder than any other Olympian creature he'd known, and he'd grown fond of the dryad over the years. Their relationship had started from mutual selfishness: he'd wanted an ally on the mortals' side, and she'd wanted a god's favour. Selfishness and self-preservation are often the foundation for the strongest alliances, or so Agnar, his host, seemed to think. The idea had grown on him over the years, along with other less useful personality traits, such as compassion and prudence.

Odin felt an overwhelming urge to hug the queen.

"Thank you, dear," he whispered, holding her tight. It just felt right to say it.

She grew stiff in surprise but returned the hug. "Thank you for what, uncle?"

"Everything." He took her hand and patted it gently as he often did, and this time left it there, caressing her smooth skin. Had he been younger – and free – she might call him something other than uncle. Other times; other lives. His dryad's body craved warmth and constant contact while his soul was a wreck without the Olympians' light. He could not sustain himself much longer. What would happen when all strength and pride left him?

"Are you certain this is a good idea?" Arianh asked, her voice small in the dark. She knew little of the goddess of the soul, apart from how much she unsettled the other gods.

Odin smiled, a reassuring expression lost in the gloom. "I fear we are out of good ideas, dear. Don't worry, I'll be all right. She can't do anything to me I haven't already done to myself."

Arianh turned her gaze to the snake. "Aedan's been…" She cleared her throat. "*Interrogating* Psyche for days with no success. What makes you think she'll talk to you?"

"She wants to be free." If there was one thing Odin was sure of, it was how much Psyche wanted to be free and as far away from Niflheim as possible. He could relate. And he would use that blinding desire to his advantage.

The silence stretched on. Aedan was taking his time, burn him. Since the Fell, Odin had been grooming Aedan as one sharpens a blade. Now he was sharp as a razor's edge, and he wouldn't rest until he cut someone. Odin hoped it wouldn't be Psyche. Cutting her would be like cutting the Hydra.

"I want to know what's behind that wall," Fenrir growled, intent on the wall opposite the vault.

"We all do," Arianh sighed. She and Aedan had tried the Suzerain's master key on every panel and teleportation ring. All worked, except that one. The gods were too focused on the main portal to give it much thought. They figured if there was something living behind it, it would have made an appearance by now. As a god, Odin would probably have thought the same. As a Wyrd…

The snake glowed alarmingly. The panel in front of them slid aside, and heavy footsteps thumped in their direction. Aedan looked ready to freeze the sun. Odin figured the conversation had not gone well again. *Stupid boy*, he thought, smiling despite himself. Aedan would get nothing out of Psyche through force or by insult. As a former human, she was used to men trying to break her with those blunt weapons. Women like Psyche had to be handled with words and praises. Freya was another such woman. It had taken him ages, but he'd learnt how to manipulate her to his will.

"Get in," Aedan barked to Odin. He sounded more aggravated than usual, if that was possible.

Odin took in the artificial glare around Zeus and Ileana and the unnatural way their bodies defied gravity, and he swallowed. Odin understood gods, and he understood mortals; he understood women, and he certainly understood Wyrds, but the Nephilim were something else. Something anathema to his comprehension. Something he could neither fight nor relate. Everything about them worried him. Nevertheless, Odin gave one last pat to Arianh's hand and moved towards the unnatural lights, because that's what gods do.

"You stay here," Aedan ordered Fenrir. The bark that followed was loud enough to shake the walls and for a moment Odin thought the teleportation ring on the surface had been activated again. Aedan's reply was barely audible in the aftermath of such protest, but the ball of energy sparking between his fingers left little room for argument. Fenrir stared at it and took a step back, snarling. Odin wanted to laugh at the wolf's indignation. Gods may have their powers compromised inside the Stump, but Aedan could wield a god's power just fine, it seemed. Hel made a huge mistake by not inspiring fear of the gods in her creations. Respect is good, for sure, but fear is better. All mortals should fear their creators; otherwise… *otherwise creatures like Psyche and the Dharkan take advantage of it.* Even in the dark, Odin could see Hel's downfall. If there was any justice in the Universe, Loki would see it too. After all, the Trickster took Odin's son; it was only fair he lost a child of his own.

"I wish to talk to Psyche alone," Odin stated.

Fenrir shifted his growl from Aedan to him, his yellow eyes burning like dying suns. "I wish to tear you apart and piss on your entrails. We don't always get what we wish," he said in a voice not of a boy but of a man, a powerful grown man about to lose his patience. Well, so was Odin.

"Spare me from your wet dog smell for a few

moments, burn you! You know I'm not going any-where. Look inside. There's nowhere to go!"

"I won't leave you two alone," Aedan said.

Odin raked his hair in frustration. "Be reasonable, for Hel's sake. Psyche won't give in with either of you there, you know that."

Fenrir hesitated, his yellow eyes burning brighter than ever. He held a grumbling growl for a long mo-ment, then sat on the floor. "I'll wait here," he said, literal to his words.

Aedan took longer to relent. The room got colder and colder until Arianh sneezed. "Get in there before I change my mind!"

Odin sighed, relieved, then cringed as he walked in, leaving the poor girl alone with the two monsters. She would be all right, wouldn't she?

The panel closed behind him.

∞

Zeus and Ileana floated side by side in the middle of the room like spectres in a dark, empty sky. Odin clicked his tongue, disgusted at the sight. Psyche was a few steps away, hunched down and curled up into herself, shivering and murmuring something unlady-like in the primitive tongue humans had once used in Midgard. Odin hadn't heard that barbaric language spoken in ages and could go longer without the dis-pleasure.

"Hello, Butterfly," he said in the common language of the gods.

She lifted her head but kept her hands pressed

against her stomach. The Dharkan must have been extremely persuasive this time. *Stupid, stupid boy…*

"Allfather." Her voice was soft, warm and slightly breathless like she'd been running. The voice of a human, far from the clear fruity tones of Arianh or Ileana; farther still from the assertive, powerful voices of Hel and Freya. Odin found that he preferred the dryads' vocal cords. Dryads were, overall, more pleasant on all senses.

"Did you come up with the title yourself?" she asked.

"Huh?" Her question was so unexpected he momentarily forgot what he was there to say. Of all the things she could have asked him, that was the one on her mind? *Clever girl…*

Odin took a moment to properly assess Psyche in her true form. He had to use his impaired vision and aeons of wisdom instead of his Reach, but it sufficed. She was beautiful for sure, but so were many other young women. She was sharp and educated, far from unusual traits amongst the Midgard mortals of old, especially royal ones. She had been one of those too, which explained her other personality traits, such as pride, stubbornness and insolence. What she had more of than the average mortal was a god's cunning and ruthlessness.

He exhaled with a chuckle, prepared to play her game.

"Baldur was the first to call me that as a jest. I was *all father*, he used to say, never a brother, a son or a friend. Always the father… Over the aeons the meaning of it got lost, but not the title. I had no idea it had spread so far to reach the ears of a mortal girl in Midgard." Odin tried to keep the tautness from his voice and wasn't sure he succeeded. So he tried a different, more humble approach.

"Might as well be honest. It took me a while to understand what he truly meant when he called me that. Unlike me, my son did the best he could to avoid aggravating others. And so everyone loved him." *Me most of all. And that's why Loki killed him.* Anger flushed through him at the memory. *Not now, not here.* Odin forced himself to calm down. *Inhale...* He could not afford to lose this small battle of wits. He had to focus on what he needed her to do. He might not get another chance. *Loki will pay,* the Aesir King repeated to himself like a mantra, working hard to follow through Freya's breathing exercises.

"Seems you're more of an uncle now," Psyche said, fortunately unable to read his thoughts. He looked about himself, wondering about all the things he would have accomplished if he had a room like this to question his enemies in.

It was his cue to laugh. "It's Agnar's fault! An uncle is how he saw himself. The idea grew on me, I suppose."

Her mouth turned up, forming the tiniest of smirks. It was time to build a rapport. "You know how hard it is to keep the host's mind separate from your own."

She grunted something that could have been amused agreement or spiteful annoyance.

He kept silent, for the wrong interpretation may ruin the conversation. Then again, on second thought, so could the silence. Odin decided he had no use for a room like this after all. It was always more useful to have access to a god's mind than to listen to their words.

"Why are you here?" she finally asked. "Did you come to see Zeus for yourself, or is there something you want from me?"

Straight to the point. Very well, then. "Yes, I was hoping you might be able to shed some light on how a mortal can wield a god's power. Your host knew something about it, yes?"

"I don't know," she said stubbornly.

"Don't lie to me!" Odin commanded with all his fatherly authority. "I see how you fool everyone with your innocent looks and twisted words. It won't work on me. I'm old and powerless, and even so I'm more god than you, little mortal girl, will ever be. And right now, I'm the only friend you've got. So answer me, how?"

She bristled at that but kept her anger subdued. "I'm not lying! Ileana nearly broke my mind, remember?"

Odin waved her comment away. "I remember a panic attack. They are common in these vessels. Always so… emotional." He said the word with loathing.

"Perhaps… but Ileana's mind was unique. Her will was stronger than a soul. And her memories…" She grimaced.

"Explain."

Psyche rolled her eyes and sighed. "Everyone's different. They have different personalities, they want different things. That's why two souls can't be part of the same person. The clash is lethal to the mind. I didn't realise what Ileana wanted until it was too late… and if she hadn't been distracted by Aedan, I don't know what might have happened."

"Was the distraction accidental, you think?"

"No. I know it wasn't."

"Hmm…" Odin paced the room, gripping the air below his chin. "Where did the Suzerain get hold of Ambrosia? Gaea assured me –"

Psyche cut him off. "He had a type of Ambrosia, different from Gaea's: corrupted and less… *divine*. More than that, there was something wrong with his body. With Ileana's too. And therefore with their minds."

"How different?"

"I never possessed a dryad before, so I can't be sure. But she was strong. Too strong and fast and somewhat uncoordinated for a grown woman, if that makes sense. She also healed faster than normal. At first, I thought it was my power keeping her uninjured. She had taken Ambrosia herself, real Ambrosia from Ideth's stash, so… it made sense. But Alek was even stronger than her. He didn't even feel pain. Gods do…" she finished in a small voice, massaging her hand.

Odin humphed. "Indeed. Dryads were created with aesthetics in mind, not strength."

He looked up at Zeus. *'Did you suffer much?'* There was no answer.

"Tell me what happens in this world's future," Odin said, keeping his sight on the Olympian King.

Psyche's temper frayed. "Is this a test? Your host, Agnar, knows what happens."

Ice, but the creature fought like a wild animal when

tested. He had no time to soothe her. "Just answer the damn question."

She took a long, deliberate breath, apparently familiar with Freya's exercises. "There is none. The Dharkan go first. If they don't die out, they leave Aegea early on. Then the Anann fight – and by *fight* I mean *avoid* – the Narrum for generations in the Gharb, but in the end, without the Suzerain to cull their numbers, they destroy every living creature and every tree in Aegea. After that, the land consumes itself, ice melts, rivers dry out." Psyche shrugged. "Everything and everyone dies in the end, basically."

Odin bobbed his head. "Yes, that matches Agnar's memories. We are all living on borrowed time. *Time*, huh. I wish I understood why Chronos did such a thing." There was genuine resentment and puzzlement in his tone. Chronos never disguised his dislike for the other gods, but he never harmed them either. Well, technically, he still hasn't, he'd only harmed their worlds. Odin glanced at Ileana, and suddenly he understood the thing that had been in his mind all along. So simple, so… cruel. Time, the thing gods always took for granted, was the only thing mortals truly cared about, for they never get enough of it. The gods brought their destruction upon themselves by creating mortals. With them, they became obsolete and Chronos finally found a purpose for himself in the Universe. He had no need to attack the other gods, he just had to destroy their worlds and wait. And the God of Time was nothing if not patient.

"I believe Chronos is trying to save us," Psyche said.

"What?" He turned around to face her.

"After Zeus, er…" She glanced at the lifeless deity. "After I got free, Chronos brought me to his presence."

"You met Chronos? *Here*?" *That's highly unlikely*, he thought.

"I don't know where it was. I couldn't Reach anything useful. He said the Universe was changing and that he needed our help. I think in his strange way, he's trying to protect this world from whatever is out there."

"Protect?!" How could she be so naïve? "Destroy it along with as many gods in it as possible is more likely," Odin added pointedly. "You haven't considered that, have you?"

Psyche twisted her mouth. "I have. I just… don't believe it."

Odin curled his lip in disgust. "Faith is for mortals, girl! You're a goddess now, think like one!"

She narrowed her eyes. "Very well. This is speculation, for Chronos never actually said it, but I got the impression Kali is in trouble. Now, am I the only one who thinks it's strange Gaea is in Niflheim while Kali is not?"

Good point. But he would not allow the conversation to derail further. "Gaea treats Niflheim as her back garden. And a good thing she's here. What do you think is keeping this world alive without the Tree?" That gave her pause. "The question you should be asking is: Why did Alek leave Ileana behind?"

Her frown deepened. "She wanted to stay."

"Did she? Are you sure?" Odin couldn't read her face in the darkness properly, but he reckoned if she was sure, she would have insulted him by now. "Think: Why would Alek Dveer leave his precious daughter behind? I think the reason for your being here goes deeper than a misplaced prayer. Don't you want to find out who set you up?"

The glare in her eyes said she did, and the knitted brow above them that he had just been added to her list of suspects.

"Why did you take Agnar?" Psyche asked. "Yes, yes, I know his memories were useful to you, but a god as powerful as yourself could have accessed those memories by other means."

He fought the urge to clutch his absent beard again. "True. But Agnar volunteered, and the three of us worked out the best way to proceed."

"Three?"

Damnation, he didn't want to reveal that part just yet. "Agnar, Zeus and I."

She made a good show of being surprised. She might have been, who knows? Perhaps she wasn't as clever as he thought.

"So you got into bed with the Olympian King."

"We never got that far," Odin said, trying not to take offence. "It was an 'enemy of my enemy' kind of situation. Zeus came with Hermes to Aegea after the Fell to see it for himself. The Merge hadn't bothered him much, but this" – Odin cast about him, referring to the whole Stump – "perturbed him deeply. I think Zeus understood the danger better than I did at the time, and I now wonder what else he kept from me…

"He was determined to prevent such a thing from happening in one of his worlds. Or so he claimed. The plan was to figure out a way to infiltrate the Stump and put matters straight, for no god's will, not even Gaea's, was enough to destroy it from the outside. As you can imagine, working together was not our forte, and while we argued, the Suzerain's power grew. We would probably still be arguing if not for Agnar."

He was talking too much. The memories triggering emotions he could not afford to indulge in. Not there; not with her.

"I see. So, Agnar came to you?" she asked suspiciously.

Odin shook his head dutifully. "No. Agnar went to Zeus first, and then to all other Olympians he could find. I was his last option."

She smiled at that, looking more human than ever. He hoped she was warming up to the conversation. Women love to listen to a man being humble. *Keep going, she'll yield.*

"Anyway, Agnar got himself back in the Suzerain's good graces and resumed his role as his chief adviser. He hated the man, though. Hated what he did to the world, to his people, to his family, and being aware of a god's ability to hide amongst mortals, he offered himself to Zeus, so Zeus could do what he, as a dryad, could not. Zeus, of course, lacked the balls to curse himself, but I wasn't so averse to the idea. You see, in the old days, Wyrd meant fated: as in, in control of their fate. Gods without a world became Wyrds to escape the boredom of their existence. Being a Wyrd was not a punishment but an escape, a chance to taste life and mortality without suffering the repercussions of intruding in another god's domain. Playing mortal used to be fun!" Psyche raised an eyebrow at that. Odin shrugged. "Well, it was… for a short time. Punishment is an Olympian concept. The Aesir believe in reward: you fight well, you go to Valhalla; you live well, you get to continue existing in the Underworld and in the songs. It's only if you waste your life that you're punished with oblivion. To us, being forgotten is the worse punishment either god or mortal can suffer."

He was digressing again, and judging by Psyche's crunched-up face, she disagreed with his statements.

"As I was saying… As Agnar, I was able to get inside the Stump and be close to the tyrant. I wanted to learn everything about his gods and then destroy him when he least expected." Odin sighed. "It seemed like a reasonable plan."

"What happened?"

"That's what I would like to know." Odin's hand was on his chin now. He left it there. "The Suzerain knew immediately who I was. He threw me off the top of the Stump." Odin's hand massaged his lame leg. "This body was never the same afterwards." *Neither was I*, he thought bitterly. Nothing teaches fear more thoroughly than pain. "It took me quite a while to heal." In truth, it was just a few days, but with almost every bone in his body broken, they felt longer than all his existence as a god and a Wyrd combined. "And when I went looking for Zeus, he had vanished. At first I convinced myself he had betrayed me. The Suzerain had been one of his creatures, after all."

"Wait. You said the Suzerain knew who you were? And knowing what I intended to do as Ileana, you didn't mention that back in Relicum?"

Odin moaned with what he hoped sounded like shame, then waved his hand. "I doubted he would do that to you. Alek wouldn't have broken his daughter's body. And besides, you are better at hiding your nature than I am. Poor Iosh could swear you were her." He smiled mischievously. She didn't smile back. "Anyway, it seemed like a good idea at the time. And hey, I'm still alive!" He chuckled bitterly. "They are not. I take that as a victory of sorts…"

"What made you realise Zeus had not betrayed you?"

"Every Olympian I came across was acting strange, concerned. They didn't know Zeus' whereabouts either and blamed the Aesir. Then Hel disappeared, and the Dharkan left the Shadow. It was chaos…

"Years later, one of the Wyrd told me in confidence she'd seen Zeus inside the Stump. I kept waiting for an attack that never came and figured she might have been right. Still, I never considered he'd be…" Odin muffled the words when he gripped his chin harder, looking at the Olympian King, "in here… like this…"

"Understandable," Psyche said dryly.

"Glad you think so." He was still struggling to understand it himself. "The rest you already know, or can deduce. Zeus had no part in Hel's 'vacation' in the Underworld, and in her absence I've been hiding and plotting and did all that I could to destroy the usurper." He chuckled bitterly and opened his arms wide. "And now I've succeeded!"

Odin raked his host's long hair and looked up. Zeus' face was frozen in a sort of surprised horror. Not the expression one would expect to see in a god.

Odin wondered what went through his mind at that moment. The moment he realised Kali had come for him. Or worse… Psyche.

"Is he truly gone?" he asked her.

She made a resigned grunt. "Yes. I saw it happen. I felt it. Still do… I was Reaching for the Suzerain's soul and found Zeus' instead. I felt it dissipate, like mist under a hot sun. I tried to take it, but… it just vanished. That shouldn't have happened. A soul can exist without a body, after all."

Odin considered this. "A god's soul is linked to his power. Maybe Aedan –"

She shook her head. "It's not in him, trust me." She looked up at Zeus and lowered her voice, as if the next words were a secret she'd share only with herself. "He pleaded for my help, sobbing like a child. The last time I'd seen the King of Olympus, he'd tried to kill me. He was mighty and baleful, while I was the one crying, begging for mercy. I hated him for so long." She fixed her eyes on Odin, two dark pits of fury. "I wanted to kill him. I'd imagined my revenge often. And now… Funny how things turned out."

Hilarious, Odin thought sarcastically.

Between you and I, Odin wanted to say, *I know you took Zeus' soul. The Dharkan are hazardous to gods, true, but to take their souls… Only you can do that, girl.* He didn't say it though. She wouldn't admit to it, and he needed her on his side.

"I'm still not sure how to feel about it all." Psyche kept musing to herself. If she expected any sympathy from him, she was deeply mistaken.

"You don't decide how to feel. Just how to act,"

Odin said, quoting one of Freya's mantras. She had at least one for every existential dilemma. It pleased Odin he now had the opportunity to use them on another.

He stepped closer to Zeus. Like Psyche, he'd wanted him dead for so long. He'd hated him, envied him, and blamed him. Sometimes he hadn't even known why. Even now, his long immaculate beard offended him. Odin wanted to tear it from Zeus' face. Where did that animosity come from? When had it started? He no longer remembered. But he'd rather have Zeus alive to keep fighting with than this empty victory.

"Congratulations, you pompous, arrogant prick! You are a greater fool than me!" He spat at Zeus. Even that boast felt empty under the circumstances. "He always thought a lot of himself. Zeus would not fight the Suzerain. Oh no, he wanted to befriend him, to learn what he knew before he smote him. The idiot thought he could control the Suzerain." Odin chuckled. "So did I, to be honest. I thought I could control them both! I'd gain victory over two rivals from one battle." He glanced back at Psyche. She looked sad, and he wanted to hit her for that.

"Do not pity me, girl. Save it for yourself. You'll need it."

Her expression hardened. "You don't deserve my pity. You should be up there, with him. How did you even know how to protect yourself from Alek?"

Odin shrugged. "I didn't. Taking Agnar as a host was a means to gain access to the Stump."

She nodded. "Still, you cursed yourself. That took courage."

"Well, I thought I was being smart, not brave... I

suspected a trap or foul play from Zeus, but we can't curse those already cursed, eh? I should have been less specific in the deal, though."

"What was the condition?"

"Zeus' victory."

"Oh, I see… I'm sorry." She sounded genuine.

"So am I…" He laughed, but his voice betrayed how he really felt. Going like this, the conversation would end up with him in tears. He had to stop talking about himself.

"Tell me, Wyrd to Wyrd, what do you make of this prison?" He cast about himself.

"I'm no longer a Wyrd. As for the prison… this is a very intricate box, but a box nonetheless. This world is the real prison."

Clever girl, indeed. "True. If I may ask, how did you break your curse?"

"I'm not sure."

"I thought we were being honest with each other."

She raised an eyebrow at that. "Alek put something inside me, er… *Her*." She glanced at Ileana. "The corrupted Ambrosia. It acted too fast for me to heal. But I'm not sure that's what freed me."

"What do you mean?" Odin wished he knew more about this rotten Ambrosia she kept mentioning. Gaea, who was most concerned about it, took what was left to study. She had not returned since.

"I don't know what my curse condition was to begin with," Psyche explained. "Her death, or his death, or maybe Zeus' death. It all happened at once. Still, I'm free of her, and for that I'm grateful."

Odin sensed Psyche's guard slacken and shifted

to the offensive. "You should be. And I hope you're happy. For Baldur's sake, girl, it wasn't enough to start a fire, you had to come back and put more fuel on it?"

"You're blaming *me* for this?" She was taken aback. *Good.*

He spread his hands. "You have to admit, things went from bad to worse after you showed up, and it is somewhat convenient that your greatest foe is now dead."

"How dare you!"

She's getting angry, even better.

"The Universe was at peace and the gods were safe before you came along. There's been no peace since your apotheosis. And now this? I think the Merge, the Suzerain, Zeus; all these events and you being here are not a coincidence."

"Think whatever you want. Gaea started this, not me."

"If she started it, you'll end it."

The goddess clenched her jaw, bristling with outrage. Guilty or not, she did not see it that way. It didn't matter. He just wanted her angry. People make mistakes when they're angry. He should know.

"I don't want to fight," he said tiredly.

"It sounds like you do."

"Old habits, apologies. Let's stay on the subject. We don't have much time." He glanced at the door, surprised it was still closed, and wondered if Arianh had anything to do with it. Psyche, fuming with outrage, was right where he wanted her. "Just answer me this: Can you free me?"

She pursed her lips. "I can take your soul if that's what you're asking."

"It is."

The way she looked at him made him feel dirty. The loathing, disappointment, resentment, it was almost too much to bear. But he would. He had endured worse.

"Go fuck yourself," she said.

He was speechless for a moment, then burst out laughing. "You humans and your swearing. Fuck myself? Since when is that a bad thing?" He laughed more than he expected to, more than he wanted to, but it was so funny. She obviously didn't think so. He tried to stop, but the laughter took over to the point he had to sit on the ground, clutching his stomach. Loki was also fond of the word, he realised, and suddenly the laughter stopped and a horrible sinking feeling replaced it.

He looked up at Psyche as if he'd just seen her for the first time, remembering that indescribable dread he experienced when they met back in Relicum. He had seen it then but failed to comprehend what it meant. For ages the gods wreaked themselves trying to figure out what had made Ambrosia work on her: a mere mortal, with no god's blood in her veins. Even Gaea didn't have an explanation. Now, it all made sense.

She'll do it, he knew. *She just needs a reason.*

"I'm sorry. These emotional vessels are maddening, as you know. I only ask, for if there is a way you can set my soul free from Agnar, even if just for a while, I would be grateful. You've been a Wyrd for days; I've spent decades like this." Odin debated whether he should cry, and settled for letting one tear roll down his cheek. "I'm worried. I haven't had news from Asgard in years. It's not like Thor to stay silent. He loves to inform me of his every little feat."

"With the Tree cut down, how…" She trailed off and looked at him askance.

Good, take the bait. He waved his hand. "Oh, there are other ways."

"What ways?"

Yes, he saw her eyes spark in the dim light. That got her interested. Finally.

"Does it matter?" Odin asked casually.

"Yes, it matters. Stop the cryptic shit. I'm not one of your 'nieces'." She sighed, then sat down with him, so it wouldn't look like she was lecturing.

"We are cut off, under attack by an enemy we don't understand. If there's another way to contact Asgard, to get help, it'd be worth it. No?" Her tone changed; her voice was soft now, almost pleasant. She smiled warmly as she spoke, and for the first time Odin saw she was in fact lovely when she chose to be. She sounded so reasonable, so gentle. *Yes, I see it now. How could I've been so blind?*

Odin reached for her hands. One was broken, the fingernails black from frostbite: Aedan's work. She winced at his touch, and he let them go, shaking his head for dramatic effect.

"It's safer if the knowledge stays with me," he said, touching her shoulder instead. "These walls have eyes and ears." He then leaned closer to look her straight in the eyes and lowered his voice. "I'm dying."

"No," she said. Not a refute to the statement but the answer to what she knew was coming next.

"I am," Odin insisted, channelling all those fallen warriors begging for their swords so they would gain entrance into Valhalla. "You can help me die well."

"You'll have to wait for Kali. Or ask Aedan. I bet he'd do it even if he's not hungry, just for the joy of it. I'm sorry, Allfather. I won't help you. Not with that."

Stubborn little wench, he almost said. "Give my soul to Hel, and I'll tell you how to get to Asgard. Free me!" Odin inhaled long and deep before he uttered his next word. It had to be done. "Please."

She tried to pull away, so he held her chin, the way she had his back in Relicum, forcing her to take a good look at his face, at Agnar's wasted face. "I'm using my remaining strength to keep this body alive. Niflheim was never meant to hold life, let alone Wyrds. Without the blue sun… it's too taxing. I'm tired, girl. I'll be more useful on the other side. And besides, Baldur's there. I'll be reunited with my son." He smiled a genuine smile at the idea. "Eternity in the Underworld with those you love is not so bad." He saw sympathy in her eyes and, pleased with it, continued. "My fate was linked with Zeus. There is no salvation for me now. Don't you understand? I'm already dead. Even if we still had the sun, Fenrir won't let me live, and he'll make it worse than you. Much worse." Of that Odin was sure.

"No. You brought this on yourself. I will not be your executioner," she said, pushing his hand away.

"You'll be my saviour."

The wall clicked open. *No. Not yet, burn it!*

With no time to spare, Odin hugged Psyche tight and pretended to cry. That should at least confuse the Dharkan, if not the wolf. He leaned closer to her ear. "I never killed Agnar. He still has a chance, if I go. He'll know how to get to Asgard, and much more..." he whispered. "It would be a kindness to us both."

The room turned cold the moment Aedan entered. Fenrir stopped at the threshold and snarled at the walls while Arianh followed the Dharkan, open-mouthed, staring at the floating bodies with fascinated horror.

"What are you two doing?" Aedan asked, surprised to find them hugging on the floor.

Psyche swallowed, pushed Odin away, and stood up. She was very pale and deadly serious.

"Will she help us with the Crafter or not?" Aedan asked.

Odin grimaced. He'd completely forgotten to ask about Hephaestus.

Psyche looked up at Aedan balefully. Then down at Odin, puzzled.

"Yes, Psyche agreed to have a word with Hephaestus."

She frowned.

"He's the best one to enquire about how the bracelets and the portals work. Right?" Odin stood up with some difficulty; his vessel was truly failing. "Maybe, maybe he'll even be able to craft something that will help us fight whatever is trying to get through the main portal, eh? After all, when an Olympian wants a weapon to fight another god with, he's the one to talk to." He winked at her.

Psyche blinked and let her lips part a moment. Odin's heart skipped a beat. Had he read her wrong? The silence dragged on and on until his heart nearly stopped altogether. Finally, she closed her mouth and nodded.

"Hel will be pleased with that," Aedan said. He did not sound too pleased with it himself. "Come then. The goddess wants to see you."

"I'm not hiding," Psyche spat. "Is Hel not goddess enough to come here herself?"

Odin cringed. Psyche's temper was her weakness and no match for Aedan's. The Dharkan turned around and gripped her arm hard enough that Odin was sure he heard something break. She gasped in pain.

"You will respect the goddess," the Dharkan said. "You're only alive because of her. If it was up to me –"

"Yes, you made it very clear what you'd do, you fucking –"

"Aedan! For frost's sake, pick a fight with someone your own size," Arianh said, storming in front of him like a queen. She was a woman who knew how to properly use her temper, and Odin felt a pang of sadness at the thought he wouldn't get to watch her achieve her full potential.

She spared another troubled glance for the deceased, then blinked a few times at Psyche, as if having some difficulty coming to terms with her human appearance.

The Dharkan, out of surprised indignation more than respect for Arianh, reined in his anger long enough for Psyche to get her wits back.

"I can walk by myself, you brute." She pushed him away with her good arm.

Aedan stormed from the room. As they all followed him out, Psyche leaned closer to Odin and murmured "Damn you, *Allfather*," through clenched teeth. Then she let Arianh take her place at Odin's side.

INTERLUDE 3

Willpower

"Oh, burn me." Odin gags the moment he steps out of the ring.

"Stars! Did you do this, Dharkan?" Psyche asks.

"No," I reply with indignation.

The question offends me, for the state of the Stump's main hall is indeed appalling. The viscera and carcasses of the Suzerain's faithful have been cleared – or swallowed – away, but their rancid fluids remain spattered on the floor, the walls and the ceiling. No Dharkan would ever make such a mess of their prey, especially inside their shelter.

"The *pup* did it." I use Hel's nickname for her brother ironically, for to call him a pup is like calling an avalanche a snowflake; Hel's idea of a joke, I reckon. Gods have an odd sense of humour.

"Pup?" Psyche asks with a raised eyebrow.

"Woof," says Mika, showing her his teeth proudly.

Psyche, who until now has avoided even looking at Mika, narrows her gaze at the boy and twists her mouth. She does that a lot. And I've seen the same affectation on Ileana. I assumed it was hers. It looked better on her.

"Mika," Psyche says coldly, and the boy's grin deepens. "Good to see you again – with my own eyes."

"It's good to be seen," he replies with the most unsettling glare.

The goddess doesn't seem too perturbed by it, and I question the accuracy of her vision. Mika's real form belongs in a nightmare.

When I first met Ileana, I thought the 'pup' had been following her, aware of her relationship to the Suzerain. Too late I realised he'd actually been following the Wyrd. Now I wonder what Hel's brother's interest was in the goddess of the soul. Was he protecting her or hunting her? Judging by how he follows the other Wyrd around, probably both amount to the same thing to the wolf.

"Didn't your mother tell you it's rude to stare?" Psyche asks him, twisting her mouth again.

"She did, but my father is of a different opinion, and I agree with him," Mika says, staring deeper.

Hel clears her throat, demanding attention.

Despite the limitations the Stump imposes on the gods, she has somehow found enough power to transmute the Suzerain's oversized chair into crystal clear ice and now sits on it with glacial authority. Hades stands by her side, looking both supportive and pre-eminent above her, leaning on the back of the chair as if he might fall over without it. Another compromise, I suppose. All relationships are complicated; none as much as the one between Hades and Hel.

I do not see Ideth, and Arianh has gone back to the surface to catch the last rays of sunlight. It's for the best. Fewer opinions demanding to be heard.

Psyche steps forward and says, "Goddess." To my surprise, she even inclines her head in deference to Hel. I sense something odd coming from Psyche, not fear – never fear, burn her – but something close to it. *Good.* Not so good is that a similar emotion oozes from Hel herself. If I didn't know any better, I'd say they've confronted each other before.

The wintry goddess grips the armrests on her throne, and Hades stands at attention. The gods claim to be powerless inside the Stump, but I bet my left hand that something beyond words just passed between them. Gods have a very different definition of 'powerless' to the rest of us.

"Hello, Butterfly," Hades says in a friendly tone.

Psyche's eyes shift from Hel to him. "Hades. You worthless piece of shit." There's no mistaking the vitriol in her words. She starts towards him. I hold her back by the arm I was sure I'd broken just moments ago. It's not broken now, and neither is her hand. *Definitely not powerless, then.*

"Come now, Butterfly. Isn't it good to be yourself again? Free?"

"Fuck you," she spits.

Hades laughs and leans on the chair again, sipping the contents of an overflowing goblet conjured from thin air.

"Hel," Psyche says. "You have my deepest sympathy for the harm inflicted upon you. You and those in Niflheim did not deserve what happened, nor what is still about to happen. I wish –"

"And what exactly do you think is about to happen?" Hel interrupts.

Psyche blinks, then twists her mouth again before answering. "Spring."

Hades splutters his drink. "This is a land of perpetual winter, Butterfly. There is no spring," he says, wiping wine from his goatee.

"Are you sure, Hades? From where we came, *spring* always follows winter. A powerful curse, is it not? I believe I sense the seasons changing as we speak."

Hades' jaw slackens. The way she said the word *spring* implies many other unsaid words. Burn the gods. No wonder they are always at odds with each other; would it kill them to speak what they mean for a change? *Humph, perhaps it would.*

"What is she talking about, Hades?" Hel asks without taking her eyes off the Olympian goddess.

"It's nonsense, my lady." Hades smiles, but there is no mirth in it. Psyche is also smiling: a lovely smile, a dangerous smile. She catches me staring at it and purses her lips.

"Goddess of Niflheim," Psyche starts again in a formal tone, far from the spiteful tease she used with Hades. It's the tone of someone accustomed to both addressing audiences and giving orders to them. She might have been a mortal once, but she sure talks like a goddess now. "You've taken your world back. I am glad. This usurpation should never have taken place. I imagine you must be eager to set matters straight, cull the remaining unwelcome visitors, and so forth. I am one such visitor, and you know I do not wish to be here."

Hel's expression is one I hope she never uses on me. "Goddess of the soul," she returns with the same formal, icy tone. "I have to thank you for your contribution to our meagre victory. We couldn't have done it without your… intervention. You've done much for my family and Niflheim, and I fear I can never repay you properly, unless –"

"My apologies, but I disagree," interrupts Psyche. "I can think of at least one thing you can do: cast me away, and I'll never return to your world. You have my promise."

Hel raises her voice. "You wish to leave. Yes, we're all aware of that. Unfortunately, it's not that simple."

"Oh, I believe it is," Psyche says through a rictus grin. Hades peers out from behind his cup without drinking. Odin mutters a curse. The tension between the goddesses is like thin ice over a lake and every word a perilous step across it.

Hel mimics Psyche's smile before speaking; it looks scarier on her. "Goddess of the soul, Niflheim is isolated from the other worlds. In case you haven't noticed, the World Tree is dead."

"Hard to ignore; even harder to believe," Psyche says dryly and makes a show of glancing around the room. Her eyes land on Odin, who all but shrinks from her gaze, groping his chin. "Fortunately, I do not wish to travel to other worlds; the stars will suit just fine."

"That is not possible either."

"And why not?"

"I will ask one more thing of you," Hel raises her voice again, talking over whatever Psyche was about to say in outrage. "Since you are so eager to leave my world, perhaps you can persuade others to join you."

"You overestimate me, Hel. I have no power over

anyone, nor do I have friends in any pantheon." There's no mistaking another stab at Hades. He seems as hurt as one can be by a mosquito sting.

Hel stands up and advances in our direction with the slow, majestic motion of a glacier. A goddess in every sense of the word. Compared to her, Psyche is barely more than an animal. Which I suppose, as a former human, she is.

"I know exactly how much power you have and over whom, goddess of the soul. You will do as I command."

Psyche lifts her chin to face Hel, both out of defiance and necessity. She's as tall as Ideth, while Hel is of a height with me.

A deadly silence follows. Psyche has her mouth twisted again and seems to chew on something. *It's her cheek!* I realise. Did she make Ileana do the same? What sort of sadist would make a dryad chew on her own flesh? My dislike for the creature increases.

"What if I refuse?" Psyche asks.

Hel looks ready to strike the little Olympian. *Do it,* I pray to her.

She spares me an annoyed flicker of her eye in reply. "Do you know why you're here?" Hel asks Psyche.

"Punishment?"

Hel sighs. "Yes, I suppose your pantheon's Underworld is a place for torment and punishment. Niflheim used to be a civilised world before the Merge. Now… What is the purpose of punishment again, Hades?"

"Humility, my lady. And the punishment always fits the crime."

"Does it?" The distaste in Hel's voice expresses what she thinks of that statement. Hades grimaces into his cup but says nothing.

"I've committed no crime," Psyche says.

"Of course you did," Hel protests. "A mortal rising above the gods is a grievous crime. And let's not forget, you killed Zeus."

"For the last time: *he* killed Zeus." She points at me.

"Aedan might have taken his life force, yes, but what about his soul? We can't find it anywhere. Nor Ileana's soul either. So, where are they?"

"Ileana had no soul to speak of, and Zeus' was obliterated."

"And who has the talent to do that?"

"It wasn't me."

"You are the goddess of the soul."

"It was not me! I care nothing for the souls of gods. All I want is to leave this world. Hela, I –"

Hel freezes over in a fury. "No one's going anywhere until I get what I want!"

The goddesses stare at each other like wild manticores. The animosity is palpable. I can see now why Hades suggested the meeting take place down here. If the goddesses had their full powers, I wonder what would they do to each other. Behind me, Odin whimpers.

Hades cuts the tension. "Perhaps there is a way to redeem yourself, Butterfly."

"Did you hear a word I said? I'm innocent of Zeus' demise."

"We disagree."

"Then have your pet Dharkan end my existence and be done with it! I'm sick of this." She stomps her foot.

"If only it was that simple," Hades muses.

"It can be." I smile, pleased with the direction the conversation is going.

"For fuck's sake… what do you want from me?"

"I want to give you a chance to earn your freedom," Hel says.

Psyche snorts, crossing her arms. Stubborn, just as Odin predicted. She reminds me of Cornus again. Whenever he did not want to go a specific way, he would plant his hoofs to the ground and nothing could move him.

"The transition didn't go as smoothly as we hoped. You might have noticed this structure has been, hmm, unstable."

"Get to the point."

"We need to make it stop, and we think we know how."

Psyche tilts her head in a way that says 'go on' impatiently.

"We can't control half the stuff in this place, but we think we know someone who can. I need you to convince Hephaestus to work this metal and close the portal for good."

Psyche cackles a mirthless laugh. "Anything else?"

"Yes, I also need you to tell us all you know about the Nephilim, of course, and news of the Suzerain's absence has spread. The settlements are in uproar. Someone needs to appease the Narrum. Relicum's governor, Guilho –"

"Goddess of the soul!" Odin interrupts Hel, stopping Psyche from uttering whatever obscenity she was about to. He walks closer to us with the difficulty of a man at the end of his life. I don't believe it's all pretence. "Please excuse Hel, she gets carried away sometimes. We know you have no influence over the Narrum of this world." He sends a scolding look in Hel's direction. "But you might have over Hephaestus. Remember, you already agreed."

Psyche was silent for a long moment, working her jaw like a ruminant.

"Sure, I can talk to him. But I won't promise he'll listen. We are not exactly friends, and gods have their own minds. Or some of them do." Another pointed comment to Hades, I reckon.

"You will?" Hades seems surprised.

"Sure. Anything to get me out of this place, if not the world." She shrugs. "And if I do this for you, Hel, I need your word that you'll let me out of Aegea." She pauses. "And protect me from your family."

Mika acts offended. The two goddesses stare at each other, lips pursed, jaws clenched. The room turns icy cold. Odin sneezes.

"I need your promise," Psyche insists.

"You have it," Hel finally says.

"What?!" I blurt out. "Goddess, with all due respect, you can't promise her –"

"Aedan, be quiet," she demands, eyes flashing an angry blue.

'Why do I bother with words if you don't listen, Aedan,' she speaks directly to my mind. *'Think. What did I say? Are we* family?'

I remember the goddess's words and smile. She said nothing about leaving Niflheim, just Aegea, and no, as much I'd like to be, we are not family. Hel is indeed the daughter of a Trickster.

'Now, play along. I need someone to watch her. And Fenrir… well, he is family and too volatile for the task.'

Gladly, goddess.

Meanwhile, Psyche has been whispering with Odin, and I missed what they said.

"Very well, I will do this for you." She extends her hand to the Wyrd. He takes it.

"Don't!" Hades shouts, spilling red wine all over Hel's crystal-clear throne, but it's too late. The Wyrd takes Psyche's hand in both of his, smiles, then rolls his eyes and collapses at her feet. She looks down at him, her head tilted as if she doesn't understand what she sees, then murmurs something under her breath. It sounds like a prayer, except gods don't pray.

"What have you done!" Hel gasps. Frost fills the room.

Psyche looks up at her, serene. "What he asked me to."

Mika shifts into a giant wolf. Ruffled brown hair turns to grey fur; amber eyes flare to a burning red, and his teeth… burning goddess! He could rip the head off a Jötunn with those. Suddenly the huge room looks small with him in it.

"How dare you? He's mine!" Like Chiron, the words sound through him, his mouth never wavering in its menacing snarl.

"Not until Ragnarok," Psyche says in the usual numb tone. But this time, I sense she's anxious. Blazing light, we all are. That creature is too monstrous to react otherwise.

One deception for another. Did Psyche know she was being deceived? No, this had to be the Wyrd's doing. Again. I have to give it to the old god, he does know how to get what he wants.

The giant wolf is about to pounce on Psyche. I despise her, but she holds the only hope of me getting Ileana back, so I bar his way. A paw hits me across the chest and throws me against the wall.

"Fenrir, stop!" I hear Hel shout through a flare of pain on my side as I struggle to stand up.

"You can't make me stop, big sister."

"Fenrir, I gave her my word."

"Then you shouldn't have!"

"You vowed to kill Odin, the god," Psyche says. "Not Odin, the Wyrd. Nor Agnar, the man."

"It is foretold!" Fenrir growls, and the room, maybe the entire world, shakes.

Psyche moves closer to the beast. "Nothing is foretold anymore, pup. Chronos made it so. The future is whatever we make of it."

He will devour her, I think with mixed feelings. The giant wolf snarls and drools. His legs brace to leap, but to my surprise, he doesn't.

"Strays don't survive without the pack," she whispers with a heart-wrenching sadness. "I'm sorry."

I force myself to stand. There's no fighting that monstrosity, but maybe if I take some of his Prana…

The giant wolf tilts his head in my direction. "Get any closer, Dharkan, and I'll bite your hands off," he says, eyes still fixed on Psyche.

"He's with me, Fenrir. Odin's soul is in my realm," Hel says with relief. "She didn't destroy it. You can still have him."

"More lies."

"No. I would not lie to you, brother."

The monstrous wolf snarls and snaps his jaws shut just a hair's width from Psyche's face, then storms from of the room, his form reverting to an inconspicuous Narrum boy as he goes.

"Cerberus breath." Hades looks as shaken as I feel as he half walks, half sways across the room. "Why did you do that, Butterfly? *How* did you even do it?"

"The same way you do the things you do, Lord of the Underworld. It's in my nature."

"She was supposed to be powerless!" Hel accuses Hades.

"I'm as powerless as you are," Psyche says.

"Clearly not!"

"Taking souls requires little power; it's my talent. All I need is the will to do it," Psyche says with a deep sigh of resignation.

"You're saying you really can take our souls with just a touch?" Hel asks.

"Take them, destroy them. Change them…" She glances at Hades, then moves closer to Hel. I intercept her path. She gives me a look of pure contempt and steps aside to keep the goddess of the dead in sight. "Our deal stands?"

"Burn you, Psyche. How I wish I could throw you out of this world. *You* are the gods' bane. Yes, our deal stands. With one minor addendum: leave my soul alone."

"And mine!" chimes in Hades.

Psyche's fury is like hot pokers to my senses. "I'm not a murderer!"

"Clearly," Hel sneers, poking the Wyrd's body with her foot.

He stirs.

CHAPTER FIVE

Ideth

Ideth was still sobbing when she arrived at the surface, almost disappointed that Aedan hadn't frozen her out of her misery. Anything to make her forget what she'd seen in that kiss. And what had she seen, exactly? None of it made sense. Candles, stars, monsters – Psyche's soul was a turmoil of nonsense and wickedness. And its taste… Ideth licked her teeth, still trying to eliminate it. Never had she tasted such hate, resentment; and the thirst for revenge still lingered in her. Or perhaps it was just thirst. She hadn't hydrated in a while.

She cursed as the frosty surface bit into her bare feet, shooting tendrils of cold up her legs. Freezing Aesir and their… freezing! If it were up to them, the whole Universe would stand still, frozen in whatever configuration suited them best. At least the Olympians embraced warmth and change and passion, all the things life offered without worrying too much about consequence.

Speaking of consequence… the scowl Oreth, perched on Xylo's shoulders like a bird of prey, gave her could shatter the ice under her feet. This time she was too desolate to care and just waved at her son's bizarre guardian. Like the others, she didn't know what to make of the creature: part tree, part every other race in the land, Xylo was an enigma. After the Suzerain's death, he'd planted himself on the Stump's surface and no one, not even Gaea, had managed to move him since. He just stood there, silent, staring into the horizon. Ideth figured his mind was damaged. Broken either by the Suzerain or the lightning bolt Aedan brought down on him. There seemed to be no malice in the gentle giant though, and he was sturdy enough to keep Oreth out of trouble. That was good enough for Ideth. For now.

Chiron landed at her side with all the grace of a hoofed swan landing on a frozen lake. Ideth did not understand nor approve of Chiron's new choice of anatomy. Flying had its advantages, for sure, and she very much enjoyed when he took her for a ride across Aegea's sky. But why a horse?

She watched with disapproval as Chiron flapped his wings to steady himself before he addressed her. "Unbridled one, I was about to go back to – oh, you are upset." He nudged her with his equine head. "What's wrong?"

She refrained from pushing him away. She wanted a hug, not a nudge.

"Was it the Dharkan? Do you want me to put an end to your oath? Because I can," he said without speaking, for horses don't speak. The words just seemed to emanate out of his head.

It was hard for Ideth to see her friend in those

equine features. She missed his face, human as it was, and his smile… that half-condescending, endearing look he'd give her when she said something silly just for the joy of making him laugh. Chiron was not a creature easy to divert, always so serious under the burden of his Titan's wisdom. Ideth stared into those big brown eyes, saw his nostrils flare, and in that moment she saw no wisdom, no greatness; all she saw was a beast. Perhaps the difference between gods and beasts was not that great, she thought, then she took a long suffering breath.

"Thank you, Chiron. It's all right. Aedan's bark is worse than his bite. Don't worry. We understand each other quite well. Besides, he's the least of my problems," she reminded herself. "Hey, maybe Chronos will finally demand his due and solve them all." She regretted her words the moment they left her mouth; that was something Ileana would say.

"Don't even joke about it, unbridled one. I may be able to free you from the Dharkan, but there's nothing I can do about Chronos." Chiron shifted uneasily, as he always did at the mention of the God of Time. "I still don't understand why he spared you this long."

"Why wouldn't he?" Ideth gave him her best smile, then reversed to a heartbroken nymph. Any harmful intent would fade at such a sight, she knew. And perhaps he did not spare her at all. The last few days felt like she was paying for all her transgressions with interest.

Chiron tutted. "I trust your judgement, as always. Just… if I ever find out Aedan mistreated you." His hoof made a dent in the hard-packed ice.

She patted his mane. "Don't worry about it, friend."

"So, what happened then? Is it because of that one?" He inclined his head at Oreth. "Ideth, I understand how parents want to believe their children to be good and special, but… that one, I'm afraid he's exactly what he appears to be."

Oreth, realising they were talking about him, hurled back a flurry of insults.

Ideth sighed. "No… It's the goddess of the soul."

Chiron lifted his head high. "Psyche? You saw her? You've been inside the room! Is it… er… true what they say? You've seen Zeus too! I can't believe they've locked her down there with him." His wings fluttered at each sentence like a distressed chicken attempting to fly. It suited him for peeking into her thoughts. Ideth reckoned her mind was quite the unpleasant thing to Reach at the moment.

"She's fine," Ideth said dryly. "The room is, you know, it's not much stranger than the other rooms." *Especially the one next to it,* she almost said, but there was no point discussing the Stump's eerie architecture. "Except I can't feel Orion there. It's like the rest of the world ceases to exist when you're inside it. And yes, Zeus is there, so is Ileana. Both up in the air, wrapped up in light like sprites." She shook her head at the memory. When she died, she'd like to be buried, not put on display.

Chiron moaned, a disturbing sound in his present form, and pressed his huge swan's wings tight against his equine body.

"The goddess of the soul. She's not… right," Ideth admitted. "And it's not just because she's human," she added before Chiron could defend the goddess on that account.

"No god is 'right' from a mortal's perspective," he said. "I mean, look at me. Do I look right to you?"

"Not even slightly. Why do you have to look like that?" she asked, too tired to refrain herself. "Why not a dragon, or a manticore or, ice, even a gryphon would make more sense than a horse with wings."

Chiron's ears perked up with indignation. "The horse was Gaea's first sapient creature. Many gods wish they could take this form. It's a privilege."

"But Gaea looks human," Ideth pointed out. "Why isn't she a mare, then?"

"We all have our flaws," Chiron said tiredly. "Gaea's corrupted by vanity."

"Vanity? Is that why Zeus also took human form?" Ideth heard Hades calling him vain often enough.

Chiron shook his head. "Zeus could take any form. His flaw was complacency. He just got more worshippers looking the way he did, as humans don't react well to other races."

"Then why don't you? You're always complaining the Narrum are hostile to you because of how you look."

"I'm a Titan!" he said as if that explained it.

"But you used to at least be part human!" Ideth said, exasperated.

Chiron shook his head exorbitantly again. In his current shape, she reckoned that meant impatience, not disagreement. "The Titan Prometheus shaped humans in his image. They resemble us, not us them."

Ideth rolled her eyes. At least the conversation kept her mind off Psyche and her troubled soul. "All right.

Why don't you change back to a centaur, then? You no longer need to fly Aedan around."

Chiron spread his wings and looked about himself. "What's wrong with this form?"

Ideth gaped. Could her friend really be so clueless? "It has no face!"

"Oh," he said. "I see... well, if it makes you happier, unbridled one, I will change it when I get back."

"Why not now?"

"Because I need wings now. The forest needs me."

"Whatever." She was too tired for this conversation and already regretted starting it. Let Chiron wear whatever shape he wanted. "I have another question for you before you go."

"Yes, unbridled one?" he said patiently.

"Have you ever been to the stars?" Ideth looked up. There was only one star in the grey sky, too bright to look at without shedding more tears.

"Yes..." he said cautiously. "That's where gods go to be forgotten. A boring place. Very lonely. Why?"

"Is Orion there?"

He stepped back. "What? Of course not! Did Psyche tell you that?"

Ideth glanced up at Chiron and saw something she'd never been able to notice in his human features, but his equine ears gave it away. He was lying to her.

She wanted to accuse him, to hit him, to scream at him. Had he known of Orion's fate all along?

His nostrils flared. Frost, she'd thought too loud again. He knew she knew he'd lied.

"I'm sorry, unbridled one. I suppose I owe you an explanation."

"You do."

"I didn't want you to find out this way. It's not what you think. I…" He looked to the horizon. "I need to return to the forest now, before it gets dark." He kicked the ice again. "When I return, I'll tell you about Orion."

Ideth felt sick, furious, betrayed. "Just go. Get out of my sight!" She pushed him away, and he took flight. She wasn't sure she wanted him to return.

Was Orion up in the stars with the other forgotten gods? Would he be able to watch over her from that far away? Over their son? How did he get there? Why?!

More tears welled up. Ice, she'd need to hydrate soon, going like this.

Something fell on her shoulder, and she almost screamed in fright. Xylo towered behind her, his big mouth stretched wide across his wooden face in something like a comforting smile. The touch on her shoulder was surprisingly gentle, given how his wrists looked like branches. She bet they were as heavy, and yet she hadn't even heard the big creature approach. They stared at each other. Her neck and mind straining to hold his gaze. He said nothing, and she had nothing to say to him.

Oreth broke the silence. "Suits you," he said, relishing in her misery.

Xylo's greenish eyes narrowed at the boy. Ideth put her hand over his. His skin resembled the bark of a beech tree: soft and surprisingly warm. A tingle spread up her arm, over her shoulder blades and down her spine.

"Oreth," she said, turning her attention to him. "I

understand I upset you, but can't we at least be cordial to each other?"

"No," he spat. "My father was going to turn me into a god. And your friends killed him. I hate you all!"

"Alek was not your father," she said tiredly.

"He was. He was the only father I knew. He was going to save me from time."

Xylo smiled at that, and Ideth felt a proper shiver lifting the hairs on her nape. She'd been standing on ice for too long.

"Is that what it will take for you to forgive me? I can make you immortal."

"You mean Ambrosia? Frost your immortality and your Ambrosia. I want to be timeless!"

"I don't understand," she admitted, desolate. First Chiron, now Oreth. Maybe she was the one dull-witted. Even Ambrosia would not restore the mind as efficiently as sleep, and she hadn't slept in… slush. She didn't know that either.

"Of course you don't understand, because you're stupid!" Oreth cursed and returned to sulking.

Ideth dried her eyes and patted Xylo's hand, now starting to feel slightly heavy and possessive on her shoulder. She tried to smile, a vain effort under the circumstances. Xylo nodded and moved away with his charge to the edge of the Stump to stare once again into the distance.

What do you see? she wondered. Aegea looked lush from up there. A lovely world, rich in colour and abundance of life under the clear skies. The ground around the Stump was always dry, and it hadn't rained since the Suzerain's demise, but the ice kept melting from the mountain peaks feeding the river, the brooks and, *hmm*... Now that Ideth paid attention, the Boiling Lake, steaming in the distance, looked more active than usual.

"There you are!" Arianh said, tiptoeing in Ideth's direction, despite wearing sandals.

Oh no, not you too, Ideth thought.

"Here I am..." She sighed. "Is Aedan looking for me?"

"No," Arianh said, hugging herself and staring longingly at the setting sun.

Two ravens cawed above them, restless. "Where's your 'uncle'?" Ideth asked. The birds never strayed too far from their master.

One raven perched on Arianh's shoulder, and she scratched him on the head while blowing kisses at it. "The gods are meeting in the great hall," she said.

The other raven attempted to land on Ideth. *Don't even think about it*, she thought, and he flew away with a loud "Kraa!"

"They left you out, huh?"

Arianh grimaced. "Have you seen the state of the hall? All that blood... no, thanks. I left myself out. It's all right, uncle will be up soon," she said to the bird on her shoulder, then uttered soothing noises to the other raven that had landed on her forearm, cawing for her attention.

"You should make Occa clean the hall," Ideth suggested, wincing when Arianh kissed the bird. Ideth liked ravens as much as any dryad but would never let one get that close to her face. Ravens liked to peck at shiny things, especially eyes.

"I like your suggestion. Mother always said that hard work improves character, and Occa's definitely needs improvement." The hint of mischievousness in Arianh's voice reminded Ideth of the old queen.

"You look like her," Ideth said without thinking.

"Occa?"

"Your mother."

The resemblance was striking, but only superficial, like a reflection in a pool. The old queen had been a woman whose presence had commanded the attention of a room, while Arianh merely decorated it. Still, whenever Arianh forgot to worry about how she was perceived, glimpses of the old queen's personality slipped through.

Arianh sneezed violently, and the raven perched on her shoulder flew away. "I heard you two were friends," she said, holding her nose to stifle the next sneeze. If the queen had the sense to wear a proper cloak instead of a flimsy dress, she wouldn't be cold all the time.

Ideth shook her head. "Your mother didn't have friends. She surrounded herself with people who agreed with her and exiled those who didn't."

"Ah... I understand the appeal." Arianh snorted and let the second raven take the vacant place on her shoulder. An indignant caw came from somewhere above them. "What else can you tell me about her?"

The last thing Ideth wanted to do was reminisce. She'd much rather sleep for a year, but she was too hungry after Aedan's treatment, so she decided to indulge the queen while the sun still shone.

"She was thorny. Hard as oak, bitter as crab apple."

"Tell me something I don't know." Arianh sounded bitter herself. Ideth could well imagine Arianh's childhood. The old queen had shown no inclination for motherhood whatsoever.

"Your mother had to be tough, though. It couldn't have been easy, to be taken from home at such a young age and thrown into an alien, hostile world to serve as livestock," Ideth said.

That caught the queen's interest. "Do you remember the Homeland?"

Ideth shook her head. "No, I remember little from my childhood, actually. I guess it's been a while." She smiled sadly. "Memory's the first thing to go when you live too long."

Arianh gave her a wistful look. "Mother did. She said it was a lush woodland, fed by waterfalls and a generous sun, with tall, ancient trees. We built our shelters in their branches, and the forest stretched along the coast of a peaceful and warm sea, where you could swim all the way to the horizon. Try as I might, I could never quite visualise such an ocean, having only the freezing tumultuous waters ridden with monsters that batter the cliffs of the Gharb as reference." Arianh sighed. "It does sound too perfect to be real."

"Chiron says memories are just different versions of delusions. But he's full of dung," Ideth said bitterly.

"All gods are," Arianh said in a similar tone. "They become less and less divine the better you know them."

Ideth agreed. Arianh's personality grated on her sometimes, but maybe the Aossi queen wasn't half as birdbrained as she appeared to be.

"Chiron's a strange one, isn't he? Must be good to fly, though," Arianh mused.

"Must be..." Ideth said. Where would she fly to? Could she fly to the stars? She pushed those thoughts, and the hot hatred that came with them, away and focused back on Arianh.

Her attention had drifted to Xylo, who had his head turned in their direction while Oreth was busy shooing one of the agitated ravens threatening to land on him.

"I really don't like the way that creature looks at me," Arianh whispered. "Are you sure it's a good idea to leave Oreth with him?"

"No. But I don't want to leave him in a cell all day, either." The gods knew he hated her enough already.

Xylo's stare could be eerie at times, Ideth agreed, especially since he seemed to have no proper eyes, just two eye sockets filled with moss where eyes should be and they sometimes shone like mirrors when the light hit them. Still, Ideth had seen worse.

"Yes, keep your gaze on the horizon," the queen murmured to herself when Xylo looked away.

"Why are you still here?" Ideth meant the Stump. "Don't you have a realm to rule?"

Arianh sighed in a way that told Ideth how much she looked forward to going home. "I do, and that's why I need to be here to see this through. I don't trust Occa, or Aedan, not even uncle to see to my people's safety. With the Suzerain gone, the gods are the threat. And what a threat..." She frowned at the icy floor, and for a moment Ideth thought she'd sneeze again. "At least with the Suzerain we didn't have to worry about freezing to death."

Ideth grunted agreement. It was a good enough reason, but she'd seen the queen with Iosh, Relicum's pretty shrine, and suspected the real motive was more personal than political.

"Do you think the Suzerain's gods will return to destroy the world?" Arianh asked, pointing to the portal.

"I think they'd rather own it than destroy it. Don't worry, Hel and Hades will never let that happen." Or so Ideth hoped.

"No, I don't believe they will either. But at what cost?"

"What do you mean?"

"Hel only cares for the dead, and Hades only cares about Hel. Where does that leave us? I need to know what the gods plan to do next and make sure the Aossi are included in their plans."

"I see. Just don't expect any favours from the gods; everything has a price with them. 'Never trust a god; you won't survive it'," Ideth said in a deep voice.

"Who told you that?"

"A god." Ideth glanced at Oreth again. He looked so much like Orion, but of course, that had only been the dryad he took. What Orion's real form was, she never knew.

The two women stared at the world in silence.

"How could you have allied yourself with the Suzerain?" Arianh asked, breaking the silence and almost succeeding in keeping the judgement out of the question.

Ideth kept her gaze on the horizon. She had no

obligation to explain herself to the woman, queen or no. Arianh had no children; she would not understand.

But perhaps she should…

"How little choice women have on how to live their lives in Aegea revolts me too. This *civilisation* the Suzerain imposed is unjust and built with foundations of rotten wood. It's bound to collapse. But before, when the forest was little more than a few trees on a hill and the Dharkan were many and hungry, we didn't live at all; we merely survived. Always running away or hiding in fear." Ideth's eyes rested on the ruined patches of land between the icy mountains and the forests, where humans had built their settlements. "At first, we thanked the Narrum for keeping us safe from the Wraiths. Then they began cutting down our trees. When we protested, they turned their hostility and superstition towards us. And the moment they realised we couldn't fight back…" She would not cry again! "The Suzerain's way is flawed but kept their greed contained. Thanks to him, dryads were able to live in a sort of peace and raise their children, or most of them… I allied myself with the Suzerain because it suited my needs as a dryad and a mother, for I couldn't let him take my baby. Not just because he was my baby, but… never mind. I just did what I thought was right for Oreth."

Now, Ideth wasn't so sure it had indeed been the right thing.

Arianh sighed again. "Yes, I agree the Narrum were not an improvement on the Dharkan. At least the Dharkan can be reasoned with. They have other sources of sustenance, while the Narrum…"

"Are the plague of the land," they said in unison. Then both smiled, understanding each other.

"It's good to know you're still on our side," Arianh said.

Ideth guffawed. "I'm always on my side, *queen.*"

Arianh pouted. "Easy for you to be selfish. You're immortal. You have time. Time to learn, to make mistakes, to travel. To live! Of course you don't need a side..." she grumbled bitterly.

"Immortal? Pfah! Zeus was immortal. Look what happened to him! Ileana was immortal too. I wonder how immortal I'd be if I jump off this edge or if Aedan decides I'm no longer of use to him. Immortal..." She tutted and pulled out a black feather caught in her hair. The ravens seemed frantic now. "I'm just not like other women, and immortality has nothing to do with it."

"And what makes you so special, then?" Arianh demanded.

Ideth had to think for a moment. So many things made her special: a strong survival instinct, a pragmatic mind, and let's not forget the cursed ability to taste souls. She shrugged. "I make my own rules."

"You sound like my mother. Do you know what happened to her? She aged, got sick and died, just like everyone else. All her work passed on to me unfinished, and even if I live a century, it won't be enough time to finish it. Especially if I have to spend years breeding and raising a new version of myself to carry out the work after me. Like she did," the queen said resentfully.

Ideth gave her an appraising look. "It's time you

want? Pray to the Chronodéndron. Chronos will gladly give you time. Take the rest of the Ambrosia while you're there and you'll stay alive and young even longer!"

Arianh pinned her exquisite violet eyes on Ideth. "What did you say?"

Ah frost, Ideth thought. *Again, one sentence too far.* Tiredness always made her tongue carry on producing words after her brain had shut up.

"You know where it is, the Ambrosia?" Arianh insisted.

What was the point in hiding it now? It wasn't like the hunter was coming back for it. Besides, it wasn't his to begin with, it was Orion's. "Yeah… Some…"

"Please. Tell me." Arianh held her hands as if in prayer.

Ideth considered the queen: naïve, misguided fool that she was, she had a point. Even limited immortality was better than none. It's frustrating enough to be weak as a twig in a world of gods and predators. A ruler needs every advantage they can get to succeed in such a world. And if the right ruler lives long enough to see their work through… *What would the old queen have done with Ambrosia?* Ideth wondered. Probably there would be no more Narrum in Aegea. Arianh seemed to be of a similar disposition as her mother in that regard, and she would not let Ideth go without an answer. *Oh well, where is the harm?*

Ideth lowered her voice and leaned closer to the queen. "I buried it at the Chronodéndron. Where else, right?" She winked.

Tears of joy and relief ran through Arianh's flawless

cheeks. "Thank you," Arianh whispered and squeezed Ideth's hand. "Thank you, thank you!"

Above them, the ravens all but screamed, flying in spirals.

"What's wrong with them?" Ideth asked, not sure she wanted to know.

"I don't know… I've never seen them like this."

Arianh's bracelet made a clicking sound. Aedan's angry voice followed.

"Arianh, find Ideth and meet us at the top. NOW."

"Oh, no…" Ideth sighed.

INTERLUDE 4

The New Ruler

I walk the long tunnel to the top of the Stump with the Wyrd's unconscious host over my shoulder while Hades and Hel, a few steps ahead, argue about the differences in intellect between the sexes, neither apparently aware of the irony in their disagreement.

Psyche huffs out a long-suffering sigh, as unamused as I am. "Are they always like this?"

"Worse," I admit. The Underworld couple seem to use words to subdue their frustrations as a Dharkan uses heat to subdue their hunger.

We arrive at the surface to find Ideth and Arianh holding each other's hands. That's odd. Ideth will have to explain to me what the gesture means amongst dryads. If they made some sort of pact, I need to find out what it was about. Above us, the Wyrd's black birds make a terrible racket when they see their master. Hel whispers a few words at them in a language I don't recognise, and they fly away, silent.

"Uncle!" Arianh cries the moment she recognises the burden on my shoulder. "What happened?"

"Ask her." I nod at Psyche and drop the body on the icy surface. The temperature – or the impact – makes him spasm.

"Pick him up, you idiot! The sun's about to set. He'll freeze faster than he can feed." The queen, realising how she addressed me, loses all colour from her cheeks. I put on my best scowl. She bites her lip. "Apologies, Aedan. Can you… oh, for frost's sake, just take him off the ice, will you!"

With a thought, Hel breaks the ice away from the spot where Odin lies, exposing the wood beneath. However strained her relationship is with the old god, at least she doesn't want his host to suffer.

"What did you do to him?" Ideth asks Psyche suspiciously. A torrent of unpleasant emotions ooze from the nymph. I can relate.

"He's free," Psyche replies.

"You have strange notions of freedom," Ideth scorns, keeping her distance from us both. A strong self-preservation instinct on that one.

Psyche just tilts her head, gazing at the moaning, drooling man on the ground, then kneels at his side.

"What do you think you're doing?" Hel puts an icy hand on Psyche's shoulder before her hands can touch the Wyrd's skin.

"What I can," Psyche says.

"I think you've done enough," Arianh hisses, pushing her aside. Unlike Ideth, her self-preservation instinct is practically non-existent.

Psyche brushes Arianh's hand away and touches the half-conscious man's forehead. He settles into a deep sleep. "There. I healed what I could. You should take him inside now. It's nearly dark, anyway. Tomorrow, bring him back up to bask. He'll recover. You can thank me later."

As if on cue, the sun disappears behind the Mountains.

Xylo sits down, as is his custom once the sun sets, uninterested in our dramas, dragging a reluctant (and very much interested) Oreth with him.

Arianh's violet eyes open to their full width. She looks far from thankful. "What's this now? All I keep hearing from you people is how dangerous she is, how she cannot be trusted. And now she's here acting as a healer and giving out orders. What has she done to my uncle?!"

No one answers.

"Is she controlling your minds or something?" Ideth asks us, wary.

Psyche laughs. "I wish."

Hades gives both women an exasperated glance. "No one's controlling anyone anymore, and your *uncle* is probably better than we are. Do as she says. Take him inside and stop interfering in the affairs of gods, *mortal.*"

Arianh gapes with outrage but has enough sense to remain quiet. Even if not obedient.

"What's wrong, my lady?" Hades asks.

Hel has gone perfectly still. That Hades had to ask for her thoughts puts me on edge. *Goddess, let it not be the burning ring again.*

"I sense a new presence in Niflheim," she whispers.

"Where?" Hades asks, looking around as if searching for it. One corner of Psyche's mouth lifts ever so slightly.

Hel pays him no attention. "I have to go. Aedan, you're in charge of the Stump until I return."

"Me?!"

"Yes, Aedan. I rule the dead, not" – she casts around the small expanse of defrosted land the mortals call Aegea – "*this*," she says, curling her lip. "Niflheim is a vast world beyond this place. I've neglected it for too long. Yes, I know this is not what you want, Aedan, but someone needs to hold the fort, so to speak. I trust the task to you."

No! I think, but Hel gives me no opportunity to voice my protest.

"You are the one with free access through the Stump since its shield doesn't affect you; you hold its prisoners, wear the Suzerain's ring, sleep in his bed, and you're even able to walk in daylight now. This Tree and realm are my gifts to you. Take them."

I blink. "I'll be burned if I will!" My existence was far from perfect before, but how in the flame has it come to this? "Goddess, with all due respect, I'm a Dharkan! I should not be dealing with the living except to change their state of being. I am the creature other creatures fear, not who they look to for answers and guidance. I live in dark, icy caves deep underground, not atop giant trees. I'll be burned if I lost Ileana for such a 'reward'."

"Prince Aedan of Shadowfrost." Hel, now the divine personification of cold anger and impatience, her eyes flashing a fierce blue, stalks in my direction. "How does a Dharkan become king?"

I grind my teeth and remind myself she is a goddess, my goddess, creator of this world and my people. "By seizing the power of the previous king."

Hel nods. "Congratulations, *Your Majesty*." She steps close enough for me to feel her power on my skin. Such power. My reaction to it is not fear or intimidation, just… hunger.

"Make me proud."

"Excuse me." Arianh steps between us. "He can't rule – no offence – but on behalf of all dryads, we can't have a Dharkan ruling in Aegea!"

Hel casts a freezing glance down at the hand Arianh used to push her aside, and I'm surprised it doesn't shrivel. I move it away before it does. The queen doesn't seem to notice how close she came to being iced.

"Why not?" Ideth asks with an amused tone. That one loves the sound of wood burning, she does.

"They feed on us!" Arianh shrieks.

"So, you're saying Alek's rule was acceptable because he was a dryad?" Hel asks, well aware of Arianh's feelings towards the Dharkan and their gods.

"No. It was not acceptable and so he's gone. Aedan doesn't even want to rule. For frost's sake, Hel. You have a queen right *here*!" She points at herself with indignation.

"Maybe the two of you should get married and rule together," Hades suggests. Arianh's face turns crimson, nostrils flaring. Hel shakes her head, and even Psyche covers up a smirk.

"What did I say?" Hades asks, confused. "That would solve the problem, no? But – fine! Keep arguing, then. This conversation is pointless anyway until we find a permanent way to stop whatever is trying to get through that portal."

"Goddess," I say cautiously. "Arianh is much better suited to rule Aegea than I am. Her experience in the role alone makes her a better candidate. Besides, Hades is right. There won't be an Aegea to rule if the portal is breached. You saw what happened earlier. I alone am no match to stop whatever tried to get through that."

"Gaea will stand guard at the portal while I'm away."

I cannot believe it. It's not for me to question the goddess of the dead, but… since no one else is doing it. "The Goddess of Life?"

"Why not? She's more talented than she looks."

"She's the Goddess of *Life*," I repeat, hoping that realisation dawns on Hel. "You want to leave *her* in charge of defending the enemy's portal?"

"Yes. She has as much to lose as we do, trust me. She'll defend this world until the Universe burns out."

"She didn't lift a finger when they took it the first time!" I protest.

"They caught her off guard. She will be ready this time."

I glance at Hades, and he all but gestures for me to keep quiet. "If you say so," I say, fists clenched in frustration.

What is the point in arguing? Sounds like everyone's wits have left them. Let the gods play their games. What do I care? Every creature that mattered to me is gone: Cornus, Aecius, Father... Ileana. It was all for nothing, it seems.

"What about the Dharkan gathered in the forest? Chiron said they –" Arianh starts.

Dharkan in the forest? This is news to me.

"What about them?" Hel thunders.

Arianh flinches but continues. "You need to stop them."

"The Dharkan have free will. If there's one thing I can't do, it is stop them. I…" Hel turns to me with mischief in her eyes, and I know I will not like what she's about to say next.

"Fine. This is how it's going to be: the faithless Dharkan need a leader, someone able to change their minds. Aedan, if you don't want to stay here or rule the living, you'll go to them. Show them what you've achieved and convince them to restore their faith in me. You" – she points at Psyche – "go to the Blacksmith, make him craft something to seal this burning portal. Use any means necessary. If he refuses to help us, take his soul. When you're done, return here and help Gaea. She still wants to talk to you, by the way, so don't even think of escaping; you won't succeed."

"Oh, I'm well aware of that, thank you. I can't even translocate," Psyche says bitterly.

"What do you mean you can't translocate?" Hades asks with mock suspicion.

"I just can't," Psyche replies, annoyed.

"It was the first thing you did!"

"And I still don't know how I did it."

"It's so simple," Hades says. "You visualise where you want to go in your mind, and then you're there. As long as you know where 'there' is, of course. It helps if it's somewhere you've been to before."

"Believe me, it's not for lack of trying!" Psyche hisses at the Underworld Lord.

"Not all gods can translocate within the worlds of others," Hel says coldly. "Father says it's a sign of youth. Only the elder gods can manage it – or prevent it," she adds pointedly.

"Sure, he would say that, he's as old as time. I'm young and manage it just fine," Hades says. "Oh wait, does that mean this is indeed my world too?"

"Don't push it."

Hades grins and focuses back on Psyche. "What about flying? Can you fly, Butterfly?"

"Can't fly either." Psyche looks at the sky wistfully. I'm sure she would fly away if she could, just to get away from Hades. He's even more aggravating than usual, almost manic. As torments go, it is not what I would have chosen for her, but it pleases me to see the frustration on the goddess's face, and if she really can't translocate, at least I can stop worrying about her sudden escape.

Hel's face is not a merry sight. "Where's Chiron?"

"Went back to the forest," Ideth says with what sounds like loathing.

"Burning horse. Never around when you need him." Hel blows an icy breath. "Fine. Take one of the Suzerain's mounts, then. What do you call those flying skiffs again?" Hel asks Hades.

"Gliders," Psyche answers, a bit too excited for my taste.

"Right, of course." Hel rolls her eyes. "And if you

try to deceive me again, goddess of the soul, I'll bury you in Helheim for eternity. Understand?"

"You made it perfectly clear the first time."

"And you." Hel turns to Hades. "Go with her. Make sure she doesn't 'free' any more Wyrds along the way."

"Can't, sorry. I too have a lot to do in the Underworld…" Hades goes very still, ears drooping. "Actually, I really must go. Now." He vanishes.

Ice cracks around Hel's feet. "Burn you too!"

"I'm perfectly capable of getting there on my own," Psyche says.

"I'll go with her," I say, to both goddesses' surprise. "Psyche still hasn't told me what I need to know, and until she does…" I turn to Psyche. "Until you do, I'm not letting you out of my sight."

Hel puts her hands on her hips and scrutinises us through slitted eyes, her demeanour colder than ever.

"Fine! Aedan, go with her. You're going in the same direction anyway, and at least you're safe from her touch. Keep her on a tight leash and make sure she applies herself to the task." Hel turns to Arianh. "You want to rule, mortal? Then rule. I want every dryad in Aegea to know whose world they live in and that neither I nor the Dharkan are their enemy. Or they won't be once Aedan sets them straight, right? And you…" She fixes her cold stare on Ideth. "You're coming with me."

CHAPTER SIX

Ulcan

Ulcan held up a snake's skin and grimaced at the sky. There was no sign of the blue sun again that morning. *How can a sun just disappear?* The question formed in his mind, unbidden. Like so many other questions he had regarding the world he lived in, Ulcan didn't really care to know the answer. Whatever the gods had going on between them, he just hoped it wouldn't affect the white sun as well, for he'd rather not have to hunt in the dark. As for the skin… it was still moist.

The snake that shed it could still be nearby, so Ulcan had no time to speculate about the whims of the gods. He spat, adjusted his hat, made sure he had a firm grip on his blade and walked up the Nymph's Bosom.

It was an accurate enough appellation, for the outline of the hill ahead did resemble a young woman lying on her back, down to the perky breasts defined by a nipple-shaped boulder perched on its round peak. Ulcan figured these hills and their network of caves had been the work of a lusty deity. Then again, the whole of Aegea had been the product of one god or another. He often wondered if all worlds had been created the same way, and if so, why had the gods responsible for this one showed so little consideration to the mortals they brought to live in it?

Ulcan had been one such mortal; he'd come from a world filled with sunlight and oceans brimming with fish. He remembered running along an endless beach with fine white sand stretching on alongside a clear blue sea, its colour almost indistinguishable from the sky above it. When the tide receded, he'd join the other children helping their mothers pick shellfish hidden or latched onto the rocks waiting for the sea to return, and gather the fish trapped in their nets. His people were never hungry, neither had they ever fought each other out of greed like the other tribes. They were peaceful and content with what they had, for it was enough. Most importantly, he remembered they were happy.

His family worshipped the gods who they believed were responsible for replenishing the ocean with delicious creatures after each tide, and naturally so did he. When the mighty Thor himself proclaimed they'd been chosen to travel to a new world, a better world, where they would be able to prove their worth, he felt exited, special even. But the moment he arrived in Aegea, his faith in the god's good intentions shattered.

"Mother, I don't like it here. I want to go back," had been the first thing Ulcan said when he came out of the great Tree, sick and shivering, one hand held tight to his mother's, the other clutched around his torso for warmth. Everyone had to be naked for their rebirth in the new world, and it was cold... so cold. There had been no sky nor sun above them then, just branches as wide as brooks, their leaves large and thick as blankets, smothering the sunlight. He made his way barefoot down the roots of the great Tree feeling as small as an ant. If there was one thing the gods knew how to do well, it was to make mortals feel small.

"Hush, child, we've been chosen. We must be grateful and honour the gods," his mother had said.

He hadn't felt grateful then, and he certainly didn't feel it now after a lifetime of struggle.

Once out of the Tree's shade, his mother cheered along with the others. To them, this was a world filled with promise and opportunity. "If we do well, we'll be allowed to join the great warriors in Valhalla. Don't you want to be with your father?" she had asked him, and he nodded. The truth was, he'd much rather be with his friends back on the beach. He'd never even met his father.

They set about rebuilding their life in Aegea, and for a while it wasn't so bad. The gods were kind to them, especially the Wyrd, forced to live as mortals do. And the colossal Tree, when seen from a distance, was the most magnificent sight anyone had ever beheld. Like with the hill, one had to gain some perspective to truly appreciate the mighty Tree's magnificence.

The ocean, however, was far beyond the great Tree's reach, so Ulcan had to learn how to climb and hunt for the animals living in its branches instead, and he soon discovered that he much preferred hunting to fishing. Every animal in Aegea fascinated him, especially the ones that could talk. And there were so many of them then! Of course, there were also the ones that could eat him alive and the ones who hunted in the night. Those took some getting used to… but overall, life in the new world was good until one day the great Tree was gone.

They call it the 'Fell' but in truth, the crown of the World Tree never actually fell, it vanished. And the thousands of birds, squirrels, rodents and other animals that lived there and provided sustenance for the Narrum vanished with it. Suddenly there was nothing safe to hunt, nothing between them and their predators. And no way to return home.

In the Stump, magnificence turned to austerity. The tools used for hunting became weapons for survival when the Wraiths came from their icy Mountains in large groups to claim their world back and avenge their goddess. They forced families to unite back into tribes and barricade themselves in settlements, for only in great numbers were they able to keep death at bay. Unable to hunt without being hunted themselves, many died from hunger then, including his mother. The tribe leaders, all men, used orphans like him to bait the Wraiths, claiming they were offerings to the gods. That was when he ran to the forest to join the tree huggers. There, one of the Wyrd found him and took him under his protection. He was a proper hunter and the one who taught Ulcan to hunt with snares and traps, for he was hopeless with a bow. He knew how to use it well enough, but his host's eyes failed to see across great distances. Then the Wyrd, despite his poor eyesight, managed to find love and died shortly after…

Ulcan, left alone once again, joined other orphans like him, and by the time the Suzerain put an end to the

Dharkan's raids, he was too accustomed to the forest. Settlements made him uneasy. He no longer missed the ocean, nor the blue skies. He had no use for those memories either. The forest became his home, and once he'd gazed upon the world from every vantage point, he saw Aegea for what it was: a world meant only for gods, monsters and those who hunt them.

Ulcan followed the snake's trail, for fresh skins always fetched a higher price. Snakes were hard to track and even harder to kill. You had to get close to do it properly, and that could be hazardous. Not for him, though. Killing the legless monsters was Ulcan's specialty. Let other hunters hide behind bushes with their bows. For him, there was nothing like feeling the life drain from his prey. More than that. It was a matter of honour to give the prey a chance to defend itself.

The trail led to a gap in the rock where he knew rattons liked to nest. Snakes were nothing if not predictable; they were always hungry after shedding.

He pulled the sunstone hung around his neck from behind his vest and rubbed it until it shone a bright white. Then he took another knife out and squeezed through the gap in the rock.

The cave was empty of rattons, a sure sign a snake had been there recently. Something was off, though. One cloak was missing from the hooks above. "Hmm," he said, taking a closer look. Someone had ripped it down, judging by the small piece of fabric caught on the metal tip. A child, maybe? No, most likely a small female. Children never lasted long in the caves, being little larger than rattons themselves and far less cautious.

That someone had been brave or desperate enough to come here in the first place was a bad sign. The only thing people feared more than snakes was superstition, hence the reason he'd hung the cloaks in the first place. Making others believe these caves were entrances to the Underworld kept them free from runaways. Then again, hunger made heroes out of all creatures. Ulcan sighed. The last thing he needed was competition, or to have his prey disturbed. Too many snakes had already moved to the Boiling Lake, and there were other, more dangerous predators taking residence there.

Ulcan removed his boots. Snakes were practically deaf, but they could sense the slightest vibrations on the rock. He held the light overhead, then lay flat on the ground and crawled through the opening to the next chamber. Ulcan knew every nook and cranny of these caves like the back of his hand by now, but the light provided by the sunstone was supposedly undetectable by snakes, and he could use any advantage he could get. Besides, he still had to be able to see the snake in order to kill it.

The black rock looked cold in the white light, but it was far from it. Heat radiated from deep below, making it a perfect place for a snake to digest its meal. And sure enough, there it was. The monstrous creatures never hid. They had no predators, except for him. This one looked deformed, so swollen was its abdomen from its last meal. Not the largest snake Ulcan had ever hunted, but close. Its head was tilted to the side, and it breathed in steady, slow breaths without flicking its tongue. It slept, or so it seemed; one could never be too sure with snakes.

He held the knife ready in his hand. The Blacksmith had made it especially for him and this purpose, along with the sunstone. The Blacksmith was not like the other gods. He created tools and weapons, not worlds. Ulcan had to pay for the items, of course. As his mother often said: "Everything has a price." But the quality of the Blacksmith's work was worth a bowl of his blood and the awkwardness of siting on a pedestal all day watching him hammer a copy of himself.

Ulcan spoke to the blade, and the runes on the pommel glowed faintly, readying it for the attack.

The hunter approached the snake slowly, carefully, until its head was within arm's reach, then plunged the long blade through the reptile's skull with practised precision until the tip hit the rock, and immediately jumped back. The snake spasmed, trashed, and writhed. Ulcan kept his distance, behind a recess, avoiding the tail lashes, proud of yet another successful ambush.

Now, the hard part…

Skinning a snake this size was gruesome, arduous work. The sun was already on its way to the shadow when he'd finished: bloodied, cramped and hungry. He had no time to clean the skin properly, so he just rolled it up and placed it inside the bag, along with the snake's head (for those fetched good prices too).

Getting the whole snake out of the cave in one piece was out of the question. It would stay there and, due to one of the many ironies of nature, probably be eaten by rattons. Although mostly herbivorous, they didn't turn their noses when meat that didn't put up a fight was available.

Ulcan hated the idea of all that meat going to waste, though, and considered going up the hill to ask Aedan to freeze it for a later time. But he hated asking favours of the moody Dharkan as well. Last time he'd demanded a third of Ulcan's payment for the task. What need had Wraiths for currency, anyway? They did not need to eat, and his horse would not go hungry in the forest. Knowing Aedan, he would probably spend it on books or other such nonsense. No, Aedan might not have a sweet tooth for life, but he was as greedy as the Suzerain.

Thinking about the solitary Dharkan made him think about the blue sun again. He'd surely know something about that. Ulcan spat, considering his options. It was getting dark. He would not make it to Portum before nightfall, and he didn't fancy spending the night unsheltered. He spat again. He'd have to shelter in the caves, and so perhaps he should pay Aedan a visit. The Wraith was greedy, but he was not evil like that bitch, Iva, and Ulcan could not afford to make more enemies out of the Dharkan. They were not as easy to kill as snakes, after all.

∞

Ulcan was halfway up the gloomy hill, with many of its trees splintered and charred from the last lightning storm, when the stink of decay reached his nostrils.

Death was far from uncommon in Aegea, but most carcases were devoured before they decomposed. Ulcan stopped to adjust the strap on his shoulder, took out his bloody knife, spat and walked towards the source of the smell. He figured it was probably just a regurgitated ratton, for there was nothing on these hills but snakes, rattons and – a gryphon pounced from the foliage, sinking its talons into his chest.

Ulcan grabbed the creature's sharp beak before it could snap closed on his face. Ignoring the shock and pain, he pushed the predator's head aside to expose the feathered neck with one hand and sliced it open with the knife in the other. Hot blood splattered his eyes, nose and mouth. The talons sank deeper, burning agony into his ribs. The gryphon screeched a deafening call before Ulcan was able to cut clean through its neck.

"Fuck," he said, once he'd spat out enough blood to get the word out. He rolled from under the dead creature, half blind with pain, and caught a glimpse of a shadow swoop overhead.

"Shit!" A second gryphon landed on the carcass of the first and screeched that painfully eerie sound of theirs. Ulcan didn't hesitate. He got to his feet and leaped on the creature, hacking at the base of its neck with vicious intent. The gryphon twisted its head around and nearly bit off Ulcan's ear, but that was all it did before falling over, wings spasming. Ulcan stabbed it a few more times to make sure it was dead, crawled back to his feet, and waited for the next one on wobbly legs, blade tightly gripped in one hand, the other clutched to his chest, bleeding profusely.

After several heartbeats of quietude, he allowed himself to fall to his knees.

He cursed when he was able to assess the damage.

His leather vest and the snakeskin inside the satchel

had been torn to shreds by the gryphon's talons. His own skin was lacerated but not too deeply. Nothing a few stitches wouldn't fix, maybe. The hand, though... Ulcan ripped off part of his ruined shirt and rolled it tightly around it. He'd need to go to the centaur for healing. And protection. He'd just killed two of Artemis' pets.

The mad huntress would skin him alive for the insult, but what was he supposed to have done? Let the beasts feed on him? Fuck that! Fear and pain gave way to unmeasured rage. The goddess had no right to do this to him! He'd earned his kills. The snake's skin would have kept him fed and drunk for a hundred days at least. He cursed the gods, their world and all their creatures.

Then he saw it.

Beyond the foliage, the source of the stink of decay. He knew what he was looking at, but like with the sun, he did not understand how it could have happened and did not want to know the answers to the questions running through his mind.

Exposed to the elements and scavengers was the prey a hunter would never dare to kill: an Elysian horse. Cornus, his name had been. *Can it be prey if it has a name?* Ulcan pushed the question from his throbbing head and dragged himself closer.

Cornus had arrows sticking from his neck and skull. His throat was sliced wide open, the blood long soaked into the earth beneath.

Ulcan yanked one arrow from the horse's skull. It was fletched with a gryphon's feather. Only two hunters would have had access to such a luxury (he wasn't counting himself in this turn of events). The tip was ordinary metal, the shaft made of cedar. Not one of Artemis' arrows then; only special silver for the goddess. That left Bertho.

"That fucking bastard," Ulcan said, revolted. *How could he?* The sight of the rotting Elysian horse was tragic in every way.

The rivalry between Ulcan and Bertho was legendary in the forest. And rather unfair, as Bertho had the patronage of the goddess of the hunt and Ulcan only had her scorn. Had the man gotten so full of himself that he killed the horse just to prove that he could? No. Bertho was the sort of man capable of murdering an Elysian horse, for sure, but no hunter would abandon a prey to rot, certainly not a prize such as this. He hadn't even taken the horn! Something was wrong. Very, very wrong.

And if Cornus was dead, what had happened to Aedan?

Shit. "Shit, shit, shit." Ulcan pulled himself up with the aid of a sapling and ran up the hill towards the Dharkan's cave.

Close to the entrance, Ulcan smelled death again.

"There you are, you bastard," he said, waving away a swarm of flies.

Collapsed at the bottom of the slope to the cave's entrance lay what was left of Ulcan's nemesis. Broken, swollen and headless, Bertho was recognisable only by his boots and crossbow. Whether his state resulted from overkill or torture, Ulcan couldn't tell. Both often looked similar in the end.

Bertho's skill with the crossbow had been enviable,

as had his stealth. Stealth was not Ulcan's forte. As tall as most dryads and twice as wide, it was hard for him to go unnoticed. Another reason why he'd preferred to hunt snakes. Still… It seemed every hunter apprenticed to Artemis had come to a bitter end. Orion's body had never been found. Now this. Ulcan felt no pity for Bertho, for he had disliked the man intensely, but he still doffed his hat and offered a prayer for his family out of respect for Martha, Bertho's wife, who had always been kind to him.

One thing was certain, no gryphon or Dharkan had done the butchering, unless they'd developed canines. Ulcan reckoned this was the work of a rival god to the huntress and therefore way beyond him. He should leave and find the centaur. He'd know what to do. And yet… curiosity kept pushing him further up the slope.

Ulcan held the glowing sunstone high when he stepped over the loose rubble at the cave's entrance. A cold shiver ran up his spine. The cave was covered in ice, cold enough for him to see his breath. The bed roll against the wall was empty and bloodied, Aedan's possessions lay broken and scattered across the floor, and what could possibly have made those marks on the ceiling?

He heard a moan.

"Aedan?" Ulcan whispered. Dharkan often slept during the day, and it was not wise to startle one during sleep.

Silence.

"Aedan?" he called again, louder this time.

A rasping rumble answered. The hairs on the back of his neck bristled. Instinct was telling him to run away, for whatever was inside the cave he knew he couldn't fight it. He prepared to leave, determined not to end up like Bertho, when he heard a hiss. It was not a snake, he was sure. No snake hissed like that.

Torn between curiosity and terror, he turned around and aimed the sunstone towards the pool at the back of the cave.

"Fuck me…"

INTERLUDE 5

Monumental Disaster

"Look out!" Psyche shouts in my ear.

The flying skiff comes abruptly to a halt. One moment I'm weightless, flying through the air, then pain splits my skull and rattles my teeth, spreading from my forehead to my neck and down my spine.

"Ow," I hear myself say, blinking away the stars from my vision. The foliage of a large oak wobbles above. *Blazing sun, how did that tree get here?* The ringing in my ears makes the thought feel like it comes from someone else's head. The entire world shakes and shimmers while I try to set my mind in order.

"For fuck's sake!" shrills the angry goddess.

Psyche, or some approximation of her, appears scowling in my field of vision. I'm unsure of what I'm looking at. She's all wrong. Her shoulders are backwards, and there's a bone protruding from her neck.

"Burn me," I say, cringing at the sound of bone and cartilage rearranging themselves as she rotates her neck around and rolls her shoulders into something less disturbing to look upon, all while cursing my wits and masculinity.

I groan another curse, unable to come up with anything more eloquent to say in return. My head throbs. I don't need this level of hostility right now. Can't the creature see it was the tree's fault? No, it was *her* fault. She did something to the skiff. Or to the tree. This oak had not been here before. I'm certain of it.

"This is not a horse, you clot. It can't see where it's going, you need to pay attention."

"I was paying attention!"

It's agony just above my brow. I touch the source, and my fingers come back bloody. I then reach towards the piece of living wood that caused the wound, half expecting, half hoping to find it missing. Psyche, probably thinking I'm asking for aid, grabs the outstretched hand and pulls me to my feet, nearly dislocating my arm off the shoulder in the process.

"Ow," is all I manage to say again. Speaking, much like standing, is quite the challenge at the moment.

"Next time, I drive," she says.

Next time?! As if there will ever be a next time, I think.

"I'll never get into one of those things again!" I tell her.

"It was not the glider's fault."

"It was not my fault either! I did everything as instructed," I state and proceed to demonstrate. "Push handle forward to run, backwards to halt, turn wheel right to go right and left to go left. This thing is far less complicated than a horse. I did everything right. So it must have disobeyed my commands!"

"I think you broke it," Psyche says, not listening to a word I said, staring at the crumpled metal instead, arms folded across her chest. There's a spark, followed by smoke and a grating sound, like a knife sharpener grinding against a blade's edge.

Psyche's eyes widen. "Move away from the –"

The metal contraption shakes, convulses, and collapses to the ground with a sad whistle.

"It's dead," I declare.

"It's broken, you mean. It wasn't alive to begin with." Psyche scowls up at me. "Kinda like you."

I scowl back. "That thing moved, had energy running through it, responded to stimuli and commands. Obviously, it had a mind of its own and control over all its parts. The way I see it, it was very much alive. Your definition of life is narrow and insulting to the Dharkan."

She gives me a hideous look. "So it decided to commit suicide, then?"

"Why not? It's one of the Suzerain's mounts, woman! Maybe it didn't like me riding it. Or you. Maybe it tried to kill us both. Have you considered that? It nearly succeeded too," I say, cleaning blood from my face.

Psyche gapes at me and at the crumpled mount, shakes her head, then pinches the bridge of her nose and blows at the wind. "Stars, give me patience. I can't," she says to herself.

She says that a lot, and I still do not understand what it is she can't do. Take my soul, probably, since I don't have one. I don't care. At least she's not shouting insults at me anymore.

"Do you want me to fix that, or are you happy seeing

red for a while?" She points at my face. I'm surprised at the offer, but take it nonetheless. The pain hinders my reasoning.

Psyche gasps and sends me flying backwards into the tree again. Now the back of my head throbs as much as the front.

"How many times do I need to tell you to stay the fuck away from me and my neck!"

"You said –" I begin.

"I meant that I could stop the bleeding on your forehead. You don't get to feed on me again, Dharkan. Ever. I'm barely able to sustain myself as it is, especially at the rate you keep injuring me."

"What are you complaining about, creature? You're a goddess!"

"A debilitated goddess in a foreign, inhospitable world. That blue light did more than kill Dharkan and sustain Wyrds, you idiot. Now, be still and keep your bloody hands to yourself."

∞

"This is not the way to the Boiling Lake," Psyche says. It took her long enough to recognise the scenery. "Why are we here?"

"I need to do something first," I say, walking up to my shelter, head down. Whatever the goddess did to the wound helped with the bleeding, but it did nothing for the pain, and even starlight feels too bright right now.

"Aedan, wait. It's better if you don't go that way." The goddess sounds serious, trying to catch up with me.

"Why not?"

"You won't like what you'll see."

That just makes me want to see it more. I push through the ferns.

A gryphon lies dead at my feet. Another with his neck hanging by sinew and coarse skin lies next to it. I walk past them and freeze.

"This should not have happened," I say through clenched teeth. Sparks crack around my fists. Grief is the only thing keeping me from destroying this clearing with rage.

"No, no, it shouldn't. I'm so sorry, Aedan. Damn it!" Her voice cracks. She scrubs her cheeks angrily, then moves her lips silently. I've never met a god who prays. *Who is she praying to?* Herself, probably.

I'm too angry to pray. The gryphons had been feasting on Cornus. But that is not the reason for my anger. Frost spreads from under my feet to the trees. Lightning splits one of them.

"Aedan…" Psyche's voice sounds far away. Not afraid, but definitely concerned.

"I'll flay the creature who did this." The ice covers Cornus' remains, and more trees shatter.

"Aedan, calm down. Fenrir already took care of the hunter who shot him. He got what he deserved."

"This!" I point at the sheared nub of bone between the empty eye sockets of my friend. "Someone took his horn!"

"Oh." Psyche kneels and touches Cornus' bare skull. "Why would anyone take his horn? Some kind of trophy?"

"The Narrum believe it will give them power."

"Power to do what?"

"Who cares!" I shout. "Narrum attribute powers to anything to justify their own greed to acquire them."

Psyche stands back as if I have slapped her. I should have. This was her fault too. If she hadn't forced Ileana to leave the cave that morning... I take a deep breath before I bring another lightning storm down on our heads. It wouldn't have made a difference. Cornus would probably still be dead, but Ileana would be alive at least. I push the thought away and continue up the hill.

Cornus' murderer lies in pieces close to the entrance to the cave. Fenrir had been too kind to the creature; his death had been swift and final. Had I been able to lay my hands on the hunter, he'd still be breathing.

"Where's his head?" Psyche asks, searching the grass at our feet.

"Again: Who cares?"

"I do," she grumbles in a sulk. The woman has the strangest concerns.

She picks up his crossbow and inspects it with delight. "Amazing."

That's not the word I'd pick to describe the weapon that killed my best friend, and I force myself to move on before I say something I might regret.

Inside I find the cave filled with hot steam, my meagre belongings scattered across the filthy floor.

"That's disappointing," I say.

"What is?"

"I expected the mad huntress to still be here so I could finish my meal," I sneer. I could, in fact, use some sustenance and crave something more than just heat. Ever since I tasted gods, nothing quite quenches my hunger.

"It's been days. What did you expect? Stars, I still can't believe you froze Artemis. I wish I'd seen it, though. Oh, shit," Psyche says, inspecting her foot. She just stepped on the foul remains of Oric's arm. Suits her right for walking around barefoot.

The goddess clicks her tongue in annoyance but doesn't seem too concerned with the decomposing slime as she continues patrolling the room with her eyes closed.

"What are you doing now?" I have to ask.

"It's still bright…" she murmurs to herself, then bends and picks up a book. "Ah! Found it," she says, grinning up at me. She stands on the exact spot Ileana stood before she kissed me. The juxtaposition of the memory with reality makes me want to break something.

Psyche's smile vanishes. I snatch the book from her hand. Ileana had brought it with her, so it must be important. "What sort of language is this?"

"Mine," she answers curtly and takes the book back.

"What's it about?"

"None of your business."

I move closer, towering over her with a menacing frown. "Answer my question."

"The Suzerain."

"So it is my business. What does it say?"

"I don't know. I haven't read it yet," she hisses, trying to slip past me.

Lies. "Why not?" I block her retreat with my arm braced against the wall.

She chews on her cheek before answering. "Because the last thing Ileana wanted to do when she was here was read."

Psyche never misses an opportunity to remind me she had been lurking in Ileana's mind when we were together. It's not unusual for the gods to eavesdrop on our pleasure and even use us as vessels for their twisted lusts, but at least they have the decency to keep those experiences to themselves. Not her. And the way she talks makes it sound like it was torture. Maybe it was. Part of me would like to think that, while another wonders why. Had I been a poor lover? Is she so averse to men, or Dharkan?

The silence stretches on long enough for frost to form on the hot rock's surface. Psyche rolls her eyes and ducks under my arm to sit by the pool, then places her hand on the book and closes her eyes again.

Long moments pass. I occupy myself by collecting a few possessions. I had a mind to give the carved likenesses of Odin's ravens to Arianh as a gift but can only find Muninn. Burn the gods. Everything I own is either broken, stained with blood or scattered out of place.

"Well, that was pointless," Psyche finally says, putting the book down with the others.

"Explain."

She shrugs. "There's nothing here about the Suzerain that we don't already know."

"What about Ileana?"

"Again, not much beyond his obsession with her. Had I known its nature and how deep it went, I could have handled the situation differently. It's too late for that now. There is one thing that caught my attention, though." Psyche runs her fingertips over the other books as she speaks. "Seshat made a note saying she once overheard Alek talking to himself, claiming that he needed Ileana's body."

I cringe in abhorrence.

Psyche dismisses my horror. "I think he was being literal. The way you need his flesh to move through the Stump. I think he needed something of her. But for what purpose…"

"Did he get it?"

The goddess pales, breathing hard, then snatches her hand away from the books.

"What? No. I don't think he did," she says, walking away from the books and clutching her hand as if it had been scorched. "At least there was nothing missing that I could tell. Then again, I was unconscious for most of the time there. Who knows what he did to her body then."

I pick up the book that caused the goddess's distress: a boring tale of intrigue and betrayal amongst the Aesir. "That doesn't mean she was unconscious." I put both books inside the bag with the rest of my stuff.

"What did you say?" Psyche asks in a strangled whisper.

Burn it. I spoke too much. "Nothing," I reply, but I know she heard me well enough.

Psyche's dark brown eyes fix on mine. "What did you mean by 'that doesn't mean *she* was unconscious'?"

"She cannot know," Ileana had said. I can't betray her. I can't think of a lie either.

"Dharkan, you may not have a soul, but I swear by the stars I will cripple your mind and spirit in such ways you'll never have a coherent thought again!"

I blink at her. This is the most honest thing she's ever said to me. Burn me, but this goddess is indeed more dangerous than the path to Helheim. I have to tell her.

"That dawn, when she found me here. After I…" I hesitate.

"After you fed on me. Go on."

"Ileana gave me the necklace so you couldn't make her leave."

Psyche doesn't blink, doesn't breathe, doesn't move for what feels like a very long time.

"You're telling me Ileana was conscious while I was not?"

"Yes. I even thought I'd killed her host – er, you – and freed her. But apparently I only silenced you for a while and took her Ambrosia. Maybe if I hadn't, the Suzerain's poison wouldn't have harmed her. Do you think…" I could not finish the sentence. Psyche's burning stare clouded my reasoning and made me talk nonsense. She was the one responsible for Ileana's death. She'd taken her in the first place. Not me!

"I don't know what to think anymore, Dharkan," Psyche says and storms out of the cave.

∞

I catch up with her chanting next to a pile of rocks stacked taller than myself where Cornus' corpse used to be.

I stare at the rubble in disbelief. Is this her idea of

revenge? Or perhaps a message saying: 'Cross me and I'll dump a boulder on you'? *Goddess, I should never have let the woman out of that vault.*

"What did you do, creature?" I ask, dumbfounded. I thought she liked Cornus.

"The stones were already here. I just moved them around a bit," she says with a hint of pride in her tone.

My mouth hangs open. "You can't translocate, but you can do *this*?"

"It's not finished yet. Oh, don't be so surprised. It's easier for gods to do things for others than for themselves. Cornus deserved a proper burial."

"You call *this* a burial?"

She tilts her head, pondering. "I guess it's more of a tombstone, really. A monument." She nods, obviously pleased with herself.

"You put a pile of rocks on top of my horse's corpse! I've upset you, I get it. I'm not sorry, but do not take it out on Cornus!"

She stares up at me, unblinking. "This has nothing to do with you, you egotistical arse! And what would you have done, huh? Leave him as he was?"

"Yes! Undo it."

She crosses her arms and narrows her eyelids to slits. "No."

I've grown to know that expression well. She won't budge.

"Just promise me something. Do not *ever* do anything for me."

She bites her cheek. "Gladly!" She steals my bag and takes out one of Cornus' obsidian likenesses.

"Hey! Give it back."

She doesn't. Instead she holds it to her chest, takes a deep breath, and the pile suddenly glows, fusing together to take the shape of the sculpture. The result is magnificent, a lifelike statue of Cornus in his prime.

"Wow…" I say.

"You're welcome," she sneers.

Icicles sting the corners of my eyes at the sight, but I'll be damned if I let them break. "You shouldn't have wasted your precious energy with this… thing. Let's keep moving. I want to be in Portum by dawn."

"Portum?" she echoes. "You want to walk to Portum now, in the middle of the night?" A ratton shrieks nearby, and she casts about in every direction, more worried than anyone has a right to be at the sound.

"What's the objection?" I ask.

"No objection. Just… I think I saw a snake."

"I see at least two," I say, pointing in their direction. Snakes are everywhere in these hills, but they mostly keep to themselves.

Psyche moves closer. "Oh stars! They're hunting us."

"Honestly, creature, get a grip on yourself. You're far more dangerous than a snake."

She opens her mouth in outrage.

I don't wait to hear whatever nonsense comes out of it and walk away, confident that she'll follow. "If one does attack us," I shout over my shoulder, "just drop a boulder on it."

CHAPTER SEVEN

Ulla

The day before the lightning storm

Ulla's head throbbed. The blow that had nearly sent her to the Underworld was only partially to blame. The worst of it came from listening to the women's mindless talk, carried on in shouts across the room over the screaming demands of their children. *What a horrible existence*, she thought, and yet they all seemed happy enough.

Portum's temple was little more than a shed compared to the opulence of the one in Relicum, and the women all but crumpled over each other on the dirt floor with barely any space to stretch their legs, which said a lot about the conditions they'd come here to escape.

The vast majority of the breeders were Narrum, of course. It was as if their race was created especially for the purpose with their insatiable lust and enhanced fertility. Still, many dryads had embraced the joys of motherhood for a chance to see their children turned into gods. As life goals went, it was not a bad one, she supposed, but why did they have to make so much noise about it?

Dryads who didn't want to breed or be part of the Suzerain's chosen ones usually found their way to the Gharb, a place where they could be more than mothers. Others got lost in the forest and turned into nymphs, playthings for the gods and satyrs. Those probably breed as much as the ones at the temples, but at least they laughed and danced more often.

More and more Anann had joined the Aossi over the years but ironically, since few of them wanted children, the Aossi numbers were in decline. The Narrum, on the other hand, had no such problem, and their numbers kept increasing under the Suzerain's rule. Would their women do something else with their lives if they had a choice, Ulla wondered, looking at a pregnant girl with a baby in each arm and a toddler pulling at her dress. She was smiling, and her only regret seemed to be that she lacked more arms to hold all her children. *Probably not*, Ulla conceded.

A particularly high-pitched shriek from an angry child nearby sent a spike of pain through her head so intense she would have heaved had she anything in her stomach. Pain and sickness, that's all Ulla knew since her queen's betrayal and that Wraith took Fabrian from her.

They will pay, she promised herself. A mantra she'd repeated since she was a girl, now infused with a new purpose.

Payback would have to wait until she'd healed, though. She hated that she'd been forced to shelter at the temple, but there was no safer shelter between Relicum and the forest. It was hard for a woman to fend for herself alone in Aegea, especially if wounded. Ulla knew the limitations of her strength. And of her patience. She eyed that crooked child again, face covered in snot, screaming at the top of his lungs, and felt the runes on her sword come alight. Ice, if the mother didn't silence the kid, she would.

Fortunately Jonas entered the room, and a veil of silent admiration followed him. He had on a dress similar to the ones Judoc wore, except while the vain Shrine in Relicum wore his with panache, Jonas – who was not hard on the eye by any standard – did it with the ease of a dryad covered in blood. Like her, he favoured trousers and shirts – proper, sensible clothes – and had no desire for female attention.

The gaze of every woman in the room followed him expectantly. 'Take me' their eyes said. Ice, how could they not see they were barking up the wrong tree?

The man looked as miserable as she felt as he bobbed his head and smiled at the bright-eyed girls dutifully. Of everyone, the children got most of his attention. He had a soft spot for the little ones and hated the idea of them growing without a shelter, like he did. If not for them, Jonas would have never taken the role of Shrine.

"Jonas!" she shouted when he was close. Her voice barely audible above the shrieks. Few here used his name. To the women he was 'sire' or 'lord'. His head darted left and right, searching for the source of the sound. Ulla called again.

"Ssshhh," hissed the mother of the deafening child.

Ulla glared murderously at her before calling out again. "Hey, Jo!" That finally got his attention.

Jonas frowned, mouth half open. "Ulla? Is that you? *What* are you doing here?" Jonas was not an easy man to surprise, but seeing her there, amongst all the others, apparently did the trick. "What happened to your face?" he said when he got closer. She touched her sore and swollen forehead. The bruise had probably spread down to her cheeks by now. The women nearby scowled at her face, then at her clothes, as if they'd just noticed her. She bet she was quite a sight for their judgemental eyes.

Ignoring them and their looks altogether, Ulla stood up and leaned close to Jonas' ear. This caused more frowns, scowls and disapproving words from the breeders. It was impolite to be so forward with the Shrine.

"I need a drink," she said.

There was a huge basin filled with fresh water at the entrance. But that was not what she meant.

"You know the rules," he replied, prodding her sore temple. Jonas had always fancied himself a healer.

"Frost the rules! I need to get out of here before I cull the Tributes myself – please."

Jonas pursed his lips but did not take long to decide, conscious of the attention they were receiving.

"Come." He took Ulla's hand with a lover's care and guided her to the anteroom. "Wait here until after dark, then take a cloak and hide by the back door. I'll be there as soon as I can."

"Hide with the livestock?" she protested. Jonas

narrowed his eyes. She'd seen that look many times. There was no arguing with it.

The session started with the ever-boring speech of how the Suzerain had conquered the world and banished the evil gods to the Underworld. How the Nephilim spread across the stars and took them under their protection in exchange for Tribute, etcetera.

"Your children will brighten the sky alongside the stars. They'll become legends. They will be heroes, more beautiful than the Anann, heartier than the Narrum. And more powerful than the gods," Jonas proclaimed dutifully. His listeners made up for his lack of enthusiasm with widened eyes and sighs of wonderment. Ulla's lip curled as she wondered if motherhood did something to diminish a woman's wits.

After the sermon finished, the prayers began in earnest. Each participant would send their thoughts to the Nephilim, letting them know why their children deserved to be chosen while the Shrine pretended to listen to their replies and then pick at least one woman to receive the honour of his seed, which would make the child more likely to be chosen. At least that part was relatively silent, and Ulla remained in the temple until a bored Jonas took a young and childless girl to the back room, then made her way down to the settlement.

∞

"Did anyone see you?" Jonas asked, beckoning her from the tavern's back door later that evening.

She'd been in and out of consciousness, as often and deeply as her pain and the livestock stink allowed.

"I don't think so," she murmured. It had been raining when she crossed the settlement, and everyone had been too busy avoiding it to pay her any attention. "They will smell me all the way to the Gharb, though."

Jonas only snorted a reply.

She crossed the kitchen holding her breath, averting her eyes from the hanging carcasses, and shed the stinking cloak the moment she entered the tavern's common room. Between the noise and the smell, the ache in her head had increased to an unbearable degree.

The room was dark apart from a candle burning on the counter. Ulla went to take it and lost her balance, toppling over a barrel.

Jonas was at her side before she fell over to the floor.

"Frost, woman, what did you get yourself into this time?"

She steadied herself, annoyed at her weakness. "I'm fine."

"Sure you are." Jonas moved behind the counter and poured her something acrid.

She pushed it away. "Just water, please."

He gulped it back himself, fetched her a new cup and filled it with water as requested, then shrugged out of his dress with a similar disgust she'd shown to the drink. Ulla stared at him. She had seen Jonas' artificial leg before but could never get over the fact of how real it looked. It was almost impossible to tell in that light where Jonas' real leg ended and the Blacksmith's replacement began.

"So, what happened? Is the queen…?"

"Arianh's fine," Ulla replied angrily. "I was at-tacked."

He tutted. "No wonder. Walking around dressed like that," he said, putting on a set of similar clothes to the ones she wore.

Ulla had taken to wearing men's clothes from a young age when she had nothing else to wear and later kept doing it for personal convenience and safety while travelling. Dresses were easier to get in and out of for basking, but trousers were much better suited for pretty much everything else.

"What do you mean? No one expects a woman in trousers."

The way he looked at her made her feel stupid. "If you think that's a disguise, you're a fool. If you want to pass for a man, wear a freezing cloak like the Anann."

"What?"

"Oh please, not even a child would mistake those" – he pointed at her breasts – "for anything other than what they are. The only thing keeping you safe is that sword on your belt."

She touched the pommel, and the runes glowed. They always glowed whenever she thought about us-ing it. Then she stared down at her chest. It had, she admitted, expanded recently. It was one of Fabrian's favourite features to remark upon. She pushed the thought away.

"It was a Wraith."

Jonas had refilled his cup and stopped mid-swal-low. "Which Wraith?"

"Who cares! A Wraith. Dharkan all look the same: dead and ugly. He's ash now. But he should not have been there. Arianh betrayed me. She betrayed us all because of that Wyrd. Now Fabrian is dead and the women in Lagus are their captives and I can't take two steps without being sick." She covered her mouth before more nonsense came out. "Ice, I sound as bird-brained as the women at the temple," she said.

Jonas just stared at her. He had extremely long eyelashes for a male. A good thing, for without them to soften his gaze, that look would have frozen her to the bone with shame. She took a deep breath, downed a whole tankard of spring water in one go and then started again from the beginning.

She told him all about the queen's deception, the reason for their visit to Relicum and her plans to marry the Wraith. Her throat constricted at the mention of the attack in the night and Fabrian's death. Her vision blurred when she remembered how she'd nearly sliced Arianh's throat open. How badly she'd wanted to do it, so much it scared her. "They will pay," she concluded.

Jonas clicked his tongue. "Well, that explains why Judoc never showed up. Ice, if Fabrian's dead, he probably won't come for days!"

She gaped. Runes glowing. "Is that what worries you?"

"Do you want to deal with the breeders?"

"Ice no. I'd rather climb the Shadow Mountains. But I'm not a Shrine."

His expression was one of pure contempt. Jonas was a metz. His mother had been a dryad who'd ventured too close to the settlements and met a Narrum. Whether the union had been consensual or forced, he never knew. Both his parents had died shortly after the Fell. He was part of the first generation of tree huggers, orphans of the forest, like her. Two of the few who'd survived the Dharkan's incursion and returned to civilisation, such as it was. As a metz it didn't take long for him to be recruited by the Suzerain, and she never quite forgave him for that, even when she knew how little choice he must have had in the matter.

"I'm sorry, I didn't mean…" she started.

"Pfff," he said and took another swig. "None of what you said explains why you're here. Why not return to the Gharb?"

"I'm sick. This…" She pointed at her head. "… is killing me. I need a place to recover. And…"

"And?"

"I need to find Ulcan."

Jonas made a show of looking around the room. "He's not here."

"But you know where he is."

"No."

She knew him well enough to know he was lying. "Why won't you tell me?"

"If the Suzerain comes here later and asks for you, would you want me to send him to your room?"

She clenched her jaw hard enough to regret it. The pain was nearly blinding. "You know," she said, staring at two Jonases, "one day you'll need to pick a side."

"I already have. This, here." He opened his arms. "This place is my side."

"Huh," she snorted.

"It's easy for you to draw lines and talk about sides, Ulla. I was born in the middle. I had no place in Aegea until the Suzerain came. But I can't even be on his side, can I?" He sighed and swallowed the rest of his drink.

"I have a side," she said. "I'm on the side of the living."

"You do know Dharkan can die, right?"

She paused, then looked her childhood friend in his Narrum eyes. "Good. 'Cause I will kill them all."

He rolled his eyes. "You're not thinking straight. You need to rest."

"Does that mean you'll let me stay here?"

"Yes, you can stay. Out of sight, please. I have enough to deal with as it is."

She stood up, ready to climb up the stairs.

"Ulla, can I ask," Jonas started, then shook his head but asked anyway. "Why Fabrian?"

She understood the question. Even for a metz, Narrum sometimes behaved horribly. Their eating habits alone were off-putting. She had often wondered the same question herself, and the obvious answer was that he'd made her happy. While everyone in Aegea walked around in fear, holding their breath, Fabrian had breathed in all life had to offer. Never a complaint, never a grudge, never overcome with petty jealousy or greed, well, except for food. He loved to eat. But being with him had made her feel like a better person, as if his goodness were as contagious as his verve.

"He was a good man," was all she said.

∞

Ulla woke with a sharp ache behind her eyes. Ice, but the pain didn't even stop while she slept. Not that she'd slept much.

It seemed whoever took the room next to hers had some pains of their own and had spent most of the night mewing about them to the world.

Unable to return to sleep, she got up, swaying a little, and found the water jug empty. Had she drunk it all? She didn't remember. Jonas warned her to remain hidden in the room under penalty of being sent back to the temple, a directive that conflicted with her present needs. She desperately needed to hydrate. As the old queen would say: Life is made of choices between bad and worse.

There was no sound coming from the adjacent room at the moment, so she assumed whoever stayed there had either lost consciousness or died. She opened the door.

Halfway down the stairs, Ulla lost her balance and would have fallen if not for the stag's head mounted on the wall. She held on to its antlers, waiting for the pain and dizziness to subside, no longer able to tell if the headache caused the sickness or if the sickness caused the headache, only that ever since the Dharkan broke her skull, pain and sickness were all she knew.

She hadn't seen the blow coming, hardly even felt it. All she remembered was Fabrian's face before her own hit the floorboards. Better if the Dharkan had killed her. *They will pay*, she assured herself again, grinding her teeth and letting go of the dead beast. Its empty stare was not helping her feel any better. She stumbled into the common room and wrinkled her nose at the smell. Jonas' sanctuary always smelled of unwashed bodies, as if its patrons never left it. She considered walking outside for some fresh air, maybe even bask for a bit, for the sun was about to rise, but once again felt torn between the need to feed and the instinct to avoid sunlight. Any light sent needles into her skull. Besides, Eos' eye would open soon, and she definitely didn't want to be caught under its gaze. No, she was too sick to bask, but she'd still need to hydrate.

Jonas had quite the assortment of bottles, flasks, jars and decanters behind the counter. Each one polished and labelled in the neat script Seshat had taught them. All neatly coordinated by size, shape, and content. She eyed a plain container with the label 'Dharkan's ale' with disgust and kept searching. It seemed the metz had possibly every type and flavour of intoxicating beverages in his watering hole, except water. Jonas was only half dryad, but he still had to hydrate, surely.

Cursing the metz through gritted teeth, she took an empty cup and walked to the kitchen to find a young Narrum girl skinning a rabbit with practised dexterity. She was plump with hair like straw, which reminded Ulla of Fabrian's. She even smiled the way he did. The sight brought Ulla more pain. This time in her chest.

"You should be in your room," the girl said without even slowing her work. "The sire will be upset."

Narrum had a talent for stating the obvious. At that, the knot in her chest loosened, replaced with cold determination.

"Can I have some water, please?" She handed the cup to the girl, who nodded and promptly took it from her hand to dip it in a bucket by the patio door. "Here you go."

Ulla eyed the grimy content of the cup suspiciously.

"It's fresh from the river. I fetch it on the way here."

There were smudges of blood on the cup left by her bloody fingers. The girl saw Ulla cringing at them.

"I'm so sorry. Here, let me clean that for you."

Ulla held up a hand. "There's no need. Thank you." If Ulla would ever make the Wraiths pay, she had to get over her natural aversion to blood. Fabrian used to let her practice skinning and carving dead animals. The nausea never left her, no matter how often she sliced flesh, but at least she knew how to handle a blade.

Ulla pitied the girl, having to spend her existence surrounded by carcasses, and saw pity reflected in the girl's eyes as they darted from her bruised forehead to the sword at her hip. How strange she must look to the Narrum: dressed like a male, hair cropped to her scalp. Which of the two was more unfortunate? Ulla wasn't sure. Women in Aegea had long learnt to accept their fortune, but not her. Ulla refused to see herself as one of them. She was as tall as most men and spent many hours building her strength. Yet it had only taken one blow from the Dharkan to undo years of training. Sure, she'd been ambushed, caught off guard, but even in a fair fight, she'd still have lost. That knowledge grated on her deeply.

She returned to the common room and peeked through the window. As expected, blue light shone above. She scowled at it. How could the gods ever understand the plight of mortals when, even fated, they had a sun that shone just for them? Ulla warned Arianh not to trust the Wyrd. Agnar's interest in her people wasn't sincere. Marrying a Wraith… seriously.

Occa had been right. Better to marry the Suzerain instead. At least he knew who the enemy was.

She drank the muddy water, then remembered that it came from the same river Fabrian liked to swim in, the same river he was sent down to – Ulla threw the cup at the wall and buried her head in her hands, sobbing angrily. She'd once heard Agnar defining insanity as doing the same thing over and over again. Could that apply to thoughts as well? It was like her brain had lost the ability to think beyond her loss. Every thought circled back to Fabrian's death. As much as she'd loved Fabrian, this was not how she wanted to remember him.

The sound of someone stomping down the stairs brought her out of her misery. She straightened herself up, one hand on the pommel of her short sword, the other on the table for stability.

Whoever was coming down the stairs seemed to want the world to know about it. Every bang of their boots was like a blow to her temple. Ulcan had a name for such creatures: easy prey. He liked to kill them on principle. To him, any creature who made such a rattle of being alive did not deserve to live. Maybe that was why he preferred to hunt snakes. They made no sound, not even when they died.

A man finally came into view and nearly toppled backwards when he saw her. They stared at each other from across the room, neither pleased with the sight. Both carried nearly identical blades, the runes on their pommels glaring alarmingly.

"*You*," she said, caught between surprise and scorn.

"Is the queen here?" Oric looked around as if expecting Arianh to appear from thin air. At least he had enough sense not to lecture her on how women were not allowed in Jonas' sanctuary.

"No. I'm no longer with her." Ulla gripped the hilt harder. "Is the Suzerain upstairs?"

Oric smirked. "No. I'm alone."

"What happened to your arm?" she asked.

"Frostbite."

Oric was crooked and rotten to the roots, but if anyone hated the Wraiths as much as her, it was him. "You mean –"

"Nasty bruise you got there," he said, not waiting for her turn to speak. He'd always done that. It was as infuriating now as it had been when they were children, growing wild in the forest. She tried to frown, but there was no pliability in the skin on her swollen brow. "The Wraith hit you pretty bad, huh? Still, it could have been worse." Oric glanced at his missing arm, then pulled a stool from under a table to sit on. Ulla cringed, half expecting him to snap a joint while trying to bend his long frame for the shape required to sit so low. No dryad in their right mind would ever sit on those things. Jonas kept them for the Narrum children and to prevent his adult patrons from getting too comfortable. And yet Oric treated it like the most comfortable of cushions. "Were you really humping that fat –"

The blade left the sheath on her belt and came to rest at his neck in an instant. There were advantages to standing. Crouched as he was and with only one arm, Oric hadn't been fast enough to reach for his own sword, let alone stand.

He lifted his hand and smirked. "None of my business."

"No, it isn't."

He then lifted what was left of his arm and used it to point at her sword. "Nice weapon you got there. I bet the Blacksmith made it specially for you, huh? What did you give him in return? I suppose if you could hump the fat one, you'd also hump the – ow!"

Ulla cut him right across the chest. She was shaking, dazed, the water in her stomach churning like sea waves, but she forced herself to watch as the blood soaked through his stained shirt. He stood up, pulled his own blade and cut her neatly across the cheek. The heat of the runes burned in her hand. Ulla readied herself to cut Oric's throat next.

Moving faster than her, Oric knocked her sword away with his. She flinched at the blow, startled by his strength. Oric used to be a fair match for her as a boy. Not anymore, even with just one arm. Her sword clattered across the room to the edge of the fireplace, and he backhanded her face. Pain flared behind her eyes again. Ulla fell to one knee, half blind. Her hands found a stool, and she hit him in the shin with it, then punched him in the groin. As he bent over, she stood up, grabbed his hair and kneed him in the face. Filled with a rage she didn't know she had, she loosed a torrent of kicks at him until his boot somehow met her stomach and threw her over a barrel. Before she could inhale the air knocked out of her, Oric grabbed her head. "Filthy tree hugger," he said as he forced her face to the dying embers of the hearth. Her flailing hand found her blade, and she was about to plunge it into his foot when the hot coals bit the side of her jaw. She screamed, thrashing wildly, beyond pain or reasoning.

"STOP," Jonas shouted. "What's got into you two?"

"The cunt cut me!" Oric said.

"Not deep enough." She went to pick up her sword again; Jonas kicked it away before she got to it.

"Enough! You're dryads for frost's sake! Act like such! Don't you two have enough injuries already? Oric, no more picking fights with women in my shelter. And Ulla, stop picking fights with men altogether. Ice! You're not children anymore, and these" – he held Oric's knife in disgust before throwing it across the room – "are not toys! One day you'll have to explain to me why you hate each other so much."

Ulla, her headache almost insignificant now compared with the agony in her face and ribs, fixed Oric with a baleful gaze. He avoided her eyes and walked away, tending to a bloody nose she did not remember giving to him, the closest to shame she'd ever seen in the arrogant man. He knew that she knew what he'd done.

The sound of a thousand trees splitting boomed from outside.

"Icespikes!" Jonas cursed. "What the frost's happening now!"

Ulla, still sprawled on the floor, dragged herself to the window. Lightning crossed the sky, hitting the ground, the trees, the shelters and, judging by the screams, the people too. Oric, coming to stand beside her, stared out at the destruction with gritted teeth.

Jonas braced himself on the windowsill, cursing profusely. "Get back in the kitchen. There's nothing to see here. Remain indoors," he said to the startled girl poking through the door, and she did not hesitate to obey.

"It's coming from the Stump," Ulla said.

"It's the Suzerain. The freezing gods got to him!" Oric punched the wall.

Ulla saw the sky turn darker and darker as dense clouds gathered over the land. She heard the screams, smelled the smoke, but did not understand what it meant. Fabrian believed the Suzerain caused the storms. That whenever the sky remained clear, he was away. *Away where?* she would ask, and he would shrug.

The Suzerain was not a god. Everyone knew only the gods had the power to light up the sky with lightning. Was the world ending then, like the Narrum had predicted? Would the fire under the mountains finally spill out, or was it something else?

"Are they fighting?" That much was obvious. She rephrased the question. "Who's winning?"

They looked at each other without an answer. Half the settlement was on fire now. People banged desperately on the door. Jonas cursed again.

"You two: go upstairs – now. And for frost's sake, if you're going to kill each other, do it quietly!"

∞

Later that day, when the lighting storm had stopped and the fires had been put out, Ulla and Oric sat peacefully at opposite ends of the bed, her wounds throbbing and swollen, his healing nicely. There were rumours that the Suzerain's men had been gifted with such abilities. Ulla eyed him resentfully. Not just for his strength and fast healing, but because despite all his advantages, he'd still failed to kill the Wraith that killed Fabrian. The strange thing was, she felt somewhat better now that she knew the Wraith was still alive, because now she could do something else to deal with her loss besides suffer powerlessly. Now she could kill the freezing creature.

"You don't know what you're up against, woman," Oric said. "Look what he did to me. He even froze the huntress! I'm telling you, the ice gods are working through him. Maybe through all the Wraiths."

"Then we need to fight the gods as well as the Wraiths."

He laughed. "And how do you propose we do that?"

She took a deep breath, ignoring the pain in her ribs. "We need the people on our side. All of them: the Aossi, Anann, Narrum. All the living together. It's the only way we stand a chance against the Wraiths. As for the gods…"

"So basically what you're saying is that we need the Suzerain," Oric said, not even letting her finish her thought. "Well, getting inside the Stump won't be easy, and if the gods had their way, he might not be around anymore."

"Not him. The man's insane. But maybe someone like him… someone everyone likes and listens to."

Jonas eyed them silently from the doorway, keeping an ear on his patrons downstairs. "Don't look at me. No one likes me. I've made sure of that. I'd rather be respected than liked."

"What about Judoc?" she suggested.

"He's an idiot," Oric said.

Ulla had to agree. Try as she might, she'd never understand what Arianh saw in the man. He wasn't handsome enough to make up for his lack of integrity, but he was liked and well connected. "An idiot who consorts with gods and Wyrds. He came through the Chronodéndron, and he's good with words. Everyone loves him."

"I don't. Judoc is weak and vain. He seeks adoration, not responsibility. He doesn't have the balls to stand up to anything," Oric said, and Ulla felt the urge to kick him again.

Jonas, attentive to signs the conversation might derail into more primitive forms of communication, cleared his throat. "I agree he's a selfish bastard, but he has the people's ear and access to the Stump."

That got Oric nodding. "That he does. But it's not enough. We need someone with real power and no ambition, someone able to play the part."

"Seshat," they said in unison.

"And how are you going to convince the chronicler to help us?"

Oric grinned. "With a good story, of course. Don't worry about the gods, for I bet they're not worried about us either. You just convince the dryads – all of them, tree huggers too. We'll need the forest on our side to pull this off – and I'll get the civilised folk to join us, plus the perfect figurehead. Together we'll burn those ugly bastards to a crisp."

It all seemed too simple, but Ulla was out of ideas.

Oric extended his hand to her. "Deal?"

And then Ulla did something she never thought she'd do again. She shook hands with the man who murdered the old Aossi queen.

INTERLUDE 6

He Said; She Said

"So, how come the ice-cold Dharkan doesn't think twice about taking the life force of a god who never caused him harm and then spares a couple of dryads intent on burning him?" Psyche asks, struggling to keep up with my strides.

"I don't enjoy taking Prana from mortals."

"Why not?"

We've been throwing questions at each other all night. The Wyrd was right; appealing to her curiosity and vanity works much better than applied force. The goddess likes to talk about herself more than she likes to talk about Ileana. She is especially talkative when offended, which is fairly easy to accomplish. I've learnt more in half a night's casual conversation than I did in days of interrogations. The only problem is, Psyche treats information like currency. Blazing humans treat everything like currency. They only care for things they can possess, exploit or trade. Gods are no better. And so I reluctantly have to give her a few answers of my own in return.

"They always leave a bad aftertaste," I explain.

Psyche raises an eyebrow at me, demanding further explanation. I grind my teeth and grimace in search of words. Maybe *feeling* would be a better term to describe the lingering impression a creature's Prana leaves on a Dharkan, but feelings are open to speculation, tastes only to opinion.

"It's like something of them remains in me, an intoxication of sorts. It gets fainter over time, but it never quite goes away. For example, I can still taste Fabrian's sunny disposition. His lust too. He tasted of appetite: appetite for life, for food, for sex. I think his will to live was what kept me alive that night."

She falls behind, considering my answer. "Yes, Fabrian did crave life. He did not deserve to die," Psyche says reproachfully.

I know she blames me for the Narrum's death and, accident or not, I guess I am responsible. He wasn't the first, nor the last, of my kills. I didn't choose to be what I am, nor did I make the rules for the game of life and death. I'm just one of the pieces in it. There's no point dwelling over guilt for something that, as the gods keep reminding me, is in my nature. I ignore her judgement and chose another example, one that I'm sure she won't feel sorry for.

"Oric tasted foul. So much so, I didn't want to finish him. His Prana was repulsive and had no sustenance." I frown at the memory. "And Ideth…" I stop, considering what to say about the nymph. "She also has no sustenance and no flavour either. I don't know why, but it gives no pleasure to take Prana from her."

Psyche snorts. "Knowing Ideth, I can guess a few reasons."

"It's not like that between us."

She lifts her hands in a placating gesture. "I didn't think it was, Dharkan."

"Humph. My turn: Why did you kill the Wyrd?"

"Oh for fuck's sake. How many times do I need to say it? I did not kill him! I sent his soul to the Underworld."

"Same thing."

"Not to gods. In any case, he asked me to."

"Did Ileana ask you to kill her?"

She does not reply. I stop walking and turn to see the sheepish expression on her face. "Ileana prayed to many gods. I was not the first one to answer," she says. It sounds like the truth. "As to killing her..." Psyche fixes her dark eyes on mine. "What did Ileana taste like?"

"I already told you. I took no Prana from her," I say through clenched teeth.

"All right. What did I taste like, then?"

That's an easy one. "Human." She's strongly disappointed by my answer. "What did you expect?"

She sighs. "I don't know…. That maybe my life force took on something of a god's flavour, whatever that might be. Just human? Nothing else, are you sure?" She looks up at me with such hopeful expectation, I'm almost inclined to lie. Instead, I give her my most menacing smile.

"No. I'm not sure. Perhaps if I take more?" The aim is not to frighten her, that's pointless, but to unnerve her. Unfortunately, she just sulks, adjusts the crossbow strap on her shoulder and resumes walking. The hunter's weapon, a monstrosity carved of ebony and iron, is at odds with the goddess's delicate size and attire and makes me angry every time I look at it.

"Why did you bring that thing?"

"The bow? Because I like it," she replies petulantly.

"I don't. It's the weapon that killed Cornus."

"Well, technically, the arrows did."

"Looks ridiculous on you."

"Thanks. You have your accessories, I have mine."

Insufferable creature. I bet she only took it to annoy me. I'll have to take it back from her before she finds any arrows, of course, but for the moment I let her have it, for I see the way she glances at my chest and would rather keep talking.

"What's so important about the butterfly necklace?"

She stops breathing for a few steps. "I'm not sure. I'm just compelled to protect it."

"Where did you get it?"

"Prometheus gave it to me."

"You're lying."

She stops walking to look me in the eyes. "I am not."

"But there's something you're not telling me."

She bites her cheek. "Is this your special talent, Dharkan? To detect when someone's lying?"

"No. Not special. Any Dharkan can do it." She blinks. "And you're still avoiding the answer."

Her jaw muscles tense a few times before she resumes walking. "The pendant is identical to one I wore back when I was a mortal. Prometheus never saw it. He was already imprisoned when I was born and remained so after I became… this."

I hold it up for inspection, as I've done so many times before. There's nothing remarkable about it, colour changes aside, it's just a plain, poorly crafted pendant in the rough shape of a butterfly. Certainly not the work of a proper artisan. Ash, I could sculpt a better butterfly than this. "Coincidence?" I ask. Butterfly-shaped ornaments were, after all, quite common amongst the Narrum.

She looks at the pendant with such sadness I feel compelled to close my fist around it. "There's no such thing as coincidence amongst gods. Someone was trying to tell me something. I wish I knew who and what, exactly."

"Why did this Prometheus give it to you?"

"It was supposed to protect me, and I guess Ileana, from Chronos."

"You mean Ileana is not bound to Chronos? And you're only telling me this now!"

"*Supposed* to! It didn't work. Whoever gave that necklace to Prometheus lied. If it was even Prometheus, the one who gave me the damn thing in the first place. I'm not even sure of that at this point."

"Huh? Now you make no sense, woman."

She puffs a mouthful of air. "Zeus was the only one able to break the curse binding Prometheus to Tartarus – the Underworld dungeon created especially for Titans," she adds as if I don't know that. I suppose, as a Dharkan, I shouldn't, but since we took over the Stump I've become something of an expert in Olympian history.

"Hades and Loki are working on a scheme to free the Titan," I say. "If you met him in Ileana's time, that means they've succeeded, no?"

The goddess turns whiter than I am. "I don't want to talk about gods anymore. Keep the fucking necklace out of my sight."

∞

The Dharkan thinks he has me figured out.

We've been carefully trading morsels of information under the pretence of casual conversation all night. In the process, I've learnt quite a bit about Niflheim before the Merge, his race and way of life – such as it is. In return I told him what I can about his precious Ileana and her father. It's not much, for I know little, and I've taken great care not to taint his memory of her. That bitch. She had me completely fooled with her victim act. If he knew half the stuff that went through her mind… poor bastard. I'm tempted to tell him. It would at least make up for some of the pain inflicted by his freezing punishments, but what would be the point? The Dharkan is just another victim in the gods' schemes, and I'd bet my freedom that Eros was the one responsible for their mutual attraction, so antagonising the man is counterproductive, for I need his cooperation to know why and for what purpose. Was Eros targeting me or Ileana? Making predator fall in love with prey is exactly the sort of thing that amuses the god of love. And so is humiliating me. But just like Zeus could have put me in a boar's body, so could Eros have made Ileana want to fuck one instead of the Dharkan. What was Eros doing in Niflheim anyway?

I shiver at the possibilities. And how did he leave? I can't sense his soul anywhere. I don't like this.

"So tell me more about your life as a human," the Dharkan prompts with convincing interest. I suspect the late Wyrd has something to do with his newfound conversational skills and curiosity about my previous life. The Allfather might be gone to the other side, but we're still playing out his game, it seems.

I watch him put away the butterfly necklace with regret. I need to get it back. I don't why or how, just that I need to. Stars! Why do I feel this way? I don't even want the damn thing! I curse, falling behind again. Damnation, I have to take three steps to match two of his. *This won't do.*

"I was a princess," I say, catching up to him.

"Humph," he says. "Explains a lot."

"How so, *prince*?"

"Your attitude, for one. The way the gods act around you, I expected you'd done something extraordinary to have been gifted with Ambrosia. Turns out you're just privileged."

I blink several times at the insult. *Is he trying to rattle me?* That won't work. I take a deep breath. It doesn't work either.

"Yes, from being put on display and worshipped with envy by the people in my father's kingdom to then being abandoned by my family on a cliff as an offering to a monstrous god who then kept me as his pet and sex slave for years, alone, with no friends, no one to talk to, and no means to escape, I truly had a privileged life." I fail to keep the contempt from my voice. The nerve of the man to imply I just had Ambrosia handed to me! I earned my godhood! Stars, I sacrificed everything for it, went to the Underworld and back. I – *Breathe*. "You don't know what life was like then. The only achievement available to women, of any status, was to find a decent husband and pray she wouldn't die in childbirth."

"That goes for women everywhere. And didn't you end up marrying that monstrous god?" he asks, smugly. I need not answer. It seems Hades has been sharing too much with the Dharkan already.

"You don't know anything about me or what I've been through," I say in a tone that clearly suggests a change in subject.

"From princess to pet, to wife, then goddess. You must have been an outstanding pet," he snorts.

"You know I am." I regret the words immediately. In truth I was little more than a reluctant passenger in Ileana's ride. I enjoyed it, though. It was a much welcome distraction at the time.

Aedan stops and looks at me as he often did back in the vault. Horror, disgust, disbelief? I still can't read the Dharkan's expressions properly, even with Reach. He assesses me from head to toe in a way that makes me feel unclean, then scowls and lifts his hand as if to strike me but thinks better of it.

"Shame on you," he says with loathing. "What sort of god takes part in their vessels' intimacy? I won't have you taint the memory or what Ileana and I shared."

"As a Wyrd, I had no choice."

"Sure you did. And I reckon you had a choice as a princess too. You just chose to be a pet to a god rather than a wife to a mortal. Ideth is right. You are dangerous."

I gape. For Ideth to have said that is akin to the pot calling the kettle black.

The conversation dies there. Which is just as well. I hate to reminisce about my previous life. My current one has not been an improvement thus far, and the fact remains that I only truly felt alive when I was not amongst the living.

We arrive at Portum after dawn, having walked all night – if the mad dash across the woods can be called walking.

Portum looks the same as the first time I was here, minus the rain and a few burned down shelters. Beyond the hamlet, up the hill, the temple looms solid and gaudy in contrast with the makeshift, shabby structures below.

Aedan puts his hood up and walks straight to-wards what passes for a tavern in the settlement. I follow, resigned to enter that awful place again, and ready myself for whatever might come next.

"Why are we here?" I ask.

"I need to talk to a friend."

"You have friends?"

Aedan gives me a baleful look.

"Ah, yes, the bloke behind the counter. I remember. He said you saved his life."

"He exaggerated. I merely prolonged it."

"Please tell me you're not here to collect his overdue Prana."

"Seriously, creature. What sort of monster do you think I am?"

I do not reply and hurry to the porch instead. Reach tells me the whole village is now staring at us. The hood is not enough to disguise what Aedan is; his height alone gives him away even if he'd bothered hiding the long white hair under his coat. And I should have taken the time to spread some mud over my dress. I think the immaculateness of it is more offensive to the Narrum than the Dharkan's presence.

He blocks my way. "Women are not welcome inside Jonas' sanctuary, but I'm not letting you out of my sight, so behave and don't make the situation more awkward than it already is."

"Sure," I say and climb up the steps to the entrance.

He holds me back again. "That means: be quiet and do what I say. I'm going in first."

CHAPTER EIGHT

Ulcan

Ulcan pushed the heavy wooden door open with more force than was necessary, grimacing as pain flared across the wounds in his chest. He limped across the common room, leaving a trail of muddy bootprints behind him, then dropped the bloody satchel on the counter with a wet thump.

"I need a drink," he said, tentatively sitting himself on the nearest barrel. It'd taken Ulcan all night to get to Portum from the caves. Once at his destination, he finally felt safe enough to let exhaustion take over and released a long, rattling exhale.

Jonas froze mid-polish: cup in one hand, cloth in the other, and eyed him critically. "Rough hunt?"

"Humph," Ulcan replied, suppressing the urge to spit on the uneven floor.

"You need the healer," Jonas said. More an accusation than an observation. Yes, Ulcan knew he'd have to seek help from the centaur, and the idea soured his mood as much as his stomach. He'd rather stay away from all gods.

"Drink first," Ulcan grumbled without looking up at Jonas. He could well imagine the annoyance on the metz's beardless face, for he'd seen it many times before. Jonas had been born annoyed and would remain so regardless of the situation. Instead, he searched the room: empty apart from the two of them at the counter and a drunken logger slumbering by the fireplace. Nothing unusual this early in the day.

"Here," Jonas said as he placed a large tankard filled with ale in front of him, and Ulcan promptly worked on emptying it.

Jonas lifted the bloody flap on the ripped satchel with the tips of his fingers and sucked his teeth. "It's ruined."

Ulcan grunted an obscenity and kept drinking like a dryad left in the sun for too long.

From the corner of his eye, he saw an Anann storming down the stairs; one of the Suzerain's faithful, judging by his clothes. Ulcan stopped drinking when he recognised who he was. Oric. It had to be him. Few Anann wore trousers and even fewer wore weapons, but last time Ulcan saw the man, he had two arms. Apparently Ulcan wasn't the only one having a rough time lately. Then again, judging by the state of the settlement, the whole population of Aegea and its trees were having a bad time since the lightning storm a few days back.

Oric, looking gaunter than usual but still in good shape despite his missing limb, placed two slivers of gold on the counter with a respectful nod to Jonas. His gaze then fell on Ulcan's bloody rags with a mixture of curiosity and disgust.

"I thought you were dead," Oric said.

"Not yet."

Ulcan considered asking what had happened to his arm, for old time's sake, but judging by the man's scowl, he probably didn't want to talk about it. Not particularly inclined to share his troubles either, Ulcan focused on finishing the drink instead. Even as children, they were never that close. Oric preferred the company of Jonas, and Ulcan spent most of his time with Ulla.

"Ulla's looking for you," Oric said, and Ulcan nearly choked.

"What?"

"Jonas will fill you in on the plan," Oric said pointedly. "Is the mount outside?"

"Bridled and ready to go," Jonas replied sternly.

"Excellent. It's good that you're here, Ulcan. We need more men like you." Oric patted him painfully hard on the back, which did not improve his breathing, then placed two more large slivers of gold on the counter and, sparing another pointed glance at Jonas, stormed out of the building.

"What the fuck?" Ulcan said, coveting the precious metal. There was enough wealth on the counter to buy the skin of two snakes. Working for the Suzerain had its perks, apparently. "Are you two friends again?"

Jonas snorted and put the temptation away. Ulcan knew that was the only answer he'd get to his question. Oric and Jonas had been the best of friends once, they even went to join the Suzerain together, then suddenly their friendship soured. Ulcan figured a woman was probably involved in the feud. Still, the animosity couldn't be that serious since Oric kept coming to Jonas' watering hole and Jonas kept serving him. Dryads never held grudges for long. When a Narrum took a dislike to someone, nothing short of murder or relocation would do to solve it.

"You didn't tell Ulla where I live, did you?"

"Of course not."

"Good. And what's this about a plan?"

Jonas wrinkled his nose at his wounds. "We need to get you fixed first."

"Damn right. Another!" Ulcan said, lifting his tankard. "And give me the strong stuff this time."

Jonas' annoyance shifted to something closer to anger. "For one damaged skin?"

"Yes, damn it!" He unconsciously gathered saliva in his mouth and, seeing the metz's outraged glare, promptly swallowed it with a sheepish half grin. Previous experience taught him that Jonas had no tolerance for spitting and would cast out any offenders from his sanctuary, injured or not.

Subdued, Jonas ducked behind the counter and reappeared moments later with two small cups and an ornate flask carved in glass. One of the Blacksmith's, Ulcan reckoned. Only the gods knew how to turn sand into glass.

Ulcan's spirits lifted at the sight. He glanced at the drunken logger once again. The man stirred and mumbled something that sounded like a sob but seemed too intoxicated to follow the conversation. Regardless, Ulcan lowered his voice for effect when he spoke.

"You won't believe what I found."

"Try me," Jonas said patiently, pouring the intoxicating liquid into the cups.

"I have something to show you," Ulcan insisted, hoping for more interest from his listener.

"Please do," Jonas said in his annoyingly flat tone. He pushed one cup filled to the brim towards Ulcan, then lifted his own cup to his lips and tilted his head back, swallowing the liquid in one gulp. Ulcan figured the metz probably needed it as much as he did after dealing with Oric. He tried to mimic the metz's efficiency and nearly choked again. It was the *really strong* stuff, reserved for celebrations and extremely bad situations. The very smell of it made his eyes sting. Ulcan should be putting it on his wounds, not in his stomach, but he had never been accused of being sensible, so when Jonas offered him a refill, he accepted and poured it down his throat again.

Once simultaneously numbed and bolstered with drink, Ulcan leaned across the counter, closer to his apathetic listener, and opened his vest to show the contents of the inner pocket.

Jonas blinked. "What did you do!" he hissed.

"Nothing! I mean, it was already dead when I found it," Ulcan hissed back.

"Put it away for frost's sake!" Jonas considered his cup for a moment, then lifted the bottle to his mouth and drank. Finally, something that rattled the man. Ulcan had begun to think Jonas might be half Dharkan instead of half dryad.

"I think Aedan is dead," Ulcan said.

"If he's not, you will be soon enough," Jonas said matter-of-factly and poured both another dose. "You saw Oric. He claims Aedan did that to him. Ice, if Oric was stupid enough to kill his horse, maybe he did." Jonas swallowed another shot, then leaned closer as if about to say something in confidence. Drink always made the usually terse metz ramble. Ulcan suspected it was the reason he'd rather serve it to others while abstaining himself. The hunter closed the gap between their heads, encouraging the other man to share his knowledge.

"I've been sheltering Oric for days. He was delirious when he arrived. He said Aedan iced the mad huntress and that the gods made an alliance to infiltrate the Stump, kill the Suzerain and kidnap his daughter. I didn't believe any of it at first, knowing how prone to exaggeration the man is. I figured he just provoked the wrong Wraith. I mean, the day the ice gods and the fire gods get along is the day the World Tree spouts again, right? The fact remains, it hasn't stormed properly since *the* storm and the blue light…" Jonas made a show of pinching out the nearest candle.

Ulcan crunched his face. "Eh… Aedan did ice the mad huntress."

Jonas, who had served himself yet another cup, uttered a curse before drinking it. Ulcan just stared at his, remembering Artemis frozen in Aedan's pool. Her skin, capable of assuming the colours and patterns of its surroundings, black as the obsidian walls around her and her eyes – never kind and never warm – glared at him with such intensity he feared he'd never leave that cave alive. "I saw her, in his cave. Frozen solid."

Jonas cursed again. "It can't have been him."

"I understand you have a… hmm, debt to the man,

but he is a Wraith. I still remember when they came down from the Shadow, determined to ice everyone in their path."

Jonas glowered at him. "Artemis is a goddess. Aedan doesn't have the power to ice a deity."

"Maybe he was hosting one of his gods?"

"Then it still wouldn't be his doing, would it? Besides, he told me his gods left the world."

Ulcan considered this. "Any burnings lately?"

"Only one. A few days ago, why?"

"Could have been him."

The innkeeper shook his head again. "It was Aecius."

"Aecius is dead?!" Ulcan spoke too loud. The logger shifted, farted, then resumed snoring.

Jonas nodded and poured the rest of the flask's contents into the cups. Ulcan stared disbelievingly at the beverage. That was a shame. Aecius was one of the good ones. An honourable man. And a good hunter, too. Always happy to help out with killing or freezing the meat. And he never charged for it, unlike Aedan.

Ulcan sighed and lifted his cup. "To Aecius."

They drank.

"I have heard rumours… in the forest, of Wraiths gathered at the Boiling Lake. And you must also have heard what happened in Lagus," Ulcan said. Jonas nodded. "Do you think…"

Jonas didn't let him finish. "Some Wraiths might be feeding on life again, but not Aedan. I just don't believe it. If he was the one who did that to Oric, he must have had a good reason, and he still didn't kill him, did he? Something is going on between the gods and the Wraiths, though. Something bad. And whatever it is, we are the ones in danger."

They fell silent. If there was one thing Narrum and Anann had in common, it was fear of the faithless Dharkan.

∞

The door slammed open and Jonas' jaw slacked. "Speaking of the daemon..." he murmured, hiding the flask.

Ulcan shuffled painfully on his seat to witness the Dharkan's entrance for himself. Aedan, looking bigger, stronger and more wrathful than ever, halted momentarily to survey the room's occupants, then marched towards the counter. He was followed by a woman: a Narrum woman, no less, despite her unusual height. Ulcan's eyebrows arched wide, and it was his turn to gape. Maybe it was the liquor, or perhaps exhaustion and blood loss having an effect on his vision, but she was the most beautiful woman he had ever seen. She didn't even look real, seemingly walking on air behind the big man. She carried what looked like Bertho's crossbow on her shoulder, and for a moment all Ulcan did was stare bewildered while the unlikely pair crossed the room.

Jonas, equally baffled by the sight, recovered first. "Aedan! You can't bring your..." He hesitated, obviously at a loss for words to define the divine creature. "There're no women allowed in here!"

"There's at least two in the kitchen," the woman said. She had a soft and yet assertive voice. She also sounded as furious as the Dharkan looked.

Jonas' eyebrows rose high up his forehead. "Then you should go join them!" He meant it. Jonas' tolerance for women in this sanctuary was slightly lower than for spit. Ulcan reckoned it was because he was so saturated with them. Having to deal with their constant nagging daily at the temple had to make any man averse to their presence.

The woman strode up to the counter and took the tall stool next to Ulcan instead, placed her elbows on the polished surface, her chin on her hands and smiled at the livid bartender. "Cider, please."

Jonas opened and closed his mouth like a ratton caught in a snake's embrace.

"He's paying." She pointed at Aedan.

Aedan frowned down at her as one does to a carcass when trying to figure out the best way to skin it, then grunted. "Sure. It will keep her quiet."

She snorted and turned her attention back to the outraged metz.

"If you say so," Jonas said pointedly, then took a couple of large tankards from behind the counter and resumed his duties with professional annoyance.

Ulcan kept staring, entranced. She had long dark wavy hair, decorated with lilies, and wore an immaculate white tunic. Her feet were bare and filthy – *so not walking on air then*. She caught Ulcan staring at them and curled her lip, leaving him feeling like an idiot.

"The usual?" Jonas asked Aedan, pointing at a small barrel. Ulcan didn't remember ever having a drink from that one.

Aedan grunted agreement and sat on the nearest table, massaging his temples. He looked haggard as if he hadn't slept in a while and had a nasty wound along his hairline, the skin around it was a disagreeable shade of blue. His clothes were torn and dirtied, his hair grimy and tangled. Overall, he looked like a man who'd lost a fight. *There's always a larger, meaner foe*, Ulcan thought.

"Such an unexpected surprise this early in the day," Jonas said, placing both drinks on the counter. "To what do I owe the pleasure?"

"I need a mount," Aedan said.

"I'm sorry, old friend. Just sold the last one."

It did not go unnoticed to Ulcan that Jonas did not say to whom, nor that he refrained from mentioning Cornus. That was a mistake. Everyone knew Aedan rode an Elysian horse. The natural reaction to his request would be to ask for Cornus' whereabouts. Fortunately, Aedan seemed too preoccupied to notice. The woman, however, eyed both Ulcan and Jonas suspiciously over the rim of her tankard.

Aedan clicked his tongue and reached forward to take his tankard from the counter. While Ulcan tried to get a peek at its contents, the woman lifted the flap on his satchel, moving too fast for Ulcan to object, then stared back at him. "Is this your work?" There was no accusation in her tone, and yet Ulcan felt anything but pride.

"It is," he confessed, suppressing the urge to spit.

Her eyes turned dark as flint then moved from his face to his chest, as if she could see through the fabric. She gasped. And Ulcan was sure she could. *She's one of them,* he realised; one of the gods. Her gaze shifted to Aedan and she was about to speak. Thinking fast,

Ulcan kicked her foot. She paused, shooting daggers at him with indignation. *I did not kill Cornus*, he said in thought, *I only took the horn. Please, don't tell Aedan.*

She bit her cheek, considering him for a moment, then focused back on her drink. Ulcan released his breath. Aedan, fortunately again, was too busy gazing broodingly at his mug to notice their interaction.

"You just missed Oric," Jonas said, picking up another cup to polish. "He claimed you were responsible for his latest loss."

Ulcan winced. He should not have encouraged the metz to drink. It clearly dulled his wits for him to confront the Dharkan like this.

"Should have frozen his tongue instead," Aedan grumbled.

"Missed opportunities," mused the goddess halfway through her cider.

Not a lie, then, Ulcan thought before he could stop himself. If she heard him, at least she did not show it. Maybe gods need to be looking at the thinker to read their thoughts? The corner of her mouth twitched with a repressed smile. *No, they don't*, he decided.

"Where is he now?" Aedan asked.

"On his way to Relicum."

"Burn him."

"That's a thought," the goddess chimed again. She finished her drink and then did the most bizarre thing: she burped. A sound too loud and coarse to come from such a bonny source.

All eyes fell on her with a mixture of surprise and horror.

"What? Never heard a woman belch?"

"Actually…" Ulcan started.

"Fill it up," she demanded.

Jonas was seething when he glanced at Aedan.

"Just do it," the big Wraith said tiredly.

Ulcan, always attentive to opportunities, pushed his own empty tankard towards the metz with a sheepish smile.

Jonas filled both tankards reluctantly while the woman squinted at him. "Ahh! You're a Shrine! I should have known, being a metz and all… Why aren't you at the temple?"

"This is my temple. You're trespassing in it," Jonas replied dryly through gritted teeth.

She drew back slightly. "Stars, you really don't like women."

"I merely prefer the company of men."

"Fair enough." She shrugged and resumed her drink.

"Do you remember that favour you owe me?" Aedan asked Jonas.

"How can I forget?" He slapped his false leg.

"Oh, I see," said the woman, staring beyond the counter, through the tankard.

"It's time to pay it back."

Jonas' amber eyes glared at each of them through narrow slits. "Let's talk in private."

"She –" Aedan started.

"I want to talk to you, alone," Jonas insisted.

The big Wraith stood up and was about to argue against it again, but Jonas was having none of it.

"You came to me. My shelter; my rules. Otherwise…" Jonas pointed at the door.

Aedan stretched himself to his full height. The fire flickered as the room temperature dropped significantly and sparks cracked between his fingers. The woman put a hand on his forearm. "Go with him. Don't worry, I'll behave."

Aedan's jaw muscles bulged with tension. "I need your promise."

She rolled her eyes. "I promise I'll be here when you return."

The Dharkan hesitated a moment, then beckoned Jonas to follow him up the stairs. The goddess waved them a mock farewell and resumed her drink.

"Now, who the fuck are you and why did you take Cornus' horn?" she asked Ulcan the moment Aedan and Jonas were out of earshot.

"Er…" was all Ulcan's intoxicated mind came up with on such short notice.

"Answer me or I'll find the answer myself." She lifted her hand to his forehead.

"That's not polite!" he protested.

"Fuck polite!" The vitriol in her words made him grimace almost as much as her foul language. Never had he heard a woman swear like that. Come to think of it, not a god either.

"It was there to take! Do you know how much the horn of an Elysian horse is worth?"

"Actually, I'm more interested in learning who would pay for it."

"The gods, of course!" He realised what he said and grimaced again.

"Which gods?"

A shiver ran through his body. "For pity's sake,

do not make this worse. The last thing I need is Zeus' wrath." Although he could do without her wrath as well. He felt light-headed. The wounds on his chest no longer bothered him, but he'd lost all feeling in his left hand.

"Zeus is dead," she said.

Ulcan dropped his drink on the counter and chuckled bitterly. "Well… imagine that. I guess, if gods can die, I won't last long then."

"Not in that state you won't." She snorted derisively.

The room became dimmer. The woman said something else he did not understand, the words lost in a high-pitched hum. His stomach churned. He tried to speak, but before he could utter a word, the floor hit him hard on the chin.

∞

The first thing Ulcan saw when he woke was Jonas' drawn face frowning at him. Then the billows of smoke behind it.

"Welcome back." Jonas patted him hard on the shoulder then sat down on the dirt.

"Where did I go?" Ulcan asked. There were people shouting, their feet pounding the ground around them and a strong smell of burnt wood.

"You fainted," Jonas said with his usual annoyance, staring beyond him with what looked like tears in his eyes.

That can't be right. Men don't faint. "The woman! She did something to me."

"You could say that." Jonas chuckled bitterly.

Ulcan touched his chest. There were no signs of the gryphon's attack on his skin, and his hand, still wrapped in a bloody rag, was whole. He could move all his fingers, including the one he'd broken as a child and never quite bent the same as the others.

He sat up and blinked a few times. They were still in Portum, just outside Jonas' watering hole, which was now engulfed in flames.

"Fuck. What did I miss?"

INTERLUDE 7

Social visit

"Such a gentleman," Psyche says when I'm about to walk in ahead of her. *Gentleman… humph.* Never been accused of being gentle before in my life. Poison just constantly drips from the creature's mind onto her tongue. She reminds me of Hel's father. Those two would get along splendidly. Or, more likely, kill each other.

I look down at the goddess and, once again, have the impression that something's different about her. Finally, I understand what.

"You're taller," I say, bemused. It's not a question, for I'm certain of it. Her forehead is now at a height with my chin.

"Huh? Don't be absurd," she says, avoiding my gaze, and makes for the door again, looking over her shoulder at the crowd gathered to stare at us, not used to the way the living react to Dharkan.

I step in front of her. "You are! You've made yourself taller." I couldn't help but laugh. Gods sure are such petty, vain creatures.

Blood rushes to her cheeks. "I got tired of running

after you and having to crane my neck to look at your ugly face! Now, get in before they fetch the pitchforks."

I curse the blazing creature for her spiteful humour and push open the door.

Jonas stands behind the counter as usual. He gapes at me as if he's never seen a Dharkan before, then glares at Psyche. "There're no women allowed in here!" he shouts. I have no intention nor patience to explain to him what she is, and fortunately his objections subside when I buy her a cider. *Can gods get drunk?* I wonder. I buy her another one. At least she's silent while she drinks.

There's only two Narrum men in the room, and they are no threat to my purpose. One is asleep; the other, the snake hunter who likes to ask for favours, looks like he messed with the wrong prey and has already had more than his share of liquor. Even the usually sober Jonas is flushed with drink. Instead of softening his character, as drink does to most men, he's more obtuse and paranoid than ever. I'm forced to leave Psyche alone with the hunter and follow Jonas for a private talk. Perhaps it's for the best. I'd rather not have to explain what I'm about to ask him to the goddess. We stop halfway up the stairs, probably not far enough to be out of her Reach, but close enough to stop her from doing something foolish. Unlikely, given her promise, but I'll be burned if I'm taking any chances.

Jonas throws his polishing rag over a shoulder, crosses his arms and purses his lips, more annoyed than ever.

"You have some nerve bringing a woman in here.

Did anyone see you come in? If word gets out I'm serving women here, the others will demand the same privilege and I'll cease to have a moment's peace away from them and their solicitations. This is *my* sanctuary, for frost's sake!"

Had he been less colourful, Jonas would make an excellent Dharkan. He sure has the temper for it. And had he the power to match it, the whole *sanctuary* would be frozen solid by now.

"She's not a woman… well, she is. But… never mind."

I refrain from telling him that pretty much the whole settlement saw us come in. Hopefully, we'll be far away when he finds out.

"Did you really ice the mad huntress?" Jonas asks, still furious.

I grimace at how fast the news has travelled. Psyche was right about Oric, burn her. I should have iced the foul creature. "Sort of," I say.

"Are you 'sort of' feeding on the living again by any chance, one limb at a time?"

"No. Come on, you know me better than that. It was self-defence. And Oric's still alive, isn't he? The huntress is alive too. She's Hel's problem, not mine."

"For frost's sake. So it is true; the Aesir goddess is back?"

"Yes."

"And the Suzerain?"

"Dead."

Jonas whistles, then takes the cloth from his shoulder, gives it a tug and throws it over the other shoulder. "Oric is out for blood. He spent the last few days gathering as many of the Suzerain's supporters as he can."

"Can't be that many…"

"You'd be surprised," he sneers. "No one loved the Suzerain, true, but ask any man in Aegea: they'd rather have him in power than a goddess."

"Better her than Hades," I say.

"I don't care. Hel's –" He paused. "Hades? What about Zeus?"

"Er…. Zeus is gone. And that may have been my fault," I admit.

"Slush! Might as well close the place down and move to the Underworld, then. Or the Gharb." He shakes his head morosely at the idea.

"Actually, the queen is at the Stump. She's the one in charge of the living now. She intends to move the Aossi back into Aegea, under the Dharkan and the gods' protection."

"Protection?!" Jonas laughs mirthlessly. I hear shouts from the main room below and leave him to his hysterics to pay closer attention to them. Psyche is cursing, which means she's still there at least, arguing with the drunk huntsman no doubt.

"Laugh all you want, Jonas. The situation for those living in Aegea changed, and you can no longer pretend to be neutral. You'll need to pick a side, brother. I strongly suggest it is ours."

"That's the problem," he snorts, using the cloth to dab tears from his eyes. "I have no brothers. Barely any cousins either. Dryads judge me as Narrum, Narrum as a dryad, I'm a pet to the Nephilim and sustenance to the Dharkan."

"I never thought of you like that."

"Well, tell that to Iva and the others."

Ice gathers on my skin. "Iva crossed the Shadow?"

"Oh yes. She's taken a small army to the Boiling Lake and caused quite a lot of havoc in Lagus. Didn't you know?"

"Burn her." I clench my jaw until it aches. "I knew about the faithless, but I didn't know she was their leader. I should have guessed…"

"Yes, you should have. She claims she's doing the goddess's work. I always thought Iva spent too much time under the sun, but if Hel is back, well then, she doesn't sound that batty now."

"Hel has nothing to do with it! In fact, she's against it. That's why I'm here. She wants me to restore the Dharkan's faith in her."

"You?" Jonas laughs again. Burn the man. What possessed him to drink? He, better than anyone, knows the effects his concoctions have on the mind, hence the reason Dharkan only drink water.

"How many women do you have at the temple?" I ask.

He waves a heavy hand. "Oh, I've lost count. I have at least one hundred under my care now. Half of them are about to give birth, the other half already did, all with no place to go, sleeping on top of each other and their babies. Freezing Isko only said the Tribute has been delayed and if I had a problem with that, to take it up to the Suzerain. The bastard must have known he was gone."

"Who's Isko?"

Jonas scratches his head, pensive. "You know, the

weird fellow who hangs out with Seshat and Oric. The messenger."

"Ah yes…" I barely remember the creature. There is something about the man that makes one want to forget ever setting eyes on him.

"Why do you ask about the women?" Jonas frowns askance.

"I want them."

"All of them? That's very ambitious of you."

"They're not for me," I growl at the insufferable man. The commotion downstairs increases. Burn the goddess. Why does Psyche feel the need to rattle everyone she meets?

"No," Jonas says.

"No?!" I repeat louder than I intend. My patience's growing thin.

"You can't use the women to bribe your faithless brothers."

Sometimes I think the metz has some oracle's blood in him. "Personally I prefer the term, 'peace offering'."

"Call it whatever you want. The answer is still 'absolutely not'."

"You said it yourself, you want to be free of them! Don't you want your peace? Give me the dryads at least, the ones not pregnant. You can keep the children."

"I can't believe I'm hearing this – from you! Are the women property of the gods now that the Suzerain is gone?"

"No, they are *my* property. *I* killed the Suzerain."

Jonas gives him a pitiful look. "Oh, ice. Aedan… What happened to you?"

I have no more patience for this. Judging by the shouts coming from the main room, I don't have much time either. Ice forms on my fist, and sparks crack around it.

"I'm sorry, Jonas." I grip the metz's neck. His eyes grow wide with fear. "I hoped it wouldn't come to this, but you left me no choice. I asked you as a courtesy, for it is not for you to decide their fate. You will give me the women and you will tell me everything you know about the Nephilim. That is my price for saving your life all those years ago. Pay it or have it forfeit. Choose. Now."

∞

The alehouse differs from what I remember. The unfortunate severed heads are still mounted on the walls, the stink of unwashed bodies and yeast is still embedded in the makeshift furniture, but there is something warmer, almost cosier about the place. It doesn't look so dirty in daylight, nor as menacing as it did to Ileana that night. Then again, I'm not half as helpless as she was then.

I take another gulp of the cider. It's average at best, and I wonder if it came from the same batch I had before or if Ileana's taste buds really made everything taste sweeter. Her body was funny that way. She had the most acute senses, but her perception was shallow. She mostly noticed the things that gave her joy, while remaining blissfully oblivious to the rest. I, on the other hand, often wish I didn't notice half the things I do, even before I became a goddess, and I rarely take pleasure in them. For example, I really wish I hadn't seen

Jonas' leg or Cornus' horn behind the snake killer's vest. What am I supposed to do with this information? More secrets to carry around while being despised for my silence and constant dark mood. Perhaps I should just shout everyone's secrets to the Universe. Maybe then I wouldn't be so miserable. Maybe then I'd free. *Yeah, right.*

As soon as Aedan disappears up the stairs, I turn to the hunter and confront him about the horn. I know he wasn't the one who killed Cornus, but that won't stop me from teaching him a thing or two about desecrating his corpse. Sadly, he's too ill and preoccupied with what I am and what I can do to him for a proper discussion.

"I don't feel so well," he murmurs. No wonder. Instead of tending to his wounds, he sits here drinking. His mind is too muddled with it, and before I'm able to extract any useful information, he mews, rolls his eyes, then collapses to the ground, toppling two stools in the process.

Brilliant. Why do men never know the limits of their bodies? This one lost pints of blood, then tried to replenish them with booze. Not that it would make much difference, anyway. Gryphons are nasty creatures, and I doubt the huntsman would survive the slow putrefaction of his flesh, but he could have died with dignity, at least.

I finish my sour cider and strain to follow Aedan's conversation with the metz. Something about gods and women. I can't help but laugh. No wonder he didn't want me to listen to it. I leave them to their conversation and sit next to the man dying on the floor, cursing him while trying to decide what to do. *I could heal him.* "The road to damnation is paved with good intentions," Ideth once said. She was right. Good intentions got me here in the first place. Perhaps if my intentions are selfish, I won't be punished. After all, it's not like I want to heal the man for *his* sake. Of course not. What do I care if he lives or dies? I just want to know what he knows about gods and the powers associated with Cornus' horn, that's all.

The other drunk, slumbering by the fireplace, wakes up startled. His mouth hangs open when he sees me, then his eyes fall on the hunter.

"Murderer!" he screams.

I'm about to say something to explain the misunderstanding when I notice he's not talking about me, nor particularly distraught about my presence.

The two women in the kitchen poke their heads through the door. They stare at me in horror, sharing the accusation. Damnation, why do humans always believe what they see without giving it further thought? I give them a reassuring gesture, but it does not convince them. I suspect the sight of me standing there is as much a source of alarm as the unconscious man in bloody rags at my feet, regardless of the wailing one by the fireplace.

"You told them about the resin. Burn in the Underworld, you bastard!" He spits on the unconscious man.

"What resin?" I ask.

The man blinks back at me. Too drunk to stand, he collapses back on the stool. I Reach his mind: feeble, full of jumbled images – food; sex; a woman holding a baby smiles; she's missing a tooth. Fear, grief, despair. The sight of a small child with curly blond hair broken against the rocks. And the resin… red and pulsing like a living ruby.

Oh stars…

"He took her, and they killed her," the man cries.

"Who did?"

He does not reply, but the image is clear in his mind: Dharkan. Many Dharkan in the mist. Faceless Wraiths, the embodiment of death. One stands out amongst them. I Reach at her and she turns her bright blue eyes straight at me.

"Fuck!"

"She was just hungry…" the poor man wails.

Aedan and Jonas come stomping down the stairs.

"What did you do? I leave you alone for –"

"I did nothing!" I tell him, well aware of the evidence to the contrary. Then, against my better judgement, I place a hand on the hunter's chest and hope for the best.

"Daemon!" one of the women screams at the sight of the Dharkan and retreats into the kitchen. The wailing man shrieks and backs away in a panic, nearly falling into the hearth, then dashes towards the door, leaving a trail of toppled furniture and scattered embers in his wake, all the while screeching "Daemon! Murderer! May the sun burn you! May it burn you all!"

Shouts erupt from outside.

"Fantastic!" Jonas throws his hands in the air. "Now everyone knows you two are here. I'll be lucky if they don't burn the place down! Take your woman and do not come back, Aedan. Ever. We are done."

"I'm not his woman. I'm a goddess!"

Jonas throws a flask in my direction. It shatters on the wall behind me. "Woman, goddess, whatever the frost you are. You might consider adding a cock to your disguise or you're not welcome here either! Get out!"

"Gladly! You misogynistic onanist!"

"Let's go," Aedan says, dragging me away through the back door.

We exit through the kitchen into the animal pen. The women are long gone, probably to join the approaching mob. I can't help but laugh at the familiar situation, except this time I have no cover from night or rain and the whole settlement is out to get us.

"Any ideas?" Aedan asks, dodging a goose.

"Run."

We run to the forest's edge, the shouts of angry people not far behind. Stars, how I hate mobs. And I can't help wishing I had Ileana's powerful long legs at my disposal for the occasion. Once concealed in the trees, we look back to Portum. Black smoke billows from the tavern.

"They are burning the place down," Aedan mutters in disbelief. "Why? They saw us get away. Why do Narrum always have to burn things?"

"Narrum are humans, and there's nothing more spiteful and destructive than scared, frustrated humans in large numbers. They've probably been looking for an excuse to burn something since the lightning storm." I sigh. "The gods brought fire down on them, so they will on others. It's their nature."

Aedan's scarred lip curls up in disgust.

"Is Jonas safe?" he asks.

I Reach into the flames. "He is. Destroyed, like his sanctuary, but alive. So is the hunter. One goat, tethered to the fence by a chain, wasn't so lucky."

He snorts.

"You are right," I whisper. "I did choose to be a pet to a god rather than a wife to a human." And despite all the suffering my choice brought, I'd still choose it again.

I don't expect the Dharkan to understand, but I think he does. Disgust turns to something dangerously close to pity. It doesn't last long.

Aedan shakes his head. "That was Jonas' world. He'll never forgive me."

"You can hardly be blamed for human nature."

He avoids my gaze, and I sense there's more to forgive than the flames.

I take his momentary vulnerability to ask the question burning in my mind. "Who's Iva?"

Dharkan don't pale. They are as pale as it gets. But Aedan's complexion changes. It turns bluer like water frozen in a lake and so I know, Iva is trouble.

CHAPTER NINE

Hel

Hel puffed out an icy breath while she contemplated the steaming, empty pool where Artemis had been. Odin would be so disappointed in her. She had crossed a line, she knew. She also knew it was too late to cross it back.

"We had an agreement." The male voice echoed in the cave.

She had no desire, nor need, to turn towards the speaker. Apollo's light blazed through her Reach. The Olympian sun god always loved to blind her.

"Yes, we had. We agreed you wouldn't blind me every time we met," she said.

He feigned confusion. "How else would you notice me? It took the light of a hundred suns to get your attention in the first place. And it was worth every single one of them." Apollo spoke in the captivating, self-assured way of an oracle. He had the power of making everyone listen to his every word. Worse, he had the power of making everyone believe in them as well.

She bit her lip. Yes, she'd been dazzled by his radiance once, when she'd been young and foolish. She knew better now.

"We also agreed your burning sun would only serve to keep the Olympian Wyrd happy."

"Ah, what can I say? All power has side effects. Besides, it takes a special kind of sun to melt Niflheim." She felt the warmth of his breath on her neck and quickly moved away. "Come on, you can't blame a sun for shining."

She turned around to face him. "No, I'm blaming *you.*"

He showed her a row of pearl white, perfect teeth. Flickering light rippled over his golden skin, and his eyes shone bright as stars. Apollo always shone, even in the darkest places of her realm. Like most Olympians, he'd forsaken clothes in favour of trinkets and carried significant objects instead of weapons. In his case, an adder-stone around his neck and a lyre. Apollo was not a warrior; he was a poet. He used music and words as weapons with great effect. His melodies could mesmerise the most powerful beings into submission, she knew, for she'd once been one of them.

Hel looked at Apollo's perfect features and saw herself, sitting at the bottom of his golden throne with a silly smile on her face, listening, entranced by his sweet music, hanging on his every word and movement, certain she'd seen nothing as beautiful as his golden curls and cleft chin. The memory shamed her.

He feigned hurt. "So what if the world melted a little beyond what we'd agreed. Blame Eos, the Titaness always gets carried away with her pursuits. It was unwise to leave the sun in her charge. It won't happen again. By the way, you don't happen to know where she's taken it, do you?"

"No. I don't know where your burning sun is. You'll have to ask Loki." She grinned triumphantly at his fury and braced herself for his worst, but he only dimmed and began pacing the room, away from her. He picked up an obsidian figure from Aedan's collection: Huginn, one of Odin's ravens. The Allfather must have sent them there regularly to keep an eye on the Dharkan.

"Yes, I heard the Trickster was free. That's unfortunate. I figured it had to be him. It takes a powerful will to hide a sun," he said appreciatively.

Hel watched as the obsidian raven glowed and melted to nothing in Apollo's hand.

"No matter. I can create more suns. Better suns."

"Your sun burns my Dharkan to ashes!" Hel snapped.

Amusement shone in Apollo's flaming eyes. "Then perhaps you should have made them more inclined to stay in the shade," he taunted.

"You –" she started, ice creeping towards him. He stepped over it, leaving a puddle of steaming water behind.

There was no warmth in his voice when he spoke. "*You* agreed no Olympians would be harmed."

"Odin agreed to that. *I* made no such promise. Besides, your sister was the one who broke the truce. She came after one of mine and he defended himself."

"Zeus wasn't so lucky," Apollo said, glaring in her face.

There was a time when Hel welcomed his heat, a time when she longed to take it, to be consumed by it. Now she saw Apollo for what he truly was: a god of destruction. "Zeus ran out of luck the moment he allied himself with the Suzerain," she said. "You're the oracle. You should have seen it and warned him."

"Who says I didn't?" He grinned, pleased with himself. "And I saw through your deception too, dear Hela. You found a very dangerous way to bend the rules. You clever girl." He poked her nose with his finger.

"My father taught me that survival requires creativity," she sneered, slapping his hand away from her face. "And don't call me that!"

Apollo went deadly serious. "The Dharkan are too creative for my taste. I demand the blue sun to be returned to the sky immediately."

"How dare you make demands of me, in my own world!"

His eyes blinded hers. "The Dharkan are hunting my beautiful nymphs as we speak!"

"Someone has to keep their population down. All they do is breed!"

Apollo burned impossibly bright, but his words were ice cold. "It doesn't matter now, anyway. Where is my sister?"

"Where she can't cause any more trouble."

Apollo's beautiful face twisted in ugly ways. "Hel, cheating gods is one thing. Forcibly making them cross realms is, however, quite another."

"I hope you're not accusing me of what I think you are. I'm still bound by Kali's rules."

"So why can't I Reach her?"

Hel remained silent.

Apollo sighed dramatically. "I don't blame you for Artemis. Sometimes I wish I could freeze her myself. Poor Arty, her mind was never quite right, especially after what happened to Orion." He shook his head. "And I'm not here to tell you how to run your world either. I'm here to take her away, that's all. So, one last time, where is she?"

"Safe. From herself and others. You have my word."

A different, more urgent sort of heat burned thought her Reach. Apollo's rage dazzled something much worse. "Hel, we don't have time for wordplay. Artemis' rage burst through stars all across the Universe. *They* heard her too," he whispered.

Hel blinked.

"I'm faster than they are. But they will be here soon, especially now that they know how interesting this world is."

"I thought Niflheim was already of interest to them," she said, taken aback.

Apollo shrugged. "As a source of unusual creatures, yes. The Suzerain was cunning enough to keep the best out of his reports. I don't think he fully understood just how important this world is, but in wanting it for himself, he protected it from them. You and your pride have destroyed our best defence against the Nephilim. Now they are curious and mightily displeased. They're coming your way with everything they've got. I've seen it. There's no place under the light that you can hide now. Except, maybe, in my light. Hel, give me back the sun and my sister, and maybe, just maybe, you might get a chance to elude them."

"I don't need your light; I have darkness on my side now," she said, feeling sick.

Apollo laughed. "Hades, really?"

"What can I say: opposites attract."

"And then what? Annihilate each other?" Amusement tears shone in his eyes. "You never struck me as a goddess who likes to share."

"Does such a creature even exist?"

"Oh, poor Hela. Hades is using you." He sounded as if he cared.

"As I'm using him. Pfah, you call yourself an oracle? Tell me something I don't know," she said, hoping to steer the conversation away from her personal life.

"Odin can't protect you anymore."

"He never could. I don't need Odin's, or any god's, protection."

Suddenly his eyes rolled back, lips quivering. The beautiful sun god was a pitiful sight when taken by his talent. "You will," he said in an ominous tone. Not a statement – a prophecy.

Hel swallowed and waited for him to recover. "Apollo – what have you seen?"

He sat down by the pool, seemingly exhausted and free of pretence. "It's hard to explain these things… my talent, that is." He shook himself as if to clear his vision. "Sometimes the vision is as clear as you are, standing there, uttering one word after the other in a coherent way. Other times… like now, everything happens at once. I can't tell what causes what. Memory and time are always at odds with each other.

Sometimes I remember things that haven't happened yet. And then I forget things that have happened, like they never did… you know what I mean?"

She didn't. In her realm, the closest thing to time was a sense of before and after born of cause and consequence. Even in Aegea, the passage of time only truly became relevant after the Merge.

Apollo glowed alarmingly bright. "I don't think we have time on our side, Hel. Where is Artemis? Take me to her, *now.*"

"I told you, she's safe," Hel said. "Tell me what you saw."

"Take me to her first," he insisted.

It's too late to cross it back, she reminded herself and held out her hand to him. "Fine. Come, let me take you to your sister."

CHAPTER TEN

Hades

Hades knew Persephone was there even before he Reached her. The curse that bound his wife to him and the Underworld went both ways. She always had to return to him, and he always had to meet her before it allowed her to leave again. This, however, had not happened since the Merge.

He almost convinced himself that the Merge had somehow severed the link between them and Persephone would not be able to return to the Underworld again. But no god can undo the designs of another, not even Chronos. Hades' curses were particularly difficult to break. They had to be, otherwise every Titan locked in Tartarus would be free.

Persephone had been a whim of youth, the most beautiful thing he'd ever seen, when he'd barely seen beauty at all. He'd kidnapped her hoping she'd bring something beautiful to the Underworld from the world above with her. In his dreams he'd imagined her turning the dark and dull Underworld into a garden to rival Elysium, but instead she only brought turmoil and misery to its souls. Every god makes mistakes, and when a god like Hades makes a mistake, those mistakes can affect even eternity. Over the ages, her beauty offended him more than her words or actions. And now, he could barely look at the shallow creature.

She waited for him in his chambers – or should he say, *their* chambers – displayed on the bed, absently picking the petals from a rose, making the bud regenerate each one she threw away. Judging by the amount of discarded petals on the bed, she'd been there a while. A curse on the Stump and its telepathic shield.

"Hello, husband. Did you miss me?"

"No," he replied curtly. The room had a pungent odour from a combination of several fragrances: rose, lilac, daisy, jasmine, gardenia… One scent alone might be pleasant; all combined gave him a headache. Did she always smell like that?

"The feeling is mutual, husband. But here I am, as is my duty. Shall we get on with it so I can leave? I'm kind of in a hurry," she said petulantly. Her voice was high-pitched and girly, almost childish. He used to find it sensual. Had he been deaf?

Hades scratched at the base of his right horn. This was far from what he had planned for the day.

"Oh, but not while you're like *that*. I'm not bedding a goat," she stated with disgust.

The goddess of spring spread herself on the bed, surrounded by infinite shades of pink petals. The sight made his blood boil, just not exactly in the way it used to.

There was no point in asking why she was doing

this. The curse specifically required they be united before she could go back to wherever she went when she was free of him, but he very much wanted to know *how* she got there *now*. And *why*.

"I came with Apollo," she answered before he asked.

Hel would not be pleased with that, Hades reckoned. "What business has the Olympian sun god in Niflheim?"

"He received a call for aid from his sister. She sounded so cold, poor thing. You don't happen to know anything about that, do you?" She smirked, enjoying his discomfort. Cerberus breath, it was disturbing how easily she could Reach him – a side effect of their marriage, not the curse. Could she know about *everything else* as well?

He cleared his throat. "Has Apollo met with Zeus yet?"

"How would I know? I've been here waiting for you. Come on, change out of those hoofs and get this over with. I have stuff to do."

Hades bristled. He would not be treated like one of the Suzerain's shrines. "What *stuff*, exactly?"

"Friends to visit; places to see. This is a whole new world! Have you seen it from above? There's so much to explore beyond the mountains. And the ocean… ah, Poseidon would love the ocean. I hear the forest even has its own Chronodéndron. Is it true? And it's a proper one too!" She laughed. "The Aesir are better than us at creating worlds, I'll give them that."

"Did you miss the felled tree on your way in?"

She grinned. "Fabulous, isn't it?"

"That's not the word I'd choose."

"And that's just the landing platform. Can you imagine the chariot? I for one don't want to be around when it lands. So come on, hurry up. I'm getting bored."

Hades took a deep breath, regretting the fact that, this curse, he brought it on himself.

CHAPTER ELEVEN

Loki

Loki stormed into the room in a shower of crumbling masonry.

"That son of a whore!" he growled, seething with anger.

Seshat, sat at her writing desk by the window, put down her quill to gather the scattered sheets of papyrus back into their stacks and chuckled to herself. "Why do men always blame the mothers?"

The god of mischief halted, momentarily confused. "What?"

"'Son of a whore.' Whores rarely have children; they know how to avoid such a hindrance to their trade, and mothers rarely get a chance to choose who sires their sons. Especially amongst humans. And yet men always refer to prostitutes as if they were not their source of income and blame their wives when they don't like their offspring."

"Do not get philosophical on me now, Seshat." She had a point, but Loki was in no frame of mind to pursue it.

Seshat touched the top of her quill to her chin, still

musing. "It's a pertinent question, the idea common across many pantheons and civilisations. I'll make a note to study it further." She scribbled something in midair. "In this particular case, the father is the one you're angry at, correct?"

"I'm angry at the whole fucking family!"

Seshat chuckled again. "What else is new." She sighed and resumed drawing her thoughts on the pages.

Loki exhaled some of his tension and sat on the bed, still fuming, but not about to catch fire. The question and the rational nature of Seshat worked at dispersing a fair amount of his anger. A good thing, for he had to think. Anger and thinking never worked well together. If they did, he'd be the greatest mind in the Universe.

"So, how is Baldur?" The goddess of writing enquired once he settled.

"Well enough," he said grudgingly. Baldur was actually happy in Helheim. He didn't miss the living nor the gods and had no desire to return to life. Loki envied him.

Seshat grinned at him over her shoulder. "Better than us, then." Nothing escaped the cunning creature. He liked that in her. Her composure and cold logic were refreshing amongst the gods. She kept him calm. Right until the point her complete lack of imagination made him furious. Still, she was right. Baldur was better off than all the other gods stuck in Niflheim with the living. And that infuriated Loki the most.

The sunny Baldur always shone brighter than everyone else, even in death. He didn't even hold a grudge against the one responsible for his demise. Which was fine. Loki's outrage was enough to carry a grudge for both. If only he knew who it had been who framed him for Baldur's death, then he could stop being angry about it and channel his temper to something more constructive. So far, he knew it had to have been an Asgardian or someone able to travel between worlds without a Tree, for the bridge was locked immediately after the event. Someone vain, jealous, and ambitious enough to restart the war between the pantheons. Someone fairly skilled at archery and with a personal grudge against him. Well, that last feature was irrelevant; pretty much every god in the Universe held a grudge against him. Loki took great pride in that.

Baldur admitted he had known all along who put the mistletoe arrow with the others but could not bring himself to point the finger. He was too good for that. Good, bah. Loki had another word for such creatures: weak. Of course Baldur could afford to be 'good' because he had Loki to do his dirty work for him. Loki always had to be the one who spoke the harsh truths, the one who got blamed for the bad news. He had to be bad, so others could be good. Loki didn't mind. Being good was boring, after all. He knew survival required ruthlessness, for conflict was never between good and evil as they taught the mortals. Conflict was always between evils, and through his whole existence Loki had endeavoured to be a worse evil than his enemies.

This train of thought depressed him.

Loki shifted his attention back to the goddess of writing with her head bent over neat piles of papyrus.

Warm light radiated from her skin, illuminating the room. Her straight black hair brushed her shoulders as she wrote. She looked so young and fragile, almost mortal. And so damn sexy sat naked behind that desk.

Sensing his mood, she put down her quill and joined him on the bed with a teasing smile.

"I've never been to the other side. What is it like?" she asked, bright orange eyes burning with curiosity through their thick outlines of kohl. She then stretched alongside him like a lazy cat in the morning sun, her head propped on an elbow, waiting for an answer.

Loki dismissed his anger and lay back next to her, mimicking her leisure. "Dull. Boring. There's nothing to do there but tell stories. You'd love it, actually."

She laughed. "So the living tell stories about the dead and the dead tell stories about the living?"

"Not quite. The living tell stories about the dead to remember their lives, while the dead tell each other stories to remember being alive."

Seshat's eyes shone like the Midgard sun. "How interesting."

"You think so?" He found it sad.

"I always wondered how memory worked on the other side," she said.

"Same as it works on this side: not very well." Loki said it as a jest, but the gods knew Mnemosyne had a lot to answer for.

"'We only truly die when we're forgotten'," Seshat said to herself, then chuckled bitterly.

"Who told you that?" Loki asked, paying close attention to the lines of her long neck. She had an ink stain just behind her ear he found particularly endearing.

"Kali," she replied. A torrent of angry thoughts followed the name. He pretended not to notice. It was rude to eavesdrop on another god's thoughts. Not to mention dangerous. Especially Reaching into a mind like hers.

"Is that why you record everything, so it's not forgotten?"

"It's one reason… I'm trying to record as many events as possible in order to compare them with how they are remembered."

"What for?"

"To make sense of a few discrepancies I've found in the narrative of our Universe."

"How so?"

"It's hard to explain."

"Try me."

She sat up and studied him with a quizzical expression. "Why do you care?"

"I'm curious, that's all. This" – he pointed at her work – "is obviously important to you."

"Very well," she said, lying back down. "There are many ways to tell a story, but you always have to pick a starting point and an end point. That doesn't mean there's no more story to tell before or after those moments, and often, in order to tell a story properly, you might need to include events that happened before the events you're describing for context, or skip some of them altogether. It is impossible to record every single moment of every single story. Believe me, I've tried. Sometimes you may even need to describe events from a completely different perspective while still telling the same story. The point is: in a story, before and after only exists in the memory of the storyteller. Time is irrelevant."

"Tell that to Chronos," Loki said, amused.

Seshat shook her head. "To call Chronos God of Time is like calling me goddess of writing. I write, yes. I record things, but that's not all I do. It's not the things I write, but how I write them that make me who I am. I de ine what I write, turn it into history. I make stories real, the same way memory makes time feel real."

"So, is that why every creature experiences time differently?"

"Exactly. Events are remembered in different ways, by different minds. The best way to keep track of everything is to focus each story on one charac-ter. I observe and record the events surrounding that character so I can compare them with how they are remembered by others, for I believe memory has been distorting events the same way it distorts time. I mean, we all know how one moment in agony lasts forever and one of joy, nothing at all."

"Hmm," Loki mused. He had to agree with that one. The time he spent in the Underworld felt longer than an age. And yet...

"And yet time also has the power to distort memo-ries," he said, considering the implications.

"Or erase them altogether," Seshat agreed. "But there's more," she said, seemingly alight with excite-ment. "For example: How well do you remember your dreams?"

"Not well," he admitted.

"That's because there's no concept of time in the realm of dreams. Same goes for the realms of the dead.

Now you understand why I find it interesting that the dead use stories to remember their lives?"

"Huh. What about illusions? They're timeless. How can you tell if a memory is real or an illusion?"

"That's easy." She traced the lines of his handsome face and smiled sadly. "By the scars they leave."

Loki laughed. "We don't scar."

"Yes we do. Up here." She touched his temple.

He bristled. This conversation was giving Loki a headache. He regretted having started it. "Oh, let Chronos and Mnemosyne play their games. We're gods. Souls are what define us, not memories. So what does it matter?"

"It matters to me," she said flatly, then looked away.

Loki stood up and walked to the window, tried to open it and was left with the broken handle in his palm.

"Couldn't you afford something better?" he asked her, annoyed.

To say the room's condition was precarious was a kindness: dilapidated walls, crumbling masonry, a floor made more of rubbish than stone. Loki knew that to Seshat the sheds and palaces of mortals all looked alike. The gods of her pantheon build huge pyramidal structures, able to withstand the harshest punishments of time and nature; they used architecture to reflect power and immortality. To them, nothing a mortal built lasted because they themselves did not last. But this? Seshat's willpower was probably the only thing keeping the shelter from crumbling down entirely.

She made a sound half tut, half hiss. "This house has the best view. I can Reach the whole forum from here and see all the way down to the Grove besides."

"It's falling apart."

"Don't be so dramatic. It was hardly held together to begin with. Don't worry. It won't crumble while we're inside. And even if it did…" She paused and glanced at her work. "Actually, that would be a nuisance." She closed her eyes and, although nothing changed to the casual eye, the room seemed to have somehow straightened itself. "There. It won't fall just yet."

Loki shed his own clothes and returned to the bed.

The shelter was indeed a prime location in Relicum. Stuck between the market and the temple, nothing happened in the settlement that the goddess wouldn't know about. What he did not understand was why she cared. Come to think of it, why did she still dwell in Aegea, hidden inside a building, especially one in this state. If he didn't know better, he'd say she was hiding. He took a good look at the goddess while licking his fangs with the tip of his tongue.

"Seshat, why do you want to Reach outside?" he asked almost menacingly.

"Listening to their stories amuses me. You won't believe how creative merchants can get in order to sell their wares."

"Really? You've been around mortals for too long if you're that easily entertained."

"It's safer than being around gods." Something in her voice inflated his interest.

"Oh, I thought you liked wicked gods." He bit her shoulder.

She looked cross for a moment and then spread herself on the bed, arms over her head, smiling at him. "I do. And I like it here too, believe or not."

Loki cupped a breast, small and perky. "Do you? Better than Asgard?"

"Well, to compare Asgard to Niflheim is like comparing a pyramid to a hut," she purred.

He pinched her nipple.

"Ouch!"

"Don't speak ill of my children's world. Niflheim is unique."

"Sure it is." She chuckled.

"Seshat. Why are you here, truly?" Loki understood why Seshat was originally drawn to the Suzerain and his gods. The Nephilim were new, and what they had done to the Stump was more than impressive, was a demonstration of power to the other gods. 'This is what we can do to your world Tree,' it said. 'Imagine what we can do to you.' But he did not understand why she remained.

"I told you why. There are good stories here. What?"

"You never cared for mortals, Seshat. 'Short stories,' you always called them."

"So what do you think I'm doing here, then?"

"Hmm, I bet you're writing the story of a god. Is it mine?" He slid his hand further down her belly.

She chuckled again, parting her thighs. "You're not that interesting, Trickster. There's only one twist to your story, it gets old."

He kissed her. The heat from her lips burned like a hot summer's day. "Easy for you to say. You have the talent to assume any character. I can't help being what I am."

"True."

To prove the point, she shifted into a handsome male dryad, with black hair at his temples, otherwise untouched by age. Loki frowned, amused and slightly intrigued by her choice.

"The Suzerain's story is over. Why didn't you leave after he died? Hel and Hades have the world under control, or they will have, once they get themselves under control," Loki grumbled.

"Hel got her taste in men from her mother," Seshat said in the Suzerain's deep voice.

"Very funny. Don't try to change the subject. Why are you still here?"

She reverted to her real form. "I just told you. I like it here. Niflheim is rich with interesting characters." She guided his hand between her legs. "And there's so much more to enjoy, besides."

He grinned, giving her exactly what she wanted. "You flatter me. Now, tell me the truth." His tone, like his touch, was gentle, disguising the threat behind it.

She moaned, a faint glow rippling under her tanned skin. "The truth is: I have nowhere else I wish to be right now."

"And if you had?"

"I have no means to get there." She gasped.

"Bullshit. You're a goddess of light. You can go anywhere." He roughly pushed his fingers inside her.

She tried to push his hand away in protest. He held her down. "What are you hiding, Seshat? You do it well, but not well enough. No one can hide their truth from me."

She tried to leave the bed; he didn't let her. "Not so fast. Not until you tell me what really keeps you in this shit hole, scribbling endlessly."

She stopped struggling and changed into Hel. An impressive resemblance. "Make me talk, daddy," she purred.

Seshat loved to play games, to change characters; it was the most exciting thing about fucking her. This choice told him he was onto something. He wasn't even that curious before, but now… "You think I won't hurt you or fuck you looking like my daughter? Seshat… surely you know me better than that?"

She shifted into a human with fair skin, chestnut hair and dark eyes.

He snarled, deep blue eyes burning. "Enough games! Tell me what I want to know."

Seshat burst with light, searing his skin and hair. Chuckling, she pushed him over and straddled him, rolling her hips against his hardness. "You're lucky I like you with skin on."

He never forgot how easy it would be for her to burn him beyond repair. Torment in the Underworld was nothing compared to what she could do to him if the mood took her. Her danger aroused him. If she crossed the line, he could make her believe the same torment, of course. And neither wanted to find out who could make better use of their talents.

Such was the nature of relationships between gods.

They came together. Biting, scratching, nearly tearing each other apart in their lust. Two powerful forces battling wills with all the might of their souls. Their bodies kept them grounded in reality, for some pleasures only exist in flesh, after all.

After they were done, Seshat sat up, her skin glistening with starlight and sweat.

"What's going on outside?" she wondered aloud.

The populous of Relicum was in uproar, nothing particularly unusual amongst mortals, always trying to bring the gods' attention on themselves, the fools. Loki ignored them and focused back on Seshat. The pleasurable distraction hadn't been enough to make him forget the question that had prompted their encounter, and so he asked again, straight to her mind. *'Why are you still here?'*

Seshat glared at him. *'If I tell you, you need to promise not to tell anyone. Not even Hel.'* Her voice seared his mind like a solar flare. She definitely wasn't playing anymore.

"I can keep a secret." He grinned.

She narrowed her eyes into two thick black lines. "Oh, you can keep a secret, all right. Can you stop yourself from acting on it, though?"

He clicked his tongue. She knew him too well. "Not often."

She did not chuckle. A bad sign.

"Seshat. You know I won't let this go. I'll find out eventually, so you might as well just tell me."

He could sense her apprehension in every muscle,

every cell. He tried to comfort her; she pushed him away. He let her. A sign of goodwill. One thing he knew about women: they don't like to feel pressured.

"It's too late, Loki. There's nothing you can do about any of it. You've been away for too long. The Universe has changed."

His patience was running thin. "One more reason for you to tell me what I've missed."

She was about to, then hesitated. "Cats! The Shrine lost his mind. Are you paying attention to what's happening at the temple?"

"No!" Loki shouted. He was growing dangerously bored with her now. "I don't give a fuck about their little rebellion. I'm paying attention to you. So, once and for all, what happened?"

She took a very long breath before she answered. *'Ra is dead.'*

His first reaction was to laugh, but her look quickly put an end to that idea. "How?"

"You're right. I didn't use to care about the lives of mortals. Not until their actions closed books all over the Universe with half-finished stories."

"Whose stories?"

"Ra, Marduk, now Zeus and Odin."

"Odin?!" Loki practically squeaked the name.

She studied him. "You didn't know? Well, you probably just missed him."

"Odin is with Baldur? That fucking – Arrrggg!" Loki punched the wall, and half the roof collapsed. More shouts erupted from outside.

"Great. Now we have to move. There's no way I

can repair this without bringing more attention to the building."

Loki ignored the goddess. Odin did not deserve to be with his precious son. After all he'd done, the All-father still got the better of him. The outrage was such that Loki could hardly think.

"How did he get there?"

"Guess." Seshat began gathering her manuscripts. Outside, a mob was gathering in front of the house.

Hel wouldn't send him, he was sure. That left… "Psyche wouldn't…"

"She did."

The goddess of the soul must have had a good reason. She must have.

"You are right, Loki. I came here because of the Merge," Seshat said, scrolling through sheets. "I took a ride with Apollo when he came to create the blue sun. Ra was furious. He and Marduk were about to set off to burn the fake gods, and Ra wanted me at his side to record the victory. But Chronos always was such a re-clusive God, one almost forgets he exists. Then he does something like this? I had to record it. I only learnt of Ra's death after the Nephilim's arrival. The Suzerain made sure I learnt it from him. By then, Apollo had left. I figured he took Hel with him. And so I found myself alone in a cursed world, with no friends or pantheon. I had two choices: become a Wyrd – no thanks – or join the Suzerain." She shook her head and seemed to have dimmed, somehow. "I've recorded Ra's battles since the moment I came into being, and then I wasn't there when he lost. Maybe it's for the best, but I promised myself I'd learn how to defeat this enemy, for his sake. After everything that's happened, I still don't have a clue how to do it. But I suspect you do." She burned her stare into him. "Don't you, *Trickster*?"

"Odin is dead?" Loki repeated, pretending not to have heard a word the goddess said.

Seshat's eyes glowed a dangerous red. "Get out!" she hissed, and he did not wait for the flames to reach him.

CHAPTER TWELVE

Iosh

Psyche, Psyche… How do I know that name?

The question had been burning in his mind since that dreadful morning. He had heard the name before; he was sure. But where? When? Iosh ripped the meat off the chicken thigh and grimaced. Like every other meal Toman prepared, it was unseasoned and over-cooked.

"Where should I put the women and children, sire?" the boy asked, again.

Iosh swallowed the barely chewed meat, enraged at having his thoughts interrupted. "I don't know! Put them on the patios, in the baths, on the roof for all I care!"

"Already have, sire," Toman said in a small voice.

"Then find some spikes and start hanging them from the walls!"

The boy opened his eyes wide at the idea, then pressed his lips, looking up at the stone wall in front of him, as if considering how to go about it.

Relicum's temple, despite being the largest in Aegea, had no more room to accommodate all the women and their children – especially the children. Their incessant cries, more grating than a gryphon's mating call, seemed to come from everywhere and were draining Iosh's sanity.

He took another bite of the flavourless meat and tried to calm himself. His mind searched for a solution while his mouth chewed loudly in an attempt to muffle the unpleasant din. Toman, his new assistant, still waited expectantly for instructions. Fabrian's replacement was devoted to his work, ate a lot less, and was obedient to a fault, but he showed no initiative whatsoever.

"Use the meeting room and my chambers for the heavily pregnant ones, the rest send to Portum. Let Jonas deal with them for a change." Jonas had evaded his duties as Shrine for too long. Iosh had gladly agreed to sire the man's lot in his stead, but not to suffer the consequences of it as well.

"I heard Portum was greatly affected by the storm, sire. Many of its buildings burned down, and being so close to the forest, it might not be safe for –"

"I don't care!" Iosh snapped, spluttering bits of chicken meat from his mouth.

It was all the gods' fault. They didn't care either, so why would he? They forced the women on him under the pretence that the Stump wasn't safe for the children. Horse shit. If gods could not protect the children, how could he? They couldn't care less for him or any of the mortals in their world. Even Arianh, that – no, he would not be rude to her, not even in thought – even Arianh had stayed at the Stump, with the gods, instead of returning with him or to her people at the Grove where she belonged! No surprise there, she'd always wanted to be a goddess. They'd all forgotten about him. It'd been days – days! – without word, days without assistance, days without a solution. Oh, he bet that in their minds he was the solution. And why? Because he was a metz. The living proof their creations could breed and that therefore they were not so dissimilar as they'd intended. *I will not be treated like this. I'm not just a man!* Iosh repeated to himself, chewing vigorously.

What would happen to him now? His power in Aegea was linked to the Suzerain. What happens to Shrines when their god ceases to exist? Was he free now or just – he could barely bring himself to think the word – insignificant? No, Judoc of Relicum could never be insignificant, could he? He was the most handsome, most worshipped mortal in Aegea. The god of love himself had gifted him! He'd worked too hard, sacrificed too much, he'd prayed to Chronos, and He found him worthy to cross time to be where he was now. Iosh knew his worth, and he would not be treated as an ordinary man!

"Sire, people are asking questions. Governor Guilho..." Toman started timidly.

Of course they were. People loved to ask questions and conjecture on answers even more. And Guilho could go hump a goat for all he cared. He took a deep breath.

"I've already explained to the governor that the Tribute has been delayed."

"Yes, but… sire." Toman's guileless face crunched up in thought. He looked constipated. Thinking did not agree with the boy.

"What is it?"

"It's just that it's difficult for me to do my job if I don't know what has happened at the Stump. Obviously something has. Something bad." He attempted to step closer. "You can trust me, sire."

Iosh considered his new assistant for a moment. He did not know who to trust in this strange turn of events, but Toman was not even on the list of potential candidates. He never thought he'd ever miss the old Wyrd, Odin. At least with him Iosh knew where he stood, and he always knew what to do. But Odin was a god; though fated, he'd always choose the gods' side. *And which side do you think the other gods will choose?*

"Everyone saw the lightning storm, and no one has seen any of the Suzerain's men since. There was ice over the great Stump's roots," Toman added in a conspiratorial whisper.

Iosh closed his eyes, took another deep breath and forced himself to swallow.

"Very well. I suppose you should know: there's been a problem with the main portal. A sort of, of…" What was the freezing word, again? Ah, yes. "Glitch. A malfunction in the uh… mechanism of the ring – the thing that allows travelling to other worlds." Yes, that made sense, Iosh thought. Toman made that constipated face again while he moved his lips trying to memorise the new strange words.

"And because of it," Iosh continued, growing confident in his narrative, "the Suzerain's delayed off world. Therefore, the Tribute is also delayed until the issue with the uh… device is resolved and he's able to return. Until then, he's left me in charge of keeping both the peace and the Tributes safe. The rest is non-sense. There is nothing to worry about." There, that should do it.

The boy's face lightened. "Ah, that's a relief, sire. Fear makes people say the strangest things. You should hear the talk in the forum. Tales of flying horses, Dharkan hunting in the forest and monstrous gods hiding amongst us, disguised as young boys. The baskers go as far as to proclaim our Lord is dead." He made a stern face. "It's not right, sire. You should make an an-nouncement to put matters straight."

Iosh's expression must have showed his opinion of this suggestion.

"I'm sorry, sire, I didn't mean to –"

"Tell me what to do? No, I sure hope not." The annoying thing was, it was exactly what he should have done, had he not been so focused on his own grievances.

Could he still do it? He should. After all, he spoke for the Lord. Now that the Lord was gone, he could say whatever he wanted. The people would listen to him. At least the Narrum would for sure. They always had to be told what to think. The Anann would take more convincing, and the Wyrd… well, he might not convince them at all, but what could they do? Reveal themselves? They wouldn't dare, especially without their sun. But then what? What would happen if he said "your Lord is dead, and by the way, the old gods are real and they have returned and they don't give a splinter about you" and they believed him? There would be chaos. The dyads would go back to their forests to protect their precious trees. Narrum would hunt them again, and the Dharkan... good grief, the Dharkan. How would he even begin to explain that one of them was probably sitting on the Suzerain's throne as he spoke? The idea made him dizzy.

Toman was still there, staring at him expectantly. "Do you think you can go do what I asked you to and leave me alone now?"

"Yes, sire. Of course, sire," replied the boy enthusiastically. "Thank you." He inclined his head and ran out of the pantry. His dedication might be annoying at times, but he was diligent. If only Iosh could get the town dedicated to him the same way...

Iosh braced himself on the table, his appetite overtaken by a sudden knot in his stomach. His head split in agony as a familiar voice whispered behind his ear. Iosh listened. Then he grinned. Of course he deserved more, he *was* more. He could do whatever he wanted.

Hurried footsteps interrupted his thoughts.

"Governor Guilho, what an unpleasant surprise," Iosh said without turning back. He'd recognise the jingle of his ornaments anywhere. Guilho was a man who liked to compensate for his lack of worth with gold and precious stones.

"That assistant of yours wouldn't tell me where you were! The insolence."

"How did you change his mind?" Iosh asked, still smiling at his thoughts.

"I didn't. I've been searching for you everywhere! This is the last place I thought to look."

Well done, Toman, Iosh thought. There might still be hope for his young assistant, after all.

"So here you are, hiding like a rodent." The small man looked mightily displeased, as he always did. This time there was more than resentment in his frown; he was worried.

"Here I am," Iosh sighed. The voice went silent. "How can I help you, Governor?"

"I demand to know what happened at the Stump."

"Demand?" Iosh guffawed. "I'm not one of your boys."

Guilho prickled. "You'll answer my question, you glorified shrub!"

"You would not believe me if I did. I suggest you go there and see it for yourself."

Guilho pulled the sleeve of his left arm. "Someone stole my key!"

"They did you a favour, trust me." Iosh turned his back to the little man, poured water into a wine cup, turned back around and drank. He disliked wine but knew how much Guilho was fond of the beverage. He had to be thirsty, sweating as he was. The way the old man coveted the cup pleased Iosh no end.

"Trust you? You're a beast, no more than a pretty ox to cover the cows with daemon spawn."

"A beast? Careful, Guilho, for you're in my den," he said, showing him his teeth. "What would Alek say if he heard you? He's a dryad too."

Guilho was not intimidated. "We both know he's a lot more than that. I'll never understand the Suzerain, or his plan. But I never questioned it either. We Narrum learnt long ago not to question those in power.

We take what they give us and are grateful for it. It's hard not to make enemies of beasts when you need their flesh and fur. All that matters is that the Suzerain provides for us. If we have to sell our females for peace and a full stomach, so be it. It's not like we're lacking children." He grimaced as if mentioning the children made their cries louder. It seemed that the governor shared Iosh's aversion to the sound.

"It's always possible to find common ground with the adversary, and use it against him," Odin used to say. He was wise.

"But you are not the Suzerain, tree hugger," Guilho said.

Iosh let the insult wash over him. He knew well how much Relicum's governor despised and resented dryads. He knew he was a metz, but in his eyes, half a dryad was still a dryad.

"You dryads think just because you call it 'basking' it makes your kind less unnatural than the Wraiths." Guilho tutted. "You are not!"

Iosh ripped another chunk of meat from the bone. Guilho's anger gave way to momentary confusion.

"We are more alike than you imagine, Governor. I only bask as part of my job, to keep up appearances, and a good skin tone."

Guilho scowled at the notion of having anything in common with him. "I can eat fruit too; it doesn't make me an animal."

Iosh picked a bit of tendon from his teeth. "Guilho, you're in my temple. Again, I suggest you show me some respect."

"Your temple is in my city! You owe *me* respect – whatever breed of creature you are," he added with disgust.

"It's the Suzerain's city, and I'm his Shrine. I speak for him."

"Then answer the question! What happened at the Stump?"

Iosh grimaced. How he hated the little man. Odin was wrong. Some adversaries cannot be reasoned with. He wondered what disgusted the governor more, that he was part dryad or that he genuinely enjoyed women. In Guilho's eyes, there was no difference between women or mares. Just walking uteri to fill with progeny.

Iosh's mind wandered back to the gods and what had happened that dawn. The Suzerain had been right. The way the gods used mortals never ceased to enrage him. They took their bodies, their lives, even their will. People weren't puppets, they should not be used and discarded or silenced as if their voices, as obnoxious as they might be sometimes, didn't matter. In that moment, filled with a powerful resolve, Iosh decided he would not be disrespected by either god or mortal. He was important. The people in the city came to him for advice. Its own governor had less power over them than he did. Most children in Relicum were his. He already had a temple of his own. He was more than a servant, more than special, he was extraordinary. And extraordinary men don't have to put up with insults from their lessers. The voice in his mind agreed. His eyes came to rest on a small carving knife lying on the table.

"The Suzerain is dead," he said casually. Once spoken, the words no longer bothered him. They freed him.

This was the moment Iosh'd been waiting for all his life, and now he knew exactly what to do. Iosh may never be a god. But he could be a king. He would rule both Anann and Narrum, as it had always been his right. The Suzerain knew it too. That was why he sent him here, to unite the people and create a new race. The Metz would send the Dharkan back to the Shadow Mountains from where they should never have left. He knew it was the right thing to do. He had seen the future, after all. And the gods, the gods would do nothing because the Nephilim would take care of them.

The look in Guilho's eyes was priceless. "Dead…?" he murmured.

"Send him my regards when you see him." Without hesitation, Iosh did the next thing that came to mind; he took the blade and carved open Guilho's throat from ear to ear.

Guilho's eyes bulged. He tried to speak, but Iosh accidentally put enough force in the blow to cut the man's sinewy neck all the way to the bone. No words came out, only blood.

He stood there, fascinated, while the blood, hot and thick, gushed all over his toga. The smell of it made him salivate. "Tree hugger, you called me. Can tree huggers do this?" He licked the blade, relishing how the blood tickled his tongue, then plunged it again into Guilho's chest. The man fell back on a sack, eyes bulging, a trembling hand lifted halfway to his throat.

Iosh pulled the knife out to stab him again and again, the feel of flesh ripping under the blade more euphoric than sex. "My temple. My settlement. My people. My rule," he said with each stab.

Iosh looked down and saw Guilho had pissed himself. "Ew." That ruined his appetite. Gods, but the man just wouldn't die. He just stared up at him in horror – or could it be awe? – mouth open, struggling for breath.

I am better than a god, Iosh decided when Guilho finally died at his feet.

∞

A clapping sound came from the doorway. "Well, well. Who'd have thought? I didn't think you had it in you, pretty man."

It was Oric. *Had he been there all along?* He had his left sleeve wrapped up in a knot by the shoulder, and his complexion was worse than Fabrian's after death. Still, he was laughing. The man was laughing at him! Iosh, filled with bloodlust, advanced on the one-armed man.

Oric immediately put his own weapon between them. "Now, now. You're not the only basker who can wield a blade. And mine's bigger," he pointed out with a lewd smile.

"Size doesn't matter."

"Wanna bet?"

Iosh bared his teeth. "I just butchered your governor. Do I strike you as being in the mood to be taunted?"

"He was not my governor. Had half a mind of killing him myself a few times. Same goes for you, *Shrine*. But I can be reasonable now that I know of your hidden talents. In all fairness, I've had more than my share of fights, lately."

"I noticed." Up close, Iosh could see Oric not only had a black eye and a split lip, he'd also been sliced across the chest, judging by his shirt. "Found someone with an even bigger blade, did you?"

Iosh didn't know what made him say that, and for a moment he thought Oric would gut him right then and there. Instead he gave him the sort of appraising look a livestock merchant gives his wares. "I always wondered what the Suzerain saw in you. Seems your balls are not just for breeding."

"And what did he see in *you*? Apart from an arrogance greater than his own."

Oric smiled as if he'd received a compliment. "Opportunity. We're not that different, you and I. You see, I too am a metz."

"Horseshit," Iosh said, taking in the man's flawless sycamore skin, azure hair and light blue eyes. "If that's so, why aren't you running your own temple?"

"My talents lie elsewhere."

Another Jonas, Iosh thought. That would explain their friendship, but little else. Iosh practically had to lock the women away when Oric came to stay at the temple. It was all pretence, apparently. Well, he had no patience for this. The blood on him was turning cold and sticky, and he'd very much like to wash before anyone else saw him. "What do you want, Oric?"

"That." He pointed at the bracelet on Iosh's forearm.

Of course. He'd lost his when he lost the arm, probably. Iosh doubted the man would ever have given up his bracelet otherwise.

"What if I refuse?"

The maimed man feigned surprise. "You just killed the governor. What will you do when the mob comes to lynch you?"

"Me?" Iosh answered in a similar tone. "I'm not the one who likes to boast about his kills, waving bloody blades around as if they're torches for everyone to know what a cold-blooded killer you are. I'm just a harmless metz. The Suzerain's living Shrine. Loved by the people and the most important man in Relicum, followed by the governor over there. The governor you cut down, or so I'll say."

"And who would believe? Look at the state of you!"

"I tried to help poor Guilho. I bravely overcame my visceral aversion to blood in an effort to save him, and when I couldn't, for I'm just a Shrine after all, I held him in my arms to comfort him in his last moments."

Oric smirked. "Why haven't you screamed, called for help?"

"I was overcome with emotion! And terrified. You are one of the Suzerain's trusted knights! If you could do this to him, what would stop you from doing the same to me?"

They stared at each other for a moment, then laughed. They laughed until their stomachs hurt and tears wet their eyes.

"Well, looks like we can either stab each other or talk like the reasonable men we are," Oric said.

"Give me your blade, as a sign of good will, then

we'll talk." Reasonable or not, Iosh was not about to make the mistake of trusting the man.

Oric hesitated but did hand him the weapon.

Iosh put both knives away, took off his dress, drenched a cloth in a bucket of water and began washing the blood off his skin. "Go on, I'm listening."

"You know what went down at the Stump?" Oric asked.

"I do."

"Who controls it now?"

"Gods. Both Olympian and Aesir, along with your pale, scarred friend. He's acting as the new ruler."

Oric sucked his teeth, seething. "That is unfortunate. What's stopping the gods from killing us all?"

"Arianh, I imagine."

"They hold the queen hostage?"

"No, no. She's there of her own free will."

Oric frowned, unconvinced.

"She's a woman, and women are drawn to power. She's exactly where she always wanted to be, trust me."

Another woman came to Iosh's mind. Psyche. *Gods, why do I know her name?* Unlike Arianh, she was not there willingly. He felt a surge of regret and frustrated anger at the thought. He should have done something to help the goddess. He would have to find a way to free her from the other gods, for somehow he knew, deep within his mind, that she belonged to him. Why else would Chronos send her to him disguised as Ileana, his first love, if not as proof of their fate?

"Where is Seshat?" Oric asked.

"Huh? How would I know?" Iosh hadn't seen the chronicler since the last burning. He knew he owned a shelter somewhere in the forum and was probably there, buried in papyrus, oblivious to the world. His location didn't seem important to share with Oric, though. They had agreed on a truce, not an alliance.

Oric tapped his finger on the wall, thinking, then said, "I know something you don't."

Iosh had to bite his lip to stop himself from laughing at the man. He would never believe the things he did know. "Is it something you want to share?"

"They haven't killed the Suzerain. The Suzerain can't be killed."

"Looked pretty dead to me," Iosh snorted, remembering the shattered head at his feet. "I know he heals in a blink of eye and can't feel pain. But it's hard to recover from a shattered head. I saw it. Trust me. He's dead."

"You don't know him."

"I've known him all my life! I've known him since well before he became the Suzerain!"

"That Suzerain, sure. But he's not the only one."

Iosh, his ablutions concluded, sat down on a corn sack, arms crossed. "Explain."

CHAPTER THIRTEEN

Arianh

Arianh tentatively lowered herself onto the frozen throne. The cold bit through the thin fabric of her dress and into her thighs, eating through skin, muscle and bone until her teeth clattered.

Occa, on her knees in the corner of the room, watched her with a smirk.

"Eyes on the floor!" Arianh shouted. "Go on, keep scrubbing. If this will be my hall, I want it spotless."

Her sister pouted and resumed her task.

What would Mother think if she could see me now? Arianh wondered. Would the old queen be proud or appalled? She'd probably make a face similar to the one she had just before she died choking on her own vomit. More importantly, what would the Aossi think? Arianh knew she could not rule the Gharb from Aegea, and with the Suzerain gone and the Dharkan on her side, she wouldn't have to; her people could finally move to the settlements, or into the forest if they preferred. Some would even move with her into the Stump, or so she hoped. They'd have to if this would be her new seat of power, and now that the Stump was hers she'd make it a lush and worthy seat for her and her people. Yes, she would.

Sat on the icy throne, Arianh tried to imagine how exactly she would turn a place deprived of life and sunlight into a place suitable for dryads. The Stump was a tree, for sure – it was The Tree, actually – but it was dead. Ice, the whole place was colder and gloomier than a cave. She tapped her lips in thought. *Perhaps flowers would do the trick.* She would ask Gaea to create flowers that require no sunlight. The task shouldn't be a problem for the Goddess of Life, surely. Or she could ask Seshat to put a tiny sun in each room. No... she didn't want to ask the gods for more favours. Maybe Arianh could set up her audiences on the surface and bask while she ruled. Yes, she liked that idea better.

A violent sneeze followed by a full-body shiver brought her back to reality.

This will never do, she decided, standing up. Her backside and hands had gone numb with the cold, and the back of her dress now featured an embarrassing wet patch. Whatever Hel had done to Alek's ostentatious chair made it impossible for her to use it. The cold was more than uncomfortable; it was as if it drained life from her. *No matter. Dryads don't need chairs.* She took in her grim surroundings again: their oppressive design, the rotten stink in the stale air, the specks of dried blood still visible on the walls...

Oh, what the frost am I doing here? she asked herself for the hundredth time. She should be on her way to the Gharb, or out in the Grove, enjoying herself for a change. Instead, she'd chosen to remain. Why? Pride? Fear? Both? She wanted to stay close to the gods, and she couldn't let a Dharkan rule over Aegea, that much was certain. The very idea of it gave her chills. Then again, Alek had been a dryad. He'd also given her chills. Goddess, everything gave her chills these days. She groaned in frustration and moved away from the icy throne.

Her mother and all her training had not prepared Arianh for this. And the truth was, no title, education or willpower would ever put her on equal ground with the Suzerain or the gods.

The gods... what a bunch of idiots! The things she could accomplish if she had their talents, and all they ever did was use them to bicker at each other. Whenever she'd imagined herself amongst the gods, basking in their power, this was definitely not what she had in mind.

What would she do? Allow herself to be their puppet? Absolutely not. As to the Dharkan... She could call herself a queen all she wanted, but she knew that to them she was merely livestock, a pet at most. Uncle had been right. She'd have been in a much better position as Aedan's wife. Sadly, that bird had flown the moment he set his eyes on Ileana. Smart woman. It was as if she knew, of all the Dharkan, that Aedan was the one to enthral. Well, Arianh would be smarter too if she had a goddess guiding her thoughts. It was not fair!

I'll take the Ambrosia, Arianh decided. That would give her some leverage, or time if nothing else. Maybe even turn her into a goddess like it did Psyche. Then she'd be powerful and free from the gods' rule and the Dharkan's hunger. A true queen; an *immortal* queen. If only she could get to it now. But how was she to walk all the way to the forest and beyond alone? She didn't even know the location of the Chronodéndron. Ulla knew… She'd grown up in the forest, but she'd abandoned her. Like her mother and her people and the gods and Aedan and even her uncle had abandoned her. And where the frost was Judoc when she needed him?! The lying metz couldn't wait to get back to his precious temple. The man needed adoration like a dryad needed water. Without it, he'd shrivel up into the weak, insecure boy he really was. They'd all left her to fend for herself alone in this tomb. Goddess, she wanted to scream with frustration.

The teleportation ring lit up, and for a moment the thought that it might be Judoc, finally coming to rescue her, made her heart race. She could almost see him, kneeling at her feet with a declaration of undying love and a promise to never leave her again or even look at another woman.

She all but ran to the light. "Judoc! Oh…" Disappointment cut through her like one of Aedan's freezing moods. "Uncle –" She stopped herself again. This man was not her uncle either.

Agnar blinked at the wall a few times then turned to face her. "Ah, there you are – my queen." He smiled timidly when he bowed his head at her, then waved at Occa. "Hello."

Arianh was not impressed with this Agnar. The man without the god was almost pathetic. His raven hair made him look as distinguished as an old oak, but his skittish, clumsy demeanour and boyish features showed he was no better than a willow sapling.

"Wow," he said, looking about, mouth agape. "I've seen it before but now… it looks so different."

"Better or worse?" Occa asked.

He blinked and scratched his head. "Emptier."

Arianh kicked her sister into silence, who after a moment of glaring hesitation, pouted and continued to scrub the floor. "I think this area is clean, Occa. Move on over there, if you please."

Agnar glanced at both women with a mix of sympathy and pity.

"How did you get one of those?" Arianh referred to the gem key on his forearm.

"Lady Ideth said I could use it."

"Did she." *Lady Ideth takes too much pleasure in aggravating Aedan*, Arianh thought. She often wondered if they'd become lovers, or if the suspicion was just the product of her own lonely imaginings.

"What are you doing here?" she asked Agnar petulantly.

"I wanted to talk to you, dear." He covered his mouth. "Er, apologies, old habits."

"Very well." She beckoned him to move out of Occa's earshot and, remembering the state of her dress, kept facing him, walking backwards. "What do you wish to talk about?"

"I am intrigued by your people, the Aossi. You are dryads, correct?"

She gave him a long-suffering look. "Do I look Narrum to you?"

"You look beautiful to me," he said casually.

Arianh knew for a fact she was beautiful. She had

been praised at length on that account, just never in such an honest, aloof way.

"Er, well. Thank you. What about the Aossi?"

"It's just that I don't remember other dryad tribes besides the Anann."

"Oh. What do you remember?"

They had reached the throne. Instead of sitting, Arianh merely circled around it, always keeping the back of her dress to the wall.

"From my old life, all of it, I think. But how will I ever know for sure if what I remember is all that I knew if I don't know if what I remember is all I used to know?" He giggled to himself. Arianh just stared at the man, convinced his mind was broken. He cleared his throat. "In any case, there is much Odin kept from me. Him-self most of all, and it doesn't help that he thought in the Aesir's language. But over the years I learnt to listen."

"So you speak their language?" Arianh was impressed. She'd lost count of the times her uncle left her out of conversations. The gods' ability to talk without using words was bad enough, but when they purposely used words she did not understand, it was maddening.

"No, I just understand it. It's... how to explain... I still don't know how much I know, if that makes sense. It's like I've been living in a dream. More like a nightmare, if I'm being honest... But I remember you well. Especially in recent times. I've made an effort to be aware whenever we met."

"Why?" Arianh asked. The man could not possibly

be infatuated with her. All she saw when she looked at him was her uncle, and even if she didn't, Agnar was… he was… Well, he was not Judoc.

"You cared for him," Agnar said simply. "Everyone else didn't. Odin was… he was a difficult creature to understand, let's put it that way, and almost impossible to like. His intentions were noble, true; however, the way he did things… well, it often did no one any good."

She waved her hand. "Gods never take into consideration the lives of mortals in their actions."

"I suppose…" Agnar sighed, sounding unconvinced. "But the thing is, even in his mind, the Aossi were a mystery."

"Huh, that is strange…" She considered the throne again and decided to sit on the floor, filthy as it was. Agnar followed suit without taking his eyes from hers, as if pulled by her gravity. "We were brought to this world by the gods, same as the others, I believe."

"Do you know from where?"

"No, I was born here. Even my mother was too young to remember where she came from properly. All I know is that unlike most dryads, she hated the forest. She used to say it was a fake forest with fake trees and a murderous sun." Arianh shrugged. "They always seemed real enough to me. I guess wherever we came from was just better."

"Is that why you live in the Gharb, because your mother disliked the forest?"

His eyes were bright with curiosity. She almost laughed. It was like talking to a child.

"No. We live there because it's the safest place in

Aegea for us. The only way to get in is through a ravine just wide enough for two people abreast. Easy to block. Then two days walk with no shade. But what am I saying? You already know all this. You came from there right? In the future, I mean."

"Yes," he said, looking away in reverie.

"You think the Aossi and the Anann came from different worlds?" she asked.

"Maybe. I'm not so concerned about where the Aossi came from, but where they went." Agnar scratched his head again. Arianh, concerned with the possibility he might have lice, moved away slightly.

"Do you know what happened to your father?" he asked after a short silence.

She laughed. "My mother happened to him. I never met my father. Rumour has it my mother hardly knew him either. All I know is that he was not the same man who sired Occa." *Thankfully*, she almost said, eyeing her sister grudgingly.

It was uncomfortable to think of her mother as a woman. Especially since the old queen had had only one use for men. Arianh tried a similar approach. She picked the best stud in Aegea, but instead of an heir all she got was a broken heart. She shook her head at the realisation. "Why do you ask?"

"You look familiar, that's all." He hesitated, inspecting the throne, then he smiled shyly. "I used to pride myself on knowing all there is to know about this world and the people in it. Of course, this was a scarcely populated world in my time with no history, just stories. One reason I travelled through Yewlow was to see and live its history, confident that I knew it all by heart and would be able to change it. And then when I got here, there was so much I discovered I didn't know. This Tree, your people, the gods. The Suzerain," he added bitterly. "It's the same world, but…. to my mind it isn't, you know?"

She didn't. "Well, I'm sure being taken by a god will play tricks on anyone's mind."

"Indeed… Some of Odin's memories are good, though. Asgard, for example… oh, I wish I had the talent for drawing. There are no words to describe it: the grandeur, the light, the beauty of its halls." Agnar grimaced at the dull grey walls around them, clearly finding them lacking. "It really doesn't compare…" He sighed and fell silent, lost in whatever imagery he saw in his mind.

Arianh began twisting her mouth impatiently. The last thing she wanted to hear about was descriptions of places she'd never see. "Was that all?"

"Pardon? No. I'd like to go to the Grove. I don't like it here."

"You're free to go. You're not a prisoner. Certainly not *my* prisoner." She smiled encouragingly.

"Would you come with me?"

She blinked. *Yes*, she wanted to say. "Why would I?" she said instead.

"You don't belong in here."

"I'm a queen," she said. If she said it often enough, maybe the role would finally fit her. "The gods put me in charge."

He seemed confused. "Is this what you want? To be the dryad queen of the Stump?"

Her lip quivered. "What's wrong with that?"

His eyes opened wide. They were stunningly green. "You're giving the gods exactly what they want. Listen, Odin taught me a few things about how they think. And more importantly, how the Narrum think. When they realise Alek is gone, they'll look for culprits. The most obvious one is the person sitting on his throne. They'll look for someone to follow in his place, and they will never follow a woman. Instead, they'll blame you for their troubles. They'll blame the Aossi. They're killers, you are not. What will you do? Call the gods for help. The gods do nothing for free. It's like it's against their nature or something. The price they demand may be too high for you and your people to pay. I fear that is why I've never heard of the Aossi."

Arianh swallowed. *The gods are not that bad*, she told herself. They barely paid any attention to her or her people. Granted, Hel might want all dryads off her world, but Hades, he doesn't mind, does he? *Nor does he have a say in what Hel does in her own world, no matter how he likes to think otherwise.* No, Chiron definitely cares for the tree huggers. He would not allow the Aossi to be harmed, surely. *Even if he also cares for the Narrum… he cares for them a lot.* And then there's the Dharkan… "Aedan and I are friends," she thought aloud. "He's in love with a dryad. I believe he has no intention of –"

"Perhaps, but Aedan's but one Dharkan," Agnar said. "This is what I know for sure from my own memories: when we arrived at the Gharb, there was no one living there."

She took a shivering breath. "I would love to be anywhere but here. There are so many things I'd like to do; staying here isn't one of them, believe me. But I'm afraid if I leave, that is what destroys the Aossi. I need to be where I can have a say in these troubled times."

"But your instinct tells you to go."

"My instinct is slush," she said, thinking of all the wrong choices she'd made in her life. "I have to trust the knowledge my mother taught me. And I believe she'd have stayed. She'd be sitting on that freezing throne, telling the gods to pull themselves together. She'd make Gaea herself create a forest just for us and have the Dharkan as her personal army against the Narrum. Why can't I do that?"

She had not noticed when she'd begun to cry.

Agnar touched her cheek tenderly. "Come with me."

Mika entered the room. He snarled upon seeing Agnar, and the man shuffled behind Arianh for protection.

"Mika, I thought you'd left with the others," Arianh said, wiping her tears. He wore his boy guise, and the way he looked at her, like a Narrum at a piece of raw meat, was another thing that gave her chills.

"Someone needs to guard this place."

"Gaea should be up at the portal."

"I can smell them," he growled, sniffing the walls.

Occa glared at him. "I'm doing my best, all right? It's not my fault you spread their guts all over —"

"Not them. Behind the walls. In places I can't Reach."

"Who?"

He howled and left. *What a strange creature*, Arianh mused.

Agnar held her hand. "Arianh. I may not know half as much as I thought I did, and what I know challenges my sanity at the best of times, but I do know one thing: you do not belong here. Please, come with me."

"I can't leave. I'm sorry, I just can't. They'd win if I do."

He raked his fingers through his hair again. This time he did it as her uncle used to do when he was frustrated. "We'll come back. Right now, your people need to see you."

"They know I'm here. They know I'm working on their behalf."

"Yes, but they need to know how much you've done for them already. Once they know how much you accomplished, they'll be grateful and come back with you. You need their support."

"You really think they'll come?"

"Of course! You're their queen. They know you can't do everything by yourself, nor should you. But you need to go to them first."

She nodded, dumbstruck that someone finally understood her. "I'll go with you to the Grove and then return..." she said more to herself than him. "I do want to go, Agnar, but I can't be away for too long. In case..." She looked at Occa, who was frowning at her in disbelief.

"We can take a glider." He pointed at his bracelet. "We can go anywhere you want and be back before nightfall. Come on, you deserve it."

"Anywhere?" she asked. *Agnar knows where Yewlow is!*

"Anywhere you want!" he repeated passionately.

She smiled. "Actually, there *is* one place I'd like to go."

CHAPTER FOURTEEN

Hel

Hel left Apollo with his twin, where he could cause no more harm, and willed herself to Hades' quarters in the Underworld. Distraught as she was by the latest events, she did not Reach he had company until she was already inside the room.

"I warned you of the consequences of betrayal!" a woman shrieked in a childish voice. She lay on Hades' bed wearing nothing but her skin, and she was – Hel had to admit – to her what a garden was to a glacier.

The goddess of the dead had never come across that particular soul before – an Olympian soul, of that she was sure, as she was sure she did not give her permission to enter her world.

Equally disturbing was the fact that Hades, also naked on the bed, had a new appearance: dryad-like, with long red hair, jet black skin and smouldering eyes. Hel froze at the sight, and the couple stopped their argument the moment they Reached her presence.

"Oh, look who's here: it's the Aesir bitch."

It took Hel a colossal amount of effort not to pierce

the flowery goddess with a million ice needles. "Hades, who's your charming friend?"

"I'm his wife, Persephone."

Hel blinked.

"I see you forgot to mention to your new captive that you were married, *husband.*"

"More like shackled!" Hades protested.

"And whose fault is that!" Persephone hissed.

Hel thought about the day Hades kidnapped her to the Underworld. How she convinced herself, upon feeling his presence, that he was not there and how she let him take her to his realm, making him believe he took her against her will when in truth she'd wanted to be taken for reasons she'd yet to come to terms with. Up until now she'd been flattered – flattered! – that the Underworld Lord had gone to such lengths to have her attention. When, apparently, he'd risked a lot more than her displeasure.

"I'll take my leave," Persephone said, glaring at Hel. "The room just got too cold for me. I'll be with Medusa. She'll be dying to know the news of the worlds."

"Go! The stars know you'd wither without gossip. I hope a snake bites you in the eye," Hades shouted at her. Persephone vanished with a triumphant smile.

Hel studied Hades with pursed lips, her arms crossed tight against her chest, holding her together. "How long have you been married, Hades?"

"Oh, since before you were born, probably. But who cares about time in the Underworld, right?" he snorted mirthlessly.

"When were you going to tell me?"

"Never, ideally." He covered his face with his hands.

"Huh," Hel said. She felt cold. Cold in a way she never felt before.

Hades peered at her from behind his fingers. "That's it? No insults or attempts to freeze my balls? Hel, just say something please, the silence is creeping me out."

"I'm not sure about the new look," she said casually.

He grimaced. "Believe it or not, this is my real form. The other I wore so I could roam incognito in the forest and keep an eye on the horse. I can go back to satyr, if you prefer, or be invisible altogether. That is my talent, after all. To convince others I don't exist, to the point they can't even see me." He covered his face again. "I'm particularly tempted to use it now."

She left.

'*Hel?*' Hades called after her. She didn't Reach back. The truth was, she had nothing more to say to him.

It was only some time after, when she was assigning new tasks to a group of Dharkan in the Underworld, that she remembered why she'd gone to see Hades in the first place. By then, it was too late. Loki had returned.

CHAPTER FIFTEEN

Loki

Loki found Hel deep beneath the World Tree, where her world and Hades' Underworld met, busily giving orders to a group of Dharkan. She seemed in a terrible mood. Well, so was he.

When she sensed his approach, Hel swivelled her head and put on a smile. "Father, welcome back. What took you so long?"

"I ran into Odin."

The smile vanished.

"So it's true. You let Psyche free his soul."

"I didn't *let* her do anything," Hel snarled. "The woman does whatever she pleases, at least when it comes to souls, anyway." She sighed. "And you should be grateful, for Odin is now under my care. I can do with him as I wish. Or, as *you* wish, Father. Isn't that what you wanted?"

She dismissed the group of Dharkan, who bowed and made their way towards Helheim, looking flushed and highly intoxicated from the heat, while another group prepared to descend to the Underworld's pit.

Loki remained silent long enough to unnerve her.

"Daughter," he said ominously when all Dharkan were out of earshot.

"Father," she replied, eyeing him askance.

"When were you going to tell me about you and Apollo?"

Hel lost her footing on the ice, too attached to gravity to compensate for something as negligible as a slippery surface. To her credit, she recovered both her balance and her wits quickly. "Since when do I need to inform you of my lovers?"

"Since one of them put me in the Underworld for a millennium!" he growled.

Hel froze. Then laughed. "Don't be ridiculous. Why would he do that? *How* would he do that? We both know it was Odin who put you there."

"And he knew very well I was innocent," Loki said sourly. "Had I killed Baldur, I'd not have stuck around waiting for all of Asgard to lynch me. Apollo was there, at the feast, wasn't he? Disguised in one of them." He pointed at the Dharkan. "I remember you brought a group to the contest to prove to the others that even the goddess of the dead could create life – or something like it." He frowned at her creations.

Hel did not contradict him; she had no need to.

Loki gave a mirthless laugh and began pacing the cavern. "I do applaud your audacity to bring an Olympian to Asgard and parade him right under their noses. All these years, even after I've learnt of the extent of the Dharkan's talents, I never figured it out. I knew it had to be someone with access to Asgard but not Asgardian, for all Aesir loved Baldur, even Thor. And Baldur's death was no accident. I always assumed it had been a coup to put me away or revenge for some petty offence. How self-centred of me." Loki's eyes turned a burning blue. "Then Baldur told me it had nothing to do with me. That it had been an act of jealousy. Now, if memory serves me well, Baldur always shone brighter than Apollo. Were I a sun god, that would have made me jealous. But more importantly, it had to be someone who knew about the mistletoe, the only thing that could harm Baldur. Freya wouldn't tell a soul about her lapse in judgement, and I only told you, dearest daughter."

"Oh," she said, the word muffled behind the hand covering her mouth. "Father, I'm so sorry. The whole thing started because of you."

"How so?" he said curtly.

"Apollo and I were… er, talking. He told me about this nymph, Daphne. How Eros made him fall in love with her and then made her hate him using different types of arrows. I wanted to find out more about them, for your sake. Somehow the conversation turned from that to how certain plants can counteract the gods' magic… That's when I told him about the mistletoe. He said he needed to see it. I didn't think much of it at the time, for he does have a thing for herbs and healing." She shook her head. "It was just a prank, something worthy of the Trickster's daughter. How better to repay the way the Aesir always underestimated me than by bringing an Olympian to their palace? I was naive. I'm so sorry, Father."

"What did you find out? About the arrows."

She cringed. "Nothing. He never told me the details, and the matter was forgotten. After Baldur, I encouraged him to get far away from Asgard. I'm so stupid…"

Loki had never raised a hand to any of his children. At that moment, he was tempted.

"But I have something that will make up for it!" Hel said triumphantly.

"It had better be good."

∞

"So this is the Stump…"

Loki ambled across the large common room, shaking his head disapprovingly. It was as if the Nephilim had taken his imagination and tainted it with dullness.

"They want to be like us," Hel said. "This is their idea of how gods live, I suppose."

"They don't think gods have fun? Or an aesthetic sense, at least?" Loki curled his lip. "Do they think we just stand around in empty halls plotting against their pitiful mortal lives?"

"Pretty much, yes. Blame the Olympians for that one."

Loki snorted. "And how's the King of Olympus during these troubled times? Is he enjoying the other side as much as Odin?"

Hel grimaced. "He's not there…"

"Good. He deserves to spend eternity in his own Underworld."

"Er… he's not there either."

Loki frowned. "Then where is he?"

"Well, that's what I'd like to know. He's not in any realm in this world. Even Psyche can't Reach him anywhere. As far as we know, he's not alive nor dead in this Universe."

"Hmm," Loki mused, unconvinced. Gods, unlike most living creatures, don't just disappear when they perish. He suspected perhaps the goddess of the soul hadn't been as diligent in her search as she should have been, or as honest.

"And what was that thing I just put myself through?" He pointed at the dark ring on the floor. He felt diminished, as if it had left a part of him behind.

"A teleportation portal. It moves you from place to place within the Stump, since they can't, well, do it by more natural means."

"Hmm," he said again. His own ability to trans-locate was indeed cut off inside these walls. He tried other abilities: all compromised, except his talent. "Is it like this everywhere inside?" A disturbing thought.

"No. Some places are worse. Come."

∞

Loki's mouth was dry, his hands clammy, and beads of sweat covered his forehead as he stared at the wall with the glowing snake chasing its own tail – a poor choice of insignia, if there ever was one. He hadn't been this uncomfortable since he'd escaped that other snake in the Underworld.

"So this is where you found Zeus?" There was nothing in the small chamber but an awful eerie feel-ing and the snakes glowing at each other in different colours.

"No. Behind this is where we found him." Hel

touched a modified gemstone to the snake's eye, and suddenly the wall moved aside.

"Fuck…" Loki said when the wave of frustration hit him. He had to give it to the Nephilim; they sure knew how to make a god feel powerless. Prometheus would be so impressed.

What he saw afterwards took his breath away.

"What have you done?" Loki murmured, taking a good look at his daughter. He barely recognised the goddess standing in front of him. Without her powers, her true form came through: a creature who was both dead and alive, able to cross both planes of existence at will.

She shrugged. "Well, I had to take Artemis out of that pool eventually, and I couldn't leave Apollo free in the world either, threatening to burn it down, could I? The blue sun was his creation – or should I say, his deception. The sun was only supposed to help sustain the Olympians in Niflheim. But the sun god had other intentions." Hel tutted. "Olympians… you can't live with them, can't deal with them, so why not just put them away? After what you told me about Baldur, I'm glad I did it. Well, he's all yours, Father. You're welcome."

Apollo's eyes widened at the realisation that Loki was aware of his deeds. His sister only glared.

Loki's attention, however, shifted to his son.

Fenrir, also wearing his real form, took up most of the room where Apollo, Artemis, and the Suzerain's daughter hovered next to Zeus and snarled at his father with such aggression, Loki had to force himself to remain calm.

"You have something to say to me, pup?"

"Odin was mine," the wolf growled.

Loki cleared his throat. "He still is. At Ragnarok."

"Ragnarok might have already happened while we're stuck here, for all we know."

True, Loki had to admit. Ever since the Merge, time had been erratic to say the least. And without the World Tree, who knew what might be happening in the other worlds. Still, prophecies like Ragnarok existed outside the whims of time and always came true.

Fenrir moved closer. Loki stood his ground, looking up at him with a slight tilt of his head.

"Don't look at me like that," Loki said, more annoyed at the overall discomfort of the room than intimidated by his monstrous offspring. Fenrir wasn't the most intimidating of his children, especially now that Hel had revealed this whole new side of herself, but he still made an impression. And he had a good reason to be upset.

"You tricked me." The wolf barked.

"You allowed yourself to be tricked!" Loki shouted back at him. "And not by me. Did I touch a hair on Odin's head? No. Was I the one who freed his soul from the dryad's body? No. Is he out of your Reach? No!"

"I'm not going back to the other side," Fenrir stated.

Loki glanced at their audience. "Son, do we have to do this now, here?" Family arguments were a nuisance in private, but when performed in front of enemies, they could be deadly. There was always a risk of saying something they could use against you.

"Yes," Fenrir roared.

"Is this how you thank your sister? Look, she even brought you the huntress!"

"She's a poor replacement," Fenrir said, scowling at Artemis, who all but shrank from his canines. "And what I am supposed to do with them, huh? Their flesh doesn't regenerate well in here. I'll get a couple good bites out of each, at most."

"So just nibble!" Loki massaged his forehead to dissipate the migraine forming behind his eyes. Being a father sometimes felt close to torture.

He left his ferocious pup to his own predatory musings for a moment and turned his attention back to Apollo. "My daughter gave you to me. Jörmungand knows I have reason to take my revenge on you, you bright piece of shit. Just answer me this: Was putting me away part of your plan to get rid of Baldur's light?"

Apollo's eyes burned at Hel before he answered. "It was nothing personal, Trickster. You were just convenient. To be honest, it surprised me how easily everyone believed you were to blame. They all wanted it to have been you, so they could finally put you away for the many crimes you did commit unpunished. Well, here I am, bound and powerless. Have your revenge, coward. I dare you."

Loki grinned. He could take his revenge. There was nothing interfering with his talent inside the room. A good thing, for it allowed him to keep his image intact. He glanced up at Fenrir instead. "I have better things to do than listen to your screams, Apollo. My son, however, shares my dislike for bullies and hunters. And he is in a peckish mood, as you can see. Do you have better things to do, Fenrir?"

"No," the wolf snarled.

Loki made a show of being assaulted by one of Apollo's prophecies, like the Pythias back in ancient Midgard. "I foresee you're about to experience a considerable amount of pain, oh beautiful sun god."

Fenrir licked his lips with a wolfish grin.

"Happy nibbling." Loki winked at his son and turned to leave. He could not stand being inside that room for much longer. Hel was already on the other side of the wall, both halves of her face easy to look at.

"They're coming. Without my sun, they'll erase this world from reality. You'll see it as I have seen," Apollo shouted at them.

"Looking forward to it!" Loki shouted back at him.

"You'll get what you deserve, Trickster." This time Apollo spoke in his oracle's voice, calm and foreboding.

Loki fought to remain with his back turned to the Olympians as the wall closed shut behind him. The last thing he heard was Apollo's triumphant laugher being cut short by Fenrir's growls, but he knew it was too late. The oracle had spoken, and oracles never lied.

"Happy?" Hel asked.

Once free from the suffocating pressure of the vault, Loki let his rage take over and rounded on her.

"You better be prepared for the consequences of what you've done, young lady."

"I am. There's plenty more room in there."

"That's your solution? Hide away your enemies?"

"Why not? Now I have my own private Tartarus." She sounded pleased with herself.

"Nothing stays hidden forever, Hel! Especially not

in Tartarus." Loki often forgot how young Hel was and how little she knew of the monsters of old.

"It doesn't have to be forever. Just until I have my world sorted out."

"You better do it quick, then. Because if Apollo's right..." Loki could not bear to even think about it. "Where are we on the Prometheus situation?"

Hel's face froze in contempt. "Nowhere. We ran into other problems while you were away. They took priority."

"Prometheus *is* the priority!"

"He is *your* priority! Not mine. You leave us alone for an age, then show up, give a bunch of orders and disappear again. I know there is much you're not telling me, father. I know you had something to do with the Nephilim. Don't deny it! Now, I fulfilled our bargain. You hid the blue sun and in return learnt who framed you. We are done! If you want Prometheus free, you must figure that one out with Hades. I'm done with him too! Zeus' death did not release the curse on the Titan, so maybe Psyche can do it. You'll have to ask her. Because the dead know I won't! Owing one favour to that woman is enough. I will not compromise myself with another. Not even for you. So there!" She barked each word in his face with a fury that would put Fenrir to shame. Loki had to take a step back at her every statement. When she finished, he was pressed against the wall.

He could not blame Hel for her choice of priorities, not knowing what he himself had done and how critical Prometheus' freedom was for the future of her world. But he would not be talked at in this way. "Now, you listen to me young lad –"

"I will not! Prometheus, Psyche and the Nephilim are *your* problem. What is that you always told me? 'You have to solve your own problems.' So, grow a pair and solve them!"

Loki blinked. Hel's rage chilled him to the core. He never thought she had it in her, but apparently, of all his children, she turned out to be the most dangerous one. He felt simultaneously proud and intimidated by her anger.

He smiled. "Very well, daughter. Just get me out of this place. I can't stand those damned snakes glowing at me."

∞

Loki could not wait to reach the surface. Not even when he was chained in an Underworld pit with a venomous snake had he felt this claustrophobic. Once outside, he sucked in a lungful of air and let out a mighty breath of relief.

"There's nothing as comforting as breathing, don't you agree, Trickster?" Gaea said in a mocking tone, proud of having spread her affectation to the entire Universe.

Will this day never end? Loki thought.

The mother of life was in much better shape since he'd last seen her. More voluptuous than ever and wearing a gown that seemed to have a life of its own – the Goddess of Life always loved to splurge her talents on such frivolities – she seemed to be inspecting the leaves on Xylo's head, just as a monkey might inspect another for lice. The Suzerain's idea of a Jötunn was not enjoying the attention one bit, judging by the way he glared at her.

"Gaea," Loki grumbled, not bothering with Reach. "I can't deal with you right now." This new turn of events with Hel and Apollo had not been part of his plans. He had to think.

Gaea stopped her prodding and was about to speak when Hel intervened.

"Any new activity?" she asked her.

Gaea took a deep breath. "The ring rumbles and glows occasionally. Nothing even a talentless god can't handle. Seriously, Hel, as if keeping Niflheim habitable isn't enough, do you need to insult me further with this minor task? I have more important work to do."

"It was no minor task earlier," Hel said bitterly.

"For you, maybe."

"Where's Oreth?" Hel asked, pointedly ignoring Gaea's smug comment.

"I put him back in the cell," Ideth said grudgingly. "He was upsetting the *great Mother*."

"I had to teach this girl a few things about motherhood," Gaea stated in her matronly tone.

"Yes. The Goddess was just explaining to me how Life ends the moment motherhood begins," Ideth sneered.

"Oh, so you were paying attention," Gaea sneered back.

Ideth faked a smile. Dangling her feet off the edge, she looked about ready to jump off the Stump just to get away from Gaea's preachings. Loki could relate.

"Hel, I demand to see Psyche – now. Bring her up," Gaea commanded.

"Again? You've got nothing from her the previous times."

"I will now."

Hel rolled her eyes. "She can't tell you what she doesn't know, and even if she did, she made it perfectly clear that she won't speak to you. Besides, you created the flaming resin. You should have known what sort of effect it would have on mortals."

"She'll talk this time," Gaea insisted.

Cold spread through them. "Why?"

"Because he's here." Gaea grinned at Loki. *'Oh yes, Trickster. The Underworld vacation is over. You will have to deal with me now.'*

"Well, Psyche's not here," Hel said, unaware of the savagery taking place through her elders' Reach.

"What? Where is she?" Loki asked, feeling faint.

"I've sent her to the Blacksmith. Hades said –"

"Alone?!"

"Of course not, Aedan went with her."

"Fuck! When did they leave? Never mind that. Where are they now?"

"Why? Father, what is it?"

"Where are they now?"

Hel closed her eyes and frowned. "On their way to the Lake... Still? Burn them. Why are they on foot?"

Loki didn't care. He took the information and left, hoping that this once he wouldn't be too late.

CHAPTER SIXTEEN

Hades

Hades knew Hel was there even before he Reached her. The Aesir goddess's presence was like a breath of fresh air in the stuffy Underworld. He wished he could breathe her in for eternity.

"Leave, now!" Hades hissed at Persephone, who was still on his bed, berating him for every grievance their marriage caused her.

"I warned you of the consequences of betrayal!" she shrieked, then turned to stare at the goddess of the dead.

"Oh, look who's here: it's the Aesir bitch," Persephone said with causal spitefulness.

"Hades, who's your charming friend?" Hel asked coldly.

Lying naked on a bed of crushed rose petals next to another goddess, Hades knew the truth would be as bad as any lie, and so he remained silent.

"I'm his wife, Persephone."

In all the millennia they'd been married, Hades had never heard her say the word *wife* with pride before.

He expected the room to freeze, maybe even the whole Underworld, but Hel just blinked. Cerberus breath, that was much worse.

The Aesir goddess stood there with her arms crossed for long moments after Persephone had left, while he answered her questions and babbled nonsense to fill in the silence that followed them.

"Will you just say something," he pleaded. The silence was crushing him more than the shame. For the first time since they'd met, he actually felt hot in her presence. *Why isn't she freezing something?*

"I'm not sure about the new look," she finally said, tilting her head.

He explained that this was his true form, but that he would change to any form that would please her. He'd do anything to please her, he realised with mixed and extremely intense feelings. She only grunted, turned around and left.

'*Hel?*' he Reached. There was no answer.

He was about to follow her when a tremendous disturbance shook the Underworld.

"No. No, this can't be happening!"

The wave broke through the fabric of his being as if reality itself had fractured. He'd never experienced that before, but he knew exactly what it meant: Tartarus had been breached.

∞

Hades found Hel atop the Stump with Gaea and Ideth. No sign of Loki. That was a relief. Hades knew there was no way he could hide the events that took place in the Underworld from the Trickster. He would have to know, sooner or later. *Later*, Hades decided. First he had to make amends with Hel.

"My lady, thank the fates, I've been looking all over for you. We need to talk."

"We have nothing to talk about. Go back to your wife, *Olympian*," she said. The heat in her voice chilled him more thoroughly than any of her freezing moods had.

"Yes, we do." Hades pulled her aside, half expecting Gaea to intervene in Hel's defence, but the Mother of Life appeared to be entranced, staring up at Xylo alongside Ideth like thralls to their master. He tried to Reach them and found nothing. It was like their minds weren't even there. "What's the matter with them?"

"I'm not sure… They were fine a moment ago." Hel moved closer to the trio with her eyes closed. "They seem to be having a private conversation of sorts. I cannot Reach any of it. Gaea, whatever you're doing, stop it. It's not funny!"

Hades probed Gaea. Nothing. He passed a hand across Ideth's eyes. Nothing. He shouted at both, and Xylo turned an eerie gaze in his direction. Hades instinctively took a step back. "Maybe we should give them a moment."

He dragged Hel down the ramp, feeling somewhat safer inside the Stump than on the surface with the entranced trio. She followed, struggling half-heartedly against his pull.

"This is far enough! Father or Aedan might need to Reach me."

"Hel, I know you're angry at me – and you have every right to be – but I need to tell you something important. You will not like it, but please just hear me out."

"There's no need. I already know kidnapping is common practice for you."

"Who would come to the Underworld of their own free will?" Hades replied, furious with himself for not telling her of Persephone sooner. Well, Psyche had gone to the Underworld of her own free will, true, but the goddess of the soul was not a good example to present to Hel at the moment. "And I didn't kidnap you, no more than Paris kidnapped Helen. I can be charming, when the occasion calls for it." He tried some of that charm and got a scowl in return. "You could have left at any time."

"Could she?" Hel asked.

He grimaced. "No. Her binding is real. I knew she'd leave me otherwise."

"Release her!" Hel demanded.

"I can't. The seed is forever. Even if you unleashed your Dharkan on me, she'd still be bound to the Underworld. You think I'd still exist if destroying me freed the souls in there? Persephone herself would have iced me long ago."

"I might still unleash them on principle," Hel hissed with a glimpse of her playful coldness.

"No, you won't. I know how much you care for the dead. And me. Just a little?"

"No, I don't. And I told you, I don't like that new look either."

"Why not?"

"It's too… too… dark," she said, biting her lip.

He grinned. "I see." He kissed her. A risky move, but the right one.

"I'm not asking you to forgive me just yet. I have more bad news and… I need to ask a favour of you."

"You've got some nerve."

"You wouldn't like me half as much if I didn't." He smirked.

"Ask."

"Persephone arrived here with Apollo. Now, you wouldn't know where he is, would you?"

"Me? Why would I know?"

"You can find out the whereabouts of every free god in this world, can't you? A sun god shouldn't be hard to find."

Hel fiddled with her earlobe. "No… He must have dropped her off and left while I was inside with Father and Fenrir, studying the vault. I never Reached a thing."

"Huh…"

"What?"

"Nothing. Just… you're lying," he said.

She cursed. "He's with his sister, all right? Now, don't ask me more than that."

"You iced Apollo?!" Hades was so aroused he could have made love with her right there.

"Not exactly. Drop it. I mean it. What's the bad news?"

The passion drained from him. "Right… so, you know my bitch of a wife?" Hel froze. He inhaled the cold air with delight before continuing. "She broke into Tartarus and took blood from the Hydra. She

must have convinced Medusa to help her somehow."
He shook his head. "Poor Medusa."

Hel shrugged. "What's a Hydra?"

"You've never heard of the Hydra? A serpent with
many heads."

"No. Have you heard of my brother, Jörmungand?"

Hades blinked. "The world serpent is your *brother*?
Cerberus breath. You must explain your family to me
one day."

"The Hydra…" Hel prompted.

"Right. Long story short: the Hydra's blood will
make any god mortal."

Hel laughed. "That's not possible."

"It is. Trust me. And Persephone now has a box
filled with it. I'm afraid you're in danger."

"Well, well. Is that so?" Xylo said.

CHAPTER SEVENTEEN

Chiron

Chiron arrived at the cabin with a heavy heart and Bertho's head in his hands.

He didn't know what to say to Martha. In these situations he wished humans could Reach, for words alone were not enough to express how he felt. Certainly not enough to offer comfort, let alone explain the circumstances of the hunter's death.

Martha, like all humans living in the forest, knew about the gods' existence, but she didn't know much about their pantheons, their legendary grudges, nor all the things they were capable of when fighting each other. Chiron always made sure humans saw the gods, the Olympian gods especially, as friends in Aegea. To the point he now suspected many thought of him and Pan, and even Artemis, as something closer to intelligent animals than deities, which was fine, he supposed. Let the Narrum think of the Suzerain and the Aesir as the evil gods and of them as the benevolent forces of nature they should respect and obey.

Martha was busy stretching an apron across the

washing line while Ben ran around the front of the house, tormenting the chickens.

"Xiroon!" the boy screamed when he saw him.

"Hello, young man. What is this?"

The boy held a miniature crossbow in his hand. By the intricate detail of the mechanism, Chiron could tell it was not just a toy.

The centaur frowned. "Where did you get this?"

"Mine!" the child screamed, running away before the centaur could take the crossbow from him.

Chiron tried not to take offence. Being a friend to mortals had its disadvantages, like not being given due respect sometimes. Children, in particular, required a lot of patience in that department.

Martha stopped her work to watch him, unsmiling. Not that she ever smiled as a rule, but her expression was definitely more forlorn than usual. Her eyes, sunken with grief, settled on the bundle in Chiron's possession.

She knows. "Martha I –"

She silenced him with an impatient gesture and took the bundle, unfolding the cloth carefully with shaky hands.

"I advise you not to," he said.

"I have to see him."

Chiron had eliminated the rotten smell and arrested the decay with his will, but he'd been unable to reverse the damage done to Bertho's flesh for it had been done by Fenrir.

Martha stared into the skinless, half-eaten face of what used to be her husband for a long moment. Motionless, expressionless, silent.

"My condolences," Chiron said. It was the appropriate thing to say, he knew. But what he'd really like to say was something like: 'He should never have joined Artemis.'

Martha gave out a single sob, then wrapped the head again carefully and placed it on the table, out of arm's length from Ben, who was getting curious about it.

"Where is the rest of him?" she asked.

"You really don't want to –" He stopped himself. "I sent him down the river," Chiron lied. The truth was, he couldn't even bring himself to bury the man. Chiron stopped feeling sorry for Bertho once he learnt about what he did to Cornus. To kill an Elysian horse? Just the thought made him mad. He did feel genuinely sorry for his family, however.

Martha's chest rose and fell alarmingly before she pointed an index finger at him. If there was something about Narrum females that deeply unsettled Chiron when they got angry, it was that finger.

"You promised us safety. Yet you'd always choose the gods and the dryads over us!"

Chiron reared on his hind legs to keep some distance from the accusatory digit. "That is not true!"

"Ruling the forest is all you ever wanted, *Titan!*" She spat the word with loathing.

Well, that *was* true, he had to admit, but not the cause of Bertho's untimely death. And how did she even know he was a Titan?

"How are you so well informed about the gods and what I want, Martha?" Last he checked, Artemis was still frozen in that pool. He hoped Hel would leave her there a while longer. At least until he could clean up her mess and his name in the forest, which apparently would take a lot more work than he previously thought.

"Ulcan told me everything," she said.

"Everything?!" What did the snake hunter know about *anything*? He hadn't even seen the hunter in years, not since he had to heal his liver, ravaged from a lifetime of excess drinking. He'd presumed the man dead already.

"He gave me this," Ben said proudly. He now had a tiny arrow cocked in the crossbow.

"Give me that. It is not a toy – ow!"

The small arrow hit him above the knee of his back leg with just enough force to pierce the skin. Blood welled around the metal tip, and suddenly Chiron's entire sense of reality changed.

"Oh no," he said, the way Ideth often did when she was in trouble. It felt like such a silly thing to say, as if denying something would make it go away somehow. He looked down at the child, who was jumping in arcs of joy, thrilled with his accomplishment. Then to Martha, slightly embarrassed by her son's behaviour but still oozing righteousness and resentment. He saw how small and ignorant and ungrateful they both were. How wishing for gratitude from these flawed mortals had been a mistake. Ideth had been right all along: Narrum were sick creatures. They would never learn; they would never appreciate gods like him and all they could do for them.

And they would not grieve him either.

Chiron tried to end their lives there and then, but

he had no power to do it. The Hydra's poison acted fast, too fast. His back legs collapsed first, then his whole body tumbled over to the ground.

Martha abandoned her anger to kneel by his side. "Lord, what's wrong?"

Ben, fed up with trying to cock another arrow in place, just stabbed it straight into Chiron's exposed flank, laughing. "Mum, Mum, look, I got him. I'm the best hunter in the forest, like Dad."

Chiron was forced to breathe through the pain. His lungs demanded it. An intoxicating scent of over-ripe roses and jasmine pierced his senses.

"You…" he croaked. Then they came. And the next thing he heard was Martha's dying scream.

INTERLUDE 8

Boiled Up

"Who's Iva?" Psyche asks.

The name triggers instant hostility. Sparks crackle between my fingers, and I clench my hands into fists. "Where did you hear that name?"

"It's on everyone's mind: yours, the hunter, Jonas, even the poor drunk man by the fireplace. She's quite the popular girl, it seems."

"Humph." I do not wish to say more, but Psyche's curiosity is a thorn about to pierce my skull.

"She used to be a friend."

"Used to? Oh, a special friend," she teases.

I glare at her.

"That's a yes, then."

"That we were once lovers is neither here nor there." I see the goddess smirking through the corner of my eye. "It's a long and complicated story," I explain.

"Great! We still have a whole day of walking ahead of us. By all means, entertain me with your story."

I grind my jaw tight. The last thing I want to do

is talk – especially about Iva. But I know if I remain silent, Psyche will just keep poking my mind, and I don't want her finding the wrong answers.

"We grew up together. When the Merge happened, the world burst with energy, and for the first time in memory we could stray from the world's core and venture to the surface. It was bliss. Then the living came and, with them, Prana. The Dharkan were of different opinions on how to deal with this new source of sustenance. Some believed, Iva included, the gods put the living here to serve and feed us. It's because of her they now burn Dharkan in the settlements. Icing the Suzerain was her idea; the failed attempt her fault. She escaped. My brothers and I paid the cost. I haven't returned to the Shadow since. It seems she's been busy in my absence gathering followers. They call themselves the faithless. She wants to rule Aegea, as Hel rules Niflheim. The end."

Psyche's expression remains blank. "A long and complicated story, you said." She half shakes her head. "You explained it quite well, thank you. So Iva developed a taste for the living, the same as you did for gods. I see."

"You see nothing!" I growl. After what I did to Jonas, her judgemental ignorance burns me deep. "What do you know of the Dharkan? How can you understand our needs, our ways, let alone our disagreements? How can you, not even a natural-born goddess, understand what Prana is to us? What it *does* to us? I do not pretend to understand why your kind eats some flesh raw, other roasted or boiled. Or why you name your meals. Breakfast, lunch, dinner; do they taste any different or nourish you in different ways depending on where the sun is in the sky when you eat?"

She opens her mouth then closes it again, pressing her lips tight together. "Perhaps if I understand, I can help."

"You can help by dealing with the Blacksmith. I'll deal with Iva."

She chews on her cheek for a moment, then cocks an eyebrow. I walk away before she has a chance to utter the sort of obnoxious comment that normally follows such affectation.

"Her name was also in Ileana's mind," she calls after me.

I freeze.

∞

Aedan stomps in my direction, a large bulk of freezing fury crushing the ferns in his path. It takes a considerable amount of courage not to recoil from the Dharkan.

As is his habit, he roughly grabs me by the shoulders and shakes hard enough to break bone. "That is not true. You lie! I have never mentioned Iva to Ileana. She could not have known. You broke into my mind, you –"

I push him away, thankful for my perks as a deity, for the Dharkan might actually kill me during one of his anger outbursts without them.

"'Iva and the oracle'," I say, and see Aedan has no idea what I'm talking about. "That's who Ileana blamed for the destruction of Aegea. I didn't know who Iva was or what oracle. I always assumed she was a Narrum. After all, there were no Dharkan in Ileana's

time. Oh, forget it, maybe the name is just a coincidence."

"What else?" he demands, unconvinced.

"There's nothing else. I don't even know why
Ileana blamed them, or what they did exactly. The
name first appears in one of Ileana's childhood memories – which, by the way, are the only ones I have of her
I trust – as part of a legend told to her by her uncle."

"Then you've lied to me again. You said you remembered everything!"

I bite my bottom lip. *Fuck...* "I didn't lie. Not exactly. I remember her thought process, her feelings
and personality. Her actual memories are not so clear.
There are fragments here and there I still struggle to
make sense of. It's hard to distinguish what is a real
memory and what is a story she told herself. Only the
memories infused with a strong emotion are clear.
And she had a whole array of strong emotions associated with Iva."

"You lied... All you do is lie. Why?" He looks so
sad when he asks this. Outrage is all that's keeping
him together.

"Because the truth is..." I sigh. "No one really
wants to know the truth. They think they do, but truth
is often either painful or disappointing. That's why
we tell stories to ourselves and others. "And how can
I be sure if what I know is the truth when it's based
on second-hand memories tangled up with conflict-
ing emotions? That is not truth. At least not a truth
I can trust. Now, events are better than truths. I can
work with events. From what you said, your former
friend Iva is about to do something memorable. And

if there's one thing I remember clearly, it's how this world ends." I touch his arm. "Aedan, for all our sakes, you have to stop her."

"What do you think I'm doing?" he growls, back to being furious. "Iva's up at the Boiling Lake, ready to launch an invasion on Aegea. I will drag her back to the Shadow by myself if I have to."

"Help," says a feeble voice.

Lightning bursts from the Dharkan through my arm, and I yelp at the pain. The jolt makes me bite my tongue. Had I been mortal it would have stopped my heart.

"Who's there?" he asks, sparks in hand.

"Over here," I say, Reaching beyond the trees and cursing the volatile creature. As if freezing was not bad enough, now he has the power to literally shock everyone with his touch as well. Going like this, no mortal or deity will be safe from the man's temper.

I follow my Reach to a nearby stream where a naiad lies partially submerged in a small pool.

Stars! I remember her from the first day I arrived in Aegea. "Agua." I move the hair off her face, and she blinks her full black eyes at me.

"Do I know you?" she asks.

I shake my head, and truth be told I don't know her either. "What happened?"

Her gaze falls on the Dharkan, and she raises her hand to point at him. "Help me," she says.

"I won't let him harm you, I promise."

Agua looks back at me, confused.

Aedan dips one hand in the pool and cools the water around her. The naiad sighs in relief and submerges deeper into the pool. "Thank you," she says to him. The Dharkan shoots me a pointed glare.

"I'm sorry I haven't been there, friend," he says to her. "Aecius…"

"I know," Agua says. "News travels faster through water than land. He will be missed."

"Why are you so close to the Lake?"

"I was foolish. I thought your victory meant the Dharkan were there to make things right with the world. I was wrong." She winces and stares back at me. "Was I wrong about you too, Aedan?"

"No. But I can't stay."

She nods. "It's too late anyway. Thank you for not letting me die in pain."

"Plenty of frozen lakes in Helheim," Aedan says with what sounds surprisingly like compassion.

Agua smiles at him. "If only your gods welcomed Olympians in their realms."

"That will change," he says, avoiding her gaze.

Agua shakes her head. "Perhaps. I just wish things went back to what they were," she says miserably.

"They will. Just hold on." Aedan pats her hand fondly, then begins to freeze the pool's surface. Agua gasps and submerges completely, out of sight and out of Reach.

"What just happened?" I ask, unable to make heads or tails of their exchange.

"As I said, goddess of the soul, there is a lot about the Dharkan you do not understand. Let's go."

∞

We resume walking up the hill, towards the dense canopies and the mists.

The Dharkan stops, turns and clenches his jaw a few times, then drops his head, looking almost vulnerable as he speaks. "I know you're still hiding the truth. I don't know why. And I won't host you to find out. Not ever. No, don't try to convince me it's for my own good; you care for no one's good but your own. Just answer me one thing: Will I see Ileana alive again?"

I bite my cheek. "That depends. How long can you wait?"

"However long it takes. I can wait on the other side. Hel would not deny me that, I think."

"The thing is, there is no other side in Ileana's future. No gods, no Dharkan, not even cockroaches. And it seems it all starts with this Iva of yours. Perhaps if you were more forthcoming yourself, I could help."

I hear his teeth grind. "You accuse me of lying?"

"Yes, I do. Can you look me in the eye and tell me you're not hiding something yourself? For example, how can the Dharkan cross realms if they have no soul? And what just happened back there?"

I think for sure his teeth must crack under the pressure of his jaws. "There are things a Dharkan can't share. We are bound to our gods."

"And I am a goddess. If I say there are things I cannot tell you, then trust me, I cannot."

"I'll never trust you."

He walks away.

Fair enough, I think. Some days I barely trust myself, but this will get us nowhere. I take a deep breath and walk after him, for what else is there to do. I can't just tell him what I know. Even if it were what he wants to hear, it's never wise to play the oracle. Anything I tell Aedan about the future will only make it more likely to come to pass, for the more you try to avoid something, the closer you get to it. No. I need to focus on my own predicament and let events in Aegea unfold as they must. I've done too much harm already by aiding Ileana in killing her father.

I catch the scent of sulphur just before sunset, and shortly after, we're wrapped in the Boiling Lake's mists. I'd be blind without my Reach, and Aedan, whose night vision cannot penetrate the dense vapour clouds, would be blind without me. Not that he will ever admit it, of course. He walks slightly behind me, squinting and scowling at the trees as if they offend him.

I remember the first time I arrived in this strange world, powerless and wearing a stranger's body. Ileana's senses were so acute, tailored to appreciate the beauty of the forest green, the diversity of sounds produced by its vibrant life, to revel in its many scents. Everything looked perfect. This time, I'm able to Reach the forest's true colours, its miasma and how thin the layer between it and the Underworld really is. I can see all the creatures previously hidden from Ileana's senses. They are many, all around us, curious and so terrified. Damaged souls with barely any will left in them, but smart enough to hide from our path.

This is indeed a cursed world.

We arrive at the lake. Dozens of Dharkan – tall, stern faced, with long, ghostly white hair and all clad in black leather – are gathered at its shore.

"Hmm. Who'd have thought you're actually the cheerful one," I say in a light-hearted attempt to lift the Dharkan's mood. Aedan gives me a sour look in reply. I sigh and consider our distance along with the poor concealment of the vegetation between us and them. "Is this too close? Can they see us?"

Aedan squints. "It's far enough. I can't see them properly, so they can't see me either. What can you see?"

"Everything," I reply with my eyes closed.

"What are they doing?"

"Nothing. They are just standing there. Is that normal?"

"Yes. They are waiting."

"For what?"

A figure separates from the ranks. As tall as the others and similarly fashioned, she has androgynous features, but I can tell she's female by the sway of her hips. She addresses her audience with purposeful and expansive body language, uncommon for a Dharkan.

"That's Iva," Aedan grunts unnecessarily. "Look at her," he tuts. "She always liked to dictate."

That might be so. There is, however, something different about her from the other Dharkan. Something other than vitality. I turn my gaze to the Dharkan next to me, not liking the similarities I see.

"Is she, er... royalty, like you – prince?"

His silver eyes narrow askance. "No. My father spoke for the Dharkan, but he was no king. Humph. Odin likes to simplify things in his terms. We have no royalty as your people understand it. I'm my father's eldest son, but I have no right nor desire to take his place. My brother, Emil, will probably do it. Burn me! That's him, over there. He… he's changed."

The man standing next to Iva is a near identical copy of Aedan, minus the scars and a few pounds of muscle.

"Changed how?"

"He's a man now." Aedan shakes his head as if it's an offence to his own manhood. At least some things are common across the different races. "Burn her, she's gotten to him too! Foolish boy."

I cock an eyebrow at that. He looks no fool at all. Unlike the others, he is, if Reach does not deceive me, smirking at Iva's speech.

"What's she saying?" Aedan asks.

"Oh… something like: 'We'll take what's ours, feed our hunger, show the gods what we are made of, blah blah.' Unlike you, she seems to enjoy telling short, simple stories at length and with many complicated words."

His scarred face twitches into a smile.

"What's this about women and children?"

Before Aedan can give me an answer, a woman with flawless dryad-like features and long strawberry-blond hair comes into view, clad only in flowers and leaving a trail of petals in her wake.

"Wow. Who is she?" Aedan asks, wonderment in his voice.

While Iva looks like a spectre, seemingly ethereal under the starlight, Persephone looks every bit the goddess she is. She could define feminine beauty. In fact, her beauty is so coveted, Aphrodite once made me go to the Underworld to fetch some of it for herself. Something I'm sure she bitterly regretted afterwards.

"That's Persephone, Olympian goddess of spring. Her beauty matches the ugliness of her soul," I warn him.

"Olympian? What is she doing there, with *them*?"

"I have no idea."

I'd sensed Persephone's soul when I was still at the Stump and didn't think much of it. She's the queen of the Underworld, after all. But to find her there, amongst the Dharkan, that's a surprise. Whatever the reason is, it can't be a good one. "Oh fuck, I should not be here, she might be able to Reach me." It's too late to hide, even if there was anywhere to hide, and if Persephone can Reach me, she doesn't let it show. This has to be a trap.

"Is she your friend?" Aedan asks.

"She's Hades' wife."

"Can't you stop lying for one moment, woman?"

He's about to protest further, and I shush him. "It's the fucking truth," I hiss.

Aedan gapes back at me. "Hades is married?"

"Yes. Be quiet."

"Does Hel know?"

I glare at him to be silent, and for once, it works.

Persephone and Iva embrace like old friends, then the goddess conjures a small box into existence and presents it to the Dharkan.

"What's that?" Aedan asks.

"A box," I whisper.

"I can see it's a box. What's in it?"

"I don't know! She can confine anything inside a box, beyond anyone's Reach. It's her talent."

∞

The mist thins enough for me to see as Persefore, or whatever her name is, presents Iva with a small black box. Iva bows – bows! – to the Olympian goddess as she takes it, then lifts it above her head for all Dharkan to see. They cheer. *Burn the Olympians.* You cut one down and two take their place.

"I'm putting an end to this right now," I say, standing up.

"Aedan, wait. You need to pray to Hel. Tell her…" Psyche hesitates, chewing her cheek. "Fuck. Just tell her what's happening."

"I can't tell her about this!"

"She needs to know, and we need her help."

"No, we don't. These are my people, my problem. Hel sent me here to solve it. That's what I'll do."

"You're fighting them all by yourself?"

"If I have to!"

Psyche, her attention divided between me and the other Dharkan, is not as confident as I am.

"Don't be stupid, Aedan. Persephone might not even be the only deity there," she whispers, a hint of apprehension in her tone.

I sometimes wish I possessed this ability the gods call Reach. Not right now. The more you know about something, the less resolute you become. Hesitation can be as fatal as recklessness.

"Do you Reach other gods besides her?"

Psyche gnaws at her cheek again. "No… maybe… How can you tell when a Dharkan is hosting one?"

"You ask him," I say dryly. She just frowns at me. "Don't worry. The Dharkan won't harm me, not even possessed by the will of a god. We are vessels, not puppets, and if the Olympian interferes, I'll ice her. You either come with me now or go convince the Blacksmith to help us with the portal. Whatever happens, we won't return to Hel empty-handed, understand?"

Psyche's face tells me she'd rather swim in the Boiling Lake than come with me. I can't blame her. Were I a god, I wouldn't come close to this many Dharkan either. *Why does Persephone?* I wonder. Is she a fool or just ignorant? This is a trap, if ever there was one, but I'll be burned if I'll just stand here and watch.

"I'm coming with you," Psyche says half-heartedly, and I sense actual fear from her. Her fear gives me pause. I know I can protect myself, but will I be able to protect her from my brothers? Would I even want to at this point?

"No. I'll do this alone," I decide. "Stay here." To my astonishment, Psyche nods and does as she's told for once.

I march towards the lake's shore, angry enough to freeze it and the Olympian goddess both. Iva sees me before I can do either and grins.

"Aedan. I'm so glad you finálly decided to join us. I expected you sooner. You almost missed the best part."

"I missed nothing. What do you think you're doing, Iva?" Sparks crack between my fingers.

She shifts her attention to them, a smirk on her lips. "I see you found new ways to express your anger."

I ignore her comment. "Iva, being faithless is one thing, putting your faith in this Olympian creature, quite another. Goddess of spring, is it?"

Persephone pouts with amusement. It's like her full lips were designed for that very purpose, making her both irresistible and highly intimidating. "So this is the mighty Aedan, murderer of Zeus. How delightful." She smiles, and the momentary spell she had on me breaks. There's no warmth or beauty in that smile, just meanness. "Well, Aedan, you have my thanks for accomplishing something my family never even came close to achieving."

Suddenly it all becomes clear. While Hades seduced Hel, his wife seduced the Dharkan. With Zeus gone, they'd have the world to rule by themselves. And Psyche knew it. She mentioned spring back at the Stump. I glance back at the trees. Sure enough, she's no longer there. I curse myself for being so wrapped up in my own grief and need for answers that I did not see their plot sooner.

"Hello, brother."

I glare at the young man standing behind the Olympian goddess. "Emil. What are you doing? What possessed you to join this madness. If our father could see you here –"

He laughs. "Good thing Father can't see much of anything anymore."

"How dare you? He burned for us! The fight with the Suzerain and the living is over, brother. We won. There's no need for this."

"You call this a victory?" Iva says. "Look around you. We're all that's left."

I blink. "How?"

"Hel called the rest of our people to the Underworld to work as slaves for her lover. They haven't returned. Oh, I see the icy goddess forgot to tell you about it."

"It's true. There are more Dharkan than Titans in the Underworld right now," Persephone says maliciously.

She had to! I think. "You're insane," I say to both women.

"You iced the King of Olympus, *brother*, so don't you dare lecture them on sanity." Emil's words burn with hate.

My brother would never care if I iced the entire Olympian pantheon, and he would never talk to me this way either. Emil is a man now, far from the shy boy I left in the Shadow, but he is more than that. He's too confident in speech and posture. No one matures this fast. "Are you hosting, brother?"

"Oh, Aedan," Iva says in a condescending tone. "We are taking our world back, with or without you. Personally, I'd rather it was with you. You brought down the Suzerain after all, and the sad fact is" – she lowers her voice close to my ear – "I know they'd all rather follow you than me."

I lean away from her. "I didn't do it for them. And I don't want to be *followed*."

"I know. You did it for yourself and for a *girl*." The contempt in her voice burns each word. *You couldn't do it for me, but you did it for* her, her tone said more clearly than her words. "You're weak, Aedan. Your motives are weak. We are your people! Not them." She points out at Aegea. "What can the dryads give you, huh? Do you really want to spend your days in the sun and the nights atop a tree? You're one of us; you belong with us in the shade. This is our world, not theirs."

"Careful, girl. I understand the need to boast during a lovers' spat, but this is not what we agreed," Hades' wife says.

A glance passes between Iva and Emil, and he seizes Persephone from behind.

"Hey! Take your hands off me, how dare –" Alarm suddenly bursts through her. "You!"

"Me." Emil smiles and nibbles at her ear. There is something simultaneously erotic and revolting in the act.

"Everyone stand back," Iva orders the other Dharkan.

The goddess of spring struggles in Emil's grip, but he has his arms locked tight around her. Still, she's a goddess. She should be able to overcome him. *But not if he's hosting.* "Apollo will be here any moment! He'll burn you all to ashes!" she cries out. Everyone laughs except me. I have no idea who she's talking about, and I'm far from amused by her threat.

"You cannot do this. We had a deal. You promised!" Persephone shrieks.

The rose petals on her dress wither as Iva steps closer. "I'm not a goddess, as you often like to point out. I don't make deals. My promises mean ash. Aedan, behold: this is the best part."

Iva wraps both her hands around Persephone's neck and feeds.

For a moment I just stand there, torn between horror and jealousy. I want to join Iva, to feed on the goddess's Prana. I can almost taste it, but Iva's not just feeding on Persephone, she's killing her. I didn't know the Suzerain was linked to Zeus when I iced him, and however right it felt in the moment, I know it was wrong. The dead god's power roars in me in protest, and without further thought, I pour it into one mighty lightning bolt and bring it down on Iva. She screams as she's thrown to the ground billowing smoke. Half her clothes have burned away, exposing the scorched flesh beneath. *I'm sorry*, I almost say, but in truth I relish the pleasure along with the shame of my action, standing over her, triumphant. Persephone still lives, gasping in Emil's arms.

He whistles. "Not bad, *brother*. You finally learnt to cast it properly. Well done."

At our feet, Iva coughs and moans. *It's not possible.* She rolls over and sweeps my legs from under me, and before I can react, she has a dagger against my throat.

"You're not the only special one, lover," she hisses, smoke billowing out of her mouth.

The bolt I brought down was strong enough to burn any mortal, and yet Iva's not only alive but healing before my eyes. She sees the surprise on my face and laughs.

"Burn me, that hurt," Iva croaks to the other Dharkan. "I think I lost my appetite. She's all yours."

I glance up at Persephone, still breathing, still struggling, her eyes wide with terror. Emil hushes her, showing no effort to restrain her and no emotion either.

The Dharkan advance slowly as one. I recognise them all. They were once my friends, once loyal to Hel and my father. And I also recognise the hunger in their eyes. They swarm on the Olympian, her screams muffled by the frenzy of their feeding. When they finish, all that's left of the goddess of spring is a scattered pile of frozen petals melting on the hot rock. Emil, the only one who didn't feed, turns on his heel and walks away, whistling to himself with the black box in his hand.

"And now we are all special." Iva traces the thick scar on my cheek, then stands up with difficulty, cursing at the state of her clothes and skin alike.

The Dharkan don't look special; they look drunk, laughing and dancing gleefully. They are different all right, more active, louder. *More alive.*

"You think Hel will reward you for this?" I ask Iva.

She laughs. "Oh, Aedan, Hel would never punish us for ridding the world of one of them. Just because you're her favourite doesn't mean she doesn't love us too or us her. We would never act against our gods."

"So, you're saying this was her plan?"

Could Hel have known of the Olympians' deception all along and played us to have her revenge? That, too, would make sense.

"No, Dharkan. It is *my* plan." Iva's voice changed, and her eyes flash a bright purple. She shakes herself.

"Who said that?" I demand.

She sighs. "You're not the only one honoured with a god's soul, Aedan."

"Except yours is taking over!"

"No wonder. You just brought the sky down on me. I have her under control, don't worry. Here." Iva helps me get up. My hands are shaking. "Just take a deep breath. Like this: inhale and exhale. There, don't you feel better? Come, we have work to do."

I stare at her, revolted. "Iva, this is not the time to restart a war with the Olympian gods. An enemy far greater approaches. We need the gods to fight it. All of them."

"The Nephilim. Yes, I know. Why do you think I'm doing all this? We needed to be prepared." She hints at the Dharkan. "Now that they have tasted real Prana, they won't want anything else. The Nephilim won't even know what hit them."

"No, Iva. The Nephilim are not like the other gods. They have powers we don't understand."

She pushes me away. "It's you I don't understand! After what you just witnessed, do you still doubt? The Dharkan deserve this new world; they deserve life. Burn you, Aedan! You never fought for us."

Ice spreads around our feet. I point at the scar burned on my face. "I fought for us. I fought while the Suzerain did this to me. I fought while the blue sun got our brothers, one by one. I fought, even when it got to me. I fought and kept fighting after you ran back to the Shadow. I fought until the very end. And I won! He's gone. Where were you while the Wyrd and I planned it all?"

"The Wyrd, bah. It was Odin's recklessness that brought us to this point. Had he had any sense and remained free, this skirmish with the Suzerain and his gods would have ended years ago! You ask where

I was, I was with them." She points at the Dharkan. "They all wanted to go after you. To avenge our brothers. Someone had to keep the Dharkan protected in the Shadow, united. Someone had to prepare them to fight at the right time. Let the gods settle their scores, I said. When they're done, we'll take over. Everything I've done was for us, for our people, so we can rule Niflheim together."

"Those were not my father's wishes."

"Your father stopped being a leader the moment you joined the living. He was so disappointed, I think he'd rather the Suzerain had killed you. He knew there was no negotiating with the tyrant and so he sacrificed himself for you. To bring you back to our side."

"That was not what I heard."

"Of course not. Aecius would never speak ill of your father. He promised to protect you until you decided to return to the Shadow. But you never did. He too died for you while you were rutting a tree! You betrayed us all."

"No, Iva, I may have betrayed you. The rest is sheer madness."

She clenches her jaw and rips a strip of leather from her ragged clothes to tie her hair back, exposing a patch of pink skin on her neck, the last vestige of the burns she sustained.

"We are ready, Aedan. We'll take what is ours. With or without you."

The Dharkan, now sober, nod their agreement. Some extend their arms in invitation for me to lock mine in them.

I imagined this moment so many times.

"Let the past be behind us. I forgive you, Aedan. We were always meant to rule together," Iva says, her own arm extended, a genuine smile on her lips.

This is exactly what I wanted for so long. And a part of me still does. But… *Ileana.*

"Not like this."

I walk away to the forest, the lake's water freezing in my wake.

I do not look back.

CHAPTER EIGHTEEN

Seshat

"Get out!" Seshat hissed, bursting into flames.

The fire spread to the bed covers, the desk and the papyrus on it. She tried to stop the flames with her will. Unfortunately, the goddess was only good at starting fires, not putting them out, and in just a few moments all her latest work turned to ashes.

"Cats!" she cursed.

Seshat was old. Older than Odin, Jehovah or even Zeus. She'd witnessed the birth of countless stars and their deaths. She'd seen entire civilisations and even pantheons rise to glory and fall into oblivion. She'd recorded more stories than all the worlds that ever existed in the Universe, so she had definitely gathered enough wisdom over the aeons to know perfectly well she should not have got herself involved with the Trickster.

This had not been the first time, nor the twentieth, that he'd left her ablaze with rage in the wake of his affections. He was to her what her flames were to the papyrus she wrote on. A bane to her work, and herself. He would be her undoing, she knew. And still, after everything she wrote about him, she still had no words to describe how he made her feel.

"A clowder on you, Loki!" she said as she stood there, letting the flames soothe her frustration.

"I really don't get what you see in that one."

Seshat flared at the speaker.

"Hey! Careful. The eyebrows are my best feature."

She disagreed. Hermes' host had no good features whatsoever; he'd chosen the defective dryad for that very reason. His choice of character was counterintuitive but efficient, for no one was able to describe him properly, and few even cared to look at him twice. His approach to survival amongst mortals was to be ignored by them. Thus, he went everywhere unnoticed and was aware of everything that happened in the world. One day she'd write his story.

He now stood by the door, keeping his distance from the flames, waving a palsied hand at the smoke, as if that would clear it.

"Have you been there all along?"

"Of course I was. I'm lonely and bored. What else is there to do?"

Hermes was a Wyrd. A privileged Wyrd, but one nonetheless. He basked directly in her light in exchange for being her eyes and ears amongst the gods, unable to Reach his presence and unwilling to Reach his thoughts. Unfortunately, that also made him hard for her to Reach, and the idea of him spying on her was not a pleasant one.

"By the way, a mob's gathering outside. Your little argument shook the foundations of a dozen houses. The fire isn't keeping things discreet either."

"So what?"

"Mobs are like methane: they stink and are easily flammable. All they need is a spark to ignite. This is a pretty big spark. We should go – now." He coughed.

"Indeed…"

He was right. The last thing she needed was to bring attention to herself. Besides, there was nothing left for her in there, and if her senses didn't deceive her, history was about to be rewritten by a couple of blood-thirsty idiots. Seshat took a deep breath, changed to her male form, conjured on a cloak and escorted Hermes through the flames. Once outside she took him by the hand and began ploughing their way through the crowd.

"Where're we going?" he asked, alight with curiosity.

"To the temple. Oric's been praying to me for days. He claims he has important information about the Nephilim. I had no inclination to answer him, but now the Shrine has lost his mind," Seshat said when they were across the forum far enough from the burning house. Behind them, the mob split into those who organised themselves to put out the flames and those standing back to watch them burn.

"I'm confused," Hermes said, unable to Reach the many thoughts attached to her words. "What do Oric's prayers have to do with Judoc's sanity?"

Cats, being a Wyrd must be the most frustrating thing in the Universe, she thought. She'd perish out of boredom alone if her mind had so little to work with. "They are writing their own stories now," she explained.

"Hmm, that's good. Perhaps this is the opportunity we've been waiting for."

"To do what?"

"To take control of the narrative," Hermes said with a rueful grin. It looked disturbing on his host's mismatched features.

"I don't want to take control of anything. I observe and record, that's all. I just want to know who the Nephilim are, where they come from, and how to destroy them so I can move on and write about something else!"

"You know, I used to be like you. I've spent most of my existence carrying messages back and forth. A neutral party in every conflict. I always knew what the messages said and often I didn't agree with them, but I stuck to my task. I never tried to change the message or influence how it was received. I never held information back or used it for myself, and I never sugar-coated a bad piece of news either. And you know what I got? Hatred. Blame. I got this." He pointed at his body. "An eternity as a mortal in a shattered world. You know what I've learnt from it all?"

"That you should have been more tactful with the information you dealt?"

"That I should have interfered. I had the power to say whatever I wanted, claim it as someone else's words and get away with it. I could have stopped many wars or played them out to a reasonable resolution. I could have united lovers whose families wished to keep them apart. I could have made kings or deposed them. Directed the pantheons as I saw fit. I had all the information, which meant I had the control. And all I did was pass it along and watch as they played their games. I even carried the order for my own punishment, can you believe it?"

She could. Gods like her and Hermes were bound to their talents and their elders. Many times Ra made her write down events that had not happened so they would be recorded as truth when she knew they were anything but. Funny how all it takes for a lie to become truth is for it to be written down by a god.

She chuckled. "Is this about your conspiracy theory regarding Titans and the Underworld?"

He lowered his voice. "You don't think it's slightly strange they cursed me right before the Merge? Why would Zeus want one of the few gods who can cross worlds in an instant to be stuck in the one isolated from the rest, hmm?"

Seshat tutted. "You cursed yourself the moment you used a Chronodéndron."

"I had to!"

"What message was so important it required you to travel through time to deliver it?" Seshat had asked that question of him many times, and every time it resulted in either silence or an abrupt change of subject.

Hermes put his hands in his pockets and kept walking. *So it's silence this time, then.*

They entered the crowded temple and went straight to the inner patio unnoticed. Toman had his hands full trying to organise the women for their journey to Portum.

Jonas will be furious, Seshat thought, knowing how much the metz hated his duties. It was because of him she'd chosen a disguise resembling the Suzerain. If she could not be herself in his sanctuary, then she'd make him look at the man who inspired his ill temper. It seemed petty now… especially since it had pleased the Suzerain a great deal – after he'd made sure her form was less attractive than the original, of course.

∞

"I speak for the Lord!" The Shrine was saying.

"But your idea sucks!" Oric replied.

"Bah, what if your idea is better – and I'm not saying it is – you can't even put two words together without boasting about it."

"And no one will believe your modesty either. I'm telling you, only the Suzerain will convince them."

"In here." Seshat followed her Reach to the pantry where Judoc and Oric were arguing.

She lowered her hood, and the metzes stared at her as if they'd just seen a ghost.

"Gods, Seshat, for a moment I thought you were him," Judoc said. Sat naked on a sack of vegetables with the governor's bloody corpse at his feet, he looked like a proud puma. No mortal should ever look this good, and she was not some half-crazed goddess of war to feel this aroused by the sight of violent death. She took a step back, cautious of whatever gave him such power.

"Seshat, glad you finally decided to answer my prayers. Oh, where's your bracelet?"

"I gave it away, so you can stop interrupting my thoughts now."

"What? For frost's sake, Seshat, why would you do that!"

"I don't want it, and I won't return to the Stump either." Not after what she experienced inside its vault. The way the room extinguished all light from her being was… she shook herself. "Oric, what's this nonsense about Alek's return?"

"Could you hear us talk from across –"

"I can hear you think, mortal." She glared at Judoc's astonishment.

"It's not nonsense. It's the truth," Oric said. "And when he returns, he will reward those who kept doing his great work."

"He would skin you alive, that's what he would do. Your plan sounds a lot like world domination, which is easier said than done, even for a small world like Aegea."

"It's world salvation," Oric insisted. "The Dharkan are coming."

"Tsk," Seshat said. "The Dharkan have problems of their own. Trust me. And trust me when I say the Suzerain is dead. I was there when it happened. You should be more concerned with the living. The whole of Relicum is in uproar and you just killed the only person able to calm them down."

"Didn't you hear? There is more than one Suzerain, apparently," the Shrine sneered.

Seshat was about to become flammable again. "And where is he, then?"

"At the Stump."

"Eck. Dead governor gonna stink," Isko said.

"Stop talking like that," she hissed at him. Sometimes the Wyrd took his character a bit too far.

"You're no fun, Seshat. Here, Oric, I still have my

bracelet," Isko stated, pulling back his sleeve proudly. "Na ha, you can't just take it. Make me a deal."

Oric frowned at him. "You're a god too?"

"No, I'm a Wyrd, and she's technically a goddess, not a god." Hermes grinned at her indignation.

"I don't believe it," Oric said.

"Appearances are deceiving, my boy. Come on, Seshat. Show him."

Seshat rolled her eyes and shimmered back to her real form. Judoc gaped, looking her up and down. It made her want to burn his eyes out, so she changed back.

Oric whistled. "After all these years… no wonder you were so dull."

She hissed at him.

His expression brightened. "Hey, Seshat, could you make yourself look even more like Alek?"

Toman burst into the pantry, panting. He spared a brief glance at everyone before he spoke. "Sire! The people. They're coming."

"Coming for what?" Judoc asked.

"Answers. Blood." He frowned, looking down. "Is that…? Oh, sire, they're here already?"

"Cats. He's right. The mob's lust for violence has escalated. We'd better leave immediately."

"We can't leave. You have to harness their power," Oric said.

"With what?"

"Words." Oric grinned. "From their Lord himself."

Seshat's eyes went wider than Toman's. "I don't tell stories. I only record them."

"I have the perfect story right here." Oric pointed at his temple. "All you have to do is read it out loud."

"To them?!" They would not be asking her to do this if they could hear all the hateful, rabid thoughts inside their minds. There were no words capable of putting that fire out.

"They won't harm you. You're their god." Oric grinned.

Toman gasped and immediately prostrated himself in Guilho's blood. "Oh Lord, I'm so sorry, Lord, I should have recognised you. Forgive me, Lord."

"Oh, for frost's sake. Get up!" Judoc scolded. "Go fetch me some clothes and find something clean for yourself as well."

"But sire."

"Go!"

"You know, for once, I agree with the metz. Both of them, in fact. You need to do this, Seshat," Hermes said.

"You too?" she hissed at the Wyrd.

'Do you want this story to end well for us, the gods?' Hermes whispered in her mind. *'This is our chance.'*

Seshat took a deep breath, reminding herself she was dealing with mortals and she had to do her best to explain things in a way they might understand. "Oric: me, outside in front of all those… creatures, is a bad plan. You see, crowds make me upset. I get flammable when I get upset," she hissed through clenched teeth.

"Actually, a little fire display wouldn't go amiss," Hermes mused. "We need to reinforce the people's belief and fear in the mighty power of the Suzerain. Just keep it small. It would send the wrong message if you accidentally incinerate the whole settlement."

Seshat was speechless.

Toman returned with fresh clothes and handed a bundle to Judoc.

"Does that horrible man still keep his pigs behind the temple's yard?" Judoc asked his assistant. The boy nodded. Seshat Reached his thoughts and cringed.

"Seriously?" she asked him.

"Unless you have a better idea. Can you make him disappear, *goddess*?" Judoc asked her, pointing at Guilho's body.

She could, but she wasn't inclined to. She had more pressing concerns, for example, how to make herself disappear.

"Oh, cats… they're here," she said. *To a clowder with this.* Seshat willed herself to translocate and failed. That had never happened before. She tried again. Nothing. She summoned her mount, and when that failed too, her whole narrative collapsed.

"Come on. You can do this." Hermes practically dragged her outside, while Oric and Judoc subdued those around them with promises they were about to witness something extraordinary.

Seshat was sweating; she never sweated. She finally understood why Psyche loved the stars so much. The emptiness of space seemed pretty ideal right about then. She willed herself to translocate again. Nothing. *Oh, cats!*

"I don't interfere. I just write. I don't take part in the stories. I don't take sides," she repeated to herself, staring at the unrestrained rage on the faces of the populous.

"Seshat." Hermes voice came from far away, or maybe it was his thoughts. She couldn't tell anymore. There were throngs of thoughts in her head.

"Yes…" she replied faintly.

"You once told me you let yourself be captured by a black hole to write about what was on the other side."

"I did… twice…"

"If you can do that, you can pull yourself together and address these people."

She glanced back at Oric and Judoc. One mind held the plot, the other the words to put it together. She Reached for both and began to speak.

And the crowd listened. Sceptically at first, but word by word, their rage cooled, gradually replaced with agreement and adoration.

Seshat had written words her whole existence without ever understanding their true power. When she fell silent, a great cheer rose, and for the first time in her very long existence, she felt like a true goddess.

CHAPTER NINETEEN

Arianh

"That was amazing!" Arianh stepped out of the glider with a wide grin plastered across her face. That had been the most fun she'd had since she was a girl.

"Glad you think so, dear," Agnar replied, limping after her, looking a bit shaken himself.

She went to help him out of habit. "Shame we're already here. Are you sure this is the right place? I thought the Chronodéndron was farther away."

"And I thought these things had speed limits." Agnar's voice was the same as her uncle's, but the way he talked, completely different. He made the words sound more musical and gentle, even when he was being facetious. In the daylight, his black hair no longer made him look old. Instead, it looked somewhat striking when combined with the forest green of his eyes.

Arianh got momentarily lost in them before she spoke. "I'm sorry. Was I driving too fast?"

Agnar opened his mouth, then smiled and shook his head. "No. Not for a mortal."

She punched him on the shoulder playfully and he

nearly fell over. Goddess, but the man was frail. "So, where is it?"

He pointed at a gap through the boulders ahead. They were halfway to the Gharb, and some of its features were showing. "That way, beyond the trees… wait!"

Arianh left Agnar to steady himself and ran to the rocks. She just couldn't help herself; she had to see it: Yewlow. The Chronodéndron responsible for half of her problems and also the solution to the other half.

There it was.

"Wow," she said. It was the ugliest tree she'd ever seen: too wide and shrubby, like a huge bush instead of a proper tree, with swirling black bark and leaves shaped like arrowheads. But there was no denying its power. Arianh could feel it from fifty paces away as a sort of hum inside her mind, getting louder as she got closer.

Odin's ravens, flying above her, cawed alarmingly.

"What are you doing here?"

She recognized that voice. "Chiron?!"

He stood on the other side of Yewlow and no longer looked like a horse with wings. His regular form – half man, half horse – was not an improvement to Arianh's eyes, especially when the man part resembled the Narrum. He looked so sad, though, and somehow diminished in that form, she almost felt sorry for him. "I could ask you the same thing."

"I'm gathering my courage to do what needs to be done," he said, stepping closer to the tree.

But of course, she already knew why he was here. "Ideth sent you ahead of me, didn't she? That weed!

Do you have it already? Please, you have to give it to me. I need it. More than you ever will!"

The centaur stared at her for a long moment, then laughed. A manic sort of laugh, with no mirth in it.

"What's wrong with him?" Agnar asked, catching up with her.

"He's a freezing god, that's what's wrong with him. Do I amuse you?"

"No, he's no god, my queen." Agnar held her back. "Look." He pointed at the viscous mucus oozing from Chiron's hind leg. Flies buzzed around the wound and, now that she saw it, she could smell it too: putrefaction, the smell of death. "He's mortal."

Arianh's eyes went wide at the notion. "You mean, he's a Wyrd now?"

"No. I mean, he's dying," Agnar said.

"Ah, unbridled one," Chiron said to himself, wiping tears from his bloodshot eyes. "Thank you." Then he awkwardly knelt by the Chronodéndron and began to dig.

"Don't you dare! The Ambrosia is mine." Arianh started towards him, but Agnar held her back again, sternly this time.

"Let him dig."

"Why?!"

"You don't want to accidentally trigger the tree."

She saw fear in Agnar's eyes. Something she'd never noticed when he was her uncle. "How so?" She looked back at Yewlow, torn between the need to find the Ambrosia and the caution inspired by Agnar's words. "Don't you have to pray to Chronos first?"

"Prayers are just thoughts aimed at a god's mind.

Like words, they can be misspoken or misinterpreted. And thoughts are a lot harder to control than speech. Calm yourself, first. Clear your head. You don't want to be thinking the wrong thought while touching the tree."

Something about the way Agnar spoke gave her pause but also made her curious. "What did you pray for? When you... you know..."

"I've been asking myself that question a lot lately. What I prayed for was to be sent back to the start."

"The start of what?"

"Exactly." He smiled wearily. "I should have been more specific. But the thing is... I'm not sure that's what I actually thought in that moment. Arianh, I –"

"Ah! Found it!" Chiron said triumphantly. "Oh... No, it's just a bulb."

"I can't let him take it!"

Arianh pushed Agnar away and ran to the Chronodéndron. The only thought in her mind was that she had to find the resin so she could become immortal. There was no danger of misinterpretation.

The soil was hard with the lack of rain over the last few days. Two nails broke as she frantically scrabbled for the resin. She didn't care. It couldn't be buried too deep if Ideth had buried it by hand, could it? Or too far from the tree. Slush, she should have asked for more details. Far or near, there was no avoiding Yewlow's roots, protruding under and above the ground, knotted around each other like vines.

Chiron's hands were larger that hers. He was uncovering more soil and faster than she was! Another nail broke. She felt it come right off, cursed at the pain and kept digging. She could barely see what she was doing this late in the day, under the dense tree's shade. *Icespikes, what does Ambrosia feel like, anyway?*

Her raw fingertips found something softer than rock or root, simultaneously warm and cool to the touch. *That's it*, she knew. It had to be. She smiled. Chiron stopped digging to stare at her, such hunger in his eyes. "Give to me," he said, stretching his hand. Mortal or not, the Titan was intimidating. She almost obeyed his command out of reflex. "Give. It. To. Me. Now," he thundered, advancing towards her. He would take it, she knew. Without further thought, she put it in her mouth.

"No!" Chiron bellowed.

Arianh chewed: resin, dirt, worms and all. The taste sickened her. She bit a small stone and a tooth cracked. Tears filled her eyes. It took all her willpower to keep chewing. The centaur was on her now despite Agnar's struggle to keep him back. She forced the resin down her throat, against her rebelling stomach, the Titan's strong grip and all her instincts, and when Chiron finally pried her mouth open, it was empty.

A fit of coughing followed. She braced herself against the tree.

The thought in her mind was the same as it had always been.

INTERLUDE 9

Forged

Clink.

Clink.

Clink.

The incessant ring of metal on metal Reaches me well before I'm able to hear it. Hephaestus doesn't just crafts things, he also infuses them with power. Each blow is like a rune, adding definition to its true purpose.

There's no proper entrance to the cave, just a hole in the volcanic rock with a chain dangling into it to aid the descent of those unable to translocate inside.

I consider the darkness at my feet and the foul odours emanating from it, reluctant to climb down.

Stars, give me strength, I pray as I grab the chain, aware that getting in will be a lot easier than getting out.

The immense heat hits me first, followed by the suffocating smell of sweat and iron. The last vestiges of starlight pouring through the opening above are snuffed out by the smoke and leave only the angry glow of the forge to guide visitors in. Beyond the smithy, the lava cave seems to stretch out into the depths of Tartarus itself. The Blacksmith always liked to dwell in dark, grubby places.

Clink.

Clink.

I fight the urge to breathe when I let go of the chain. My mind demands it for comfort, but my body can well do without it. The stale air is so hot, I fear it might sear my lungs. There's no need to make this more painful than it has to be.

The rock underneath my bare feet is also unbearably hot. I will myself not to feel it and notice the place is warded against a god's will: a similar ward as the one used in that dreadful room back at the Stump; more natural, less severe, but equally effective. I circumvent the limitations of the ward by willing into existence a pair of thick-soled sandals instead and continue my descent into Hephaestus' personal Underworld.

Clink.

Clink.

I wince at every clash of the hammer on the anvil. It's hard to think of Hephaestus as a god of creation, but that is his talent. He shapes matter, gives it purpose and beauty – when he's inclined to. He is to rock and metal what Gaea is to flesh and wood. Hephaestus could simply use his will to create the things he forges, but he'd rather beat them into shape instead. He claims that destruction is just another form of creation. The truth is, Hephaestus is a god who just likes to hit things.

Clink.

I can see him clearly now, exactly as I remember him.

He's grotesque, misshapen, like he's taken a few beatings himself. His legs are stunted and bowed. One is shorter than the other, and he looks slightly off balance, keeping his weight off his clubbed foot. The spine of his disproportionally long torso is twisted, and his overdeveloped pectorals protrude like masculine breasts over a distended abdomen covered in soot and coarse hair. His arms, long and hairy to the shoulders, with biceps as large as a normal man's thighs, are also asymmetrical. His right arm and hunched shoulder twice as large as the left reminds me of the crabs found in saltwater marshes. And his face, with one eye set lower than the other, is a horror of warts and patches of greasy beard growing between the scars left by countless flecks of incandescent bits of metal striking it over the aeons.

Could those be the same clothes he had on last time I saw him? Likely yes. Gods get attached to a specific image. He could have chosen any form, any attire, but to my knowledge he's never reshaped himself. There would be little point, anyway. His ugliness goes beyond his appearance. What the eyes see is merely the faint manifestation of his true ugliness. The rancour, envy and wrath in his soul is present in his every movement, every expression, and attitude. These traits can be seen even through the most perfect of bodies.

Beyond the forge, piled on crooked tables or discarded in heaps against the black walls, lies the fruits of his labour: blades of all sorts, shields, arrowheads, chains, pegs, nails, tools and even jewellery. Through my limited Reach I can see their details. The Blacksmith might be flawed, but whatever he crafts is exquisite perfection. And he has been busy.

Clank.

"Well, well, well. What do we have here?" He pauses mid-strike to inspect me with his mismatched eyes, mouth set in a spiteful twist. "Psyche: princess, goddess, lover, wife, whore – not necessarily in that order, of course. And let's not forget the more pertinent titles: traitor, coward, liar – murderer." Hephaestus punctuates each word with a blow to the anvil. I can't help but see myself in the place of the dagger he's working on. I reckon he does too.

I've never met a god who despised me more than the Blacksmith. He's never done me any harm, mind, but I know he would very much like to. The way he looks at me now, hammer still in hand, makes me want to step back. I don't think he'd actually hit me, it's just that Hephaestus is a god who inspires wariness and distance.

And he had the nerve to call me a whore. I bite my cheek to avoid saying something I might regret, such as enquiring after his beloved wife, Aphrodite. Would he even know where she is? Or with whom? *Breathe…* I tell myself without actually breathing.

"It seems every despicable creature finds its way here," I say instead.

Clink.

Clink.

"Speak for yourself. I had to earn my place in Niflheim, deep underground and out of sight, just like in Olympus. Pretty gods frown upon looking at ugly creatures." He lifts his head to face me, proving his point. If there was a universal depiction of ugliness, he would be it. From the matted patches of greasy hair on his scalp, to the protuberant forehead, the bulbous nose and a mouth filled with rotten teeth, there is no uglier creature I've ever seen, and I've seen my share of ugliness in the Universe.

Hephaestus was against my union with Eros and wanted me dead as much as Zeus or Aphrodite. "Mortal beauty is not meant to last," he had told me then, tracing a calloused finger over my cheek. I remember thinking at the time how I understood why his own mother threw him away at birth.

I know that even now I'm not a goddess in his eyes. Only a mortal girl. *A mortal girl capable of shredding his soul,* I remind myself. Doing my best not to let my discomfort show, I focus on the task at hand. Hideous or not, he is a god, selfish, greedy and rotten to the core as most gods are. All he wants is to be treated like one, and so I do my best to show something like consideration when I speak.

"I bet you feel more at home with the Aesir."

The Aesir's definition of beauty is more broad, after all. Thor, Baldur and Freya aside, they are more used to creatures such as Jötunn and Dwarfs. To be fair, they also find beauty in things like battles and torture, so one would assume Hephaestus would fit comfortably in their worlds.

His face twitches. It could have been a smirk or a spark hitting his eye. "I like the mountain view. Don't you?"

"I prefer the stars."

He laughs. It's not a pleasant sound. "Sure you do. You were never satisfied with simple things. Always a goddess, even before you tasted Ambrosia."

I'd like to take the bait and use my divinity to hammer some respect into the beast, but Hephaestus is a brute and nothing good ever comes from arguing with brutes. *Enough small talk.* I take another mental breath and focus on what I came here to do.

"I heard you killed Zeus," he says before I have a chance to speak.

"For fuck's sake! If I have to say it one more time... I did not kill –"

"Yes you did!" he shouts back and throws the hammer against the anvil with such strength it leaves my ears ringing. I jump away from him and instinctively will myself to flee to the stars. I fail, of course, like every other time I've tried since I woke up 'free' in this forsaken world.

"Zeus died the moment he failed to kill you," he spits. "I almost feel sorry for the bastard." He raises his huge hammer and points it at me menacingly. "You have a lot to answer for, human cunt."

Stars, he truly hates me. He hates me more than Zeus, Eros and Aphrodite combined. It doesn't even matter why, such hate cannot be reasoned with. I realise asking for his aid is pointless. Anything I say will only make things worse.

"I am a goddess. I answer to no one," pride demands me to say before I leave. As a mortal, I always had to answer to my parents, then to my possessive husband, then to his family. Upon my apotheosis, I promised myself I would never answer to anyone ever again.

Hephaestus blocks my exit. He has no problem translocating inside the cave, it seems.

"Gods answer to other gods," he says through foul breath.

"But not to you."

He laughs. "Before this is over, you'd wish you could." I dislike the sound of that and push him aside to leave. Better to take my chances with the Nephilim than this monstrosity.

"Hades said you might come by," he says from behind my back.

Hades. Always Hades. Wouldn't he like to see me return empty-handed? And Hel… stars! She will never let me leave if I do. I'll spend the rest of my eternity inside that room. An easy prey for monsters worse than this one. I turn around.

"Did he? It's almost as if he arranged it."

"He knows his guests well."

"Are you his guest, then?"

"No. I pay Tribute to the rightful ruler."

That gives me pause. *The bracelets*, of course. Hades knew, he'd known all along.

"You ugly bastard. Tell me, traitor to traitor, what's on the other side of the portal. And how can we stop it?"

I'd rather look at anything but that corrupted, mismatched gaze, but I have to see his reaction to my words. The grin he gives me is one of scorn and pride.

Then he shakes his head. "Nothing can stop them."

"You'd better be wrong about that."

Something catches my attention. I walk back, past him and the forge to one table almost at the edge of the firelight and pick up a dagger similar to the one he's working on, except this one is made of obsidian, not steel. It looks familiar: large, crooked and sharp with no visible ornamentation. *Ileana's dagger.*

"Will you give me the answers I seek? If not, we're done here. You're Hel's problem, not mine. She'll freeze you and your forge until Kali comes for Chronos."

He guffaws. "Hel's so beaten she can't even see the hammer anymore!"

Hephaestus returns to the forge and resumes his work.

Clink.

Clink.

Negotiations are an act. It's all about presentation, tone, and bluff. Especially amongst gods. The trick is to get the information you need without revealing much of the reasons behind why you need it. Of course, that's easier said than done. Natural born gods have these skills imprinted in their minds from birth, and they've lived a lot longer than I have to perfect them. I had a good teacher, but sadly not enough time to practice.

Oh well, I have no intention of playing his game. Especially not when he has such a low opinion of me. *Maybe Aedan will have better luck with the Dharkan.* As I think this, something odd Reaches my senses. A disturbance strong enough to penetrate Hephaestus' shield, but it feels more like an absence than a presence. *Aedan!* I rush to the exit.

"I have a question for you, *goddess* of the soul." Hephaestus puts enough scorn into the word *goddess* to make me feel soiled. I stop. He doesn't wait for my reply. "Between a mindless soul and a soulless mind, which one is more dangerous?"

What sort of question is that? I wonder, annoyed. Something terrible just happened outside and I have no mind for riddles. "Neither. Souls are not consciences."

"That was not what I asked."

I bite my cheek hard enough to taste blood while reconsidering what answer to give him. "A soul on its own is a closed box, waiting to be opened. Its contents will shape themselves to the mind that opens the box. All sentient creatures have minds, and minds don't need souls to guide them through life. They work pretty well, maybe even better, without souls."

"What about love?"

"What about it?"

"Is it connected to the soul or the mind?"

"The mind. Love is an illusion. A fantasy and an excuse for selfishness and lust."

He stops hammering and chuckles bitterly. "You're wrong. Love is the strongest force in the Universe. It corrupts both mind and soul. It makes you do things, things you would never consider otherwise. Things you never even knew you were capable of."

And there it is again, the admission of guilt written all over his ugly face. He not only crafted the gem keys, he turned the World Tree trunk into the Stump for the Nephilim… Stars! The knowledge comes to me straight from his own mind. I know it to be true, as clearly as if I'd been there to witness it. I drop the dagger to the floor, having cut myself with it accidentally with the shock of this revelation, and watch the blood spill from my skin, while trying to make sense of the implications of what I've just learnt.

"How could you? I mean, why? Do you hate the Olympians that much? I expected it from Hades maybe, but not from you." As the words leave my mouth, I rethink them. If ever there was a contest for who had reason to hate Olympians more, those two gods would probably need to share the prize. Someone had to lead the Nephilim into Niflheim in the first place. Someone whose world would be safe from mortals and magic suns. Someone with access to the greatest forge in the Universe to offer as a reward to a like-minded ally. *Oh stars, could it be so?*

Hephaestus goes silent for a long moment while poking the burning coals.

"They have her," he whispers. Even in a whisper, his voice sounds harsh, grating to the senses.

"Who?"

"Aphrodite."

"What for?" The thought escapes my mind and runs through my mouth before I can do anything about it.

Aphrodite is not a warrior, nor a leader. She has no world of her own, doesn't command any of the elements, nor has power over life or death. What could they possibly want with her?

"Aphrodite is older than Zeus," Hephaestus says. "The Nephilim value beauty as much as power. And they value the elder gods most of all," he says, Reaching my thoughts. I put more effort into shielding them.

"So they blackmailed you. You did what they wanted, but they didn't give her back. And you're still here?! Don't you want revenge? Come on, you can create any weapon. Help us fight them. Or close the damned portal at least!"

"I can create weapons, yes. But I can't wield them against the Nephilim. Neither can any of the gods. But maybe I can customise a solution."

"Maybe?!"

Hephaestus shrugs and dips the dagger into a bucket of water. The sizzling sound hisses through the long cave. Then he holds it to his eyes and nods appreciatively.

"Definitely. With your help."

I raise an eyebrow at him, waiting for more specifics.

"She never loved me. I know that," he speaks to the blade. "The goddess of love placed all her love into her son and left none for the men she slept with. Such are the hearts of gods." He gives me a pointed look. "But she didn't need to love to make others feel loved. That's her talent. She always made me feel like a man. If you know my meaning."

I know only too well.

"She chose human form because she thought it would make her stand out from the nymphs. She made herself as beautiful as humans could be. Until you came along, none even came close. Everyone said you were more beautiful than her: a fair assessment."

Suddenly his calloused hand is on my chin, lifting it. "Yes, very pretty indeed. But are you as much a goddess as she is?"

I push his hand away. "Different talents," I sneer.

His eyes shine with amusement. "Is that so? For years you fucked your husband without ever even knowing what he looked like. In the dark, you made the poor boy believe you loved him. You turned his own talent against him." He takes my chin again, roughly. "You can keep your eyes closed if you like."

Fuck this. I will not prostitute myself, especially to this creature. With eyes open or closed, Reach would let me see and feel the experience in great detail. I push him away and again head for the exit.

"I promise I will help you, Butterfly. But a god's help always comes with a price. I know their weakness. I've created a few myself. Or you think I'd be foolish enough not to?"

"I don't know what to think. Right now you seem pretty foolish to me if you expect me to –"

He covers my mouth when he overtakes me.

"I can provide Hel with weapons especially tailored to fight the Nephilim when they come. For they will come. And I've been crafting those weapons in expectation, as you can see. I just need one special talent to infuse them with: your talent, goddess of the soul. You see, the Nephilim are nothing without their souls." He shows me a double-edged blade. Long and narrow, the sort of blade that would cut through anything. "See this one here? I've made it especially for you. You'll need it to get back to your stars."

I try to take it from his hand, but he throws it away onto the pile with the others.

"How badly do you want to be free, Butterfly?"

"More than anything…" I whisper. *Especially from you*, I want to say, but what would be the point? He won't let me go, especially if I plead. Anger is the only thing keeping me together right now. I want to scream, to cry, to fight, but I will not give him that pleasure, at least.

"Do we have a deal, goddess of the soul?"

I close my eyes.

CHAPTER TWENTY

Ulcan

Ulcan couldn't wait to get home. It had been the longest and most bizarre day of his life, but he was alive and uninjured, thanks to the weird goddess and Jonas, who pulled him out of the fire in time. Poor Jonas, what would he do now without his sanctuary? Ulcan had insisted he come back to the forest with him, but he refused. "I'm a Shrine," he said, as if it were a curse, and went to the temple instead. Still, Ulcan wasn't too worried about the metz. Knowing Jonas, he'd probably have the women and children building him a new sanctuary in no time.

Despite the earlier events, Ulcan was in a strange mood – a good mood. He whistled cheerfully and loudly now that he had crossed the labyrinthine thicket of trees the Olympian nymphs liked to call home. In truth, he'd never felt this good. That goddess had done more than fix his injuries. Even his back pain, a constant throughout most of his adulthood, was gone and his mind was less strained with worry. He felt like he did after a good meal: satisfied and… happy. Too happy to even worry about being happy, in fact. He hoped this emotional inebriation would pass soon, for there was little room in Aegea for happiness.

On his shoulders he carried Bertho's crossbow. How it survived the fire or why the goddess had it in the first place barely crossed his mind. Ulcan learnt early on never to question the gods' motives. Besides, he really liked that crossbow. Bertho used to boast that the crossbow was enchanted so each shot always hit the target. Well, he'd see about the verity of that statement at first light. Maybe he'd catch himself a gryphon, now that Artemis no longer guarded the beasts. He smiled at the idea, wondering what it would taste like. Eagle or lion? Well, he'd never tasted lion, so – He stopped, dropped the crossbow on the ground, unsheathed his blade and took cover behind an elm.

"Fuck," he said to himself.

His cabin lay just ahead, cleverly concealed by the trees and the mists pouring down from the Boiling Lake, and its door was wide open. He'd not left it so. Ulcan sucked his teeth and spat, surveying the area. There wasn't much to see this late in the day under the canopy's gloom. He sniffed the air. Nothing but the faint rotting sent from the Lake. He listened. All was quiet, but not too quiet. Birds still sang, small critters scuttled about. He moved closer, cautiously creeping from tree to tree until there were no more trees between him and the cabin. He kept his eyes on the open door, wishing he could see into the shadows like a Dharkan. Could it be them? No, they wouldn't dare. The runes on his blade grew hot. He gripped it tighter. Satyrs also knew better than to play pranks on him. Ulcan still kept the horn of the last one who tried. Maybe someone desperate or foolish enough had the nerve to steal from him. Who would dare, though? Better to kill him than steal from him, as he would chase that fucker through the Underworld itself. Everyone knew that.

Ulcan walked up to the door, considering the possibility that maybe he had left it open, when a figure appeared at the threshold: tall, big-boned, with purple hair cropped short and one eye nearly forced shut by the swollen lump above. She had a nasty burn on her jaw, a bottle of Jonas' best liquor in one hand and her short sword in the other. She looked ridiculous, dressed like a man, but it was her all right: Ulla. "Fuck," he said out loud. He'd much rather face the mad huntress or a Wraith than this one.

"Hope you don't mind, I let myself in and" – she lifted the bottle – "I was thirsty." She took a swig of the liquor and grimaced, spilling most of it on her sleeve.

He spat out the bile that filled his mouth. "How the fuck did you find me?"

"I asked around."

Next time I see Jonas I'll flay him.

"You're not welcome here. Get out."

She turned on her heel and went back inside, swaying slightly. The bitch had just turned her back on him, drunk! He followed her in, determined to drag her out by her ears if he had to.

Ulla placed her short sword on the table, runes still gleaming, pulled out a chair and sat on it. Unlike most dryads, she could use a sword and also knew how to use a chair. Well, sort of. She sat on it with her legs spread out to steady herself in an almost provocative way. He knew the pose was incidental, Ulla was simply an expansive woman who used a lot of space in every move and action she took.

She looked older, harder and utterly exhausted, like she hadn't slept or fed properly in days. She probably hadn't. If the blue sun vanished, maybe there was something wrong with the white sun as well. As a Narrum, he couldn't tell. Still, her injuries didn't look like the type a dryad recovers from with a nap and a bit of sunlight, though.

It didn't matter.

"I'm not going to say it again. Get out!"

She shook her head slowly and reclined on the chair.

He took the bottle from her hand and drank what was left in it. The liquid burned its way down his throat and scalded his empty stomach in a pleasurable way. His body might protest later, but his mind was grateful for it. He put the empty bottle on the table and wiped his moustache with the back of his hand, feeling slightly less aggravated.

"I haven't seen you since before I could grow a beard properly," he said, gripping a handful of facial hair. "Since you proudly left me to join your people. After everything we'd been through, you still chose your own kind. You bitch. Do you remember what I promised I would do to you the next time I saw you?"

She lifted her chin as if trying to peek from under her swollen brow and leaned back further on the chair. "I promised I'd never look upon your face again," she said, looking straight at it. "Promises can be broken."

"Not mine."

"Prove it."

Whatever had brought Ulla to his house after all these years had to be important. She was many things, but not nostalgic. He also didn't think she'd break a promise lightly. But then again, people change.

He stared at the bruised face of the stranger that had once been his entire world.

Back when there was only her, Jonas, Oric and himself. Four orphans who'd lost their families during the Fell and had run into the forest like so many others. None had trusted each other at first, but they were all they had. Together they'd learnt to survive. Then they'd grown up and… He let go of the memory, trying to focus on the present. He did not love her, had not for a long time, and that was a relief. He did not desire her either, though that might change with more alcohol. What he certainly didn't want, he realised with shame, was to talk with her.

He spat. "Why are you here?"

"I've left the queen's service."

He couldn't help but smirk. "You will regret it," had been the last thing he'd told her before she left for the Gharb.

She produced a resigned grunt, guessing his thoughts. "You were only half right. The old queen was worthy of my service. This new one… is not."

"I see. So you've joined the Suzerain?" he asked, considering her attire. That would be worse. But Ulla was an ambitious woman.

She narrowed her eyes in pure outrage. "No. There's only one thing I hate more than that man. Freezing Wraiths," she added to herself.

"What happened then?"

"The Suzerain's dead."

"So I've heard."

"The ice gods put out the blue sun."

"So I've noticed."

"The Wraiths are coming for us all."

He eyed the empty bottle wistfully. This was not a conversation he wished to have sober. "No, they aren't," he said tiredly. "The Wraiths, like most predators, are only dangerous when hungry or provoked."

"Tell that to the women and children they took from the temple in Lagus. Now they are all gathered at the Lake. What do you think they'll do next?" Ulla's eyes burned with fervour. Maybe she had a fever.

He scratched his now healed chest, found Cornus' horn and placed it on the shelf with the other trophies. "There's only a score or so of them at the Lake. They have more sense than to take on the thousands living in Aegea, with or without the blue sun." He shrugged. "The Dharkan just want the heat from the land and a bit of fun."

"Fun?! They're raiding the settlements! Taking the women and children from the temples against their will. We are nothing but cattle to them! Yes, I reckon they're having fun. I won't let them do this to us again."

"It is not happening again. There's too many of us now, Ulla," he said, growing weary of the conversation.

"I have a plan."

"Good for you."

"I came here because I need your help to escort as many people out of the forest as we can back to Relicum where it's safer and easily defensible. Then I need you to help me train them, so we can kill the Wraiths. All of them."

At that, Ulcan just snorted. "Is that so? Just how hard did you hit your head, woman?"

She stood up in a fury. "Do not patronise me! How can you not care about this? They're feeding on us again!"

"So you want to kill them all?"

"To the very last one."

Ulcan took a deep breath and sat her down. Ulla was obviously distressed beyond reasoning, so he tried to be gentle as he spoke.

"Ulla. I have not forgotten what we've been through, and I know this is not easy for you to accept or understand because you're a dryad. You do not need to kill to survive. Dryads – No, hear me out. All you need to stay alive is the sun, water and a bit of fruit, and because of that you think you're better than us."

"That's not true. I've never thought that."

"You don't understand the struggles of life. Prey and predator are part of Nature. Am I evil because I kill?"

"You take no pleasure in it."

He laughed. "Sometimes I do."

"It's not the same. No. The Dharkan don't need to kill either."

"Perhaps. And that's exactly my point. Some don't kill. You want to murder an entire race because of the acts of a few?"

"You're defending them?"

"I'm just saying: select your prey wisely. In case, you know, the other Dharkan decide you are indeed worth feeding on."

She gasped, eyes wide, picked up her sword and sprang from the chair.

CHAPTER TWENTY-ONE

Loki

Loki hated blacksmiths. They were as dull-witted as fighters: all muscle and no brains. He supposed there wasn't much difference between swinging a sword to cut an enemy down or swinging a hammer to forge that same sword. Such basic creatures. Always hammering or waving their weapons about, shouting at each other. Mostly Loki found them frustrating. Either with words or through Reach, they just did not speak the same language. And every time he had to dumb himself down to communicate with one of them, his hatred grew a little bit more. Except for Hephaestus. Loki already hated him as much it was possible to hate anyone, even Odin.

Loki cautiously walked the length of the hot, stinky cavern that was the Blacksmith's personal Tartarus. It spoke volumes for the god's personality that this was where he felt comfortable.

The hideous Olympian was beating yet another weapon into shape with vigorous intent. Hephaestus could probably craft anything from any material, but working metal was brutal, angry work, and it suited his temperament. The sour god needed to hit something often and hit it hard. Might as well be metal.

The beating continued until well after Loki arrived at the forge. Hephaestus knew he stood right behind him, and this was his way of showing he was not intimidated by his presence. The insult grated on Loki, but he made an effort to put his anger on hold and patiently waited for the Blacksmith to address him.

"I was surprised to hear you got out," Hephaestus said without taking his eyes from the glowing metal he hammered on. "Of course, if anyone could escape the dungeons of the Underworld, it would be you." He smirked.

Loki laughed dutifully, unamused and already bored with the conversation.

"How convenient, wouldn't you say, that after everything that happened, you found yourself free right on your own doorstep."

"Technically, it's my daughter's doorstep. As for convenient… there's nothing convenient about torture."

Hephaestus grunted. "I suppose not. Odin always was a sadistic prick. How is the old fart? Still basking with the nymphs?"

"He's retired to the other side."

"That's a shame. This side could use more like him."

"More sadistic pricks? Nah, I think we have enough of those already," Loki said. He just could not help himself.

Hephaestus looked up from his work with a lopsided smirk. Loki fought the urge to comment on the sight. Hideous or not, he had more strength in that arm than Zeus had in his thunderbolts. He was a creature built for destruction, and Loki would rather keep his own good looks intact.

"Wyrds, I mean. Some gods should learn their place in the worlds."

"And some gods should keep to their pantheon's worlds. Hel tells me you've made yourself quite at home here."

"I have. Thank you." The Blacksmith showed his teeth in a mockery of a grin. It was all Loki could do to restrain from making him believe he had a mouthful of hot coals.

As alluring as the idea of Hephaestus howling in pain was, Loki was not Odin. Besides, he had more pressing matters to address, so he focused on what he was there to do.

"Did you get it?"

Hephaestus pointed at a long dagger resting on a table nearby. It was fairly unimpressive. Nothing like the sort of weapon a god would own. Loki picked it up.

"Careful you don't cut yourself," Hephaestus said. The tone implied a certain invitation to do so.

The long blade was sharp. Very sharp. Loki licked the tip of his bloody thumb defiantly.

"It's fairly harmless on the skin – as requested. It would take a proper stab to the mind to do the trick. But the side effects of a cut can be… unpredictable."

Loki sliced his palm open, shivered, then smiled with closed eyes as if listening to something beautiful and distant.

Hephaestus grunted and brought the hammer down on the anvil with extra strength.

"I am impressed with your work," Loki said.

"It was a pleasure. I am, after all, the god of craftsmanship." There was a bite of pride in his tone.

"Was it necessary to be so… diligent in your research?" Loki asked, straining to keep his rage under control.

"You wanted the power of the goddess imbued into the blade. That is what you've got."

Loki paced around the forge. "Correct me if I'm wrong, but a simple handshake would have sufficed, no?"

The Blacksmith snorted. "Some things can't be Reached by handshakes, Trickster. I had to be thorough."

"I see," Loki said coldly, turning the dagger in his hand. "I guess I never took you for such a perfectionist."

"Everything I craft is perfect. Otherwise, it goes back in the forge. Only amateurs keep their mistakes," Hephaestus said pointedly.

"Ah, Prometheus should have taken lessons from you before he started playing with clay," Loki replied, aware of the direction the conversation was going.

"He did. I wish he'd told me for what purpose."

"So you could have taught him properly?"

"So I could have stopped him."

Loki scowled. "Come on. You must have known what he was up to."

"I thought he wanted to create more Titans to put Zeus in his place."

"That was the original idea, yes." Loki admitted.

"And then you came along and convinced him to try something different. Something new and exciting."

Loki cleared his throat.

Hephaestus fixed his hateful gaze on him. "By the stars, Trickster. How can you live with yourself?"

To be asked that question by a creature such as Hephaestus was beyond insulting. It was humiliating.

"And now you're here, free in your home world while he's still down there, having his liver ripped out of his body and eaten before his eyes, over and over and over again," the Blacksmith said, indifferent to Loki's anger.

"I'm working on that."

"Work faster! They are coming our way, and all this" – Hephaestus pointed at the piles of metal around them – "will not be enough to defeat them, if anything can defeat them at this point." He tutted, bending to dip the blade in the water trough next to the anvil.

Well, one more reason to get this over with, Loki thought.

"The mind, you said?"

In a flash, Loki was behind Hephaestus, plunging the dagger through the back of his neck and up into his brain. The tip popped out of his left eye with a squirt of sclera. Hephaestus gasped, then dropped his hammer and tried to get a hold of Loki. Loki twisted the blade inside the Blacksmith's skull and forced his misshapen head into the burning forge.

The corpulent god thrashed violently, but Loki held him still with a willpower he hadn't known he had, born of pure hatred.

He watched as Hephaestus' flesh sizzled, wondering what souls look like. Would he see his in the rising smoke? He'd like to.

He sent a thought to Hel. *'Daughter, I'm sending you your next guest. Make sure he never sees a forge again.'*

The Blacksmith stopped twitching and finally went limp. Through Reach, Loki could clearly see the inside of his skull and his brain, but no soul. *Shame.* He supposed some aspects of a god's talent cannot be replicated no matter how thorough the intent.

"Thank you, master craftsman. This works perfectly," Loki said to the corpse.

He cleaned the dagger while watching the flames take the rest of the Blacksmith's body. The stench of burned hair and scorched flesh filled the cavern as he left it.

INTERLUDE 10

Panic

I stumble through the forest without bothering to look where I step or dodge the branches in my path. The pain they inflict on my skin keeps me connected to reality and distracts me from other, deeper pains.

I don't know where I'm going, I just want to go away, far away from the Blacksmith and his forge, to anywhere but here. *Why can't I do it?* It was the first thing I ever did as a goddess. I just willed myself away, like I'd done so many times before. Away from Zeus, from Olympus, from the gods, from everything. Just away. And for the first time in my life, it worked. That's how I found the stars. My desire then hadn't been as strong as it is now, and still, I can't even will myself to the next tree!

Ideth's right. Something's wrong with me. I'm damaged, broken, corrupted. I know I'm not like the other gods; situations like this never let me forget that. But I'm not as I remember either. I'm losing my strength, my power, even my talents are weakened. I'm a fraud, a victim, and yes, a murderer... *NO.* I command myself to stop thinking like a mortal. I have to –

I stumble and fall and make no attempt to get up again.

A small colourless bird perched nearby stops grooming its feathers to stare at my misery. The memory of a young Ileana holding a sparrow comes to mind. I remember how it felt in her hand: so fragile and fidgety. I remember how reluctant she'd been to hold it, afraid she might crush it in her grip.

And I remember the sound of its bones snapping when she did.

Ileana didn't really want to kill the sparrow, that's how she was able to do it. Gods are powered and ruled by their wills, so when they made dryads averse to killing, they did so based on their perspective. They never took into consideration that mortals often need to do things they don't want to do in order to survive. There lies their power.

One would think, as a former mortal, that I would be able to do anything, and yet here I am.

I hug my knees to myself and rock back and forth like I did after I passed through the Chronodéndron, my mind balanced in the limbo between sanity and chaos. Is this Chronos' punishment? *I deserve what was done to me*, I tell myself. It's what I've always told myself. For it's the only way I can make sense of it, the only way to gain some semblance of control over my fate. I must deserve it. After all, I am the thing everyone fears and hates. The thing I ran away to avoid becoming. The thing I sacrificed my – *no!* I can't think it. Even now, I won't let myself think it.

"I deserve everything," I say aloud, then burst out sobbing like a child and hate myself more for it. *Why am I always crying?* I punch the ground in frustration, for the thought only makes me cry harder.

"You cry because you care."

I stop. The speaker is close. For a moment I think the tree looming above has spoken, but it is not a Chronodéndron and therefore not sentient, let alone able to comment on my thoughts. I Reach out and find a satyr slouched behind it.

"I, myself, have never been able to cry," he says in a detached, mournful tone.

He has brown hair, brown eyes, and a broken horn just like… *oh stars!* "Pan?" I crawl around the tree to his side. "Pan is that you?"

He nods wearily. The god of the wild seems a mere shadow of his former self. He's emaciated, feverish and, worst of all, sad.

"What happened?"

There was never any vanity in Pan's bestial features. Unlike Hades, he looked feral, wild, fearsome. Or he used to. He now looks more broken than I do. He still inspires fear, but for him, not from him.

I take his hand and his soul screams at me. Trapped, sick, shrivelled. "You're a Wyrd."

He grins, the same impish grin that once terrified children, warriors, mortals and immortals alike now cuts through my senses in a different, deeper way.

"Been one for a long time." He drags out the last word in such a way I could almost count the ages. More than anything, he looks wasted, like candle wax melting into itself.

"How could you hear me think if…"

I know the answer before he utters it. "A gift from Hades. It goes both ways to some extent. The Underworld Lord likes to keep tabs on the minds of the Wyrd in their realm and make sure they listen when he Reaches them," he says through a meaningful glance.

That lying bastard. I remember when Hades Reached into my mind and brought Ileana's back to consciousness and wonder what else he learnt in the process. *How could I have been so stupid?* Well, whatever it might be, it's worth staying sane long enough to find out. In the meantime…

"Pan, what did you do to end up here, fated?"

"Oh, I had a pep talk with a mortal once. A god's plaything. She was ready to take her own life so she could go the Underworld in order to do another god's bidding. I took pity on her. Told her a few things she needed to know and lied about other things she didn't. She listened. Gods can be very persuasive – as you know." He gives me a hint of his once rueful smile. "I elevated her soul and condemned mine."

I shake my head, and more tears threaten to fall. Has he been here ever since? Because of me? "I'm sorry," I say, and I mean it.

He chuckles. "Don't be. That girl broke all their rules and became a true goddess. She nearly brought Olympus to its knees. I'm proud of her."

I shake my head. "Why?"

"Because they deserved it. Unfortunately, someone always has to pay the price for change. You should know that by now – *Butterfly*. 'A god for a god,' Zeus said. He blamed me for his mistake. Are you surprised?

He had to blame someone. I was the most convenient culprit."

"I'm so sorry," I say again, for what else is there to say?

He tuts. "Enough of that. Sorrows are for mortals and losers; you're neither. Besides, I've been quite happy here with all the nymphs. Well, not *here* exactly. I'm not sure where 'here' is anymore. Reality is shattered everywhere. But keeping the Narrum away from the forest has been a treat." He winks. "I was having a great time up until the blue sun vanished. Hey, did you have anything to do with that?" I shake my head again. "Then you have nothing to be sorry for. Now, why are *you* here, Butterfly?"

"Stupidity," I say, reluctant to go into the details of my latest downfall. Sometimes it's better to Reach than speak of misfortunes out loud.

"Ah… well, stupidity often turns to genius in hindsight. And vice versa…" he muses to himself. "Fuck them, I say. You're no longer fated, so just go. Fly away while you still can."

"I wish I could. I may no longer be a Wyrd, but I'm still not free."

He tuts again. "No god is free, Butterfly."

No god is free. The words seem to echo in my ears. Chronos said the exact same thing when we met. The memory of that meeting still makes me cringe. I always imagined the mighty God of Time to be more… well, godly. Anyway… "I've been told that before," I tell him.

"It's the truth. Freedom is an illusion. What you

need is to redefine your idea of freedom. Only then will you truly be free." He winks again.

"I don't understand. What do you mean?"

"Look at me, for example. Do I look free?"

"You're not."

He half smiles. "I am. Same as you. Your prison is not the flesh, or the world. It's the mind. You can't keep holding on to the morals, laws and concepts of mortals. You're a goddess now. Think like the goddess you are." He squeezes my hand in his. It's burning up.

"Of course, I could be more than free. I could be liberated."

Suddenly I understand what he's trying to say. What he's asking with those sunken eyes. The most eccentric, nature-loving god is asking me to take away his soul. I feel sick. *Is this all that I'm good for?*

"No. Not you too!"

"Come on, Butterfly. Life is not worth it without fun." He sighs. "Being a Wyrd is not so bad. You know I always preferred the company of mortals. But without the sun? No. If I'm to live in shadow, I'd rather be on the other side. Besides, I'm done. I've fulfilled my purpose. I've put fear and lust into the minds of mortals across the worlds. *All* the worlds." He grins impishly. "I've achieved true immortality. Help me move on. Help me be free."

"It's not your time," I say. Stars, who am I to decide such things, anyway? Even Kali doesn't know what she's doing, judging by the randomness of her choices.

Pan gives me a smile that speaks of wisdom older than the gods, older than the Universe itself. His eyes come to life and momentarily regain their fire. He points a finger to my temple.

"Time is not what you think it is."

∞

"I hate forests," I mutter for the hundredth time. I truly hate them, especially at night when all I see is trees. Trees and more trees upon trees! Burn them, burn Iva, burn Psyche, burn all the gods and the mortals and the Dharkan as well!

I'm about to give up on my search for the goddess of the soul when I see her conversing with a satyr.

"There you are! I gather by the way the Blacksmith threatened me that you failed to acquire his help with the portal."

"Hello, Dharkan…" she says with such weariness it melts my anger.

"Impressive," says the satyr, staring at me as if I'm a naked nymph. "If I ever get this curse lifted, I think I'll make myself look like one of those. He's scarier than I ever was. What do you think?" he asks Psyche.

"Who's this idiot?" I growl with disgust. The last thing I need is another Hades to put up with.

"Ouch! He doesn't know who I am! Psyche, just take away my soul, please. I've suffered enough."

She tuts. "This is Pan. He's an old friend, prone to exaggeration. I'll explain later. How did you find me?"

"I prayed to Hel. Are you all right?" That she isn't is plain. She looks miserable, and her once immaculate dress is filthy with sooth, dirt and blood.

"I'm fine," she says dryly. I glance at the satyr. He glances back, then lowers his ears.

"Any luck with Iva?" Psyche asks, standing up with some difficulty.

"Iva made her own luck. She's Hel's problem now."

"What will she do with her? Oh." Psyche bends over as if in pain.

"What's wrong?"

Her eyes are blank when she smiles. The smile turns into a grin. I glance at the satyr. He glances back and shrugs. *Goddess, give me strength.*

"There's one less god in Aegea." Psyche sounds delighted.

"Persephone, yes, I can explain –"

"Hephaestus. He's gone, Aedan." She laughs, her eyes alight with joy. "By the stars, he really is!"

"What? He was fine when I left him. What did you do, creature?! We needed his help. If you think I'm going to be blamed for this Olympian as well, you –"

She slaps me. Hard. Then screams in my face. No curses, no words, just a loud, long scream. I'm so stunned I can't even begin to make sense of it. I look at the satyr. He shakes his head, discouraging any reaction, and then extends his hand to me.

"I could use a little boost, if you don't mind," he says with a meaningful smile.

Between the scream and the gesture, it takes me a moment to understand what he really means. He's not suicidal, quite the contrary.

"How do you know this?"

"Is he always this thick?" Pan asks Psyche.

The goddess, still breathless, sets her dark eyes on me. "He's all right." She smiles. "Well, that felt good. That way, you said?"

The satyr nods. I'm about to speak, but she's already guessed what I'm about to say.

"Just give Pan what he needs and follow me."

"Are you giving me orders now?" I call after her.

"Yes!" she shouts back.

The satyr chuckles. "That's my girl."

∞

"Why are we here?" I ask as we approach the hunter's cabin. "We need to go back to Portum. Iva will attack there first."

"We need rest and a few more fighters on our side. We can't take Iva and all her hungry Dharkan by ourselves," Psyche says.

I wonder if she knows what happened at the Lake. She probably does, burn her. How can I accuse her of failure when I failed so miserably myself? Still, there was no reason for her to react the way she did. My ears still ring from her scream.

Loud, angry voices come from inside the cabin. *Oh great, more screaming.* I wonder why the living like to scream at each other so much. They scream when they fight, they scream when they celebrate, they scream when they hump. From the moment they're born, it seems all they do is scream.

"You're defending *them*?" shouts a female voice.

"I'm just saying: select your prey wisely. In case, you know, the other Dharkan decide you are indeed worth feeding on."

"Wise words," I say, crossing the threshold.

The hunter and a dryad with cropped hair scowl at each other. She has a short sword against his neck and looks somewhat familiar. Her eyes go wide with surprised horror when she sees me, then she lunges at me with bared teeth. The glow from the blade's pommel is blinding, but I catch her wrist easily enough.

"I've seen you before," I say.

She screams. I'm growing tired of women screaming in my face and push her away. I make sure she lands on the bed, for I don't want to harm the life growing inside her.

The hunter comes for me next. Him, I have no issues icing.

"Everyone stand still!" Psyche commands. Something in her voice makes me want to obey. Whatever it is works on the others too.

"Kill him!" the dryad shrieks to the hunter. "He's the one. He's the one who killed Fabrian!"

Ah, that's why I recognise her. I realise there's no point in trying to explain my actions that night to her now, so I just say, "I do not wish to harm you, so for your baby's sake, do not attack me again." She stares at me, even more horrified than before, then her eyes drop to her belly, dumbfounded.

"Pan!" Ulcan says, wise enough to keep his distance from my hands. "You brought a Dharkan and a deity to my house?! Are you fucking kidding me?"

"You're going to want to hear what they have to say, old friend. Believe me."

CHAPTER TWENTY-TWO

Occa

"Do you hear that?" Occa asked, pressing her ear closer to the wall.

"It's Hel. I can feel the chill," replied Oreth at her side. "She's talking to a man. I don't recognise his voice. Do you?"

"No…" Occa said. "He sounds handsome, though."

"How can you possibility tell that from his voice?"

She hushed him. "It has warmth and depth to it. Like the Suzerain's."

Oreth puffed out a mouthful of air.

"Did they just say something about Artemis?" she asked.

"Who's Artemis?"

"Ah, slush… they're gone." Occa cursed and turned her back to the wall.

It felt like forever since Arianh locked her in that cell with Oreth to go for a ride with her new uncle. For company, she said. Bah. Occa didn't need company, certainly not Oreth's company. She needed to be outside, doing things and basking before she starved. What the frost was her sister thinking anyway, playing queen with the gods? If mother were alive, she'd put her in her place. She'd hoped the Dharkan would do it, but he was another one with more passion than sense. All he cared about was his precious Ileana. The old Wyrd was right. Their union might have actually worked out well for the Aossi if not for the Suzerain's daughter interference.

Occa prodded her sore cheek and licked the space left by her missing tooth. Her gum had finally stopped bleeding, thank the goddess. Occa had tasted nothing but blood since her fight with Ideth. Fortunately, the taste of blood no longer sickened her; it tasted similar to the rusty saltwater running through the Gharb, and she'd learnt how to overcome the disgust associated with it at a young age. What she didn't learn was how to prevent tasting it in the first place. Who would have guessed that after all her study and careful preparation, her fate would come down to a fistfight? She shook her head, thinking of all the times she'd sneered at Ulla's training. What sort of dryad fights like Ideth anyway? The angry nymph had a daemon in her, she was practically Narrum in her viciousness. Occa moaned at the memory.

"Don't worry. Father will be here soon. He'll get us out, you'll see," Oreth said, completely misinterpreting her mood.

"Your father is dead."

"My father cannot die, stupid."

"Who are you calling stupid?"

"You," he sneered. "I saw you, all smiles and eyelashes, trying to seduce him."

"I did seduce him," she said proudly. The memory made her cheeks hurt; blushing was painful when half your face was badly bruised. The truth was, she didn't know much about seduction or sex, and there had been some disturbing differences between her experience with Iosh and whatever the Suzerain had done to her that night. She tried not to dwell on it. Goddess, it was no wonder her mother had hated the idea of a husband. But still, seduce him, she did.

The boy snorted. "He didn't even like you."

"He did after I told him of the gods' plan and where to find his daughter."

"And he still didn't trust you. That's why he left you behind when it was time to face the gods."

"He wanted to protect me."

"Sure. Keep telling yourself that."

Ice, but the boy was beyond infuriating. "And you're one to talk. You were up there when they came, and did nothing."

"Nothing? I watched and have been watching the gods ever since. Or until that fat goddess decided to ground me, that is," he added grudgingly.

"And now you're just sulking and being annoying."

"I'm waiting! He'll come back, and he'll reward me for what I've learnt, you'll see. What have you learnt, little queen? Besides how to clean floors, that is."

The boy reminded her too much of Ideth with those big blue eyes and high cheekbones. She wanted to hit him. And so she did.

"Ow! Freezing tree hugger!"

She ignored him.

Long moments passed before they heard voices again. This time the male voice replying to Hel was deep and taut. Far from warm, it was the sort of voice able to turn words into weapons. She was sure she'd never heard it before. Oreth didn't recognise it either. The boy was useless.

She sensed the sun falling away behind the horizon and sighed. Another day gone by without basking. Her sister was a cruel woman. Occa could not wait to make her pay for all the offences she'd given her.

"There's that knocking again. Can you hear it?" Oreth asked.

Occa had been hearing it all day. It sounded like the dull, restless thump of someone with nothing better to do. She figured one of the children had been left behind.

"Maybe it's the wolf," Oreth said.

"No. That one is always silent in his patrols."

With nothing better to do, she pounded her fist on the wall, matching the other knock.

"Who's there?" the voice came from a ventilation hole in the corner. It sounded strangely familiar: feminine and fruity. It was probably one of the women. The Stump had been filled with them. "Can you hear me?" it said.

"Yes. Who are you?" Occa asked.

"Who's asking?"

Occa exchanged glances with Oreth. He shrugged. "I asked first."

"Never mind, then. Are you alone?"

The nerve of the creature! Very well, Occa could play that game too. "No. I'm with the Suzerain." She winked at Oreth. He giggled.

"Father?"

Occa's stomach sank.

"Finally!" Oreth said. "Ileana's awake."

"Ileana Dveer is dead," Occa chided him, displeased with the poor taste of the jest being played on her. "That's the Wyrd who took her. Don't talk to her."

"No, stupid. Father broke the curse, the Wyrd is free. That is Ileana. She's reborn. Which means Father will be here soon."

"What the frost are you talking about?"

"Ask her where she is," Oreth said.

"Why don't you ask her yourself?"

"Because I don't have a warm and deep voice," he sneered.

Occa felt the urge to hit him again but did as he asked. "Ileana?"

"Yes?"

"Where are you?"

"I'm in the lab. I can't get out."

"What the frost is a lab?" Occa hissed to Oreth.

"Ask her if she's wearing any jewellery," he whispered.

"Do you have a ring or a bracelet on you? Anything with a gem?"

"Yes, several. Why?"

Oreth cheered. "Ask her –"

"No. I won't ask her anything else until you explain to me what is going on."

Occa's cheeks hurt, this time from smiling as she listened to Oreth's explanation.

"Hello? Are you still there?" Ileana asked.

"Yes," Occa said, barely able to contain the elation from her tone. "Now, pay attention. This is what you need to do."

CHAPTER TWENTY-THREE

Gaea

Loki vanished with a curse. Gaea had seen him do this enough times to know he always did it when he was about to get caught, which proved her theory was probably correct.

Damn you, Trickster, she thought.

"Father?" Hel called after him. "Fine, leave. Again! I'll do everything myself!" she shouted at the sky.

"I wish I could just leave like that," murmured Ideth wistfully.

"You know, Ideth, so do I!" Hel told her, then marched down the ramp cursing to herself.

"Am I excused too, *Mother*?" Ideth asked sarcastically.

Gaea was too impatient to deal with her now, but the next lesson for the insolent nymph would be about how to properly address a God.

"Yes. I've learnt all I need to know about how Ambrosia affects your kind. You can go."

Ideth prepared to follow Hel inside.

"Stay."

Gaea stiffened. She knew the deep hollow rumble of that voice.

"Xylo?" Ideth asked enthusiastically.

"Hello," he said with a warm smile, the expression somehow at odds with the rest of him.

"I knew you could speak!" the nymph said, beaming at him. "Why didn't you say something before?"

"I was listening. I always listen," he said to Gaea.

Gaea pulled Ideth away from him protectively. "No. You cannot be here," she said. The words were meaningless, she knew, and yet she said them anyway, as if words had the power to change reality.

"And yet here I am. What do mortals say? 'Where there's a will, there's a way.'" He laughed in a thunderous roar. "My will is stronger than yours. Stronger than all the others. Always was and always will be, because *I am always*." The words reverberated through Gaea's Reach as blows to her soul.

"Is that…" Ideth whispered.

Xylo took her hand gently in his and bent to kiss it. "Yes, I am Chronos, my darling."

"Oh, no."

Gaea made a strangled sound before she spoke. "How?"

"This is how." He pointed to himself. "A vessel worthy of my soul."

A shiver ran through Gaea's own soul. So that's what it was. The thing she could not figure out about the hybrid creature. She should have known. No creature alive would ever be able to host Chronos, she made sure of it. Xylo was alive, but the source of his life came not from her.

"You're a Wyrd?" Ideth asked. She still had her hand in his! How could she be so calm while touching him? Ignorance, Gaea decided. Pure ignorance.

"Not exactly. I do have… what are they called? Limitations." He looked at the sky. "The way starlight cannot penetrate solid rock." He thumped the surface. "And it seems I'm affected by gravity. How interesting." He chuckled.

"Why…?" Gaea whispered.

"My reasons are my own," Chronos roared. "I dislike exchanging words with you, Goddess of Life, so I'll say this only once. When the portal activates again, you will let them through."

Ideth snatched her hand away.

Gaea opened and closed her mouth, gasping for words and air alike. "Chronos, please. Don't –"

"Quiet!" He tilted his head. "And, for once, listen…"

Presented with no other choice, she did.

CHAPTER TWENTY-FOUR

Ileana

Ileana considered the body floating above her. She'd always imagined she'd look like her mother when she got older. That wasn't the case. She was indeed her father's daughter.

"Frost, I look so old. How long did you leave me on those cliffs, Father?"

"Too long, love. But you are here now, and you made me so proud." He put his arm around her and kissed her temple.

She smiled, leaning into him, then her gaze shifted to the dark grey walls around them. "This is not how I imagined a World Tree to be."

Her father sighed dramatically. "I know. The Nephilim have different ideals than us. They are, after all, related to the Narrum."

"Huh," she grunted. That knowledge vexed her more than anything. She'd hoped her father got rid of the Narrum, not forged an alliance with their eccentric cousins.

"How's your memory?" he asked.

"Foggy," she admitted. "Psyche's mind was more cluttered and jumbled than an old forest. It'll take a while before I can make sense of it all."

"Any idea how she severed my link with Zeus?"

Ileana shook her head. "All I remember is Psyche trying to help him. She found his soul and… then it was gone. I couldn't stop it."

The idea had been to transfer Zeus' soul into her father's body permanently so he could become a true god since the link provided by the Nephilim's technology, as effective as it was, only worked up to a certain distance from the source.

"Hmm. And the Dharkan?"

She winced. "I remember him well."

"Do we need to have a conversation about it, love?"

"No, Father. It was all the goddess's fault," Ileana lied.

"Shame that the poison didn't work on her. But don't worry, love. She will pay for what she did," he said, tugging her closer.

"I'm sorry we didn't get the gods you wanted. Will they do, you think?" Ileana looked up at the couple suspended next to her old body. Apollo and Artemis, trapped in the force field and unable to move or speak, glared back at them.

"They'll have to. They're all we've got. For now," Alek said.

"A huntress and a sun god," Ileana mused, considering the possibilities of such a combination.

"A sun god? Ah, that's perfect!" He laughed. "I was growing tired of controlling the weather. Had to put on a storm every night, can you imagine? The sun is much more useful against those Wraiths." The hatred in his words made her shiver.

"The male is badly damaged, though," Ileana pointed out. "It will take him a while to heal in this chamber."

"Don't worry, the Nephilim will be here soon."

Ileana frowned at the restrained gods. Something did not add up. "How did they end up there anyway?"

"I brought them," Mika said proudly by the door.

"You? Put them in there. By yourself?" Ileana asked sceptically.

"The gods were too busy fighting each other to understand how the shield affected them until it was too late. They stepped through the rings by themselves, convinced that it would protect them from Hel and her Wraiths."

"You gave them that idea?"

The boy grinned. "Always willing to help the ignorant."

"Like you helped me," Ileana sneered.

"Hush, love. Mika is a good boy. Aren't you, Mika?" The Suzerain walked out and ruffled the boy's hair. Mika's grin widened. Behind them a group of newly synthesised faithful stood on guard, intent on his every move. He held Mika's chin and turned his face to her. "Doesn't he look like the other one when he was his age?"

Her father never let her forget she once loved a metz. "Not quite," she said, curling her lip at the boy.

Alek shrugged, turning Mika's head to face him again. "They all look the same to me."

"How did you even survive the incursion?" she insisted. She just didn't trust children, Mika especially.

"I hid." The boy grinned again. There was something about that grin that deeply disturbed her. A memory, perhaps? A feeling… Which feeling though? This new body was yet too new to properly execute emotions.

Her father petted the boy again. "You did well."

"Thank you, Lord."

"Speaking of, if memory serves me, you and Iosh are *friends* now?" Ileana asked her father, trying to shift her attention away from the unnerving boy.

Alek shrugged. "I had to compromise, love. The best I could do was convince the Nephilim that a metz was better than a full-blooded Narrum for their purposes."

"How's that even an issue?"

"Don't get me started. They favour their god's image. I mean, look at them." He pointed at Apollo and Zeus. "As I said, they have different ideals than ours. However, I have to admit that the metz turned out to be quite useful, and a more dedicated subject I could not have asked for," he said to further humiliate her.

"Tsk. We're lucky the gods didn't find the labs," she said, changing the subject again.

"Luck had nothing to do with it. One can never be too paranoid when dealing with gods."

Ileana turned her attention to Artemis and her colour-changing skin. "Will my skin turn like that when we link?"

"No, love. But you'll be the best archer in the world."

"I'd like that."

"Get away from the boy!" Occa shouted the moment she materialised in the antechamber's ring.

Ileana turned in time to see Mika change from a harmless shepherd to a monstrous wolf. It pounced on her father, biting him in half. She muffled a scream and fell back as the army of faithful bravely advanced on the monster with their lightning spears. She watched as one by one, they fell to the floor, torn to pieces. What was left of her father's body lay amongst them; his legs moved as if he was trying to run. The other half… she retched. There was just so much blood.

"I'm growing tired of killing you all!" the wolf growled.

He clawed Occa to shreds, then turned to Ileana. This was the end, she knew. There was no other body in the resurrection chamber. No way to run past the giant wolf and get to the ring. No way to close the door either. Her heart was racing. The gods were laughing. She cursed.

The wolf opened his huge mouth, filled with bloody teeth, and choked. He whined, convulsed, took a few steps back and then reverted to Mika's form, clutching his stomach.

Ileana blinked. Foam dripped from the boy's mouth; his face contorted in agony and incomprehension.

"What's happening to me?" He put his hands on Ileana's shoulders, pleading for an answer, then collapsed on the floor, writhing.

"You shouldn't have done that," she said, realisation

dawning on her. Of course, Alek Dveer would never allow his flesh to feed predators again.

Blood spurted from his mouth and nose as he called out to his own father for help. She almost felt sorry for the creature.

A deafening sound boomed from above. The Stump shook violently, wood and metal groaning under immense pressure.

The Nephilim had arrived.

Acknowledgements

I'd like to thank my husband, Dave, for his constant support and confidence in my ability to write this 'wyrd stuff' and my friends, especially Callum, Cris and Maria, for their feedback and encouragement.

A big thank-you to my editor, Lisa Gilliam, for once again making sense of my nonsense, to Design for Writers for another amazing cover, and to Sarah Kempton, who did an outstanding job narrating *Wyrd Gods*.

And, last but not least, a huge thanks to all who took a chance on a new author and bought or reviewed the first book. This sequel would not have happened without you.